NEW YORK TIMES BESTSELLING AUTHOR

SEANAN McGUIRE

POCKET
APOCALYPSE

An *InCryptid* Novel

DAW
No. 1684

DAW
No. 1684

$7.99 U.S.
$9.99 CAN

ISBN 978-0-7564-0812-1

5 0 7 9 9

S > EAN

Praise for the *InCryptid* novels:

"The only thing more fun than an October Daye book is an InCryptid book. Swift narrative, charm, great world-building ... all the McGuire trademarks."
    —Charlaine Harris, #1 *New York Times* Bestselling Author

"[*Half-Off Ragnarok* is] slightly over-the-top fun, a genuinely entertaining good time, [and] an urban fantasy that, despite the title, isn't about the imminent end of the world."   —Tor.com

"Seanan McGuire's *Discount Armageddon* is an urban fantasy triple threat—smart and sexy and funny. The Aeslin mice alone are worth the price of the book, so consider a cast of truly original characters, a plot where weird never overwhelms logic, and some serious kickass world-building as a bonus."
    —Tanya Huff, bestselling author of *The Wild Ways*

"It would seem that McGuire's imagination is utterly boundless. The world of her InCryptid series is full of unexpected creatures, constant surprises and appealing characters, all crafted with the measured ease of a skilled professional, making the fantastic seem like a wonderful reality. The shifting focus of the series [in *Half-Off Ragnarok*] to a different member of the engaging and consistently surprising Price family is a resounding success, offering a new look at some well-loved characters and a new world of interesting beasts and mysteries to explore."
    —*RT Book Reviews*

"Exciting ... McGuire creates a sense of wonder and playfulness with her love for mythology and folklore, weaving together numerous manifestations of a single theme. Her enthusiastic and fast-paced style makes this an entertaining page-turner."
    —*Publishers Weekly*

"While chock full of quality worldbuilding, realistic characters, and a double helping of sass, at its core, *Half-Off Ragnarok* is a book about judging others according to stereotypes, how nurture can overcome nature, and the importance of family."
    —The Ranting Dragon

"*Discount Armageddon* is a quick-witted, sharp-edged look at what makes a monster monstrous, and at how closely our urban fantasy protagonists walk—or dance—that line. The pacing never lets up, and when the end comes, you're left wanting more. I can't wait for the next book!"
    —C. E. Murphy, author of *Raven Calls*

DAW Books presents the finest in urban fantasy from Seanan McGuire:

InCryptid Novels

DISCOUNT ARMAGEDDON

MIDNIGHT BLUE-LIGHT SPECIAL

HALF-OFF RAGNAROK

POCKET APOCALYPSE

SPARROW HILL ROAD

October Daye Novels

ROSEMARY AND RUE

A LOCAL HABITATION

AN ARTIFICIAL NIGHT

LATE ECLIPSES

ONE SALT SEA

ASHES OF HONOR

CHIMES AT MIDNIGHT

THE WINTER LONG

A RED ROSE CHAIN*

*Available September 2015 from DAW Books

POCKET
APOCALYPSE

AN INCRYPTID NOVEL

SEANAN McGUIRE

DAW BOOKS, INC.
DONALD A. WOLLHEIM, FOUNDER
375 Hudson Street, New York, NY 10014

ELIZABETH R. WOLLHEIM
SHEILA E. GILBERT
PUBLISHERS
www.dawbooks.com

For Amy Mebberson and Nikki Purvis.
Thanks for making my world a better place.

Price Family Tree

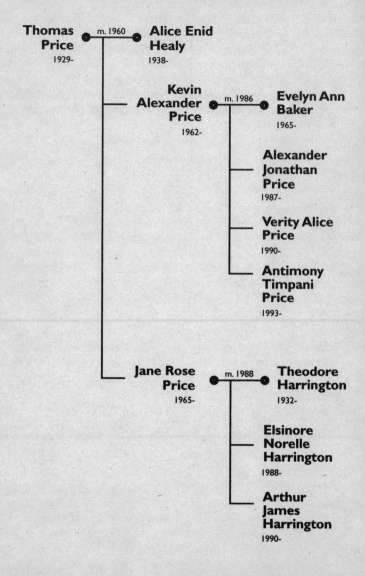

Thomas Price
1929-

m. 1960

Alice Enid Healy
1938-

Kevin Alexander Price
1962-

m. 1986

Evelyn Ann Baker
1965-

Alexander Jonathan Price
1987-

Verity Alice Price
1990-

Antimony Timpani Price
1993-

Jane Rose Price
1965-

m. 1988

Theodore Harrington
1932-

Elsinore Norelle Harrington
1988-

Arthur James Harrington
1990-

Baker Family Tree

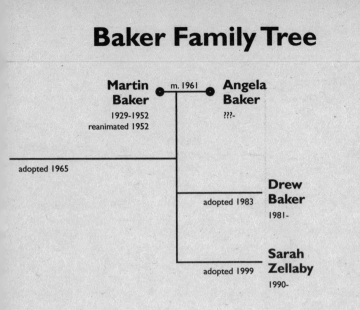

Martin Baker
1929-1952
reanimated 1952

m. 1961

Angela Baker
???-

adopted 1965

Drew Baker
1981-
adopted 1983

Sarah Zellaby
1990-
adopted 1999

Endangered, adjective:

1. Threatened with extinction or immediate harm.

Australia, noun:

1. The world's smallest continent.

2. Home of some of the most unique and varied animal life known to mainstream science.

3. A good place to become endangered.

Prologue

"Adversity doesn't exist to make us stronger. Adversity exists because this world is a damn hard place to live. Prove that you're better than the things it throws at you. Live."

—Thomas Price

A privately owned family farm near Vancouver, Canada

Seven years ago

ALEX EASED HIMSELF AROUND the open stable door, his heart beating so hard that it felt like it was going to break in two. The sweat dripping from his palms was making it hard to keep his hand positioned correctly on the grip of his pistol. Everything was silent. His parents and Aunt Jane were inside the house, looking for signs that could possibly lead them to the werewolf's hiding place. Elsie was outside, watching the road to see if anyone else was inclined to come looking. The farm was isolated enough that the screams wouldn't have carried very far—but they had carried far enough for one of the local Sasquatches to notice.

This was the area's second werewolf outbreak in a little under a month. The first had been handled by amateur monster hunters who didn't finish the job. When the werewolves came back, the locals got frightened for their own safety, and called in the closest thing they could find to professionals: the Prices.

Alex and Elsie wouldn't even have been there if Uncle Mike had been available. Alex had turned nineteen two months before, making him officially old enough for dangerous field assignments. Elsie was still eighteen. The fact that she had been allowed to come along had been the cause of much shouting at home when Alex's sixteen-year-old little sister, Verity, had learned that the rules weren't going to bend far enough to let her join the party. As loud as she could yell, she should have been a singer, not a dancer.

As he inched farther into the dark barn, Alex found himself wishing their ages had been reversed. Verity wouldn't have enjoyed the current situation any more than he did, he was sure, but at least she'd *wanted* to be there. He'd wanted to stay home with his books and his terrariums and keep studying for next week's midterms. Even if most of his research was going to be done under false identities, he needed to have a real degree to have any credibility within the cryptozoological community.

And none of that was going to matter if he wound up as werewolf chow. He took a deep, shaky breath, forcing his hands to stop shaking, and swung around the corner into the main part of the stable.

There were still bloodstains on the walls from the first outbreak. Alex looked at them and swallowed hard. Lycanthropy-w was a relative of rabies. It was primarily blood borne, but it couldn't spread through dry contact. He'd need to lick the walls to be in danger, and even then, the odds of infection were so low as to be nonexistent. He knew that, just like he knew that he'd been sent to search the stables because there was less of a chance he'd run into danger out here. He still gave the first of the stains a wide berth, and made a mental note to tell his father that they needed to put a call out for Aunt Mary. She could come and scan the ghost side of things to make sure the dead horses weren't haunting the place.

Everyone had their own set of skills and talents to bring to the table. Alex just wasn't sure that his included this particular kind of fieldwork.

Something rustled at the back of an open stall. Alex held his breath, counting to five as he listened. The sound didn't repeat, and he inched forward, scanning all the while for movement. It was probably a raccoon, or a barn cat, or something else native to the farm. Why would a werewolf have come out to the stables when there was so much untouched meat strewn around the house? The family that had owned this farm was dead, all of them, their throats ripped out and their blood left to pool on the floor. Werewolves were territorial, and they didn't like to be exposed. The creature had most likely made its den somewhere inside the house—an attic, a basement, an overlooked room.

Unless it considered the stable its territory. As Alex moved toward the open stall the creature, which had been huddled down in the straw, rose on strong, twisted legs that were somewhere between equine and lupine, yet still somehow managed to grant it a bipedal stance. Alex froze, feeling like his feet were suddenly locked to the floor. He couldn't move. He couldn't *move*.

The werewolf had no such restrictions. It stalked toward him, snapping and snarling at the air. Its mouth was a crowded jumble of herbivore and carnivore teeth, and its half-hoven claws were splayed as wide as its warping bone structure would allow.

The claws were what finally did it. Alex's paralysis broke, and he turned and ran, heading for the rear of the stable as fast as his legs could carry him. He could hear the werewolf crashing along behind him, but as he had hoped, the creature's twisted skeletal structure was slowing it down, preventing it from matching his speed. No human could outrun a horse over a short distance, or a wolf for that matter. This thing was a combination of the two, along with the unique bone structure granted to its interstitial form by the lycanthropy-w virus. It had to be a newish werewolf. If it had been more accustomed to its new reality, it would have changed forms and gone for him as either a wolf or a horse by now, not this horrifying combination of the two.

He was almost to cover. He dared a glance over his shoulder and saw the werewolf less than eight feet behind, froth dripping from its jaws, eyes red with burst capillaries. Adrenaline lanced through his veins, propelling him the rest of the way to the back wall, where he spun around, whipping himself behind a pile of hay bales, and opened fire.

His pistol was small: it held only six bullets, but all of them were silver-coated and treated with aconite. The werewolf screamed when the first one hit it. It wasn't a sound Alex had ever heard before, and it wasn't a sound he ever wanted to hear again. Like everything else about the creature, that scream was a hybridized horror, neither wolf nor horse, and somehow *wrong* in a way he couldn't put into words. It made his blood run cold and his teeth ache, and so he kept firing, again and again, until the hammer clicked on an empty chamber and the werewolf was sprawled on the stable floor, no longer moving.

Its anatomy was so twisted that it was impossible to tell whether or not the thing was dead, and Alex had seen too many horror movies to risk walking over to check. That was the sort of decision that got people gutted or, worse, infected. He sank slowly to the floor, his useless weapon dangling from his fingers, and stared at the unmoving bulk of the creature. He knew that he should run, but he couldn't get his legs to work. So he just sat there.

He was still sitting there, crying silently, when his family came running to investigate the gunshots. He didn't know what else to do.

One

"Adventure is a tricky beast that will sneak up on you when you least expect it, laying ambushes and forcing you down avenues that you would never have chosen to walk on your own. After a certain point, it's better just to go along with it. You do see the most interesting things that way."

—Alexander Healy

An unnamed stretch of marshland near Columbus, Ohio

Now

EARLY FALL HAD TURNED the leaves on the trees around us into a flaming corona of red, gold, and pale brown. The few remaining patches of green looked almost out of place: their season was over, and they no longer belonged here. Crow seemed to share my feelings. The black-feathered Church Griffin was flying from tree to tree, crashing through the green patches like a self-aiming arrow and sending explosions of foliage to the ground. He cawed with delight every time he slammed into a branch. I had long since given up on worrying about him injuring himself; his head was incredibly hard, and he rarely collided with anything he wasn't aiming to hit. Of the two of us, he was much less likely to be injured than I was.

"You know, I can stay home if I want to see scrubland and dead leaves," said Dee. She was struggling to match my trail through the patchy marsh, hampered by her sensible pumps, which weren't so sensible in her current environment. I was aiming my steps expertly for the patches of solid ground between the puddles and the mud flats. Despite having grown up in the forest not far from here, Dee wasn't very practiced at walking in swamps. That either showed a great failing or a great advantage in her upbringing.

"Yes, but can you see the screaming yams as they prepare to migrate to land that's less likely to freeze solid enough to damage their roots?" I kept walking. Dee, on the other hand, stopped dead.

I turned around after a few feet, beaming a sunny smile in her direction. Dee, her eyes narrowed with suspicion behind the smoked yellow lenses of her glasses, did not match the expression.

"What," she said.

"I told you we were coming out here to witness a migration," I said.

"Yes, Alex. You said 'a migration.' You know what migrates? Things with the capacity for independent movement. You know what doesn't migrate? *Yams.*" Dee shook her head hard enough that her wig—a sleek blonde beehive—slipped a little. "Yams are plants. I realize there's some hazing involved in doing this job. I've managed to resign myself to the fact that you're a mammal and hence by definition, insane. But that doesn't mean you're going to convince me that we're out here looking for *yams* that *scream.*"

"And see, that right there is how your colony has been able to exist for decades without discovering the screaming yam for yourselves." I turned back around and resumed my forward trek. Dee was annoyed enough that she would follow, if only so she didn't have to stop sniping at me about the yams she was so sure didn't actually exist. "Anyone who saw them would have kept it to themselves for fear of getting exactly this reaction."

"Yes, because screaming yams *don't exist*," said Dee, catching up to me. "I don't know what human parents teach their children, but gorgon parents like to stick to things that are real."

"Like Medusa?"

"Medusa was real," said Dee. There was a dangerous note in her voice, accompanied by a low hiss from inside her wig.

"Okay, bad example." It's never a good idea to drag people's gods into casual conversation. Medusa was the ur-Gorgon, the one without whom her two equally divine sisters would never—in gorgon cosmology—have been uplifted and allowed to shape their own children from snakes and clay. So maybe she wasn't a good thing to call fictional. "Look, will you just stick with me and try to keep an open mind?"

Dee rolled her eyes. "You're paying me double-time for this. Don't forget to file the paperwork with zoo HR."

"I wouldn't," I said, doing my best to look faintly hurt. "I keep my promises."

Technically, Dee was my administrative assistant at the West Columbus Zoo, where I was stationed as a visiting researcher from California. I'm not from California, and the zoo had no idea what I was really researching, but I provided enough value that I didn't feel bad about deceiving them. The denizens of their reptile house had never been healthier, and we hadn't fed anyone to the alligator snapping turtle in almost a year. I was happy about that. The alligator snapping turtle, maybe not so much.

Crow flashed by overhead with a squirrel clutched in his talons, cawing triumphantly as he passed. I sighed. Church Griffins are basically what you get when Nature decides to Frankenstein a Maine Coon and a raven into one endless source of mischief. Crow was about the size of a corgi, with the predatory appetites of a cat that had somehow been equipped with functional wings. I kept him inside most of the time, both to prevent him from being discovered by people who wouldn't know what to do with a Church Griffin, and to protect the neighborhood birds, squirrels, frickens, and smaller dogs.

"He's going to spread that thing's guts through a mile of treetops," observed Dee mildly.

"At least it means I won't have to feed him tonight. Come on: this way looks promising." Our hike had brought us to one of the more solid patches of marsh. The ground grew firmer under our feet as we continued, finally becoming rich, deep, subriparian loam. A small ring of frilly green plants poked up out of the dirt, each about three inches high. They stood out vividly against the autumnal background. I grinned. "So Dee, you were telling me screaming yams don't exist."

"Because they don't."

"Says the woman with snakes for hair. Watch and remember how much you have left to learn." I stooped, picked up a rock, and lobbed it gently underhand into the middle of the circle. It hit with a soft thump.

For several seconds, nothing happened. Then the earth exploded as a dozen screaming yams uprooted themselves and began hopping wildly around, their fibrous mouths gaping open, their characteristic screams echoing through the marsh. They had no legs, and propelled themselves like tiny pogo sticks, their threadlike root systems whipping in the breeze generated by their forward motion.

After hopping several times around the clearing, they gathered on another patch of clear ground and burrowed back down into the earth with surprising speed, becoming a circle of standing leaves once again.

"Screaming yams," I said. "If it were spring or summer, they'd have run away from us, but they're getting ready to hibernate, so they're counting on confusion to drive us away."

"Works for me," said Dee faintly.

I laughed.

My name is Alex Price, and while screaming yams weren't a normal part of my work environment, they were a great bonus. After three years in Ohio, I was still discovering things about the state and its ecology that could surprise and delight me. That was good, since I'd never expected or planned to stay this long. When I had first come to the West Columbus Zoo to oversee the basilisk breeding program established by my predecessor in the back room of the reptile house—without the knowledge of the zoo administration, of course, since basilisks supposedly didn't exist—I had thought I'd be there for maybe six months. A year, tops.

That hadn't exactly worked out as planned. Since my arrival, I had opened diplomatic relations with the local gorgon enclave, nearly been turned to stone, cataloged the native fricken species, nearly been eaten by a lindworm, fed two people to the zoo's alligator snapping turtle, nearly been killed by a Pliny's gorgon/Greater gorgon hybrid, and helped my grandparents nurse my cousin Sarah back to something resembling health after she managed to telepathically injure herself saving my sister Verity's life.

What was sad was that all of this was basically within my job description. I'm a cryptozoologist. As long as I'm working with things that science says don't exist (including my cousin Sarah), I'm fulfilling my mandate, and serving the cryptid community.

Fortunately for me, there are a lot of ways to serve the cryptid community. Verity is basically a cryptid social worker, with a side order of kicking people's teeth in when they refuse to acknowledge that "being a good neighbor" doesn't mean *eating* the neighbors. My mother is a cryptid health professional, and my father is a chronicler and general historian. (My youngest sister, Antimony, is still trying to figure out what she wants to do with her life. For the moment, it mostly seems to be roller derby, the occasional monster hunting job, and getting pissed at our parents.) I'm a life scientist. My contributions are sometimes medical—when you're working with a community that doesn't exist in the eyes of the government, you don't need to have gone to medical school as much as you need a solid understanding of nonhuman anatomy—but more often strictly scientific. If you need a basilisk bred or a stone spider relocated, I'm your man. And for the moment, I was the man in Ohio.

Dee was uncharacteristically quiet during the drive back to the zoo, sitting in my front passenger seat with her arms crossed and her eyes fixed on the road. If not for the low, constant hissing of the snakes concealed inside her wig, I would have wondered whether she'd figured out a way to turn *herself* to stone. (Dee is a Pliny's gorgon, capable of petrification under the right circumstances. They're immune to their own stony gaze, of course, but the idea of a gorgon looking in their rearview mirror and turning themselves into a statue was amusing enough to be worth considering.)

"Something up?" I asked as I turned off the freeway. Crow churred contentedly from the backseat, his belly full of squirrel and his feathers full of shredded leaves. Since both cats and birds love to self-groom, he was going to have a very satisfying afternoon ahead of him.

"I didn't think they were real." Dee's voice was flat, dull, like she was answering a question during a bad performance review. "You told me they were real, and I thought you were messing with me."

"Hey, it's okay. No one knows everything until they learn about it. That's the whole point of learning things, isn't it? We go out, we learn, we know more. It's cool." I flashed what I hoped would come across as an encouraging smile. "Screaming yams are one of the more outré offerings nature has for us around here. Mobile vegetation is a lot less common than it used to be. It's not even a Covenant thing, for once—they didn't hunt the screaming yams into near-extinction, people just paved most of the migration routes. So you have to really know what you're looking for."

"I've lived here my whole life, Alex," Dee said. The dullness dropped away, replaced by frustration. "My brother and I grew up on a farm. We should know about every kind of edible plant that grows in this state. We should be cultivating *beds* of those things if they're as tasty as you say they are. We could be helping them to reestablish a viable population *and* filling our tables at the same time, and instead we've been rotating our crops and planting things that aren't even native. We should have known. *I* should have known."

"Huh." I hadn't considered the possible applications the gorgon community would have for screaming yams. "They're endangered, but I know of five colonies currently growing in the local forests and marshes. We could transplant one of those to a dedicated bed once the ground freezes. They'll seed at a rate of about six roots a year, and most of those don't reach maturity, due to predation from the local animals. If you were willing to commit to only eating half the seedlings, and keeping the rest as, heh, 'root stock,' or releasing them back into the wild . . ."

"I'll consult with our garden planners, but we should be able to do that," said Dee. "You'll help me find good, strong roots for the farm?"

"Yeah. I think everyone benefits from that." Not the yams that would be eaten, not on a micro level, but on a macro level? The arrangement would allow more screaming yams to grow to maturity, and might even give them a chance at surviving for another hundred years. It was a gamble worth taking.

I pulled into my reserved parking space near the zoo

gates and stopped the car. "You want to go on ahead?" I asked. "I need to get Crow out of the backseat, and that might take a while."

Dee laughed. "See you at the reptile house," she said. After a quick glance in the mirror to confirm that her wig was firmly seated, she was out of the car and heading for the zoo gates with the quick, efficient steps of a woman who had no time for whatever bullshit the guard at the gate might decide to throw her way. She didn't look back. That was for the best. Our midday "field trips" were tolerated by the administration as long as they were connected to my research, but that tolerance would probably drop off dramatically if either one of us started giving off signs that we were secretly having an affair.

Not that we *were* secretly having an affair. Dee was happily married to the doctor of the local gorgon community, an imposing fellow named Frank, and I was equally happy in my relationship with the other visiting researcher attached to the West Columbus Zoo: Dr. Shelby Tanner, big cat specialist and potentially the most dangerous thing ever produced by the great continent of Australia.

I twisted in my seat, looking at Crow. "We're here," I said. "Office, Crow. Office. Can you do that?"

Crow continued preening his left wing, ignoring me.

I sighed. Chasing my griffin around the zoo grounds while I tried to keep him from being seen by anyone wasn't my idea of a good time. At the same time, I couldn't leave him in the car. Cryptid or not, he'd be killed if the car got too hot, just like a normal dog or cat—and even if that didn't happen, I didn't feel like spending the evening cleaning griffin crap out of the upholstery.

"Office," I said. "Treats."

Crow lifted his head.

"Yeah, I thought that would get your attention. Go straight there, and you can have two liver cubes." I got out of the car and opened the rear driver's-side door. Crow took off like a shot, his vast black wings straining at first to gain altitude, and then leveling off into a glide. Anyone who happened to see him pass overhead would probably take him for a raven, their minds automatically editing out the long plume of his tail and mammalian shape of his lower body in the interests of not seeing something that they knew couldn't possibly exist.

Sometimes it's convenient to have a pet that no one believes in. I'd never be allowed to bring a cat to work every day, but since Crow "isn't real," no one's ever reported him to the zoo management. Other times, I think it would be nice to stop hiding him from the world. Miniature griffins could be the next big trend in exotic pets.

Or maybe not. They did require a lot of special care.

The guard at the gate was new, and I didn't remember his name. He checked my credentials, said, "Welcome back, Dr. Preston," and waved me through. I smiled amiably and stepped inside, closing my eyes for a moment in regret. The old guard, Lloyd, had been a friendly man who'd always seemed happy to see me. Unfortunately, he'd also been a homicidal gorgon hybrid who'd resented humanity for shutting him out; he'd stabbed Shelby and tried to kill us both before I shot him dead in the forest near the gorgon community.

Still, he'd been a nice old man for a long time before that happened, and I missed him. Logic and loss aren't always great friends. Sometimes we mourn for the things that hurt us. Sometimes, that's okay.

School groups and small clusters of excited zoo goers clogged the paths between the entrance and the reptile house, all of them trying to get in one last sighting of our shy snow leopard or our playful young male orangutan before the weather turned bad and the zoo became a much less appealing destination. Ohio winters weren't exactly conducive to open-air pathways and natural enclosures. Some of the animals enjoyed the snow. Others would spend the whole winter inside, glaring at anyone who dared to open a door and let the wind in. I wove my way around the people, smiling politely when they cast curious glances at my muddy boots and zoo ID, until my destination came into view: the low round shape of the reptile house. I sped up. Almost home.

Stepping into the reptile house was like stepping back in time, into a world where the rich, dark smell of snakes and lizards dominated the atmosphere. The overhead lights were low, allowing the individual enclosures to shine just a little brighter. Crunchy, our big alligator snapping turtle, floated in his tank directly in front of the door, like a promise of better things to come or a warning about not pissing off the residents.

There were a few people inside as well as outside, but most of the zoo's visitors were eschewing the warm confines of the reptile house until later in the day, when the chill would drive them into any enclosed exhibits they could find, and getting a good position in front of our cobra enclosure would prove virtually impossible. I waved to Dee, who was wiping smears off the front of the rattlesnake enclosure, as I passed.

"You have company," she said.

I paused. "Good company?"

"You could say that." She grinned. I walked a little faster.

My office would normally have been used for the director of the reptile house. The zoo didn't have one of those right now: instead, it had me, and since I was serving the same basic function, I got to use the space. The door was unlocked. I opened it cautiously, hoping that Dee's definition of "good company" matched up with mine.

A blonde woman in zoo-issue khakis was sitting on the edge of my desk, her slouch hat pushed back on her head and her long, tanned legs crossed at the knee, so that one hiking boot-clad foot thumped against the desk's edge. She was leaning back on one hand and scritching Crow on the back of the neck with the other. My temperamental pet's eyes were half closed, and he was making small chirping noises in his contentment. As for the woman, she was smil-

ing indulgently, like she'd known all along that all she had
to do was show up and I would appear.

I stepped into the office and shut the door.

"Hello, Price boy," said Shelby Tanner, her Australian
accent pronounced in the way that meant she was about
to ask me for something. I didn't mind. Most of the things
Shelby asked me for were okay by me. "You know much
about werewolves?"

Well. That wasn't what I'd been expecting.

Two

"We try to avoid words like 'monster' when we can. They tend to prejudice people. And yet, sometimes, 'monster' is the only word that fits."

—Jonathan Healy

The reptile house of Ohio's West Columbus Zoo, visiting researcher's office

"HELLO, SHELBY." I walked past her, using the need to close the window as a distraction while I swallowed my atavistic desire to turn and run away. It only took a few seconds, but that was long enough for me to mostly recover from the shock of her question. I flipped the latch and turned back to her. "So what do you want to know about werewolves?" I asked. I was proud of myself: my voice didn't even break.

"Everything." Shelby sobered, all traces of levity slipping away. "Sit down, will you? I need to talk to you."

Those words just made the fear that already gripped my heart grow even stronger. "All right," I said, still fighting to retain my composure. I snagged my desk chair, rolling it to where it would give me a clear view of her face before I sat down. She didn't say anything. She just watched me. "What's wrong?"

"That's sort of encapsulated in the question, isn't it?" She frowned. "Are you all right? You look shaken."

"When my girlfriend comes to my office asking about werewolves, I get a little anxious." I folded my hands on my knees to keep myself from fidgeting. "What's going on?"

"I need you to tell me everything you know about werewolves," said Shelby gravely.

I wanted to ask if there had been a local sighting, but I put the question out of my mind: there was no way she would be this calm if the danger were that close. Instead, I took a deep breath and said, "All right. First off, werewolves don't exist as a species. They're individuals infected with the lycanthropy-w virus, which we believe started as a therianthrope-specific form of rabies before jumping back into a nonshapeshifting population. Anything mammalian can be infected with lycanthropy-w, although it's extremely rare for anything or anyone weighing less than ninety pounds to survive the first transformation, which tends to limit its living victims to humans, humanoids, and large mammals like horses or bears. Nonmammalian cryptids, like wadjet or cuckoos, can't be infected; their biology isn't compatible with the virus."

Thank God for that. The idea of telepathic werewolves was terrifying enough to make me never want to sleep again.

Shelby's frown deepened. "What do you mean, 'anything mammalian'?"

"I mean it doesn't just infect humans. Any mammal can catch it."

"That—seriously? Oh, that's just great. How deadly is it?"

"Lycanthropy-w is pretty hard to catch. It's spread through direct fluid transfer only, so bites, blood, or saliva. And that's a damn good thing, because every confirmed infection has eventually led to death—either through natural causes, when the strain of the transformations cause organ failure in the victim, or within a month of first change, when someone follows the trail back to the werewolf's den and puts them out of their misery."

"That's what I was afraid you were going to say." Shelby slouched, rubbing her forehead with one hand. "You got a valid passport?"

I frowned as the sense of dread grew. "I've got a few. Why?" Having multiple ways out of the country at all times was just common sense. It was unlikely that the Covenant of St. George would show up and chase me to Canada, but I needed to keep the option to run as open as I could.

"Good. We need to leave for Australia as soon as we can. My folks have said that cost isn't an issue, which means they're fronting the tickets for the both of us. They need me, and I need someone who's got some idea of what we're dealing with." Shelby paused. "I didn't ask if you'd come. Will you come?"

The words "what we're dealing with" seemed to freeze the air around them, making the situation perfectly clear. I still raised a hand, gesturing for her to slow down, and said, "Hang on. Why, exactly, are we going to Australia?"

I knew what she was going to say. I still needed to hear the words. If there was any chance that I was wrong . . .

Shelby grimaced before she said weakly, "I suppose I didn't say that either. We're going to Australia because there's an outbreak near Brisbane. Werewolves, Alex. Werewolves in Australia, which is not a place werewolves are meant to be. We're an island ecosystem, we can't handle that sort of thing as easily as a place that has more resiliency to its biosphere."

I wasn't wrong. "The biosphere of Australia can kick most other biospheres right out of the party," I said. "Still, you're right. The lycanthropy virus isn't supposed to be there." The thought was enough to make my stomach sour and my head spin. Rabies and lycanthropy had been kept out of Australia for centuries, thanks to careful border maintenance. If those borders were starting to fail, the whole continent could be at risk.

But that didn't mean I had to be the one who took

care of it. Werewolves terrified me, had terrified me since the one time I'd been forced to deal with a pack of them. They were worse than anything else I could think of in the cryptid world—worse even than petrifactors, like my basilisks, or telepathic predators, like my cousin and grandmother. All a cuckoo could do was twist you to their will and then kill you. All a basilisk or gorgon could do was turn you into lawn statuary.

Werewolves would unmake you, and make you over again in their own image. It was the ultimate loss of self, and the thought made my blood go cold.

Shelby looked at me anxiously. "So you'll come? You'll come to Australia?"

"Shelby, I don't think—"

"Because it's my family, you see, and they're in danger. It's not like we can evacuate the continent, and I'm not going to say 'sorry, you're on your own' when they're calling me for help. But I don't want to go alone, Alex. Please don't make me go alone."

She looked at me pleadingly. I looked back, every inch of me screaming that this was a terrible idea. Then I took a deep breath, and I forced myself to nod.

"We'll need to set it up with zoo management. After that, I'll have to make some calls. We're going to want people in customs who can look the other way about our bags, and we're going to want them on both ends." Neither of us liked to travel unarmed. More importantly, there's no vaccine for lycanthropy-w, and I wasn't going into a known outbreak without the herbal and chemical remedies that we knew could make a difference in preventing infection. Australia had good reasons for their strict bans on carrying fruit and dairy products into the country. We were going to have to find a way around them, at least where powdered aconite and dried mistletoe berries were concerned. Better safe than sorry, especially in a situation like this.

"I can handle the Australian end if you can manage the US end," Shelby said.

"As long as we fly out of New York, I can manage things here," I said. "Verity made a lot of contacts in the area who will help us out."

"You still haven't said. Does this mean you'll come?"

Maybe she was like me: maybe she needed to hear the words. I nodded again, this time slowly, as if my head had become too heavy to hold upright. "It means I think I have to."

Werewolves both do and don't exist. They're one of the great conundrums of the cryptid world, and one of the greatest failures of the Covenant of St. George, which may have—accidentally—created them.

There was a time when the world's therianthrope populations had their own ways of handling sickness. Infected individuals would retreat to caves or deep forests, where the majority of them would die without passing their infection along. The viruses that make up the lycanthropy family may be closely related to rabies, but they had to sacrifice some flexibility in exchange for the traits that enabled them to infect shapeshifters: they're even harder to catch than rabies itself. Most often, the outbreak would claim one or two victims and then burn out, a victim of its own deadly nature.

The Covenant changed all that when they showed up and started hunting cryptids, like the therianthropes, into extinction. A sick therianthrope looked like an easy target; more and more, they found themselves followed into the places where they tried to hide. Maybe that would have been all right, if we'd been talking about a pox or a flu—the sick therianthrope could have used the Covenant teams as a means of suicide, convincing them that there were no other therianthropes in the area. And maybe the ones who weren't already sick enough to have become irrational chose that method of death. Sadly, more had reached the stage where they bit and scratched at everything that moved. Some members of the Covenant were exposed to the virus. Most of the time that came to nothing. Jumping between species isn't easy.

But it only had to happen once.

No one knows the name of the first werewolf, or how they reacted when they felt themselves getting sick. Maybe they prayed. Maybe they raged. Maybe they hid their infection out of fear that the Covenant that had sheltered them would now turn against them and put them to death for having become one of the monsters they were intended to fight. Whatever they did, they did it long enough for lycanthropy-w to finish rewiring their bodies and rewriting their minds, until the day came that they changed forms for the first time, and all hell broke loose.

There's no such thing as a "good" werewolf. A werewolf in their original form is completely hidden, undetectable among a normal population; they can go anywhere, move freely without being detected. A werewolf in the grip of the change is a killing machine, designed for nothing more than feeding itself and spreading the virus that controls it. They feel very little pain, and absolutely no remorse. Stories of people successfully begging werewolves not to kill their own spouses or children are generally regarded as just that—stories, with no facts behind them. Werewolves kill. That's all.

Even Australia, with its own share of dangerous beasts and dangerous people, wasn't equipped to handle an outbreak of lycanthropy. No one ever was.

Shelby had been living with me since her apartment burned down, which made it easy to coordinate trip planning. We'd driven separate cars to the zoo—we didn't keep identical hours, thanks to the largely public-facing nature of her work, and the largely private nature of mine—but we could meet back up at the house after work to plan further for the trip. She gave me a distracted kiss before she left to do the afternoon big cat show, leaving me alone with my thoughts—and with Crow, who cawed after her in a way that was practically guaranteed to attract attention.

"What am I going to do with you, huh?" I asked, leaning back in my chair and looking at him. "I can't take you to Australia. There's lying to customs to save my own skin and then there's importing non-native wildlife because I want to. One of them is practical. The other is sort of a dick move." Crow probably wouldn't enjoy riding in the hold of the plane, either. We'd reach Brisbane and find that every suitcase on the plane had been mysteriously broken into and ransacked for treats.

Crow churred and began preening one wing.

"I guess I can ask Sarah to keep an eye on you. You like Sarah, don't you?"

Crow ignored me.

"I'm glad we had this talk. Keep an eye on the office while I'm away, all right?" I rose, finally taking my zoo-issue lab coat off the back of the chair, and walked toward the door. It was time to tell Dee that I was going to be taking a little time off.

I found her wiping fingerprints off the glass front of Crunchy's tank. She glanced over when she heard me approach, and asked, "Did you two have another fight? Shelby slouched out of here like she'd just been read the riot act."

"No, actually, I agreed to everything she asked me, which is either a sign of true love or proof that I've lost my mind," I said. "I'm going to be heading for the main office first thing tomorrow morning to file the papers for a leave of absence. Shelby and I need to go back to her place and check on her family. Can you keep an eye on my projects while I'm away?" I meant the basilisks, naturally; Dee was immune to their petrifying gaze, and would make a better caretaker for the chicks than anyone else I could have asked.

She straightened, lowering her washrag. "By her place you mean . . . ?"

"Australia."

Dee dropped the washrag. "Is everything all right?"

"Not really," I said. "I'll fill you in before I go, but I wanted to give you as much warning as I could."

"Well, when are you leaving?"

"If Shelby has her way, tomorrow night." That was for the best, given the circumstances. The longer the outbreak had to burn, the more people it was going to hurt or kill. "We should only be gone for a couple of weeks."

Dee frowned. "Are you sure the zoo is going to approve that on such short notice?"

"I'm not technically an employee: I'm a researcher on loan," I said. "If they get too picky about the amount of notice, I can always point out that my residency is strictly voluntary on all sides." It was a bluff that I didn't want them to call, since I enjoyed my place in the reptile house, but we'd always known that this wasn't a permanent position. If they asked me not to come back, I could get Dee to relocate the basilisks out to the farming fringe of her home community, and walk away without worrying about my responsibilities.

"I'm not sure I like this, Alex," said Dee.

"I know I don't like it," I said. "I also know it's necessary, or I wouldn't be doing it."

Dee looked around, making note of the few stragglers still peering at lizards or gazing in awe at snakes as big around as their arms. Her eyes swung back to me. "You'll tell me what all this is about later, right?"

"Absolutely," I said. "We'll talk before I leave."

The rest of the day seemed to fly by. The lull I'd found Dee in when I exited my office only lasted for the amount of time it took us to finish wiping the smudges off Crunchy's tank. That was when the late afternoon rush of chilled school groups began, packing the reptile house to capacity with shivering bodies and endless questions. All four staffers on duty were kept busy running between enclosures, explaining facts about the reptiles they contained or helping to break up small arguments before they turned into sugar-fueled pushing matches. By the time the loudspeakers announced that the zoo would be closing in twenty minutes, all of us were ready to hand-carry the patrons to the parking lot, put them down, and bid them a firm "go the hell away."

"I'm going to sleep for a year," announced Kim, one of the reptile house's junior zookeepers. She bent double, resting her palms on the floor and her nose against her knees. "A *year*. That will miraculously end right before my alarm tomorrow morning."

"Sounds good to me," I agreed. "Nelson, you got everything under control with the caimans?" Nelson was our other junior zookeeper, and it was his turn to feed the long-jawed crocodilians their supper.

"I've got it," Nelson said.

"Great. On that note, you are all amazing, and I am going home. Dee, we'll talk in the morning?"

"Count on it," said Dee.

"Great," I said again, and turned to walk to my office, where I swapped my lab coat for my wool jacket, grabbed my briefcase, and let Crow out the window with a firm admonition to, "Go to the car, Crow, *car*."

He flapped away into the evening air, wings beating hard, and I just had to hope he was doing as he'd been told. He was pretty good about following orders most of the time—largely because I controlled the food—but he was still half-cat. One day he was going to do whatever he wanted, with no concern for the consequences, and then there would be hell to pay. Maybe it was irresponsible to keep a pet that was basically a ticking time bomb of complications, but I'd had Crow for years, and I was fond of him. Maybe next time I wanted to get a pet, I'd go with something simpler, like a bulldog, or a very small gargoyle.

Oh, who was I kidding? I'd be first in line at the griffin aviary, waiting for a chick in need of a home.

I waved to my coworkers as I passed back through the reptile house, and then I was out into the sweet autumnal air of the zoo, which tasted of fallen leaves and bonfires—all the good parts of the fall, with none of the pesky leaf mold and early frost downsides. I love autumn evenings. They're the one thing about the season that my sisters and I were always able to agree on. (Verity's passion was Halloween: trick-or-treating and as much candy as she could stuff into her face during the two-day cheat period she allowed herself before she went back on her strict dancer's diet. Antimony was all about the pumpkin spice. Pumpkin cookies, pumpkin loaf, pumpkin *everything*. Attempts to make her admit that most of these products contained no pumpkin, and were just a trumped-up delivery mechanism for cinnamon and ginger, were met with violence. Antimony never found a cause she wasn't willing to die—or better yet, kill—for.)

The guards had already escorted most of the zoo patrons out. Groundskeepers and zoo employees passed me as I walked toward the gate, on their way to begin what many of them considered their real work. Keeping the public interested in wildlife was all well and good, but these keepers dedicated their lives to the plants and animals in their care. Some of them only left the zoo because their showers at home had better water pressure. I was honored to be part of their society, even if only temporarily and under false pretenses.

My time at the zoo was winding down. It had been for a while. The basilisks were finally reproducing, and my survey of the cryptid wildlife of the area was nearly complete. Before much longer, it was going to be time for me to pack my things and head off to the next challenge, whatever that might be. Maybe I'd take Verity's place in Manhattan and spend some time getting to know William, the last of the great dragons.

(We'd thought dragons were extinct until my sister was nearly sacrificed to him. The species needed help getting reestablished, and I could spend a year or two learning everything there was to know about them. It was tempting.)

And, of course, there was Shelby to be considered. Our relationship had started as a bit of fun—it was something neither of us expected to last—and turned serious when she learned that I was a Price and I learned that she was a member of the Thirty-Six Society, an organization of Australian cryptozoologists dedicated to protecting their surprisingly delicate, disturbingly dangerous island ecosystem.

The discovery of how much Shelby and I had in common had deepened our casual little relationship into something that was frighteningly serious, and was going to be incredibly hard to end. I loved her. I wanted to spend the rest of my life with her . . . but she was only in America to learn about our big carnivores. Once she knew as much as she needed, she'd be taking her education with her back to Australia, where it, and she, could better serve the goals of the Society. And that was the whole problem, because I couldn't go with her. Not for keeps, anyway. My family needed me here.

Crow was sitting on the hood of my car when I got there. He was preening his left wing in the purposefully sullen manner that meant he thought I'd taken too long, and had probably been on the verge of coming to look for me. "Thanks for waiting, buddy," I said, pausing to scratch him behind his feathered "ears" before I unlocked the driver's-side door.

He creeled once and was in the air like a shot, flying through the open door and curling up on the passenger seat before I could swing myself into my own spot in the car. "Better?" I asked. He clucked before tucking his head under his wing.

I chuckled and started the car. Sometimes it's nice to spend some time with the predictable things.

Columbus was always beautiful in the fall: I had to give it that, even as my coastal heart wished for the slower, subtler changes of season that we'd had when I was growing up. I drove through the city, admiring the Halloween decorations festooning virtually every storefront and telephone pole I passed, enjoying the brightly colored leaves that were clinging gamely to their trees, not yet clogging the sidewalks and gutters and becoming a public nuisance.

"It's spring in Australia, you know," I informed Crow, who ignored me. "I'll get to skip all the really unpleasant parts of autumn and go straight to the unpleasant parts of spring."

It was a lovely thought. It wasn't enough to balance out the thought of werewolves.

I drove on.

A surprising number of suburban homes are owned by cryptids, who enjoy the proximity to nature—even if it's in a tightly controlled and regimented form—and the relative privacy compared to the more densely packed urban environments. A lot of homeowner's associations have cryptids on their boards, helping to set standardized rules that will make individual homes more difficult to target from a distance. "The monsters live in the beige house" isn't a very helpful description when half the houses in the neighborhood are beige.

My grandparents are cryptids, and they own their house, and that's about as far as they've managed to get in the "blending in with the neighbors" division. Their house is the only three-story building on the block, towering over its surroundings with the amiable menace of a haunted house from an old Hammer Horror film. The widow's walk doesn't help (and no one's ever been able to explain why they had it installed); neither does the lightning rod on the highest point of the roof, although at least that has an obvious purpose: they use it to periodically resurrect my grandfather. Add in the eight-foot fence with the spikes on top, and it's no real wonder that the neighborhood kids never come trick-or-treating. They're probably afraid we're going to cook and eat them.

Both my grandparents' cars were parked in the driveway. Good: I didn't want to go over this more than once if I didn't have to. I pulled in behind Grandma's sedan and killed my engine, leaning over to retrieve both Crow and my briefcase from the passenger seat before getting out and heading for the front door.

It was swept open from within before I made it halfway up the walk, revealing the backlit outline of a woman in a knee-length wool skirt, her face obscured by the contrast of light and shadow. Any confusion didn't last for long, as my cousin Sarah jubilantly declared, "I did *calculus* today!"

"That's fantastic," I said, stepping onto the porch. Sarah moved aside to let me into the house. She was beaming. I couldn't blame her. "Did Grandma score your workbook?"

"I got an eighty percent!" Sarah's enthusiasm didn't dim one bit, even though the score was lower than she was getting when she was nine. For her, even an eighty percent on a calculus worksheet was an incredible improvement.

Sarah was technically my aunt, having been adopted by my grandparents when she was just a kid, but she'd always be "cousin Sarah" to me, and to my siblings. We were just too close in age to think of her as anything else.

I offered her a smile. "I'm really proud of you."

"I'm proud of me, too," said Sarah.

She had every right to be. Sarah was a cuckoo—a member of a species of math-obsessed telepathic predators. And cuckoos loved numbers. Arithmetic and higher mathematics were all the same to them: as long as numbers were involved, they were happy, and since a happy cuckoo was a cuckoo who might not be trying to kill you, we encouraged their mathematical pursuits whenever possible.

And then there was Sarah.

It hadn't been that long ago that she'd been with my sister in Manhattan. Some bad things happened, and Sarah had to choose between using her telepathy in a way she'd never tried to use it before, or letting Verity die—and confirming the ongoing existence of our family to the Covenant of St. George at the same time. She made the choice that would save my sister, and by extension, save us all.

Sarah had always been taught not to use her powers to intentionally change people's minds. That day, she broke every rule she'd worked so hard to learn, and she rewrote the memories of the Covenant team that was holding Verity. It worked, but it hurt her, in ways that we still didn't fully understand, and might never be able to make sense of, since "telepath physiology" isn't a course offering at most medical schools.

For a while, we'd been afraid Sarah would never be herself again. That fear had been gradually put to rest as she recovered. She was putting herself back together a little bit at a time, struggling to extract sanity from the jaws of severe neurological dysfunction. At her worst, she hadn't even been able to remember her primes. To have her doing calculus again was a blessing.

"Mom's in the kitchen making dinner, and Dad's upstairs making himself scarce," said Sarah, as Crow launched himself from my shoulder and flapped up the stairs to my room. She paused, squinting, and her eyes took on the white-filmed look that meant she was stretching just the barest tendril of telepathy in my direction. "You . . . want to talk to us about koalas?"

"Close," I said. "I want to talk to everyone about Australia." When Sarah had first come home from New York, we'd all worn anti-telepathy charms all the time, to lessen the risk that she would slip and hurt somebody, or herself. Now only Shelby still routinely wore a charm, which made sense. She wasn't family.

The kitchen smelled of tuna fish and cream of mushroom soup, a classic piece of Americana that was rendered only a little incongruous by the fact that it was being baked by my Grandma Angela, the second cuckoo in the family. She looked up when she heard the kitchen door swing open, flashing me a bright smile.

"Welcome home, Alex," she said. "Dinner should be ready in about twenty minutes. Tuna casserole, sweet rolls, and spaghetti sauce with ginger."

Cuckoos have a weird obsession with tomatoes and tomato byproducts. The human members of the family have learned to live with it. "Sounds good. Um, I need to talk to you and Grandpa about something. Do you want to do it before or after we eat? Shelby has to feed the tigers tonight, so she's going to be home late."

"Before sounds good," rumbled a deep, almost rocky voice. I turned to see the hulking, scarred form of my grandfather filling the doorway, a friendly smile on his terrible face. "What's on your mind, Alex?"

I took a deep breath. "Shelby wants me to go to Australia with her. There's a lycanthropy-w outbreak, and no one there knows how to deal with it."

"They don't have lycanthropy in Australia, do they?" asked Grandpa, his smile melting into a frown.

"No," I said. "None of the common forms, and none of the exotic ones either. It's one of the only horrible things in the world that Australia *didn't* get as part of the starter package. That means they've never handled an outbreak before, and from what Shelby said, I think they're pretty scared."

"They should be," said Grandma grimly. "But Alex . . . you're human, honey. Are you sure this is a good idea?"

Sarah and Grandma Angela had more in common with parasitic wasps than they did with humans, at least on a cellular level. Grandpa Martin had been human once—had been several humans once—but he'd become

basically immune to all known diseases following his
death and resurrections, since nothing could figure out
how to infect him. Of the four people in the kitchen, I
was the only one with the potential to be infected or
killed by lycanthropy-w.

Which naturally meant I was the one planning to
head for the site of the outbreak. "No," I said. I didn't
bother to keep the quaver out of my voice. "But it's the
only idea we have. The Thirty-Sixers need help."

"Maybe they can find someone in their own organization who can figure this out," said Grandma. "Let them do
what they've always done, and handle this themselves."

"Shelby helped me when Lloyd was using that cockatrice to turn people to stone," I said quietly. Grandma
didn't flinch or look ashamed. I hadn't been expecting
her to. No matter how human she seemed and how normally she often behaved, she was never going to priori-
tize the lives of humans she didn't know above the
people she considered her family.

Maybe she wasn't so strange in that regard.

"Yes, and we were very grateful," said Grandpa, before either Grandma or Sarah could say something
they'd regret. "And yes, I know she was at just as much
risk of being turned to stone as you were. Don't think we
don't all appreciate what she did for you. But, Alex . . ."

"I love her." It was a small, simple admission, and it
still burned, because it shouldn't have been necessary:
the fact that the Thirty-Six Society needed help should
have been enough. I'd never lived in a world without the
specter of the Covenant of St. George hanging over us,
but I couldn't help thinking that if it hadn't been for
them, the various cryptological societies wouldn't have
been so reluctant to help each other. Philanthropy was
so much easier when there wasn't a multinational organization of fanatics waiting to slaughter you if you dared
to show your face. "She's the only woman I've ever been
able to say that about—the only one who isn't family.
She's one of my best friends. She needs me. Her *family*

needs me. How can I look her in the eye and tell her I won't help her family after she helped mine?"

"Besides, if Alex goes to help Shelby with the were-wolves in Australia, he can meet her family, and maybe they'll approve of him." Sarah's suggestion was calmly made, and so lucid that the rest of us turned and stared at her. She shrugged. "You were thinking it pretty loudly, Alex. I couldn't not see."

"It's not that I mind you reading my mind," I said. "It's that you sounded so together. You're really getting better, aren't you?"

Sarah's smile widened. "No thanks to you, Mr. Thinks-too-loud. I should have made you ship me home to Artie. At least he thinks about soothing things."

"Yeah," I said, smothering the urge to smirk. My cousin Artie's crush on Sarah was public knowledge: everyone knew about it except for Sarah herself, who seemed to think that the rest of us were delusional when we thought about how cute they were together. Verity and I had in-dulged in more than a little private betting over how long it would be before she caught on to the fact that the cousin she was hopelessly enamored with was equally enamored of her. So far, neither of us was winning. "So I should take my loud thoughts to Australia, huh?"

"Yes." She turned to her parents. "Alex is *going* to go. I can hear it. He didn't come to ask for permission—he's a grownup. He came to ask for support. We owe him that. Don't we? He always supports us."

Grandma sighed. "You're right, honey. Alex, I'm sorry. You know we're only worried about you, right? Lycan-thropy is nothing to play around with."

"I know, Grandma, and I'm scared out of my mind," I said. Like rabies, lycanthropy—all the known varieties, from the common –w (for "wolf") all the way to the rarer –b (for "bear") and –r (for "rhino")—was incurable after the infection reached a certain point. It was just that for lycanthropy, "a certain point" meant "transforming into a giant wolf-beast." There was no vaccine, and the treatments intended to prevent a bite from progressing to an infection were potentially fatal. Smart cryptozoologists avoided outbreaks whenever possible, sending in nonmammalian allies to clean it out.

It was sort of funny. Here I was, standing in my kitchen with two nonmammalian allies and one mammalian ally who couldn't be infected, and I couldn't take any of them with me to Australia. Sarah wasn't fit to fly, Grandpa couldn't risk a TSA scanner, and Grandma . . . well, Grandma would be fine, but the Thirty-Sixers might shoot her on sight. They'd had a cuckoo infestation a few years previous. Now they habitually wore anti-telepathy charms that would interfere with her natural camouflage field, and were inclined to shoot on sight. If I went, I was going alone.

Except for Shelby, of course. Dangerous as the proposed expedition was, I had to admit that I didn't mind the idea of an international flight pressed up next to her.

"You get to tell your parents," said Grandpa, apparently reading my decision in my face. "I'm not going to be the one who informs your mother that you're finally running into absolutely certain danger for the fun of it all."

"Fair enough," I agreed. "If I give you a list of the supplies I'm going to need, can you let me know what we have in the house?"

"Of course," he said. "I'm assuming you're planning to fly out of JFK?"

"Yeah." Getting from Ohio to New York would mean hours in the car, but it would also mean going through customs at an airport where we knew people in both the TSA and the international processing side of things. It would have to be timed just right—smuggling the kind of firepower I habitually carry into a large airport hasn't been easy in more than a decade, and it hadn't been a cakewalk before that—but we'd done tight connections before, and it would mean I was heading out well-armed and prepared for whatever was coming next.

Grandma sighed again, even more deeply than before. "Just come home breathing, all right? That's all I'm asking of you here. Come *home*."

"I'll do my best," I said. I stepped forward and hugged her. Then I hugged Sarah, and Grandpa, and left the kitchen. It was time to call home and let them know what stupid thing I was up to now. On the plus side, "don't go to Australia" had never been on my mother's list of standard warnings. On the down side, it was almost certainly going to be there after this.

Three

"The trick to doing things people say are impossible is confidence. As long as you seem to know what you're doing, and never hesitate, you're very unlikely to face any challenges. People don't like to break illusions, even when they don't know that's what they're looking at."

—Kevin Price

JFK International Airport, departure terminal, three days later

SHELBY HAD VANISHED INTO the women's bathroom again, leaving me to watch the luggage. We were traveling carry-on only, which meant a backpack and a roller bag each, as well as a separate long case for Shelby's "violin"—an instrument she didn't play and wasn't carrying. But the case was treated to show the image of a violin when put through a standard X-ray machine, and she had a letter from the Guild of Musicians guaranteeing her the right to carry it onto the plane, so we hadn't encountered any issues with the TSA.

They might have gotten a nasty surprise if they'd decided to open the thing, and we would have probably been arrested on suspicion of terrorism. Luckily, Shelby was bubbly, vivacious, and wearing a low-cut tank top that made it difficult to think straight when I looked directly at her. It had had much the same effect on the TSA agents at the gate. She'd plainly done this sort of thing before.

I wasn't nearly as practiced a traveler. Yes, we maintained valid passports at all times, and yes, Verity, Antimony, and I had all celebrated our eighteenth birthdays with randomly booked trips outside of North America—I'd wound up in Finland, and had a lovely time with two huldra girls who thought I was the cutest thing they'd ever kidnapped from a tour group—but that didn't mean we traveled for *fun*. Travel was dangerous. Travel meant stepping outside the familiar bolt-holes and cultural rules of the North American cryptid communities and moving into spheres where we didn't know the lay of the land. The Prices had been members of the Covenant of St. George for generations before my Grandpa Thomas defected to the side of good, as represented by the fantastic rack of my Grandma Alice (this was reported dutifully to each new generation of the family by our living historical record, the Aeslin mice, even when we asked them nicely to please stop). In some parts of the world, the Prices were *still* members in good standing of the Covenant, which made "Hi, my name's Alex Price" a much more dangerous sentence to utter out loud.

Shelby came bounding back down the concourse, throwing herself into the open seat next to me with such violent abandon that I was amazed it didn't throw up its arms in surrender. "All better," she informed me, before pressing a noisy kiss to my cheek. Leaving her lips pressed to my cheek she murmured, much more quietly, "No unusual security activity, and most of the crowd's human so far as I can see. Spotted two bogeys heading on-shift in the caf, and there's some sort of snake-person waiting for a flight two gates down, but they're not going to be a problem." She leaned back in her seat and beamed at me.

"Ready to experience the joys of the land down under? I warn you, you might not want to come back."

"See, the problem with that sentence is simple: I've now been dating you for long enough that I know you don't talk that way." I smirked. "You cannot fool me with your stereotypical Australian ways."

"Ah, but can I frighten you with talk of drop bears and bunyip?" Several of the Australians in the waiting area around us chuckled. So did Shelby. I fought the urge to shudder, and settled for glaring at her, which just made her chuckle more.

"Oh, I can already tell that this trip is going to be *fun*," I said, through gritted teeth.

(To your average tourist in Australia—and, indeed, to your average Australian—the drop bear was a fun campfire story and something to scare kids with. Sadly, the cryptozoological world knows better. Why Australia felt the need to evolve a carnivorous, tree-dwelling marsupial that looks like a koala after it's been exposed to serious amounts of steroids is anyone's guess, but I was in no hurry to meet one. A normal koala is perfectly capable of clawing a man's face off. A drop bear will both claw it off and eat it, which doesn't strike me as particularly social. As for the bunyip . . . the less said, the better.)

Shelby twinkled at me. There was no other way to describe her smug, almost catlike smile, or the way she stretched languidly to her full length, defying both the size of her seat and the piles of luggage around her. One foot bumped my rolling suitcase, which gave out a faint cheer. She promptly retracted back into her seat, giving me a wide-eyed look.

"Sorry," I said, grimacing. I bent forward, pretending to fuss with my zipper as I pressed my mouth to the small opening in the case's side and whispered, "Hush. You promised to be quiet until the plane was in the air." Our seats were in business class. The theory was that the people around us would be so busy either sleeping or drinking as much complimentary booze as they could that they wouldn't notice the cheering of the Aeslin mice. At least, that was the hope. There were only six mice in my suitcase, chosen by sacred lottery to accompany me. If they got too loud, I'd have to improvise—but it would be better if the improvisation didn't have to start before we even got on the plane.

(Aeslin mice: talking, pantheistic rodents that worship my family as gods. They make things like "Thanksgiving," "laundry day," and "going to the bathroom" uniquely exciting. Their eidetic memories and endless fascination with everything any member of the family has ever done also makes them incredibly useful. They were living black boxes, like the ones pilots used to record the final details of a crash. If anything happened to me, the Aeslin mice would be able to tell my family. It—and I—wouldn't be forgotten. There was something comforting about that, no matter how obnoxious the mice themselves could sometimes be.)

Shelby frowned, looking uncertain. "You sure they'll be able to keep themselves under control long enough for us to clear customs? I don't want to get arrested for, well, much of anything, really. Getting arrested is at the permanent bottom of my list of things to do."

"I'm sure," I said. "They're good about following the 'quiet in the bag' command, as long as they don't feel like they've been forgotten." Plus I could always repeat the trick I'd used to get them through the TSA checkpoint: they had snuck out of my bag when I put it on the conveyor belt for the X-ray, vanished into the crowd so quickly and stealthily that no one had even realized they were there, and then rejoined me in the men's bathroom on the other side of security. Smuggling things that could move on their own and follow orders was considerably easier than smuggling boring old contraband materials.

"If you're sure," said Shelby, sounding even more uncertain than she looked. "I do wish we could have left them behind."

"It's against the rules." I gave my carry-on a glum look. "We need to have them with us at all times in case something, you know, goes wrong. I'm not sure how the mice would get back to the main colony if that happened, but they're surprisingly clever when matters of their faith are involved. And telling the rest of the family that I was dead would definitely be considered a matter of faith." Dead, or a werewolf. I was honestly more worried about the latter.

When I looked back to Shelby, her look of concern was gone, replaced by a deeper look of sorrow. "It's been hard on you lot, hasn't it?"

"I don't really know," I said. "This is just how things have always been." I was lying, of course. I don't think anyone who grows up the way I did could be blind enough to think it was normal, or that they weren't missing out on the things other people got to do. Like going to school under their own name, or traveling without worrying they'd be eaten by the first thing they saw at their destination. I know I've never regretted my life. As far as I know, my sisters haven't regretted theirs either. But we didn't choose them: we didn't decide to become what we grew up to be. Those choices were made for us.

Sometimes it seems like a lot of the big choices in life are.

The gate crew called for people who needed extra time down the aisle to line up at the door. Shelby stood, stretching so that her shirt rode up about an inch above the waistband of her jeans, revealing a stripe of tanned skin. The absence of a knife tucked into her belt was almost jarring. Travel was something that I never seemed to get used to, no matter how much I did it.

"Come on, lazybones, up you get," said Shelby, offering me her hands. I took them, letting her tug me to my feet. "You can sit for the next fourteen hours, a'right?"

"I can't wait," I said dryly.

My suitcase cheered again when I picked it up. I sighed, and followed Shelby to the line.

Airplanes: essentially buses that fly, and hence have the potential to drop out of the sky at any moment, spreading your insides—which will no doubt become your outsides sometime during the collision—across whatever you happen to have been flying over. Since we were flying mostly over ocean, I was sure the sharks would appreciate our sacrifice.

Shelby was in the aisle seat, having claimed that her smaller bladder and shorter legs made it hers by divine right. That left me with the window, which showed an unrelentingly blue ocean scrolling out as far as the eye could see beneath our plane. There were occasional smatterings of cloud, but for the most part the weather was staying good and the skies were staying clear. The edge of the horizon was brighter than anything else; the sun would be down soon, and I would have nothing to look at but the books I'd brought to read during the flight. Well, and Shelby, but she'd been sleeping since about ten minutes after takeoff—just long enough to finish her complimentary glass of business class champagne, kiss me on the cheek, and turn on her iPod.

Most of business class was asleep, in fact, having been lulled into unconsciousness by the combination of soft seats, free booze, and marginally reduced cabin pressure, which was like traveling from sea level to the Rocky Mountains without any of the normal transitions in between. It made people sleepy and a little sick to their stomachs, which most of them were treating with, yes, more alcohol. The mice were probably having a full-on bacchanal in the overhead compartment, but between the snoring and the roar of the engines, no one would be able to tell.

I sighed and reached up to turn on my reading light. We had a long way to go before we got to Australia. I might as well get a little work done.

There are very few cryptozoologist's guides to Australia—or at least, there are very few guides available to non-Australians. I assumed the Thirty-Sixers would have plenty, since they'd been studying their home continent since before their official inception as a group, and no organization larger than three or four people can survive for long on nothing but oral traditions. I was hoping to come home from my visit with some of those guides to add to the family collection. In the meantime, I had to make do with Grandpa Thomas' guide to the cryptozoological flora and fauna of Australia and New Zealand, which Dad had sent via overnight mail when I called to tell him that I was going home with Shelby. The book had been written before Grandpa Thomas met Grandma Alice, so it was almost certainly out of date. It was also the best resource I had.

I leaned back in my seat and opened the guide to the chapter on drop bears, which included some sketches that made me want to ask the pilot to turn the plane around. Give me a nice normal waheela or wendigo any day: drop bears were *freaky*.

(Yes, "give me a nice normal thing that I can find where I come from" is a statement drenched in colonialism and privilege: it supposes that the ecosystem that the speaker comes from is normal, and all other ecosystems are somehow weird or flawed. At the same time, Australia basically holds the copyright on "weird ecosystem." The only place where you're going to find weirder things is at the bottom of the ocean, and no one suggests that you go there for a fun family vacation.)

According to the guide, where we were going we would be contending with drop bears, bunyips, Queensland tigers, and other lovely, predatory things that I wasn't used to seeing on a regular basis. There were also species of coatl, although Grandpa didn't call them that, and garrinna, the marsupial equivalent of the miniature griffin. That was nice. I was already missing Crow more than a little.

I turned the page, and kept reading.

My grandfather—Thomas Price, the man who gave my family its name, along with the recessive genes that some-how resulted in my youngest sister being almost six inches taller than any of the other women in our family, and don't think *that* hasn't caused its share of resentment—was originally from England, but traveled a lot before settling down in Buckley Township, Michigan, where he married my grandmother and was eventually sucked into a dimensional portal leading to who-knows-where. (Grandma Alice is still looking for him, and continues to insist that he's not dead, even though it's been more than sixty years. Hope springs eternal, I guess, and is rarely questioned when it's harbored by a woman whose idea of "Hello" sometimes involves frag grenades.)

Grandpa Thomas had been a member of the Cove-nant of St. George. Not that he'd fit in very well, being the sort to question authority whenever he could get a word in edgewise. His travels had been the Covenant's last-ditch attempt to find *something* he could do to make himself useful: roam the world documenting the cryptid populations they had failed to find or eradicate, and then come home to England with his notes, making them available to the newest generation of monster-killing bastards in need of easy targets. Instead, he'd sworn up and down that he hadn't seen hide nor hair of anything "unnatural" while he was traveling, and that he was ready for a nice, sedentary assignment. Somewhere out of the way, where he could work on his memoirs and maybe perfect his masterwork on the snake cults of the world.

He'd been lying, of course. His guides to the cryptids of every continent had formed the seed of our family library, and we'd been improving and expanding them ever since. If Grandma Alice ever proved herself to be right—if she ever brought him home—he'd find that his

habit of dry, slightly amused scholarship had spawned
generations of extremely earnest imitators. I liked to
think that he'd be pleased.

Grandpa Thomas' stay in Australia only lasted two
years, from 1950 to 1952. During that time, he'd nearly
been killed by the Thirty-Six Society—twice—before becoming an honorary member, which may have been the
beginning of his final separation from the Covenant of St.
George. It's hard to swear to uphold the ideals and goals
of two completely disparate organizations, and from reading his account of his Australian visit, I think he liked the
Thirty-Sixers better. He certainly described them in more
consistently positive terms, and used the word "wanker"
a lot less.

During those two years, Grandpa Thomas traveled all
over the continent, documenting dozens of creatures,
plants, and hostile rock formations. Most of them wanted
to kill him and none of them succeeded, which means
Australia could be considered a sort of "trial by fire" for
his eventually being allowed to marry my grandmother.

The thing that most caught my attention as I read was
a passage in the introduction to his guide to Australia's
flora, fauna, and silicate life:

"Do not be fooled by the presence of sand, grass, and
clouds; do not be soothed into carelessness by the familiar shapes of sharks swimming in the water off the coast,
or the pleasant silliness of the fairy penguins riding in
with the evening tide," said the text. "This is not your
home: this is not a room you have visited before, transformed by new curtains and a few new pieces of furniture. This is an alien world that happens to share a planet
with our familiar climes, and to lose your focus is to, very
probably, lose your head. As I am sure you would like to
keep the latter, hold tight to the former, and do not let
Australia's many natural beauties lead you astray."

I sighed and closed the book, looking at Shelby—the
greatest of Australia's natural beauties—as she slept in
the seat next to mine. Her face was utterly relaxed, un-

lined in her contentment. She looked more beautiful than anything else in this dimension or any other, with her long blonde hair tangled in front of one eye and her mouth hanging just a little open. I tucked the book into the pocket of my seat, reached up to turn off the reading light, and leaned over to rest my head against her shoulder. There would be plenty of time to read before we reached land.

We were traveling to another world, after all.

Shelby woke me when the stewards came around with dinner. I fell asleep again after that, and woke a few hours later to find her hunched over her computer, typing rapidly. I sat up, yawning, and rubbed my eyes with the heel of my hand before I asked, "What's up?"

"Just checking in," she said, not looking away from her screen. "How did we live in an age before inflight Wi-Fi? It must have been like being back in caveman times, all silence and no shouting."

"I think cavemen shouted a lot," I said, yawning again. "Okay, I would commit a felony for a cup of coffee."

"There's a self-serve kitchenette a bit down the plane," said Shelby, pulling her laptop into her actual lap and contorting herself in a way that would have been impossible in anything smaller than a business class seat. I found I was unable to make myself stand up, more interested in tracing the tangled lines of Shelby's legs than I was in getting the caffeine my brain so desperately needed.

Shelby caught me staring and grinned. "Eyes up, and get moving. I want you half-awake when you get back. We have some strategy to plan."

"Yay," I said, without enthusiasm, and finally stood, squeezing through the strip of space between Shelby and the wall in order to reach the aisle. "Do you want anything while I'm up?"

"Bring me a granola bar or something." Shelby uncoiled herself again, resting her toes lightly on the plane floor as she returned her attention to her laptop. "Maybe an apple."

"I'll bring whatever I can find," I said, and started down the aisle toward the promised kitchenette.

Domestic airplanes are basically designed to keep people seated, settled, and sedated for the duration of flight. If they could, they would install catheters in the seats and strap the people down from takeoff until landing. International flights are a little different, due to the part where sometimes people's veins explode if they sit still in a pressurized cabin for too long. (This may be a small exaggeration—emphasis on "small," not "exaggeration." Deep vein thrombosis is the silent killer of the long-haul flight.) To combat this, international carriers often encourage people to get up, move around, and keep their blood circulating normally. Sure, it means the aisles get a little crowded from time to time, and it makes the TSA nervous, but better that than a bunch of dead passengers.

I inched along the aisle, careful not to hit any of our sleeping business class companions in the head, and made my way into the small, brightly lit alcove of our private kitchenette-slash-minibar. Unlike the self-serve zones in coach, our beverage selection included white wine and a selection of Australian beers, which was denuded enough to tell me that some of our fellow passengers were going to wake up with impressive headaches. Or maybe not: many of them *were* Australian, after all, and Shelby could drink me under the table, the floor, and possibly the Earth's crust.

The whole thing was nicely designed and laid out. Refrigerated crisper drawers held fruit, small cakes, and an assortment of cheeses and sliced meats, while individually wrapped packets of mixed nuts and granola bars were isolated off to one side, where they wouldn't pose a risk to people with allergies. I paused in the act of reaching for the cheese drawer, a sudden suspicion overtaking me. "Are there any mice in here?" I asked, loudly enough to be heard, but quietly enough that I wasn't shouting to the entire section.

The cheese drawer answered with a muffled "hail."

I groaned, leaning closer and addressing the drawer. "I told you to *stay in the bag*."

"False!" A brown-furred head poked out from behind a wedge of what I assumed was brie, whiskers quivering with joyful indignation. Aeslin mice were rarely happier than when they were arguing a point of holy writ. "You told us to Stay Quiet and Stay Still until we were in blessed transit. And truly did we heed your words, which echoed the ancient teachings of the God of Unexpected Situations, husband to the Violent Priestess. But once we came to blessed transit, we turned instead to the words of the Noisy Priestess, who did tell us, lo, You May Leave the Bag, Just Don't Get Caught. And we have left the bag, and we have not been caught!"

The mouse sounded so delighted with its cunning navigation of a point of theological trivia that I didn't have the heart to argue. I wouldn't have been able to win if I had: the God of Unexpected Situations was my great-grandfather, and the Noisy Priestess was Grandma Alice. The mice put a lot of stock in each new generation of gods and priestesses, but most of us lacked the cachet to successfully overturn Great-Grandpa Jonathan or his daughter on a point of order. Maybe someday, when I was older and had done more things to actually impress the mice.

Probably not.

"Well, just don't take *all* the cheese, all right? There are other people riding in business class who might want a midnight snack." Not that any of them seemed inclined to wake up from their alcohol-induced slumber, which was why I felt so comfortable having a religious debate with a talking mouse in the middle of the minibar.

Sometimes I feel as if my life is very strange.

"We will Leave Some Cheese," said the mouse, in the sort of reverent tone that usually meant I had just solidified a new commandment. Thou Shalt Not Denude the Airplane's Cheese Selection.

Again, I chose not to argue. If it meant the mice were happy and under control for the duration of flight, they could raid the minibar as much as they wanted. Instead, I took a plate from the stack next to the muffins and piled it with fruit, packets of nuts, and some of the remaining cheese, before filling two cups with coffee (mine black, Shelby's more than half milk and sugar) and walking back along the aisle to my seat. The mice could find their own way. They'd managed to wander off without my assistance, after all.

Shelby's laptop was closed and tucked into the seat-back pocket when I returned. She blinked at the tray in my hands, and asked, "Starving, are you?"

"The mice are in the middle of a fairly major supply raid," I said, squeezing past her and sinking back into my seat, somehow managing to do so without spilling my pilfered goodies. "I'll warn them about eating everything before we land after breakfast comes around, since that should give them an hour or two."

Shelby blinked again, slowly this time. "The mice are roving freely through the airplane?" she asked.

"Mice do not feel obligated to obey the fasten seat belt sign," I said, and picked up my coffee. "What's the situation on the ground?"

"Not so good," said Shelby, her confusion—and her levity—melting into a look of grim despair. "Mum says we've had four people bitten so far. Two of them are under quarantine. The other two ran off before we could catch them. One of them, Trevor McConnell, probably went to take care of things before anyone got hurt. The other's a relatively new recruit, Isaac Wall, and it's harder to say with him. He could be doing the right thing by the rest of us. He could also be going to ground and hoping that if he does turn out to be infected, he can figure out a way to live with it."

"There is no way to live with it," I said. "The virus wants to spread. He may have the best of intentions now, but if he changes, he'll be a monster like all the rest. All this means is that if he's infected, no one will know to be there to stop him before he starts attacking people."

I didn't have to ask what she meant by "doing the right thing." There's only one "right thing" where lycanthropy is concerned, and that's the thing that means you'll never have the chance to pass the infection on. It's a horrible, unfair position to put a person in. But viruses have never been known for their mercy, and people who have actually observed the progression of the lycanthropy-w virus within a community have sworn, repeatedly, that suicide is a kinder solution than any of the alternatives, and sadly, I believe them.

Lycanthropy-w is hard to catch. Out of every five people bitten, four of them will be perfectly fine. The virus doesn't deal well with the static virility of a nonshapeshifting immune system. But the fifth person . . .

The fifth person was doomed. The only question was how long it would take for them to admit it.

Shelby nodded, expression growing even grimmer. "We can't tell who's harboring the infection. That's the worst part. Da says they've killed four werewolves so far, but the bastards just keep on coming. There's so much open space there, we could be looking at almost anything."

"Remember that it could also be a 'what' harboring the infection," I said, and took another sip of my coffee, trying to buy myself a few minutes to think. We were going to need a way to locate the remaining werewolves, assuming they hadn't already been put down. Sadly, they didn't tend to mark their dens with "werewolves here, inquire within."

Shelby shook her head. "My folks were *not* happy to

hear that kangaroos could be werewolves, too. Not the sort of thing you want to spring on them, yeah?"

"Yeah," I agreed. It was still startling to me how little the Thirty-Six Society knew about lycanthropy. It made sense—they'd never had to deal with it before—but I kept stumbling over things "everybody knew" that were a complete surprise to Shelby. Even Grandpa Thomas' notes didn't help. There were too many holes where things that "everybody knew" had been left out to save space. "Have there been any signs that a pack is forming?"

"Not yet."

"Okay. That's good." It might be the *only* good thing about this situation, but it was more than I'd been expecting to get: I would take it.

As the lycanthropy-w virus became entrenched in a population, the victims would begin to come together instinctively, forming a semi-lupine pack structure. I say "semi" because how genuinely wolflike the pack was would depend on the original species of the people or creatures forming it, and how many of them were far enough gone to have become fully feral. A pack consisting entirely of freshly infected humans would probably exhibit the stereotypical "alpha" behavior attributed (incorrectly) to wolves by generations of naturalists, and would be incredibly dangerous until they had further devolved into skittish, cooperative pack hunters. From there, it would be a matter of them versus their bodies: as their transformations became more frequent, the strain on their hearts would become more severe, until they couldn't hold their original forms, and their systems collapsed under the strain. It could take six months. It could take six years. But it was how all werewolves ended up, if they didn't meet the wrong end of a shotgun first.

You know it's going to be a bad scene when your most fervent hope is that your opponents devolve into a mindless, primal, killing-machine state as quickly as possible.

"My folks have called my sisters in from the field. Raina's going to meet us at the airport," said Shelby, sipping from her own coffee before putting it down on the plate and leaning over to rest her head against the curve of my shoulder. "Everyone's coming to help with this one. Even Gabby, and getting her away from school is a bit like pulling a crocodile's teeth—borderline impossible and pretty damn dangerous."

"What are people pulled off of?"

"Everything. Dad's even bringing his head of security out of the field, and Cooper doesn't come out of the field for anything. Thankfully. Man's got the manners of a black snake." She tilted her head back, looking up at me. "We're leaving the rest of Australia defenseless to stop this. We can't let lycanthropy get well and truly established on the island. We just *can't*. Not if we want to stand a chance."

Australia was an island: that meant we might still be able to wipe the virus out, the way we had in England, Japan, and Hawaii. No shared borders meant no place to hide. But no shared borders also meant no place to run. If the virus was able to become successfully established, it could finally turn Australia into the unwelcoming wasteland so many people already believed it to be.

I kissed Shelby's forehead. It was the only thing I could think of to do. "It's not going to happen," I said. "We're not going to let that happen."

"Are you lying to me?" The question was mildly asked, and there was no blame behind it: she clearly understood the impulse. She just wanted to know.

"I hope not," I said, and put my arms around her, as much as the airline seats allowed. "I really do."

The rest of the flight passed quickly, or as quickly as is possible for a fourteen-hour stretch spent confined in the belly of a single moving vehicle. We read, slept, researched, denuded the kitchenette, and enjoyed our surprisingly well-prepared business class food. And all the while, Australia grew closer, like a great beast lurking out of the west.

Shelby caught me staring pensively out the window as the flight attendants were moving through our cabin with customs forms. "It's not that bad, you know," she said, pressing a pencil into my hand. "Almost no one gets killed unless they do something stupid. You have to provoke the wildlife into taking you out. Or step on a funnelweb, but they're mostly down in Sydney. We'll have a whole different assortment of deadly things where we're going."

"It's not the wildlife I'm worried about," I admitted, twisting to face front and reaching for my customs form. "The werewolves scare the crap out of me, but they're something I'm trained for. I can handle snakes, spiders, and soda made with sugar instead of corn syrup."

There was a pause while Shelby cocked her head and squinted at me. Finally, she asked, "Is this about the part where my family is a little bigger than your average snake, spider, or can of Coke?"

"That would be the issue," I said, and bent forward, trying to look like I was focusing hard on the difficult matter of falsifying my customs form. (I don't recommend falsifying customs forms when traveling. For one thing, it's illegal. For another thing, most of the "are you trying to smuggle this into our country?" questions are rooted in sound ecological reasons—no one really wants to be responsible for crashing the local ecosystem with an invasive weed or beetle. At the same time, since I was on the way to Australia to help keep them all from being eaten by werewolves, I felt like fudging the details of what I had in my bag was reasonable.)

"They're really friendly, Alex."

"I believe you."

"They're quite harmless, too."

I put down my pencil and slowly turned to stare at her. Shelby had the good grace to look abashed. "Your family. Harmless. Shelby, I love you, but if you're going to tell me lies, can you at least make them believable ones? I always try to sound believable when I lie to you."

"See, this is the trouble with a relationship founded on lies," she said. "Eventually, we stop believing each other."

When Shelby and I first met, I didn't tell her I was a Price, and she didn't tell me she was a Thirty-Sixer. I guess I thought there had to be something wrong with her; that was the only way someone as amazing as Shelby Tanner would be interested in the bespectacled geek from the reptile house. Since "secretly a cryptozoologist who will understand everything about me, and actually appreciate the work I've dedicated my life to doing" was too good to be true, it never even occurred to me as a possibility — at least not until she came into my home and tried to shoot my cousin. To be fair, Sarah *is* a cuckoo, and cuckoos are incredibly dangerous, generically speaking. It's not Shelby's fault she tried to kill one of the only cuckoos in the world who would actually be missed.

I found out who Shelby really was. Shelby found out who I really was. Sarah didn't get shot in the head. And we started over, trying to reconstruct an admittedly flawed relationship on a base of facts instead of fictions. It was still a work in progress. It might always be a work in progress. It was work that I was quite happy to spend the rest of my life doing, as long as that meant I got to spend the rest of my life with her.

Shelby was still looking at me, waiting for me to comment on the subject of her family. I sighed, checked the box on my form that indicated I wasn't carrying any plants or plant products — lying again — and said, "I'm sure they're nice, and I'm also sure that my current status as visiting werewolf expert means they probably won't shoot me without good reason. It's just that if they're anything like my family, 'he breathed' might be considered a good reason."

"Don't worry so much." She elbowed me amiably before going back to filling out her own customs form. "Besides, if they really get to be too much, you can always hide behind Gabby. She's as bewildered by the lot of us as you are."

"She's the one who's going to school to be an opera singer, right?"

Shelby nodded. "Right. See? You have a sister who's a dancer, I have one who plans to be a singer. It's going to be just like taking a nice long trip home."

I sighed deeply. "That doesn't make it any better. I've *met* my family."

The sound of the engines roaring drowned out Shelby's laughter. We were in our final descent, and one way or another, I was going to Australia.

Four

"I have never seen any place on Earth as beautiful, improbable, and beautifully ridiculous as Australia. Whatever god or devil first conceived of the place deserves some sort of award, and possibly a smack in the head."

—Thomas Price

Brisbane Airport in Queensland, Australia, international arrivals terminal

SHELBY AND I WERE walking along the concourse toward customs—she looking tediously awake and alert, like she hadn't just spent far too many hours in midair, me looking like a houseplant that hadn't been watered in far too long and was thus on the verge of terminal wilt—when a short, tan, pleasantly plump woman with a riotous mop of red-and-brown curls darted out of a door marked "staff only" and cut us cleanly from the rest of the crowd.

"Hello hello hello," she said brightly, her cheerful Australian voice cutting through the hubbub like a knife. Our fellow travelers picked up their step, getting away from what sounded like the start of something they didn't want any part of. "What are you traveling for, then? Business or pleasure?"

"Bringing the bloke to meet the folks," said Shelby airily. I gave her a sidelong look. "Bloke" might be the most common Australianism in American popular culture, but it wasn't a word I heard Shelby use very often—or really ever, except when I dragged her to Outback and she returned from the bathrooms with a scathing critique of using "Blokes" and "Sheilas" to distinguish the genders. "There a problem, officer?"

"Could be, could be," said the woman. "If you two would just come with me, I'm sure we can have it all cleared up in a jiffy. So if there's nothing the two of you need before we see to the all-important business of keeping this grand nation safe from all threats foreign and national . . . ?"

It was like being confronted with a human border collie. I blinked, too disoriented from the flight and too well trained about making a fuss in airports to know what to do.

Fortunately, Shelby wasn't so confused. "Lead the way: anything for Australia."

"Anything?" asked the woman pointedly.

"Life, limb, and love."

"Very good. Follow me." She turned on her heel and stalked back to the staff door, clearly expecting that Shelby and I would follow her. Shelby did, and so I did the same, dragging my roller bag and praying the mice wouldn't start cheering without getting permission from me first.

The door slammed shut behind us. Welcome to Australia.

The woman with the riotous hair led us down an empty hallway that could have been lifted out of any airport in the world—or any soundstage designed to look like an airport, for that matter. There's something remarkably artificial about a certain type of bureaucratic sterility, like even it can't make up its mind whether or not it actually exists. Her boots thudded against the tile floor like she was personally affronted by its reality, and punishing it one slammed-down heel at a time.

"We'll be heading for one of the main screening rooms, where you and your belongings will be thoroughly reviewed," she said, without looking back at me or Shelby. Her attention seemed to be reserved for the empty hall ahead, and while her voice remained too cheerful to be natural, it didn't match her posture, which was tight, controlled, and bordering on hostile. "I do hope my men won't find anything illicit. We've been cracking down on smugglers recently. You could find yourself banned from our country for the rest of your natural life, and wouldn't that put a crimp in your *honeymoon?*"

"We're not married, and I'd have at least called home if we were," said Shelby mildly. She sounded almost amused by the situation. Well, that made one of us. "Come off it, all right? We're in private now."

"There is no privacy in an airport," replied the border collie woman, a hint of a snarl creeping into her formerly jovial tone. She picked up the pace, forcing me and Shelby to do the same if we wanted to keep up with her. Between the jet lag, the general exhaustion engendered by spending over a dozen hours on a plane, and my growing fear that the mice were going to put in an appearance, my nerves were more than a little frayed.

Shelby rolled her eyes before shooting me what was probably meant to be a reassuring look. I frowned at her. I don't appreciate being kept in the dark, and it was clear that whoever this woman was, Shelby knew and trusted her enough to let her cut us out of the main crowd. Without an introduction, I was flying blind. I didn't like the feeling. It was really starting to sink in how isolated I was, and how isolated I was going to remain for as long as I was in Australia. Even if I needed them, my family couldn't possibly get to me fast enough to provide backup. Not even Aunt Mary. She was dead, which usually meant she could travel great distances in the time it took to call her name, but most ghosts can't cross salt-water, and I had the entire Pacific between me and the place where she died. I was on my own.

I struggled to keep my face neutral as we walked. If Shelby had felt like this during her stay in the United States, it was amazing that she'd remained as steady as she had. I hadn't been on the ground an hour, and I was already fighting panic.

The border collie woman stopped at an unmarked door. Producing an old-fashioned key ring from her pocket, she unlocked it and waved us into a small, fea-tureless room. Shelby went first. I followed close behind her, and the unnamed woman brought up the rear, clos-ing the door behind herself with an ominous "click."

"Now," she said. "We should have a five-minute win-dow before anyone realizes the camera feed from this room has failed. We've got Gabby and one of her Amer-ican schoolmates clearing customs with dummy bags—they have valid passports that match the names you flew under, so we'll have a clear record of your entering the country, and we have someone in the department ready to stamp your *real* passport when you fly back out again, assuming that you do. They'll be catching a cab outside the airport, Gabby's friend will be returning to Sydney via a flight later today, and Gabby should be home by this afternoon. Cooper's driving her. Mum and Dad are going to have your hide for bringing your boyfriend with you and making us do all of this extra work. Are there any questions?"

"Yeah," said Shelby. "Can I have a hug, Raina, or are you going to stand there being all pissy 'I had to smuggle you into the country, how dare you inconvenience me so' all day?"

The border collie woman—whose demeanor had changed completely since the door had closed, becoming dour and faintly irritated with everything around her—sighed and reached up to peel off her riotous mop of brown-and-red curls, revealing short-cut brown hair that had been rumpled by its time under the wig. She threw the wig at me, snapped, "You're so demanding, Shelly," and spread her arms as she stepped toward Shelby.

Any questions I might have had about how they knew each other were answered by that embrace: it was a hug between sisters, plain and simple. When they let each other go, Raina turned to look me up and down, taking her time with the gesture, so that it felt like the examination it was. Finally, she passed judgment:

"He's short and scrawny," she said. "I never thought you'd risk Dad's wrath for the sake of coming home with a geek. I remember your college boyfriends. Most of them could have been used as architectural fixtures in a pinch."

"I nearly got turned into a piece of lawn statuary, if that helps," I said dryly, and thrust my hand out toward her. "Hello. I'm Alexander Price. It's nice to meet you."

Raina looked at my hand like it was a dead thing before looking back to my face and saying, "Raina Tanner. We didn't invite you, we don't need you, and we don't want you here."

"Raina!" Shelby cuffed her sister on the arm. "Be nice. Alex was willing to come with me to help, since he's actually dealt with this sort of thing before, and we should treat him like the guest he is."

"I am treating him like the guest he is," Raina replied. "I didn't shoot him on sight. Now come on. Mum's waiting in the car, and you know how grumpy she gets when we make her wait." She turned and stomped to the door in the opposite wall, leaving me holding her wig. She didn't take any of the bags. Apparently, extracting us from the airport had been the whole of her service, and we could handle the rest by ourselves.

"One sister down, one to go," said Shelby amiably, as she picked her bags back up again. "I think that went quite well, don't you?"

"I have no words," I said, and collected my things before following the Tanner girls out of the room.

The door opened on a short stretch of scrubland, all brown grass and stunted bushes straining their thorny limbs toward the sky. The air smelled like petrichor and growing things: I had just stepped into an Australian spring. Given that it was autumn at home, the change of seasons was almost as disconcerting as the change of scenery. Mountains ringed the far horizon. I didn't recognize any of them. I didn't recognize anything. For the first time, I found myself worried about just how helpful I could actually be. Sure, werewolves were from my world, but this was Shelby's world. Could I really do anything they couldn't have done on their own?

Shelby had known nothing about gorgons or cockatrice when she'd helped me to fight and defeat Lloyd. I couldn't back out on her now. I took a deep breath of the spring-scented air and hurried across the empty field after her.

Raina was already almost to the street by the time I caught up with Shelby: she might have been short and irritable, but that woman could move when she wanted to. There was an SUV idling there. Raina pulled open the back driver's-side door and disappeared into the vehicle.

"That's not the sister who's been away at opera school, right?" I asked, while Shelby and I had a few seconds of what could be charitably referred to as privacy. "Unless they do opera much more violently here."

"No, Gabby's the sister who's been away at opera school, Raina's the sister who got left behind with our parents and resents the rest of us for having grand adventures while she's been stuck cleaning up after the drop bears."

A horrifying parallel occurred to me. "Oh, God, she's your Annie."

"Not a bit," said Shelby amiably. "She's much crankier." We were too close to the car to continue talking without being overheard; she shut her mouth, beamed, and walked faster, arriving at the SUV just as the front driver's-side door opened and spilled an older blonde woman with Shelby's funereal scowl out onto the curb. The newcomer looked the pair of us up and down before focusing on Shelby.

"Shelly," she said.

"Hello, Mum," Shelby replied. Her own smile faded, replaced by that same "the world is ending" expression. She always looked sad when she wasn't smiling, like she hadn't bothered to develop any of the intermediate steps between joy and despair. "Thank you for coming to collect us."

"Did you really think I'd trust you to make it home on your own? You went out for milk and wound up in America." The woman's gaze flicked back to me, her look of utter despair not wavering. "This must be your guest."

"Ma'am," I said. It seemed like the safest thing to say.

"Mmm," she replied, and slid back into the car. "Shell, up front with me. Your boy can ride in the back with Ray and the bags."

"All right," said Shelby. She leaned close to me, ostensibly to pass me her suitcase, and murmured, "Don't taunt my sister. She's been known to hit," in my ear before turning and bouncing off toward the other side of the car.

I stared after her, feeling utterly in over my head, and moved to start loading the luggage into the SUV. No one helped me. After the last piece was secure, I climbed through the open passenger-side door. Shelby's mother turned the engine back on and pulled away from the curb while I was still fastening my seat belt.

Raina was a silent lump on the other side of the backseat, her attention fixed on what looked like a Nintendo 3DS. She didn't seem to be playing Pokémon, which was my first guess; instead, she was using the stylus to flip through screen after screen of complex diagrams and complicated schematic designs.

"We're clear of the last cameras, and the TSA bought Gabby and her friend as Shelby and *her* friend," said Raina finally, looking up from her little screen. "Mum, floor it."

Mum floored it.

The declaration of success and the sudden acceleration of the vehicle proved to be too much for the mice, who had, after all, been very good for a very long time, especially by rodent standards. My roller bag cheered. Loudly. Raina jumped. Shelby's mother slammed her foot down on the brakes, bringing us to a screeching halt in the middle of the road. I winced.

"If we're trying to be unobtrusive about getting out of here, maybe that wasn't a good idea?" I said, as carefully as I could. "I think sudden stops in the middle of the road are noticeable no matter where you are." The mice were still cheering. That, too, was extremely noticeable.

"*What*," said Shelby's mother, in a dangerous tone, "is that *noise?*"

"Aeslin mice, Mum," said Shelby. "Seems they're not extinct after all. Surprise!"

"I brought a splinter colony, ma'am," I said, glaring daggers at the back of Shelby's head. "The mice get uncomfortable and distressed if any member of my family is outside their presence for too long, so we usually travel with at least a small part of the overall congregation."

"Do you now?" To my relief, Shelby's mother restarted the car, and we resumed our forward journey. "What are they worshiping?"

"Us, ma'am."

"Ah."

Raina had twisted in her seat and was peering warily back at the pile of our luggage. "Where are they?" she demanded.

"My carry-on bag," I said. "There's a nice little habitat

set up for them in there. My youngest sister makes them out of shoeboxes and toilet paper rolls. I'll let them out when we get where we're going. Assuming that it's not a shallow grave somewhere."

Raina turned her glare on me. That was quickly becoming almost comforting in its familiarity. "What, do you think we murder visitors without good reason? Or were you planning to provide a good reason? Because I'm not actually opposed to murder, especially since we didn't invite you and can easily erase all proof that you ever entered this country."

"Come off it, Raina, we can't erase the immigration records," said Shelby. "Just ignore her, Alex, she likes to take the piss as much as she can. It's what gives her such a pissy disposition."

"Watch it, or I'll be pissing in your bed," snapped Raina. Then, with no sign that anyone's mood had changed in the slightest, the two sisters began giggling merrily.

I leaned back in my seat and sighed. "There are two of them," I said, to no one in particular. "My body is never going to be found."

"There are *three* of them," corrected Ms. Tanner, from the front seat. It sounded like she was at least marginally amused. That was probably a good thing. "And what makes you think there's going to be a body? I raised my girls well."

Good thing, officially canceled. "Well, ma'am, based purely on my experiences with Shelby, I have absolute faith that your daughters could make me disappear without a trace if they wanted to. I'm hoping they won't decide that they want to, seeing as how I've just come a very long way, and I did it with the intent to help."

"Yes, and don't think we're ungrateful." She certainly *sounded* ungrateful, but that didn't have to mean anything: my family habitually answers the phone with snarling and threats of physical violence. "It's just that we didn't ask you to come, and we're not in the habit of importing Americans to solve our problems for us. It seems a little, well . . . Untidy isn't quite the word I want, but it'll do in a pinch."

"*I* asked him to come, as you well know," said Shelby.

"You refused the authority to make that kind of call when you refused to come home and let your father finish your training," countered Ms. Tanner.

"I know you didn't ask me, ma'am, but I couldn't let Shelby walk back into danger alone. Not when I could help her." For a brief moment, I wished that I were truly the emotionally detached scientist I sometimes tried to be. That man could have let the woman he loved face a lycanthropy outbreak alone. He wasn't the better man, but he was probably the one with the longer life expectancy.

"Mmm," said Shelby's mother. She was silent after that. I didn't know whether that was a good thing.

We were driving down a highway that would have looked completely at home on the California coast: surrounded by scrubland, the occasional ramshackle convenience store, and eucalyptus trees. (California has a massive eucalyptus problem. They were imported during the 1800s by people who thought they could be used to build more railroad tracks. The joke was on the people who did the importing, since eucalyptus trees are only good for feeding koalas and setting the state on fire . . . and California has a real shortage of koalas.)

Then a flock of parrots flew past, their wings flashing pink against the pale blue sky, and the illusion that I was anywhere familiar shattered. I found my hands pressed against the window without having consciously decided that I was going to move, unable to tear my eyes away from the contrast of pink wings and blue sky.

Shelby twisted in her seat to see what I was doing, and laughed. "We've lost him. He's going to want to stay in Australia forever now, just so he can keep staring at the budgerigars."

"I never thought you'd go in for a man who could be enchanted by *parrots*," said Raina scornfully.

"It's good to focus on the simple things," said Shelby. "They're less likely to eat you."

I didn't respond to either of them. Raina was trying to bait me—a behavior I recognized from spending years with my own sisters—and Shelby, who was a naturalist and who had left her entire world behind when she came to America and found herself marooned in mine, understood like almost no one else could. I was in a place where everything familiar was strange again, and the only really strange thing was that the sky still looked the way it always had. I kept watching the parrots fly, and Shelby's mother drove on, into the sprawl of Brisbane.

Australian cities turned out to be just as large and complicated as American cities, which shouldn't have been a surprise, considering. It was still odd to realize that after an hour in the car, we had barely reached the outskirts of town. We'd been driving for a little over two hours when Shelby's mother—who had been quietly listening to the radio for the last thirty miles or so—lifted her head, eyes appearing in the rearview mirror, and said, "It's time. Shelly, if you would do the honors?"

"Do we really have to do this, Mum?" Shelby sounded less annoyed than resigned, like she knew that whatever she was about to say to me would be poorly received, and felt the need to put up at least a token protest. I stiffened but tried not to show it. Too many things that start with "do we really have to do this" end with a body wrapped in chains and sinking to the bottom of a swamp. Maybe tears were shed after the trigger was pulled and maybe not; that sort of thing is only a comfort to the living.

"You know your father insists," said Shelby's mother. I realized I still didn't know her first name. It hadn't seemed important, somehow. The parents of friends and acquaintances were always "Mr. and Ms. Last Name," not independent people. Not until they were the ones holding the gun.

"Uh, what are we insisting on, and do I get a vote?" I asked, trying to keep my tone light, even amiable. The sort of tone that belonged to a man no one was planning to shoot and dump in the nearest billabong.

"Mum wants you blindfolded for the final approach to the house," said Raina. She had her Gameboy out again, and was focused on the little glowing square of the screen. "Since you're a stranger and you've been exposed to Johrlac and all, it's best if we don't let you know where we live, in case this has all been a long, elaborate plan to get yourself to where you can invite your hellish masters over to slit our throats while we sleep."

The image of Sarah slitting *anyone's* throat was enough to make me pause. Laughing felt like a terrible idea, but that didn't kill the urge. "I see," I said, in a somewhat strangled tone. "Shelby? Could've warned me."

"Didn't want to spoil the surprise." At least she sounded apologetic.

"Right." I removed my glasses and tucked them into my pocket before leaning back in my seat and closing my eyes. "You may want to tie my hands, too, if we're taking basic precautions. I won't fight you. If you try to disarm me, on the other hand, you're going to find that it's not worth your time, and someone's going to wind up with a bloody nose."

There was a long pause before Raina said, "What?"

"If you tie my hands, I can't go for a gun. I figure that makes the odds about even. That doesn't mean I'm going to let you take my weapons." I kept my eyes closed. Nothing says "willing to be blindfolded" like voluntarily giving up the sense of sight. "I'm trying to be accommodating, in part because I've just traveled a long way to help, and it would be silly to get myself put on the next plane home because I don't feel like playing your reindeer games, and in part because we're in the middle of nowhere, and I'm hoping that my being cooperative will reduce the chances of a bullet to the brain."

There was a long pause. Then: "Your boyfriend's mad as a cut snake," said Raina, at the same time as her mother said, "I'm beginning to see why you like him."

"He's pretty neat," said Shelby. There was a little upward lilt in her voice, and I knew that if I opened my eyes I would see her looking back at me, a smirk on her lips, eyes bright with amusement. Looks like that made a lot of things worthwhile . . . even the feeling of her sister pulling a strap of canvas tight across my eyes.

"Not going to chain your hands," she said brusquely. "Didn't think you'd stand for it, so we didn't bring the handcuffs. Don't give me reason to regret that, yeah?"

"I'll do my best," I said. The car started moving again.

My parents were fond of alternative teaching methods, reasoning that we were the latest—and largest—generation of a lineage that had supposedly been wiped off the face of the earth, and would thus need to be prepared for anything, because the one thing they didn't prepare us for was going to be the one that got us killed. Our training included an entire summer spent being locked in the trunk of the car and taken for long, rambling drives, after which we would be dumped by the side of the road and expected to find our own way home. Verity had made it back to the house about half the time. Antimony had never made it back, but after she had displayed her unerring gift for locating the nearest pool hall, comic book store, or arcade for the fifth time, my parents had declared that her sense of direction was just fine: it simply had a different set of priorities. And I?

I had made it back every single time. So I sat in the back with my eyes covered, and mentally mapped the route from the highway to Shelby's house with no distractions from the local flora or fauna. I was almost grateful for the blindfold. It's funny how we underestimate each other in this world, isn't it?

The car rolled to a stop after fifteen minutes. "You can take the blindfold off now, Alex," said Shelby. "We're here."

I hesitated, waiting for Raina to contradict her sister, before I reached up and removed the strip of canvas, bringing the world back into blurry color. Replacing my glasses on my nose put the hard edges back on the scene around me, and I turned to look out the window . . .

. . . only to find myself looking straight into the barrel of a shotgun that had apparently been designed to take down rampaging bull elephants. I blinked, following the line of the barrel until I reached the man on the other end. He, too, was built like he had been designed to take down rampaging bull elephants, possibly by punching them in the face until they decided to go rampage somewhere else. He had sandy blond hair, narrow blue eyes, and the sort of deep tan that only comes from spending every possible minute outdoors over the course of twenty or thirty years. I blinked. He scowled.

The car door slammed and Shelby leaped into my field of vision, hurling herself at the gun-toting mountain of a man with a gleeful cry of, "Daddy!"

For his part, the man with the gun—who had to be Shelby's father, unless their family was substantially more complicated than I'd been led to believe—weathered her impact without flinching or allowing his aim to waver. "Roll down the window," he said, loudly enough that I could hear him through the glass.

"Better do as he says," said Raina, who hadn't budged from her seat beside me. "He gets impatient easy."

"Yes, but if he was going to shoot me, you'd have already gotten out to avoid the glass spray," I said, and rolled the window down, careful to keep my hands visible. The smell of eucalyptus and freshly-cut grass wafted into the car, garnering a cry of "Hail!" from the suitcase behind me. I ignored the mice as best I could, fixing a polite smile on the man with the gun as I said, "Mr. Tanner, it's a pleasure to meet you."

"You bring any proof you are who you say you are?" It wasn't the friendliest greeting in the world. That wasn't a real surprise. Cryptozoological conservation is difficult. Not only are we trying to protect a population of creatures that can't be legally defended from poachers, on account of not legally existing, but we're trying to do it without attracting the attention of the Covenant of St. George, which is always lurking in the shadows, waiting to destroy everything we've worked for. We're friendly with each other, once our identities have been confirmed, but as far as Shelby's father was concerned, I was a semi-known quantity. His daughter vouched for me. His daughter also claimed I was sharing a house with two cuckoos without having my brain come dribbling out of my ears. There was every chance in the world that she'd been compromised.

"I don't have any photo ID with my real name on it, because that would be a violation of all known security protocols, but I may have something better," I said. "Do you mind if I get my proof of identity out of my suitcase?"

"You armed?"

"I'm a Price, sir. If I were unarmed, I would be trying to take someone else's weapons, just for the sake of my own peace of mind. But you have my word that I'm not going for a weapon. Even if I were lying about my identity, which I'm not, I wouldn't want to risk Shelby getting hurt."

"I can take care of myself, Alex," said Shelby. She was still hanging off her father's arm, and part of me insisted on pointing out that this would throw his aim slightly off, making it easier for me to take his gun away if it came to that.

"I know you can take care of yourself," I said. "I also know that making a good impression on your parents gets harder if I get you shot in the process."

"This is what you call making a good impression?"

asked Raina. I decided to ignore her. It seemed like the safest course of action.

Shelby's father frowned, his eyes narrowing further. "The ship of good impressions may have already sailed," he said. "Keep your movements slow. Ray, if he does anything you don't like, subdue him."

"Sure thing, Dad," said Raina, her attention still on her Gameboy. "If the presumably heavily-armed American does something I don't like, I will absolutely throw myself on that grenade."

"Actually, my grandmother's the one with the grenades," I said, and unbuckled my belt before twisting—oh, so slowly—to lean over the backseat and rummage through the top level of our luggage. Luckily for me, my carry-on bag had been placed with the zipper facing the front of the car, and it was a relatively easy matter for me to wiggle it open and call, "I require an acolyte," into the depths of the bag.

A tiny brown head popped out, whiskers quivering and ears pressed forward, like its owner was afraid of missing some piece of essential wisdom that would finally tie the workings of the universe together. "Hail!" piped the mouse.

"That's definitely a mouse," said Raina, who had actually looked up from her Gameboy when I started talking to the luggage. "It's not a reprogrammed Furby. Not even a little bit."

"No, it's not," I agreed. I held my hand out to the mouse. The tiny creature stepped reverently onto the pad of my thumb, wrapping its tail tight around its legs. I kept my eyes on the mouse. The Aeslin mice love it when we talk directly to them. It makes them feel like they're communing with their gods, not just serving as a really weird footnote. "Hail," I said. "Do you mind confirming a few things for me?"

"Thy Will Be Done," squeaked the mouse, throwing its head back in a burst of religious ecstasy.

"Thank you," I said. I twisted back around, returning my butt to its original position on the seat, and extended the mouse toward Shelby's waiting father. "Sir, do you know what this is?"

He blinked. "It looks like an Aeslin mouse," he said. "But that's impossible. They've been extinct for over a century."

"Not in my family's attic they haven't." I allowed myself a faint smile. "If you want to confirm my identity, ask the mouse." Aeslin mice don't lie. They never forget anything they see or hear, they preserve the history of a colony through religious dogma and ritual recreation, and they don't lie.

For the first time, Shelby's father looked vaguely impressed. "That's a clever one," he allowed, before turning his attention on the mouse. "Hello."

"Hail!" squeaked the mouse.

Shelby's father was a man trying to defend both his home and his daughter from a potentially dangerous visitor, and yet he couldn't swallow the smile that tugged at the corners of his mouth. He looked like a man who'd just been told that Christmas wasn't canceled after all—which wasn't an unreasonable response to finding out that one of the world's weirdest, most wonderfully useless sapient species wasn't extinct. "Mouse, can you confirm the identity of the man who's holding you?"

"Yes," said the mouse proudly. It preened its whiskers, looking like it had just passed a quiz of some sort.

I sighed. "You'll have to be more literal, I'm afraid."

"Sorry. I'm not well-versed in human to rodent communication techniques." He focused back on the mouse. "Who is the man holding you?"

"I stand in the palm of the God of Scales and Silence, son of the Thoughtful Priestess and the God of Decisions Made in Necessity," said the mouse.

"He wants their names," I said. It seemed almost a pity to shortcut what otherwise promised to be an entertaining bout of Man vs. Mouse, but I needed to pee, and

I wanted to get out of the car before somebody lost patience and did something we were all going to regret later. "Please tell him the names."

"Oh!" squeaked the mouse, sounding surprised. Then, drawing itself up to its full height of almost three inches, it said, "He is Alexander Jonathan Price, son of Evelyn Baker and Kevin Price, son of Alice Healy and Thomas Price—"

"—who wrote the field guide to the cryptids of Australia and New Zealand, which I have with me, so you should be able to compare his handwriting to any local samples," I said. "I know this is an unorthodox method of confirming identity, but given that 'please come to Australia with me, there are werewolves everywhere and they're going to eat my family' is an unorthodox request, can we call it good?"

There was a long pause, during which I began to fear that I'd overplayed my hand, before Mr. Tanner lowered his gun. My heart rate immediately began dropping back toward normal. It dropped further as he opened the door and gestured for me to get out of the car. "Riley Tanner. Nice to meet you. Shelly's told us a lot, but that's no substitute for actually getting to spend time with someone—and as you mentioned, there's our little werewolf issue to focus on."

"It's nice to meet you, sir." I slid out of the car, raising my hand to my shoulder long enough for the mouse to hop off before offering it to him to shake. His grip was firm enough to make my fingers ache, but I didn't get the feeling he was trying to crush my hand; he was just a man who was accustomed to shaking hands without thinking about how hard he squeezed. "Shelby hasn't told me much about her family, apart from the fact that she has sisters and parents."

"She told us the same about you," said Riley, dropping my hand. "We raised her to understand operational security, didn't we, Shelly?"

"I wish you wouldn't call me that, Daddy." Shelby finally unpeeled herself from his arm. She trotted back toward the car, pausing long enough to kiss my cheek as she passed. "I told you, it's Shelby. That's my name."

"We call Raina 'Ray,' and we call Gabrielle 'Gabby,' so you should put up with it; we're your parents," said Riley. He sounded amused; this was apparently a conversation they had with some frequency. Shelby responded with a snort.

Shelby's mother, meanwhile, had finally gotten out of the car. "The girls will get your luggage," she said, walking over to stand next to me. "You look like you're about to drop dead where you stand. Let's get you inside and to a bed before you collapse."

"I'm not that tired," I lied. The trip was catching up with my body, which was protesting the change of time zones and hemispheres in the only way it knew how: with growing fatigue. "Can I get a few old boxes for the mice to use while I'm here? They'll be less trouble if they have a designated place to go when they're not demanding I do something for them."

"Hail!" squeaked the mouse on my shoulder, like a demented punctuation generator.

Shelby's mother smiled. "I think we can find something. This way." She started walking. I followed.

I hadn't really noticed the lack of a house when Shelby's father appeared outside my window: I was more focused on the gun, and what it could mean for my future. Now that I was following Shelby's mother into increasingly thick brush, the lack of a house was becoming more pressing. "Er," I said, and stopped, unsure how to proceed.

Fortunately for me, this seemed to be the opening line of a question she'd heard before. "We don't have a driveway," she said. "This is where we park the car—and no, that's not an Australian thing, it's a family thing. We have to carry our groceries a little farther, but we don't get surprised by visitors."

"You're going to get on splendidly with my mother," I said. "Speaking of which, and I don't know how to say this without sounding awkward, but....Shelby never told me your name. I'm happy to keep calling you 'Ms. Tanner,' if that's your preference. I just wanted to ask."

"Charlotte," said Shelby's mother. "You can call me 'Ms. Tanner' if that's what you're comfortable with or 'Lottie' if you feel like being more informal." She swept aside a curtain of dangling branches, revealing a swath of wide, open ground covered with the glowing fuzz of new-grown grass. Something that I would have taken for a kangaroo, if it hadn't been covered in rosette spots like a leopard, was cropping at the grass within a small enclosure. There was also a house, three stories high and rising against the sky like a monument to human habitation, but it seemed somehow less important than the animal I'd never seen before.

Charlotte followed my gaze to the enclosure, and said, "We don't know what she is. She wandered in one morning with a broken leg—we thought she'd been painted at first, but the dots wouldn't wash off. So we built her a pen, and we've been studying her, trying to suss out her story. Could be she's a chromatic mutant. Could also be she's a member of a highly endangered species, and explains some of the periodic 'leopard' sightings that we've never been able to figure out. Either way, we're taking care of her until we understand her story a little better."

"Neat," I said. I felt immediately silly, but that didn't change the accuracy of the word. Mysterious, leopard-spotted kangaroos were definitely neat, no matter how immature that sounded.

Charlotte smiled indulgently and kept walking. I could hear cracking noises and footsteps coming from the brush behind us as the rest of the family followed with the luggage. That, more than anything, motivated me to speed up and match pace with Charlotte as she bounded up the porch steps and opened the screen door.

Shelby's sister had been grumpy enough before she was forced to carry my suitcase through a stretch of carefully cultivated forest.

"Come on, Alex," said Charlotte. "Jet lag is going to catch up with you if you hold still for too long, and then you'll fall asleep on the porch."

"That doesn't sound so bad," I said. "It's a beautiful day."

"Yes, but around four o'clock in the afternoon, the spiders come." With that, she vanished inside. She was probably kidding—Australia has a lot of spiders, but as far as I know, they don't keep to a strict schedule. "Probably" wasn't a word I wanted to risk my life on.

Charlotte was already halfway across the living room and heading for the stairs by the time I made it through the front door. I hurried to catch up.

"You'll be in the guest room, of course," said Charlotte when I drew close enough, as calmly as if I'd never lagged behind. "It has locks on both the inside and outside, and I've mostly talked Riley into not locking you in at night, but you shouldn't push it if you don't have to. He's not exactly keen on the fact that the American expert Shelby brought is also the man she's sleeping with, if you follow. Says it smacks of trying to impress him with how suitable you are, when you're clearly not suitable at all."

"Er," I said. "What makes me unsuitable?"

Charlotte gave me a look that, while kind, somehow managed to clearly indicate that I was being a fool, and should stop at once. "You're dating our daughter, and you're an American. You represent both 'our little girl is growing up' and 'our little girl is having her loyalties divided.' You were never going to be suitable. Not for a minute."

"Ah," I said, blinking.

Charlotte started up the stairs without waiting for any further reply. I followed her.

The stairs led to a hallway, which led in turn to a series

of doors. Charlotte stopped in front of one of them, and said, "Guest room, attached toilet, so you should be taken care of. Wireless password is on the bedside table, and I'll send Raina up with your bags while we debrief Shelly on the situation. You need to take a nap. No matter how much you feel like you're at top operating condition, you're wrong. Jet lag plays with your head. Gabby will be back by dinner, so I'll send someone to wake you then."

It made sense that they'd want to debrief Shelby without me around—everything that had happened since we had arrived had made sense—but that didn't mean I needed to like it. I put my hand on the doorknob, looked at her, and asked, "Is it as bad as I think it is? Shelby told me what was going on."

Charlotte's laugh was strained and tight, the laugh of a woman who has looked into the abyss only to discover that it is deeper than she could possibly have imagined. "Shelly never had much of an imagination," she said. "However bad she said it was, she was wrong. It's worse."

I sighed. "Of course it is," I said. "What would be the fun of it being anything else?"

Five

"This is a terrible, horrible, incredibly foolish idea. Let's try it and see what happens."
—Jonathan Healy

The guest room of an isolated house in Queensland,
Australia, trying to wake up

I HADN'T EXPECTED TO be able to sleep after Charlotte's
dire proclamation, but I had gone into the guest room
anyway: it was clear that I wasn't going to be left anywhere else without a chaperone for the time being, and
I wanted to visit the promised toilet sooner rather than
later. She had been speaking in the British sense—
instead of a commode in the middle of the room, there
was a narrow door leading to what my family would
have called a "half-bath," with a toilet, sink, and nothing
else. I took care of my business, washed my hands and
face, and returned to the main guest room to find my
bags propped against the foot of the bed. The roller bag
was unzipped, and the mice were nowhere to be seen.

Aeslin mice are small and have limited natural defenses, but they're also smart, and surprisingly good at
surviving, considering the massed forces the world has
rallied to kill them off. I sat down on the edge of the bed

and pulled out my laptop, trusting the mice to take care of themselves.

The wireless password was where Charlotte had said it would be, and I got it on the first try. My inbox was a nightmare sea of messages from the zoo, my grandparents, Dee, and people who hadn't emailed me since I'd left college, but had been prompted by the strange force that works to explode the email of travelers. I tapped out quick messages to the people who needed to know that I had landed safely—my parents, Grandma, Verity— before closing the lid on my computer and setting it aside. My eyes itched. I removed my glasses so I could rub my eyes with the heel of my hand, and somehow that translated to placing my glasses on the bedside table and letting my head drop to the pillow. It wouldn't hurt anything to close my eyes for just a few moments, I reasoned; I didn't actually have to take a nap.

The sound of a knock on the guest room door snapped me back to consciousness, my hand going for the gun at my belt before I realized where I was—and that I'd gone to sleep with a loaded weapon on my person. Not good gun safety. Not good anything, really. I sat up, rubbing my entire face with my hand, and noticed that the room had gone dark. However long I'd been asleep, it had carried me past sunset. "Who is it?" I called.

"Shelby," came the answer. "Are you done snoring your life away and ready to join the ongoing crisis, or should I come back in an hour? Mum's made lamb stew, if that makes a difference in your answer."

"I'm up." I grabbed my glasses, slid them on, and stood. Everything hurt substantially more than could be explained by the position I'd been sleeping in. I decided to hate jet lag. "What time is it?"

"Just past seven. You decent?"

I paused. Shelby had seen me naked any number of times, and I had seen her the same way; I could recreate the scars she bore from her years of working with predators both known and cryptozoological with my eyes closed. Being in a house with her parents was going to take some getting used to. "I fell asleep with my clothes on."

"Alex." The door swung open to reveal Shelby standing silhouetted by the light that filled the hall. She was wearing a sundress I'd never seen before, and her hair was down, tempting me to plunge my fingers into it and skip straight to getting in trouble with her father. That temptation only lasted a few seconds before my attention was caught by the creature crouching on her shoulder and watching me with wary, avian eyes. It was about the size of a small housecat or a very large ferret, with bright pink plumage on its head and wings, and the striped hindquarters of an animal I'd never seen before.

Shelby saw where I was looking, and beamed. "Alex, meet Flora. Flora, this is Alex." The little beast responded with a warble that devolved into a screech.

"I've never seen a garrinna in the flesh," I said, standing and moving slowly closer, so as not to frighten her. "She's beautiful."

"She was the runt of her litter, which is why she wound up brought into the house instead of staying in the aviary with her brothers and sisters. They all moved on to conservation sites, she stayed here with me." Shelby kissed the top of the garrinna's head. Flora responded by rubbing her beak, birdlike, against Shelby's cheek. "She's a clever girl. Can have the blender apart in minutes, if we leave her unmonitored in the kitchen. You ready to come downstairs?"

It took me a moment to follow her change of topics. I nodded. "I think I'm as ready as I'm going to be. Did your other sister get here safely?"

"Gabby? Yeah, she's here. Came in about half an hour ago with a sob story about Cooper getting them lost and being stopped by tourists and something about a kangaroo in a chemist's and anyway, she's here now, so if you're ready to come downstairs . . . ?" Shelby stopped, looking at me expectantly. The garrinna on her shoulder chirped.

I smiled. "Let's go."

The sound of voices and the meaty smell of stew greeted us halfway down the stairs, wafting from somewhere toward the back of the house. I let Shelby take the lead, since we were on her territory now, and focused instead on the things around me, trying to get an idea of what I was walking into.

The first thing: there were no pictures on the walls. Back at home, my family history was displayed in black and white, Kodachrome, and even the occasional ink drawing. Once you were in the house, you knew who we were and where you were standing, and you weren't going to leave alive unless we let you. There was no point in hiding ourselves in the one place where we should have been able to be safe. But these walls were virtually bare, brightened only by a few small watercolor paintings. There were alcoves set into the wall every three feet, and vases of bright artificial flowers had been placed in them, creating a slightly homier atmosphere.

My impression of the front room had been that it was functional but not lived in. Looking closer only reinforced that idea. All the furniture was exactly weathered enough to be believable—the sort of effect that comes either from actual use, or from carefully patronizing the local thrift stores until you've put together the right combination of couches, chairs, and slightly scuffed coffee tables. It was too perfectly flawed to be real, which should have been an oxymoron, and yet somehow wasn't. It was a television set, not a home.

Shelby caught me squinting at the couch and smiled wryly. "Should've guessed, I suppose," she said. "Well, it wasn't my call and it's too late now, so we might as well make the most of it, don't you think?"

She hadn't said anything to confirm or deny my suspicions. She didn't need to. "No one lives here," I said. "This is . . . a way station? A safe house?"

"Sort of a combination of the two," Shelby said. "It belonged to one of our founders. Anyone can use it, if they have legitimate need and can get approval from the rest of the Society. Basic furnishings and such come with the house, and we all work to keep them updated and keep the place in proper shape. It's good to have bolt-holes, when you need them."

"It is," I agreed, thinking of the family home back in Buckley. It was old and crumbling, and the walls were full of black mold, but we kept it all the same. You never knew when you might need to run away. "I thought we were going to your house." It was hard to admit, even to myself, but the fact that I wasn't seeing the place where Shelby had grown up stung. I knew less about where she'd come from than I liked; I'd been looking forward to seeing her childhood home, and starting to get an idea of what it had meant to her.

But this wasn't about me. This was about werewolves in Australia, and the danger they presented to the entire continent. I tried to remind myself of that as Shelby pressed a hand against the hallway wall and a section swung inward, revealing a hidden door. The smell of our waiting dinner grew stronger. "Seeing the places where we actually live comes later," she said. "Maybe after the danger's past. Now in you get."

"Is this a 'so everyone can aim a weapon at me' request?" I asked warily.

Shelby smiled like the sun rising across Botany Bay. "Call it a bonding exercise," she suggested, while Flora chirped and flapped her wings.

I sighed. "If they shoot me, you get to explain it to my family," I said, and stepped through the door in the wall to the room on the other side.

It was a large space, big enough to be considered a small ballroom, with several long wood tables pushed together in the center, bringing back unpleasant memories of summer camp. Half the tables were full, packed with people I had to assume belonged to the Thirty-Six

Society. Some of them were in the archetypical Australian khakis, but most were dressed like the sort of people I saw every day at the zoo back in Ohio: jeans and light shirts, knee-length skirts and tank tops, shorts and sundresses and every other combination of casual clothing that could be easily moved in while still being substantial enough to conceal a reasonable number of weapons. Some of those weapons were on display.

As soon as I had stepped through the wall, almost every person in the room had drawn a gun, knife, or sling of some sort, and aimed it in my direction. Only Raina, whose attention was back on her DS, and the thin, short-haired blonde girl sitting next to her were disinterested in threatening my life. Given placement, the short-haired girl was probably Shelby's other sister. It made sense that she'd be reluctant to attack me: the sooner we dealt with the werewolf problem, the sooner she could get back to opera school.

"Er, hello," I said, offering a small, nonthreatening wave. "I'm Alexander Price. You must be the Thirty-Six Society. I would greatly prefer it if you didn't put a bullet into my brain; it would complicate my plans for life, most of which involve not being dead."

Shelby appeared behind me, pulling the door shut as she entered. She crossed her arms, looking at the gathered crowd with the bland disinterest that she always brought to staff meetings at the zoo, and asked, "Well? You lot going to shoot us or what? Because I'm starving, and I'm going to take it personally if somebody decides to kill my boyfriend."

"Well, *I'm* going to take it personally if I get eaten by a *werewolf* because we went and shot the dude who actually knows how to kill them," said Raina, finally looking up from her video game. It was a video game now, not a monitoring device—when she tilted her screen, I could see colorful animated monsters beating the snot out of each other. "Can we all say 'yay, we waved our dicks around,' and eat our damn dinner already?"

"I think I like your sister," I murmured.

"Don't worry, she doesn't like you," Shelby murmured back. Louder, she said, "I'm Shelby Tanner; you all know me; my parents are custodians in residence of the house you're all sitting in, and my mum cooked that stew you're getting ready to enjoy; I affirm and testify that Alexander Price is who he says he is, and that he's here to help us, assuming all this nonsense doesn't scare him off. I further affirm and testify that if you don't all stop being such right twits, I'm going to take him and go find a nice motel. Dad." She turned, focusing on her father. His cheeks were red, and he looked like he couldn't decide whether to be amused or angry. "I know you're just trying to look out for the Society, and I also know that when Thomas Price came through here, he was still with the Covenant, but *you* know that he was in the process of quitting, and we *both* know his descendants never signed up at all. So can we stop? This isn't funny, it isn't fun, and it isn't dealing with the *werewolf problem* that's threatening to eat us all."

Shelby wasn't the sort of person who got impassioned. Even when her old apartment had been set on fire, she had remained relatively calm, right up until we were free and clear and passing out from shock and pain. But as she addressed her father, spots of hectic pink appeared in her cheeks and her hands clenched into fists at her sides, clearly telegraphing her frustration. I hesitated before reaching out and taking her hand in mine. She shot me a quick, surprised look, but she didn't pull away. She needed me as much as I needed her. That was becoming increasingly clear.

"Sir, even if I belonged to the Covenant, which I don't, and even if I wanted to cause difficulty for the Society, which again, I don't, I would never do anything to hurt your daughter." I shrugged a little. "I've been subverted, if you can call it that when members of two organizations that should be capable of getting along and working together start sharing information. I'm not here to make trouble."

"No, but you're apparently here to make speeches," said Charlotte Tanner, walking in through a door at the back of the room. She was holding a large covered bowl from which the scent of freshly baked soda bread drifted. Looking around the gathering, she sighed and shook her head. "Look at all those guns. I swear, half you people signed up to protect our ecology because you secretly wanted to be in an American Wild West movie. Weapons away, it's time for supper. Shelly, you and Alex will be eating with me and your father. We want to start filling him in."

"Yes, Mum," said Shelby, and pulled her hand out of mine as she trotted over to relieve her mother of her burden. It was a perfectly domestic moment, and the only things that detracted from it were the people looking shamefaced as they made their weapons disappear back into vests and pockets. In a matter of seconds, we looked more like a revival meeting or church group than we did a gathering of cryptozoologists. That was okay by me.

Raina looked over and waved, gesturing for me to join her and the third sister—Gabby—at the table with the pair of them, some people I didn't know, and Riley Tanner. Lacking any other options (and any bowls to carry), I shrugged and walked over to drop myself into an open seat. "Is dinner always this exciting around here?"

Riley shot me a flatly hostile look, but Raina shrugged and said, "Nah, sometimes we actually get to shoot people. Way more interesting, and the crocs get a snack out of it. You haven't met Gabby yet, have you?"

"You know I can't tell whether you're joking or trying to imply that you would happily feed me to a crocodile," I said. "Since I've fed several people to an alligator snapping turtle, I'll take it both ways. No, I haven't met Gabby. Hello, Gabby. I'm Alex."

"Hiya." The third Tanner sister held her hand out for me to shake, flashing a quick smile that was very much like Shelby's: it lit her up from the inside. I was starting to feel like the three of them charted a line from melancholy to joy, with Shelby on one end and Raina on the other. This sister, Gabrielle, seemed to be somewhere in the middle. "Nice to meet you." She had a sweet, liquid voice; I could understand why she'd chosen opera school. Cryptozoology isn't for everyone. Some people want to live.

"I just wish it could have been under better circumstances." I reclaimed my hand and took another look around the room. Pots of stew had been placed on three of the long tables, each too large to have been moved by a single person, and bowls were being filled by servers who clearly had experience at dishing out food for crowds of this size. Shelby and her mother were among the servers. I would have felt bad about that—my mother taught me it was never appropriate for me to sit back while women waited on me—but the other three pots were being staffed by men, and I wasn't sure I would have been allowed to help if I'd tried. I was a guest, after all, and more than that, I was an untrusted guest. The last thing I needed was for someone to get food poisoning and accuse me of attempted murder.

"Tell me about it," said Gabrielle. "I was at school, happily getting ready for midterms, and suddenly I'm being pulled out for a 'family emergency.'"

"Werewolves are a family emergency," said Raina. She managed to make the words sound halfway reasonable. No small feat. "If they ate us all while you were away at singsong school, you'd have to avenge us alone, and you'd get eaten, too. This way there's still a chance in hell you'll graduate."

"Troll," said Gabrielle.

"Shrieking kookaburra," countered Raina.

"Girls," said Riley. Both Tanner sisters fell instantly, ominously silent, watching their father with wary eyes. Riley shook his head. "We do not fight in front of company."

Translation: we do not fight in front of the visiting

cryptozoologist whom we do not yet completely trust. "I don't suppose any of you have seen the mice running about, have you?" I asked, trying to keep my tone light and casual. "They weren't hosting a bacchanal on the pillow when I woke up, so I'm assuming they're off somewhere exploring and endangering the local wildlife."

"Mice?" said Gabrielle.

"You've got that backward," said Raina. "The local wildlife is going to be endangering them."

"You haven't spent much time around Aeslin mice," I said.

Riley laughed. I smiled, pleased with myself. If I could just get things to lighten up a little bit on the personal level, maybe we could start properly focusing on the utter devastation the werewolves were preparing to send our way.

Before the conversation could resume, Shelby and Charlotte walked over with a smaller bowl of soda bread and a tray containing six bowls of stew and a large platter of roast root vegetables. They plunked their burdens down on the table; Shelby sat next to me, and Charlotte sat next to Riley, plucking the DS from Raina's hands as she descended.

"Hey!" protested Raina.

"Not during dinner and strategy sessions," said Charlotte. The DS vanished into her pocket. "You can have it back after we've finished discussing the situation."

Raina folded her arms and scowled. Gabby snickered, half-covering her mouth with one hand. Raina redirected her scowl at Gabby, which turned her snicker into a full-fledged laugh. Shelby pressed a spoon into my hand, and I turned toward her, startled.

She was grinning at me. "My sisters are better than most of what's on television, especially if you get Gabby drunk enough that she's willing to start singing the really filthy arias, but right now, you need to eat. Food's going to help you get switched over to local time."

"I don't think that's scientifically accurate," I said, sticking my spoon into the bowl.

"No, but my mum made the stew, and a bunch of people who probably aren't intending to poison us helped make the damper, just be a peach for once in your life and eat, okay?"

"Okay," I said. Then I paused. "What's damper?"

Shelby rolled her eyes and pointed to the soda bread. "Damper," she explained. *"Eat."*

"Okay," I said again, and ate.

Meals with large groups of people are always essentially the same. No one wants to do any serious strategizing until the food is done, but everyone wants to get it over with before dessert, if possible. What felt like the entire Thirty-Six Society stopped talking and bent to the all-important task of cramming stew, soda bread, and semi-identifiable tubers into their mouths.

The break was welcome. I hadn't been expecting quite this large a crowd when I arrived; Shelby's family, yes, and probably a few more of their colleagues, but not everyone they'd ever met. I do reasonably well with groups—better than Antimony, who never met a congregation outside of a comic convention or roller derby bout that she didn't immediately want to set on fire, not as well as Verity, who thinks an auditorium full of people is another word for "Heaven," as long as they're all there to see her dance—but I have my limits. Being put on display in front of the entire Thirty-Six Society was pushing them.

At least it was making me focus on my table manners with an intensity that my mother would have been impressed to see.

I scanned the room as I ate, trying to get an idea of the internal hierarchy of the place. Family groups seemed to be seated together, and the Tanners weren't the only multigenerational family in evidence. The people seemed to come from all races and walks of life; there was a woman in blue doctor's scrubs, and a man dressed in overalls who looked like he'd just come from a sheep farm. A census of the room might well have produced an accurate racial map of the country, and the gender balance was split roughly down the middle, maybe trending slightly male in the older members, but rebalancing in the younger generation. It was odd. And it was, in its own way, alienating. Thanks to my family's schism from the Covenant of St. George, I had grown up almost like a member of some fictional order of chosen heroes, Jedi or Knights of the Round Table or something equally silly. We were few, we supported each other, and if we fell, no one would do the job we had been tasked with.

Well, there were over a hundred people in this room who would be quite happy to do the job I'd been tasked with, thanks; the Thirty-Six Society was large and thriving, and wouldn't have known that I had ever lived or died on the other side of the world if not for Shelby. "Humbling" was the good way to look at it. "Terrifying" was equally valid.

Shelby pushed her bowl aside. I looked down at my own, and realized it was empty; I'd been eating air for the past thirty seconds. Cheeks hot, I put down my spoon. That seemed to be the cue the rest of the table had been waiting for, like civility said that no one could talk about the werewolves until the company was finished eating.

"I've heard worse house rules," I muttered. Shelby gave me a curious look. I shook my head. "Nothing."

"Good, because my dad's about to get started," she said. I followed her gaze to see Riley stand and walk across the room to a low podium. There was even a microphone mounted there, Toastmaster-style.

He tapped it once with his forefinger, sending a hollow thumping noise through the room. The expected wave of faintly nervous laughter followed. I guess some things are universal. Leaning closer, he said, "Good evening, everyone. I'm Riley Tanner, and I'm one of the people who organized this meeting, since it strikes me that werewolves in Queensland aren't a good thing for either long-term survival or the tourist trade."

More laughter this time, less nervous and more understanding. He was drawing them into a sense of shared camaraderie, and I envied the ease with which he seemed to be handling the crowd. Much like Shelby, who never met a zoo audience she didn't want to show off for, he was genuinely charismatic and interesting to watch. Whereas I had one of my thesis advisers take a phone call during my defense.

The laughter faded. Riley's expression turned serious. "I'll be level with you, everyone: Lottie has been doing some research, and if we don't get this dealt with soon, the buggers have the potential to infect half the people in Queensland. This could become a pandemic while we're sitting around here drinking coffee and trying to sort out the quarantine procedures.

"We all know about the four members of our Society who have been bitten. I am sorry to report that Trevor McConnell's body was found earlier today. He had removed himself to an isolated patch of land, and did what he had to do. There's been no sign of Isaac Wall since he was bitten. If you see him, do not approach, do not engage; withdraw, but mark his position, and contact support as soon as you can. We don't know whether he's been infected, and more, we don't know how long it takes after infection for a new werewolf to be capable of passing that infection to others."

"The average incubation period is twenty-eight days; they're not infectious until first transformation," I said quietly, almost without realizing I was going to speak. Shelby shot me a warning look.

Her father was still talking. "Pamela and Jeffrey Cornish remain in quarantine. We wish them the best, and are hopeful that they'll be able to avoid this infection. In addition to these members of our Society, we have confirmed fifteen bites in the general local population. We can't place them under quarantine, for obvious reasons, but we're in contact with local hospitals, and we've placed teams on their homes. If anyone shows signs of becoming symptomatic, we should know."

It was a calm, reasonable, fair way of dealing with a lycanthropy-w outbreak, and the fact that the Thirty-Six Society was adopting it made it clear all over again how little experience they had with therianthropic disease. There was no need for quarantine, just care, and constant monitoring. If the victims couldn't be restrained on a moment's notice—if they couldn't be put down without causing a riot—they should have been destined for shallow graves where their bodies would never be found. It was horrible. It was heartless. It was almost directly contrary to family policy under any other circumstances. The mere fact that it *was* policy for circumstances like these highlighted the dangerous nature of the situation.

"We're still working on finding the means by which the original werewolf entered the country. Since we don't know the identity of our patient zero, it's been slow going. We have people at the airports and the cruise ship landings, checking manifests, looking for anything out of order. Hopefully we'll have a breakthrough soon, and can isolate our original carrier, which will help us figure out who else may have been exposed. It'd be faster if we had a virologist—I'll be sure to order one from the next catalog that comes along."

Some people laughed nervously. I didn't. I was doing the math in my head.

Four members of the Society had been bitten. Fifteen members of the general populace had been bitten. What about kangaroos? What about sheep? What about the cryptid population of the area? If it was mammalian, it was at risk . . . and just like that, I realized what had been bothering me about the crowd. The people here were black, white, Asian, Indian, and Pacific Islander; they were men and women, young and old; there was even one man about my age in a wheelchair, with the defined upper body of a weightlifter and the scowl of an angry Norse God. And they all had one thing in common.

They were all human.

Trying not to look like I was ignoring Riley, who was now talking about population density in the Queensland area, I leaned toward Shelby and murmured, "Does the Thirty-Six Society have any cryptids in its active membership?"

"What? No." She was startled enough that she forgot to lower her voice. Several people turned toward us and glared, including her mother. Shelby grimaced, mouthing, "Sorry," before whispering, "No, we're all human. We don't have that many cryptids living in Australia. Not of the sort that would be interested in conservation activities, I mean. Plenty of bunyip and the like, but bunyip aren't big into doing their civic duty, yeah?"

"Yeah," I agreed grimly. Twisting back around to face Riley, I raised my hand.

"—which is why it's essential that we—yeah?" Riley stopped mid-sentence, frowning at the unthinkable sight of someone not holding their questions until the end. He recovered quickly, sliding smoothly into a new phrase. "Everyone, if you weren't already aware, we have a distinguished visitor from the United States with us tonight. My daughter, Shelby Tanner, who will one day be taking my place at this podium, has brought her associate Dr. Alexander Price, of the ex-Covenant Prices, to advise us on our werewolf issues." He stressed the word "Covenant" a little harder than I liked.

"He can advise himself back onto the plane!" someone shouted. Laughter followed. I managed not to cringe. That, right there, was why I didn't like the word "Covenant" being bandied around like it was somehow relevant to who I was and the choices I'd made with my life.

Instead of rising to the bait, I swallowed my pride and stood, keeping my hands in view the whole time. I already knew the crowd was armed. There was no point in antagonizing them. "Mr. Tanner, you seem to be laboring under some misconceptions about the lycanthropy-w virus, which is the cause of, ah, werewolfism."

"Am I, now?" Riley turned to the crowd and rolled his eyes. More laughter—but this wasn't as universal, I noted. Whatever was causing him to showboat against me, he had his supporters. I'd expected that. At the same time, these people were conservationists, if not scientists. They understood that sometimes you needed to listen to your visiting experts, even if you didn't want them there. "You going to come up here and school me on virology, then? I didn't know you were an epidemiologist."

"I'm not," I said. "I'm a cryptozoologist, which includes the study of some cryptid-specific diseases, and viruses, like the lycanthropy family, which don't behave in a manner consistent with current scientific thinking. I can't tell you how to make a vaccine or an anti-serum for most things. I can't tell you how lycanthropy works, or why it does the things it does. I can tell you how to deal with it."

Riley frowned. There was something in his eyes that I didn't like: something that warned me I was on the verge of making an enemy I couldn't afford. Not now, when I was on his home ground, and not ever, if I was intending to continue associating with his daughter. "So you think we're doing this wrong? Please, come up here and enlighten us."

"Thank you, sir, I would be delighted to do just that," I said, and stood. If he was going to offer me the podium, I was going to take it. Accepting his implicit challenge might make him my enemy, but I didn't have a choice. Saving these people from what could end very, very badly was more important than what I did or didn't want on a personal level.

"You sure, son?" he asked, voice suddenly low and dangerous. I was being offered one last warning, and it couldn't have been clearer if it had been surrounded by flashing lights and caution tape. I was challenging his authority. I could never take it away from him—I was a stranger, I was a foreigner, and most damning of all, I was a Price—but I could dent it enough to open that door for someone else. But again, I didn't have a choice. He had created this situation to force me to prove myself, and unfortunately for both of us, I couldn't afford to avoid this confrontation. There was just too much at stake.

"I suppose I am, sir," I said.

Riley frowned. Then, slowly, he smiled. "I guess you've got some balls on you after all. Everyone, let's give a warm Thirty-Six Society welcome to Dr. Alexander Price." He stepped away from the microphone.

The applause that followed me to the podium was grudging, but it was there, and that was more than I'd expected. I cleared my throat and leaned into the microphone. "I usually go by 'Alex,'" I said.

You could have heard a pin drop in the silence that followed.

Right. "I'm glad to be here, to assist you with this situation. Lycanthropy-w is a nasty virus. It's similar to rabies in that there's no cure. There are some treatments that can be effective if delivered immediately after someone is bitten."

Crickets. I cleared my throat and continued, "Since all known treatments can be fatal, they aren't typically delivered unless the individual in question is willing to provide informed consent." Which left the civilians out. It's hard to consent to something you don't believe in. "On the plus side, since they're made of things that are poisonous to werewolves, they can also be used to coat bladed weapons in the absence of bullets."

Riley folded his arms. His smile was long gone, like it had never been there at all. I couldn't tell if he was mercurial as hell, or if he just hated me on general principle. Either way, what fun. "You must think we don't know how to read a book here in Australia. We got all that out of the reference materials, and you're not telling us anything we don't know."

"How old are your reference materials?"

He blinked and unfolded his arms, looking non-plussed for the first time. "We copied most of them from your grandfather. He was kind enough to give us access to his books while he was here."

"With all due respect, sir, our understanding of lycanthropy has evolved in the last fifty years—much like the virus itself." No one laughed. Not quite no one: I heard a snort of amusement from the table Shelby shared with her mother and sisters, and glanced over to see Raina, hand over her mouth, shaking her head.

That was somewhat encouraging. I turned back to Riley Tanner, addressing him as much as I was the rest of the room, and said, "We have contacts at the CDC and within the World Health Organization, therianthropes who have gone into the biological sciences to learn more about themselves and the dangers their people face. They've done extensive research into the disease, and they've confirmed something we suspected but didn't know when my grandfather came through here: like rabies, lycanthropy-w is a spillover disease. It's cross-infectious in all known mammals. It can survive in the absence of human or therianthrope hosts, because it goes into dogs, into sheep, even into rabbits or housecats. Whatever can be exposed can be infected."

Riley's face grew stony. "We already knew that: Shelby told us. Does that mean all those things can turn into wolves?"

"Only the ones that are big enough. Most will still begin to transform, and die in the process—they need a certain body mass to successfully make the transition from one species to another—but when you factor in the fact that scavengers, most of which are large enough to survive the transformation, can be infected from eating the bodies of animals that have died in the transformation process, you're looking at ecological devastation."

Riley stared at me. Finally, he asked, "My daughter says that we can trust you, but is there any proof of this, apart from what a bunch of nonhuman science wonks told you?"

"I've seen the histology reports. I've seen the field reports. And yes, I've seen the reality of their work. An individual infected with lycanthropy-w got into a stable and bit several horses before he was taken down. The people who dealt with that incident were monster hunters, not cryptozoologists, in it for the thrill and the possibility of a payout down the road. They told one of the local breeding stations about their kill. They didn't mention the horses."

It had been my first encounter with lycanthropy-w outside of a book. Books were safe, for the most part. They didn't try to kill you. Even the scariest books didn't leave you with years of nightmares, and a bone-deep desire never to go anywhere near another lycanthrope.

Yet here I was. I shook myself out of the memory, and turned away from Riley, facing the room as I said, "Five horses were bitten. One became infected. That horse transformed for the first time twenty-eight days after the original werewolf was killed. There was no one on-site. The family who owned the farm had no reason to be on guard. They didn't know werewolves were real; they thought something had escaped from a local zoo or traveling circus and made a mess on their property, only to be recovered by its handlers. Examination of their personal effects after the fact made it clear that they were looking for the farm or zoo in question. They were planning to bring charges."

Four people had lived in that house: a young couple and their two children, ages nine and five. None of them had survived the night. That may have been a blessing. All four had been bitten several times before the horse ripped their throats open. Infection wouldn't have been a guarantee, but it had been likely. Each bite increased the likelihood of infection, since each additional fluid transfer was a whole new roll of the dice. No werewolf was a thinking creature while fully transformed—species of origin didn't matter—but there was something especially brutal about attacks initiated by werewolves that had never been sapient to begin with. It's like werewolves that were originally intelligent retain just enough self-control to make a difference.

Not enough of a difference.

Everyone was staring at me. I realized with a sickening lurch that I had been standing there for almost a minute, lost in my recollection of that terrible, long ago scene. The younger of the two children had been virtually in pieces. What was left of the body had been recognizable only through the process of elimination: we'd already found everyone else who was likely to have been inside.

I shook my head to clear the cobwebs away. It failed to dislodge the memory. Now that it had been summoned from the dark place where I usually kept it confined, it was intending to make me recall every drop of blood and every tattered piece of flesh. "The, ah, remains of the homeowners and their children were so thoroughly mangled that we initially thought that one of them had been infected during the earlier outbreak. Werewolves will begin to experience transformation seizures after roughly twenty-eight days, but may not be capable of full transformation for as much as six months. Those that are . . . we can't tell what species a fully transformed werewolf was before it was infected. We only confirmed that the horse had been responsible for their deaths after a full autopsy, which showed that the werewolf had still possessed partially herbivorous dentition." Molars didn't transform as thoroughly as canines and incisors. No one knew why.

It was easy from there, easy to turn things clinical and abstract: to become, for just a few minutes, the dispassionate scientist that so many people took me for when we first met. I didn't like giving in to that side of myself, because I could see the warning signs written on the walls of my soul, the ones that said that if I gave in too many times, I would find that the friendly, reasonably compassionate persona I presented to the world was no longer dominant. It would be so *easy* to not care about the people around me.

It would hurt less when they died.

When I stopped speaking, the room was even quieter than it had been before. Some of the people barely seemed to be breathing. They just stared at me, faces tight with worry, eyes narrow with the need to calculate the wisdom of stepping forward to defend the country they loved. Looking at them, I estimated that we'd lose maybe one in five. They would plead some duty that couldn't be avoided, and they would go home. That was a good thing, oddly enough. It would mean that even if the rest of us died trying to fix this, there would still be people standing, ready to keep the banner of the Thirty-Six Society flying.

Gabrielle broke the silence. She stood, pushing her chair back with a loud scraping sound, and declared, "I've never let anything on this continent push me around—except for my baby sister, so don't even say it, Raina—and I'm sure as hell not going to start now. You've told us how bad this shit is. Pretty sure we already knew it was bad. Now how about you tell us how to get rid of it?"

"We have to track down all infected individuals, whether they are civilians or part of the Society, and monitor them for twenty-eight days," I said. "If we cannot successfully monitor those who have been exposed, we need to consider more permanent solutions. Silver bullets work best." None of the solutions we had would be good ones. I hated to advocate for killing people just because they might get sick, but if it was the only way . . .

"How are we supposed to find all those people?" asked Riley. "We can't go door to door looking for people who've run afoul of werewolves."

"You have to remember that someone who's been bitten—even someone who's started to transform—will still seem normal in their original form. They might be irritable or unusually skittish, but they'll look like anybody else. The same goes for infected animals," I said. "How you find them will depend on the resources you have available to you. I don't know the territory or what you have at your disposal. I'd like to sit down with your leadership to discuss it as soon as possible. In the meantime, knowledge is going to matter more in this fight than almost anything else." Knowledge and silver bullets. "Sir? Thank you for letting me speak." I stepped aside.

Riley wasn't smiling—only a sociopath could have smiled after the speech I'd just given—but he looked marginally less disapproving as he stepped back into place behind the podium. He clapped me on the shoulder with one massive hand, and then I was dismissed; my part in this little drama was complete, at least for the moment.

I made my way back to the table on legs that felt like they were made half of Jell-O, slumping back into my seat. It seemed natural to fold my arms and put my head down after that, and so I did. Jet lag, speaking in front of an unfriendly audience, and knowing that I was about to face my worst fear were all conspiring to overwhelm me. I wasn't worried about showing weakness in front of the Australian cryptozoologists. They'd know my weak spots soon enough, and trying to conceal them now would only increase the odds of someone getting hurt.

A hand rested itself between my shoulder blades. I didn't need to look up to know that it belonged to Shelby. "You did good," she murmured. "Dad doesn't yield to just anybody."

"Pretty sure he did it because he thought I'd make myself look bad, but thanks." I didn't lift my head. If Riley thought I was being disrespectful, I was sure he'd find a way to tell me about it.

Shelby left her hand where it was. "My poor Alex," she said, and went quiet, listening to her father speak.

His description of the surrounding area wasn't making me feel any better about our chances of quickly and easily uprooting the infection, especially in the nonhuman population. There were sheep and kangaroos, wallabies and wombats and koalas, drop bears and bunyip and other things I'd never heard of before and would need to look up later, when I got access to their research materials. All of them were mammals. All of them were capable of carrying lycanthropy-w, and passing it on. Even the smaller mammals, like the possums and garrinna, would need to be tested.

There's only one completely reliable way to check for lycanthropy-w, and it's the same as the old test for rabies. We would have to kill sample members of each population and test their brain tissue and spinal fluid for signs of sickness. Then, after a few weeks had passed, we would have to do it again, and again, until there were no more signs of lycanthropy-w.

Animal conservation in Australia is extremely important among both cryptid and noncryptid populations, because so many of the creatures native to that continent are both uniquely Australian and deeply endangered. Killing sample members of their populations wouldn't be like killing a few raccoons or squirrels back home—painful and unpleasant, especially for the raccoons and squirrels, but not an ecological disaster. Killing the things that lived here would leave a lasting ecological impact.

It couldn't be helped. That didn't mean it wouldn't be hated.

I left my head down on the table, and listened to Riley Tanner as he calmly, carefully outlined all the ways in which we were about to get completely screwed.

Six

"It's easy to say that the needs of the many outweigh the needs of the few when no one's holding a gun to your head."

— Martin Baker

The secret meeting room of an isolated house in Queensland, Australia, preparing for the inevitable disaster

THE CROWD DISPERSED QUICKLY after the questions and answers were done. Many of the people who left had the air of soldiers who'd just been told that Godzilla was making a beeline for the neighborhood where they lived: calm, determined, and following a well-established evacuation plan. Only a few looked like they were on the verge of panic. That was a good sign. The more people who stayed calm, the more people we'd be able to count on when things got bad. Well. When things got worse.

A man I didn't know accompanied Riley back to our table. The newcomer was almost as tall as Riley, slim where the other man was muscular, with sandy-blond hair and the seemingly universal Australian tan. He looked like he was about my father's age.

"Price," said Riley. I sat up straighter, adjusting my glasses with one hand and trying to look like I hadn't just been calculating how many graves a group this size could fill. "I want you to meet Cooper. He handles security in this state."

Which meant this probably wasn't Shelby's original part of Australia, since otherwise the Tanners would have been handling security. I filed the information away as I stood and offered Cooper my hand. "It's nice to meet you."

"And you as well. Big fan of your grandfather's work." Cooper's grip was firm without being crushing. He pumped twice before letting me go. "Sorry to hear you'd been through all that with the werewolves in America, but I have to admit, I'm glad to hear you've actually seen action of some sort. Book learning isn't the sort of thing that keeps you alive in a place like this."

"I've heard a lot about the Australian wildlife," I said. "I'm almost glad to be here to help with something I have experience with—although I do wish it had been the manticores Shelby mentioned to me once, and not werewolves. Lycanthropy is nothing to mess around with."

"That's for damn sure," Cooper agreed. He frowned, the expression pulling canyons into his weathered skin. "You mentioned a treatment for people who'd been bitten. What's that about?"

"Silver and wolf's bane—aconite—have historically been used as effective weapons against werewolves. Interestingly, we think this application was inspired by the use of lunar caustic, also known as silver nitrate, in the treatment of early rabies cases, when physicians would apply heated rods to cauterize—"

Shelby rose, putting her hand on my upper arm in a gesture that was simultaneously soothing and possessive. "Alex, sweetie, as fascinating as the whole history of lycanthropy is, how about we table it for now and start in with how you're going to save all our lives, yeah?"

"Ah, sorry," I said, glancing her way. Her eyes were narrowed, and her attention was fixed on Cooper as tightly as a snake would fixate on a mouse. I looked back to Cooper. "Occupational hazard. Also, I find science less upsetting than thinking about how bad the situation could get."

"Well, this situation is fair distressing, so I can't say I blame you for that," said Cooper. "Shelby. You're looking lovely, as always."

"Cooper," said Shelby, in a flat tone. "Nice to see you showed up. Missed you at Jack's funeral."

Cooper looked uncomfortable. I just loved walking into interpersonal situations I knew nothing about. I wondered whether this was how Shelby felt when dealing with my family. Probably.

"Finish explaining your treatment, Price," said Riley.

"Yes, right," I said, grateful for the save. "Silver nitrate, applied to properly cleaned and sterilized wounds, can act as a crude antibiotic and a good way to reduce the live viral agents in the area. Wolf's bane, also known as aconite, has a negative effect on the health of the virus. We're still trying to figure out why. Not that it matters much. If it works, it works." I'd seen pictures of viral cultures that had been treated with pure aconite. They were blasted wastelands of broken cells, post-apocalyptic and incapable of supporting life. A dose that undiluted would kill a human, of course, although I'd heard rumors of cryptozoologists in Africa who had treated an infected elephant with a massive injection of crushed aconite flowers. The elephant had lived, and hadn't become a werewolf. So that was something.

"So you just feed a person silver and toxic flowers?"

"Not quite. We make a tincture of ground silver, aconite, ketamine, mercury, and rabies vaccine, which can be given to the afflicted person at any point prior to their first transformation—so within twenty-eight days of exposure, although earlier is always better. The treatment involves four doses in total, given at two-day intervals. It's . . . well, 'toxic' doesn't really cover it. It's incredibly poisonous, and difficult to make. If you get the proportions even slightly off, you run the risk of cardiac arrest or simple overdose."

"But it works," pressed Cooper.

"It *can* work," I said. "Part of the problem is that we don't have a good way of knowing whether someone has been infected before we start treatment. Only one person in five will actually be infected. That's a lot of false negatives. Out of the people who have received this treatment and lived, all but one have turned out just fine." I didn't mention the people who had died. That would just complicate things.

"And that one?" pressed Riley.

"Werewolf," I said. "Maybe the treatment doesn't work at all. Maybe he was the only one who was actually infected—even with the size of our sample pool, the inability to test for preexisting infection means we don't know. But all the lab work supports this as a prophylactic treatment, and it's better than sitting back doing nothing. Before you ask, no, we don't have a test that tells us which way it's going to go before people either cross the finish line into safety or transform into giant wolf-monsters and start trying to eat their former friends and loved ones. You roll the dice and you get what you get."

"Did you bring the materials you'd need for this treatment?" asked Cooper, sounding anxious. I thought about the members of the Society who'd been bitten and were now under quarantine, waiting to see whether they would live or die. A treatment—even one that stood a chance of killing them—would probably be the most welcome thing in the world.

I nodded. "I did. It's part of why Shelby arranged for us to be extracted from the airport. It's hard to explain to the nice customs agents why you're flying with a mason jar full of mercury and a bunch of dried aconite flowers. Fresh would be better, of course, but aconite doesn't grow on this continent."

"That's what you think," said Cooper. I blinked at him. He shrugged. "Some idiots decided to import their pretty flower gardens from England during colonization. We've got an issue with endemic invasive aconite plants. Most of the time we root them up and burn them to keep them from spreading further, but if you need fresh flowers, we'll get you fresh flowers."

"It's spring; they may not be blooming yet," I said. "Leaves and roots will do just as well, especially if there's a chemistry set around here that I can use."

"They'll be blooming," said Cooper. "Don't know how they behave in their home ecosystem, but here, they're damn near unstoppable."

"There's a medical station nearby," said Riley. "It's meant for wildlife triage and emergency care, and we basically control it. You can use that. I figure the equipment used to make snake antivenin should be good enough for you to cook up your 'tincture.'"

"It should be, yes," I said, trying to project a level of confidence that I didn't feel. My mother was the medic: she was the one who brewed the tinctures and mashed up the ingredients for the poultices. I was better with her sort of work than either of my sisters, and could generally be counted on to mix a simple remedy, but making enough anti-lycanthropy treatment for a continent was well beyond my skills, especially given the toxicity of the ingredients in question. I was going to have to be more careful than I'd ever been before, or I was going to get somebody killed.

Then again, that sentence could describe this entire trip. No one wanted me here but Shelby, and yet I was the only one with a working treatment for lycanthropy, which made me at least partially responsible for the lives of everyone around me. Most of them already didn't trust me as far as they could throw me. Oh, this was going to be *great* fun.

"Good. Now go get some sleep." Riley seemed to be looking at Shelby rather than me as he continued, "We're going to have one hell of a day tomorrow. It'd be best if everyone was rested and ready."

"Yes, Daddy," said Shelby. She took her hand off my arm as she stepped toward him, and he hugged her, and I had never felt more like an outsider in my life. These people were depending on me. That didn't mean I felt like they wanted me here.

"Come on, fancy-pants." Raina was suddenly at my elbow, taking up the place Shelby had occupied only a moment before. "Let me get you back to your room."

I didn't have a good reason to argue, and so I just nodded, and turned away from my girlfriend and her father (and her father's friend), and let Raina lead me away.

The mice were waiting on the bed when I got back to the guest room. They gave a muffled cheer at the sight of me stepping through the door, waving leaves and scraps of snakeskin and something that looked like one of Shelby's hair ties in the air in place of pennants. I rubbed my face with one hand. In my family, you learn to deal with the mice early. There is no alternative. That didn't mean I was in the mood for their inevitable celebration.

"I have a headache," I informed them. "Can we please keep the shouting and cheering to a minimum until I've managed to sleep off the existential terror of this continent?"

"We have added a new Occasion to the calendar," squeaked the junior priest in charge of the congregation. "We will spend this night in Solemn Contemplation, and there will be little shouting, or cheering, or speaking."

"Cool, thanks." I paused. "What's the new occasion?"

"We will celebrate Crossing the Sea, and Arriving in Australia, and Killing a Very Large Snake," said the priest solemnly.

Given the size of the mice and the fact that there were only six of them, the "very large snake" could have been the size of my shoelace. But they weren't demanding food, and they had a tendency to eat their kills. I decided it was better not to ask.

"Great." I began removing my weapons, stacking them with brisk efficiency on the bedside table. A thought struck me. "I don't know if anyone apart from Shelby has a pet with them. Please don't eat anything that looks like it could be a domestic companion. And try not to eat any of the parrots, either. I don't know what's endangered around here." We normally took a live-and-let-live approach to Aeslin predation—anything they killed was probably trying to kill them first. At the same time, they weren't native to the Australian continent. The last thing I needed was to try explaining to the Thirty-Sixers why I'd allowed my traveling cryptid circus to eat the last living member of some ultra-rare species of macaw.

The mice looked disappointed by my edict, ears dropping and tails wrapping tighter around their legs. The reason why was revealed a few seconds later, when the priest in charge asked hesitantly, "May we still gather feathers and bits of shell? There is so much new color here, and the livery of the faith grows faded over time . . ."

Aeslin mouse fashion tended to demonstrate an aesthetic of "we found it, and we found a way to stick it together, and now it looks awesome." They'd been known to steal ribbons, hair ties, scraps of fabric, and of course, feathers. Crow alone was responsible for the production of several feather cloaks every time he molted. "You can gather anything you find and wish to use for your purposes, providing you don't distress the birds in the process," I said. "Fair?"

"HAIL!" declared the mice, and scampered down the side of the bed, no doubt to start moving the feathers they'd already collected to whatever hidey-hole they were planning to use during our stay. I smiled after them, pulled my shirt off over my head, and collapsed onto the bed. I rolled over only long enough to put my glasses down next to my pistol, where both would be easily within reach.

Sleep came fast, which was a mercy, given the events of the evening; the change of time zones was hitting me harder than I'd expected. Wakefulness came even faster, when I felt someone slide into the bed beside me. I snapped instantly alert, thrusting my hand toward the bedside table, and the waiting protection of my pistol.

A hand caught my wrist, fingers tightening enough to let me feel the familiar shape of them. "It's me," Shelby said. "Alex, it's me. Calm down."

"Shelby?" The question came out louder than I intended, powered by both adrenaline and relief. I hadn't realized I was sleeping so deeply. I should have snapped awake as soon as she opened the bedroom door, and the fact that I hadn't was a worrisome failure on my part.

"In the flesh." She pressed herself against me, looping one ankle over mine, as if to hold me on the bed. I outweighed her by enough that it was a futile gesture; I could have had us both on the floor in seconds, if I'd needed to. And somehow, that made it okay. "I'm sorry I couldn't get here sooner. Had to wait for everyone to be asleep enough not to catch me sneaking out."

"Wha' . . ." I was still waking up, and it took a few seconds for the import of her words to hit me. When it did, I tried to push myself away, stopping only when my back thumped against the cool plaster of the wall. "Shelby, you can't be in here, your father will *kill me*," I hissed. "He will kill me, and then he will feed my body to the crocodiles. Crocodiles are very efficient methods of body disposal. Trust me, I've done it."

"Won't, shan't, can't," said Shelby, scooting closer, so that I had no way to escape without hurting her. She was wearing a thin shirt and a pair of running shorts. I was wearing nothing. Between us, we had way too little clothing for this conversation to be comfortable, under the circumstances. "I'm a grownup. I've been living with you for going on a year now. He knows I haven't had my own room that whole time—I told Raina, and I know damn well she's told him by now. That's the sort of loving sister she is. My father needs to come to terms with the fact that our relationship isn't as pleasantly chaste as he might like to think it is."

"Okay, Shelby, all my 'your girlfriend is right here' instincts say to agree with you, and all my 'you grew up surrounded by women who could kill you in their sleep' instincts say that your father doesn't get to control your life, but my 'let's try not to die in Australia' instincts keep reminding me that he's twice my size. I mean, have you *seen* the man?"

"Don't worry, Alex, if he tries to start trouble with you, I'll come to your rescue. I'm supposed to be his successor, after all. He listens to me." Shelby leaned in and kissed me before I could point out the flaws in her logic. Her lips were soft and warm and tasted like beeswax lip balm, and I was kissing her back before I could remind myself what a terrible idea this was.

Shelby pushed herself closer still, sliding one knee between my legs as she did something clever with her hands that resulted in her shirt being hiked up to her collarbones. Her breasts pressed against my chest, nothing keeping her skin from mine.

Dim reason told me to make one more effort to keep myself from being murdered by a large Australian cryptozoologist, and was promptly shouted down by my libido, which was much more interested in the present goings-on. I tugged at Shelby's shirt, and she obliged by leaning back long enough to let me pull it off over her head.

"I see you've got the spirit now," she said, and then her mouth was back on mine, and there was no more conversation for a while.

Having sex with Shelby in a house that was, at least nominally, her parents' was . . . strange at best. We'd been sexually active while we'd been living with my grandparents, of course, but neither of them was human, and neither of them cared, providing we used protection and didn't do anything messy outside of our shared bedroom.

The one time I'd tried to bring up the subject with my grandfather, who had at least started out human—before he died and was brought back to life by carelessly applied science—he had laughed in my face. "Alex, your generation didn't invent sex, and we came to terms with the idea of our descendants getting intimate with other people when your mother called home and told us she was pregnant. We really don't care."

That had been the household policy ever since, and it was a good one. I doubted *my* parents would be quite as easygoing about premarital relations under their own roof, and I *knew* Shelby's parents weren't as easygoing. And somehow, once we got started, that just made it all the more exciting. Every touch, every kiss, it was all stolen, and we were willing accomplices in the burglary of one another's bodies.

Time ceased to matter for a while. When we were finished, lying spent and sweaty on a bed that had seemed too empty before, and now felt perfectly full, Shelby dropped her head into the crook of my shoulder, sighed, and said, "Going to have to do a lot more of that, you know. We both need the stress relief."

"What, you don't find your family relaxing?"

Shelby snorted. "Do you find your family relaxing?"

"Point." I sighed, running my fingers through her hair, and said, "It's weird. When we got here ... enough of the tactics you use, enough of the policies and procedures, are like the ones we use at home that I almost fell into the trap of thinking we were the same. That everything the Thirty-Six Society did would make sense to me. I mean, you have two sisters, one of them's a misanthrope who likes video games, the other one's in the arts; your mother's friendly but deadly ... your father is sort of where the comparison falls down. Mine's tall, skinny, and academic."

"I think all families have their similarities," said Shelby. "Gabby's a little less, well, willing to play along than your sister. I don't think she's going to give up opera in favor of coming back to the family business. And Raina wasn't always so unpleasant to strangers. She doesn't trust people she doesn't know. Hasn't done since we lost Jack."

There it was. "Your brother?"

"Yeah. Raina was his favorite, you know? He and I weren't close—too similar in some ways, we always wound up wanting to kill each other, and that's no good for anyone—but the two of them were like ticks on a sheep. Where he went, so did she, always. She holds herself responsible for what happened with him."

"How? Cuckoos can get to anyone. That's part of what makes them so dangerous."

"You know that, and I know that, and even your family knows that. Raina knows on some level, I suppose, but most of her just knows that Jack stopped calling, and stopped answering her email, and she didn't sound the alarm. I don't think we could have saved him at that point—it wasn't really possible by then, you know? He was too far gone when he cut contact—but that's not going to help her forgive herself."

"No, it's not." I kissed Shelby's forehead. "I'm sorry. I can't imagine losing a sibling." Except that was a lie. I *had* imagined it, over and over, for my entire life. The idea of the loss lasting after I woke up . . . that was the terrifying part.

"Done is done, you know? Jack was a good guy. I think you'd have liked him. I know he'd have liked you. He was going to take over for Dad someday. Now he's gone, and the crown falls to me, and I don't want it." She sighed again, deeper this time, and nestled herself close. "Need to get some sleep now. It's going to be a busy day tomorrow."

"I was sleeping fine before you came in and woke me up, you know," I protested. It was too late: her eyes were shut, and she had relaxed in that way that meant she wasn't going to be talking anymore tonight. She couldn't *actually* go to sleep instantly, but had learned to fake it at some point. It was probably a natural consequence of sharing a bedroom with two younger sisters.

For a little while, I just lay there and listened to her breathing. Then I closed my own eyes again, and let sleep come back to me.

"You're both going to get murdered, and it's going to be horribly messy." The proclamation was made with incredible good cheer—"chirpy, treacle-y, Sleeping Beauty talks to the woodland creatures" levels of good cheer. I pried my eyes open and peered into the faintly bleary distance. Shelby was still asleep, her head tucked under one of the pillows and her right arm slung across my waist. That meant the tall blonde blur couldn't be her.

It hadn't sounded quite like her mother, and so I took a guess. "Gabrielle?"

"Oh, you are good. Yes, this is Gabby, I'm here because you're about ten minutes short of sleeping through breakfast, and I volunteered to be the one who came looking because it would give you half a chance in hell of Dad not finding out Shelby had switched rooms in the night. If Raina saw you like this, it'd be game over."

"You're very kind." I reached over Shelby and fumbled on the bedside table until I found my glasses and pushed them on, squinting as my focus adjusted. "We'll be down in a minute." This was the second time one of the Tanner sisters had been able to sneak up on me while I was sleeping. I was starting to give serious thought to belling the door.

Gabby dimpled at me. "It's all part of the service. You're a lot more cute than you looked under that stuffy academic shirt, aren't you? I'm starting to see what Shelly finds so appealing."

"I will end you," said Shelby, voice muffled by the pillow.

"Love you, too," said Gabby, and fled the room before sororicide could become a genuine threat.

Shelby groaned and pushed herself up onto her elbows, shooting a halfhearted glare in my direction. "Whose idea was it to come back to Australia again? Because at the moment, I'm inclined to blame you."

"They're your family," I said. "You're the one who asked if I would help them."

"Right. Damn." She stood, stretched, and began recovering her clothes from the floor. "I need to duck down the hall to get something suitable for the breakfast table. You going to be all right on your own?"

"I think I can manage getting dressed and walking down the stairs," I said.

Shelby grinned. "I'm never sure with you." She stepped into her shorts, pulled her shirt on over her head, and then she was gone, out the door and on the way to her room.

I took more time getting dressed, although I didn't linger over anything beyond getting my weapons secured inside my clothing. The mice hadn't made an appearance by the time I had my shirt buttoned and my shoes tied. I glanced around nervously, half expecting to see a mouse head on the floor under the edge of the bed. The wildlife of Australia was nothing to fuck around with. Neither were the Aeslin mice.

If any of them had met an unfortunate end, it wasn't apparent from the contents of my room. I shook my head, grabbed my jacket off the door, and left the room.

As before, the smell of food greeted me when I reached the head of the stairs. This time, it was accompanied by voices, clear and loud and close. I followed them to the kitchen, where I found the Tanners—minus Shelby, who was still getting dressed—sitting around the kitchen table, passing a platter of ham and another of fried eggs around. Only Gabby looked up when I entered, and her quick, sly smile confirmed that she hadn't informed her parents about my sleeping arrangements of the night before. For whatever reason, she was keeping that part between us . . . for now.

"Oh, hey, you're not dead." Raina raked her eyes

along the length of my body before passing judgment: "You still look kind of dead. Maybe you need to sleep more. Sixteen hours out of the last twenty-four isn't excessive, if you're a housecat. Are you a housecat?"

"Good morning, Alex," said Charlotte, apparently deciding that ignoring her middle daughter was the better part of valor. "How did you sleep?"

"Very well, thank you," I said, following her lead. "I'm not adjusted to local time yet, but I think I'll be there before much longer."

"Good," said Riley. Unlike his wife and daughter, he didn't sound chatty: he sounded like a man who'd been waiting to get down to business for the better part of an hour, and was ready to go. "Grab a roll and some ham, and let's get out of here. I have Cooper standing by at the medical station. We've cleared the whole thing for your use."

I nodded. "All right." I had been expecting something like this, although to be honest, I had been hoping it would happen on the other side of several cups of coffee.

"Here's a fun fact for you: one in three wildlife rescue stations in this part of the country is run either wholly or in part by the Society," said Charlotte, her eyes on her husband. "Come on, Riley, let the boy have a decent breakfast before you set him to brewing magic potions to save us from the werewolves."

"Oh," I said, unable to come up with a more intelligent response. The thought of having that sort of resources at our disposal was staggering. Most of the time, we had to make do with whatever the local cryptids had set up for themselves, or visit helpful veterinarians who had seen one too many immature lindworms presented as "iguanas" to remain in denial over the cryptid world. Then I paused. "Wait, what is it you're expecting me to do?"

"You said you could brew the stuff to keep us safe from the werewolves," said Riley. "So you're going to do that. You're going to keep us safe from the werewolves."

"I also said that it's not a vaccine, and it's potentially

fatal," I protested. "It's an after-the-fact treatment, and while I'm more than happy to mix some up as a last resort, it isn't going to keep you 'safe from werewolves,' and it needs to be made fresh because it doesn't keep for more than three or four days. If I made enough to treat the whole Society, I'd blow through all the supplies I brought with me from the States and then some, and it would all be bad inside of the week. Small batches are the only way to make this work."

"How small?" Riley seemed suddenly more tightly wound, like something I had said had caused the string that ran through the center of his body to contract, drawing him inward. It was unnerving, like watching a snake coil in preparation for striking. "Could you treat a dozen people without endangering your precious supplies?"

I tensed. If that was the number of new infections he was expecting within the next week, the situation was even worse than I had suspected. "A dozen I could do," I said, fighting to keep my tone level. "It would also be useful to start stockpiling more supplies, just in case they're needed. They hopefully won't be, but again, I was limited by the carrying capacity of my luggage."

"Good," he said. "We're going to the med station, and you're mixing up enough to offer the treatment to every Society member who's been exposed. Am I clear?"

Oh. "Yes," I said. "I'll be ready in a minute." The people who had been bitten before I got to Australia were on the cusp of crossing the line from "may still be saved" into "lost forever." The treatment *could* work right up until the first transformation, theoretically, but we had no confirmed instances of it working after fourteen days.

I hated to make them wait even a moment, but I knew enough about fieldwork to know that if I didn't eat now, I might not get the opportunity to eat again before dinner—if then. I'd been on a manticore hunt once that had resulted in skipping four meals in a row. Not because we wanted to; because the manticore was chasing us, and we couldn't stop to build a fire.

(Grandma Alice always said being in the field should be treated like going to war: eat when you can, sleep when you can, never put your gun down, and never get drunker than the people around you. Grandma Alice was more than a little bit paranoid. Sadly for me, she was also more than a little bit right.)

Riley stood next to my chair, not speaking, and watched as I ate breakfast. Shelby joined us while I was still shoveling eggs into my face. She took one look at her father, sighed, and said, "Mum, slap me together a sandwich, will you? I need to go get my knives."

"All right, honey," said Charlotte.

"Can you grab my go bag?" I asked. "It's the big brown one." I didn't like asking her to carry my things when I was sitting and enjoying breakfast with her family, but Charlotte didn't seem inclined to make me a sandwich, and Shelby was already going upstairs.

"Shall do, lazy boy," said Shelby, and made her retreat.

I had finished eating by the time Shelby returned, now with Flora riding on her shoulder. The little garrinna had her tail linked around Shelby's neck, providing the leverage she needed to stay upright. Riley turned and walked toward the door without a word. Shelby got her egg-and-ham sandwich from her mother, and the two of us followed him out to the car.

The medical station was a thirty-minute drive from the house, down a series of successively smaller roads, all of which Riley drove along like he was challenging the God of Car Crashes and Automotive Fatalities to do something about it. Shelby sat in the front with him, Flora shrieking challenges at birds in nearby trees as we went rocketing by, and I bounced around in the backseat despite my seat belt, grabbing onto anything I could to try and stabilize myself. By the time we pulled up in front of the small white-walled building that was our destination,

I was beginning to seriously rethink my views on carsickness.

Cooper was already outside, leaning against the wall next to the door with his hands shoved into his pockets and a vaguely disinterested look on his face. A black dog with high, pointed ears was sitting calmly beside him. Cooper's expression didn't change as we piled out of the car. Flora shrieked at the dog. The dog barked twice at the garrinna, a high, piercing sound that didn't hold any real threat, but would definitely have served to alert Cooper if Flora had been sneaking up on him. The garrinna took off from Shelby's shoulder and flew to a nearby tree, still shrieking.

"Sometimes I feel like I never left home," I muttered.

"What's that?" asked Shelby.

"Nothing," I said. Louder, I continued, "Morning, Cooper. Good to see you again."

"I go where Riley tells me to," he said, by way of greeting.

"Cooper's a vet tech," said Riley, brushing past me as he went to unlock the building door. "He's going to watch everything you do. See if we can't figure out how to replicate the process when you're not around." His tone was challenging, like he expected me to protest and claim the tincture as some sort of family secret.

If he'd been hoping for a fight, I was going to disappoint him. "That sounds like an excellent plan to me," I said, adjusting my glasses. "What are you and Shelby going to do?"

"Area patrol," said Shelby, sounding almost obscenely pleased about the idea. "Going to poke through the local brush, make sure nothing unpleasant has decided to set up camp. You know, the usual sort of work."

I blinked, looking at her. She was wearing what I thought of as her zoo clothes: a tan shirt and khaki shorts, with thick white socks under thicker brown leather boots. It was great attire for showing off with tigers in a controlled environment, but for the Australian brush, I'd been expecting something a little more platemail-esque. "Really?"

"Really." She darted forward, pressing a kiss against my cheek. Riley looked over his shoulder at us and scowled. "I promise I'll be fine. The boots'll keep anything from taking a chomp out of me, and if I run up against something that's aiming above the knees, clothes wouldn't have saved me anyhow."

"That's encouraging," I said dryly.

"Buck up, Alex. If I die, they'll probably deport you. So either way, the outcome is in your favor."

Shelby was still laughing at her own joke—and my stricken face—when her father shoved the door open and turned to stalk back to where we were standing. "How long is your little alchemy lesson going to take?"

"I don't really know," I said. "The stuff is delicate. It could be as little as an hour. It could take as long as three hours. It all depends on whether I get it right on my first attempt."

"Get it right," said Riley. "Shelly, you're with me." He kept walking, moving onward into the dense underbrush on the other side of the narrow dirt track masquerading as a road. Shelby shrugged and hurried after him, giving me a "what can you do?" look over her shoulder. The brush rustled as it swallowed them whole, and I was alone with Cooper, his silently watchful dog, and Shelby's garrinna, which was still giving off intermittent shrieks, just in case we'd forgotten she was there.

"I can't imagine why they're on the verge of extinction," I said, turning from the garrinna to Cooper, who hadn't moved since we arrived.

He didn't smile. "They're noisy because we've taught them to be that way," he said. "They're too bright colored to hide, so the ones that survived the hunters long enough to breed are the ones that got early notice when danger was coming. Hence the screams. In another few generations, it could be they'll never stop."

"Er." My sense of humor has never been the most

refined, but I wasn't accustomed to being shut down quite that efficiently for something that hadn't been that offensive. "I'm sorry. I think I'm still jet lagged. I keep sticking my foot in it."

Cooper seemed to thaw slightly: while he didn't smile, his stone-faced expression was a little less unyielding. Under the circumstances, I'd take it. "You're in a bit of a hard place, all things considered. No one's ever been willing to take a run at one of the Tanner girls before. Between Riley and Jack, it was always pretty damn clear that they were off-limits. When Shelly sent home word that she was seeing someone, Riley came close to hitting the roof. Doesn't help that it's her, either. Daddy's girl isn't supposed to fall for anybody else."

I knew from my conversations with Shelby when we first started dating that I wasn't her first serious boyfriend—far from it. She'd dated more than I had, mostly while she was away at school. That apparently didn't jibe with Riley's understanding of his own daughter. I decided it wasn't my place to bring up things she might not want finding their way back to her parents, and just shrugged. "He has three daughters. Maybe he needs to get used to the idea that they're going to date eventually."

"He was better about it before Jack died and made Shelby her father's heir," said Cooper. "People get protective of the things they love once they realize those things can be lost."

"Yeah. I know." The conversation was getting uncomfortable, and I felt very exposed having it in the middle of the road. I walked past him, into the medical station. As I had expected, Cooper followed me, shutting the door behind himself.

It was a small room, more of a glorified shed than anything else, but every inch of space had been used to the best of its abilities by whomever had overseen the conversion of the original structure into a fully equipped veterinary office. Shelves lined the walls, glass-fronted and stocked with common medicines, first aid supplies, and what looked like a surgical kit. An operating table was pushed up against one counter, where it could be moved as necessary, and there was a small wet station, complete with sink and what looked like a chemical shower.

"Water runs from a tank, not a pipe, so only use what you need," said Cooper, moving to raise the shades on the two small windows. "We have it refilled after people need to use this facility, but that's not going to be any help if your hands need washing and you've already sent all the wash water off down the drain."

"Good to know." I hoisted my go bag onto the operating table and began carefully unpacking it. I could have moved faster, but I wanted to be sure none of the seals had been broken and none of the potentially hazardous materials had managed to mix together. Piece by piece, the results of a thousand years of scientific progress and folk medicine appeared on the gleaming stainless steel.

Dried aconite. Powdered silver nitrate. Liquid mercury, heavy and poisonously lovely. A jar of rowan ash, burnt so fine that it looked almost volcanic. Another jar, this one filled with unicorn water. There were no unicorns in Australia; unless they had a native purifier I didn't know about, I was going to need to measure what I had down to the drop.

"You're going to tell me what all these things are, yeah?" asked Cooper. His dog had followed him inside; its pointed black ears appeared above the edge of the table, quivering as it listened to the noises I was making.

"I'll walk you through the whole process," I promised. "What's your dog's name?"

"Jett," said Cooper. He smiled down at the dog, an expression of absolute fondness on his face. "She's my good girl, aren't you, Jett?"

Jett emitted that high, piercing bark again, as if to say that yes, she was absolutely a good girl, and she didn't understand why it was even being questioned. There should be no room for debate. In the Good Girl Olympics, Jett was clearly taking home the gold, and might be shooting to bring back the silver and the bronze as well, just for the sake of having a complete set.

"Well, I think she's lovely, and I hate to ask, but is she all right with loud noises and strange smells? This stuff isn't exactly what I'd call sunshine and roses when it's being mixed."

Cooper's look of fondness twisted into a scowl— although oddly, it didn't come with a renewed freeze. Apparently, he couldn't go completely cold while he was talking about his dog, even if the topic at hand was "do we need to put her outside." "She's come with me to the range," he said. "If she can sit through a bunch of men shooting holes in things not ten yards away, she'll be fine for whatever witch's brew you're planning to make."

"All right," I said. I picked up the jar of dried aconite, frowning at it, before looking back up at Cooper. "You said imported aconite had gone endemic in this country. Is there any chance we could find some growing near here? The tincture will work a lot better if I can make it with fresh flowers, rather than relying on the dried stuff."

"Yeah, this is good country for the nasty weeds. I've seen them growing near here. Pretty sure I can shake us out a patch pretty quick." Cooper stooped to pat Jett on the head. "You're going to stay here, girl, and guard this place for us? We'll be back to you shortly."

Jett barked again, presumably agreeing to stay and guard, or maybe just acknowledging that her human was making sounds with his flappy face hole. It was difficult to tell, with dogs. I'd never had the experience that might have made it easier.

"There's some nasty stuff in the wood around here," Cooper explained, straightening up again. "This is bunyip territory. Better if she stays behind where she won't get eaten."

"Ah," I said, stretching out the syllable until it was several times its original length. "Shelby didn't say anything about there being bunyip around here."

"She probably didn't think of it." Cooper started for the door. "Do you say something when there's a possibility of bears in the area? Or d'you just assume that everyone knows bears are a thing that can happen, and will plan accordingly?"

I slung my now-empty bag over my shoulder before snagging a pair of latex gloves from the box I'd brought with me and stuffing them into my pocket. It would be best if I didn't touch the plants with my bare hands. "Actually, yes, I would say something like 'there may be bears here.' Bears are not a pleasant surprise for most people."

"Most people are pretty damn dull." Cooper opened the door and stepped outside. Jett moved to follow. He clucked his tongue and pointed to the corner. To my surprise, the little black dog stopped immediately, her head drooping, and gave him one last plaintive look before she slunk back to the indicated spot on the floor and lay down, curling so that her nose was pointing straight at her deceitful deserter of a master.

"I can't argue with that," I said, and followed him out.

Walking into the woods of Australia was no more or less alien than walking into the woods of Ohio had been when I was trying to adjust to the differences between oaks and alders and the evergreens of home. This forest consisted of eucalyptus, and of trees I didn't recognize, but the theory was the same. The forest floor was a mass of fallen leaves, decaying bark, and unusual bushes, some of which were infested with large, spade-shaped beetles. Something rustled in the brush to one side. I fought the impulse, ingrained in me since birth, to find out what it was. With my luck, it would be some sort of large and extremely venomous snake—and while that would normally be my equivalent of Christmas, I didn't want to explain to the Tanners why I'd gone and gotten myself bitten on my second day in the country. The black snakes and taipans would have to wait a little longer.

Cooper had thawed still further since we got out into the woods, although he had become even less conversational, choosing instead to focus on what was happening around us. I wanted to pepper him with a constant stream of questions, asking him to identify every bird and flower. I kept my mouth shut and stuck close behind, choosing to show restraint. When Shelby and her father returned from their patrol, they would find the tinctures mixed and my skin fully intact.

I was feeling so pious about my commitment to safety that the end of the trees caught me by surprise. One moment we were walking through a thick stand of healthy eucalyptus, and the next, we were stepping out into a shallow bowl of a meadow, thick with deep purple aconite flowers. A flat sheet of water stretched out on the other side of the meadow, studded with dead trees and delicate water weeds and something that looked like a log, but which I suspected of being a sleeping crocodile. There was a stand of tall, thin-trunked trees growing straight out of the watery area, so densely pressed together that anything inside their little copse was completely hidden.

"Is that . . . ?" I asked, pointing at the "log" in question.

Cooper followed the angle of my finger. Then, much to my surprise, he grinned. "You have an excellent eye for an American," he said. "That's a croc, all right. Looks like a pretty small one, too. Why, did you want to go for some authentic Australian crocodile wrestling while you were here?"

I eyed him sidelong. "You know, that's the same tone Shelby uses when she's talking about playing up the 'Crocodile Hunter' routine for the people at our zoo. I think I'll pass."

"And here I was looking forward to giving you back to them without a foot." He paused for a beat before saying, "It's not a crocodile. We don't get them this far south. Not every Australian log is going to be a crocodile." Cooper gestured to the flowers. "Is this what you needed?"

"Yes." I produced the gloves from my pocket and pulled them on. "I don't know what's around here that might try to eat us, apart from the bunyip. Can you keep watch while I gather flowers?"

"Already on it," said Cooper.

That seemed to be his final word on the subject, and so I turned my attention to what needed doing: picking wildflowers. Dangerous, invasive, incredibly toxic wildflowers that doubtless felt right at home in Australia, the continent where everything could kill you. It seemed almost like an oversight on the part of Nature that aconite wasn't native. They probably had something worse. Maybe a cousin of the vegetable lamb that had fangs and venom sacs instead of blunt herbivore's teeth . . .

I pulled aconite plants up by their roots as I contemplated Australia's potential for deadly vegetation, pausing to shake the worst of the dirt and bugs off each handful before shoving it into my bag. The flowers would retain their potency for three to five days. We could gather more after that, if we needed them. That was the nice thing about invasive plants: since they grew like weeds, there was a virtually inexhaustible supply. Even wilted, these would be a hundred times more effective than my dried flowers. They would—

The sound of a low growl coming from the direction of the pond brought my head up, fingers tightening on my handful of aconite stems. "Cooper?" I had to fight to keep the quaver out of my voice. "Is that what a bunyip sounds like?"

I wasn't sure whether I wanted him to say yes or no, but I knew I didn't want the answer that I got: "I don't know what that is," he said, stepping closer to me. He was suddenly holding a pistol; he must have produced it from inside his lambskin coat, but he'd moved fast enough that I hadn't seen him draw. "I've never heard that before. Do you have enough damn weeds?"

"I do." I stood. "Let's get out of here."

"My thoughts exactly." Cooper took a step backward, toward me, his gun still aimed at the water. There was a momentary silence, like the world was holding its breath.

The werewolf burst out of the trees that were growing in the pond. It was fully transformed, maybe two hundred pounds of hair and muscle and hatred, and it was coming straight toward us.

Cooper shouted something. I heard his gun go off three times. Everything seemed to slow down, the way it does when everything is going wrong. I dropped the bag of aconite, pulling the pistol from my belt and taking careful aim on the charging beast. *I should have woken up earlier. I might have remembered to swap my bullets for silver rounds,* I thought, and then, *Too late now,* and then the shot was perfect, the shot was as close to ideal as you could get outside the range, and I was pulling the trigger with frantic speed, trying to cluster my bullets on the center of the werewolf's forehead.

Silver does the best job of killing werewolves. It does something we don't fully understand to their central nervous systems, disrupting the connection between the therianthropic virus that gives them the power to shapeshift and the body's normal, static state. Lead doesn't come with any such bonuses. But if you hit anything hard enough, fast enough, it's going to fall down.

That's what happened with our werewolf. Cooper poured bullets into it, and so did I, and midway across the meadow it collapsed, yelping as it fell. I took a step closer, just to adjust my aim, and kept firing until the magazine clicked empty. When that happened, I opened the chamber, coolly reloaded, and then resumed firing.

"Son, I think it's dead," said Cooper, between shots.

I fired one more bullet into the werewolf's head. "Any werewolf that can still be identified via dental records isn't dead enough for me," I said.

"You really hate the bastards, don't you?" He sounded remarkably unshaken for a man who'd just been attacked by a werewolf in an open field. I frowned as I turned to face him. He'd been the one to tell me about the aconite. He'd known I wouldn't be able to resist getting access to fresher flowers. What if this had been a trap?

Looking at his face removed any doubt. He was pale and shaking, with white patches beneath his eyes that spoke of ensuing shock. "Yes, I hate them," I said, moving to pick up my bag. "I was raised never to hate anything, because everything has a purpose, but there's no purpose to waheela rabies getting into the human population like this. It was just a shitty spillover event, and we're going to be dealing with it forever. I hate them so much. I don't think there's anything in the world that I hate more."

Cooper nodded. "That's something I can understand. Come on, boy. Let's get back to work." He turned to head back into the woods, and toward the safety of the medical station on the other side. I moved to follow.

Something slammed into me from behind, so fast and hard that I didn't have the chance to turn and see what it was before I landed face-first in the aconite, so hard that the air was knocked out of me. Then teeth like knives were driven into my upper arm, the impact slamming my head against the dirt, and a wave of pain and agonized understanding took everything else away.

Seven

"We can plan and plan, we can scheme and scheme, but in the end, a single second has the power to change everything."
— Alexander Healy

Facedown in a field of aconite in Queensland, Australia, in one hell of a lot of trouble

CONSCIOUSNESS RETURNED RELUCTANTLY, like a student creeping into class on the first day of finals. I allowed it in with equal reluctance. If the world was the student afraid of being graded, I was the grad student terrified of being trusted with the responsibility of giving the grades. Or maybe I was the professor overseeing the class, or the classroom, or . . . the metaphor began to crumble, taking the last comforting shards of nothingness with it. It was time for me to wake up.

It was time for me to wake up.

It was time—

I opened my eyes with a gasp, and discovered that I was sprawled face down in a muddy field of trampled aconite flowers. Everything smelled of blood. I pushed myself upright, spitting and clawing the muck from my glasses. The motion pulled at the bite wound, sending pain shooting through my entire body. I convulsed but didn't scream. Not screaming was one of the first lessons I'd learned as a child, when it became evident that dangerous situations would be a part of my life until they inevitably brought it to an end. If you scream, whatever caused your injuries might come back for a second helping. Swallow the pain, swallow the fear that comes with it, and keep moving. Movement is the only thing that can save you.

Movement was complicated by the fact that everything was slippery with mud and water and crushed flowers, which added a nasty, sludgy sliminess to the whole situation. I couldn't put any weight on my left arm, either; even the slightest flex of my triceps sent another wave of pain crashing through me. Eventually, I managed to half roll, half stagger to my feet, looking around the decimated field with dazed eyes.

The mud on my glasses gave everything a brownish cast, making it impossible to make out any details. I made the tactical decision to risk another attack in my moment of blindness and took them off, wiping them as clean as possible on the inside of my shirt, where the mud hadn't quite penetrated. Putting them back on, I took another look around the field. Nothing moved except the flowers, which swayed in the breeze that was blowing across the water.

Nothing—oh, fuck. "Cooper?" There was no response. I pitched my voice a little louder, not quite shouting, and called again, "Cooper? Cooper, can you hear me? Answer if you can hear me."

There was no response. I took a deep breath through my nose, held it for a few counts, and started scanning the field for signs of a struggle. The purple aconite flowers did a good job of camouflaging the blood, but it stood out well against the leaves. There; that was where I'd fallen, and the drag marks showed where the—where the thing had dragged me through the field like an old rag doll. I knew what had bitten me, I had *seen* it, but my mind still shied away from forming the word, like thinking it would grant it a reality that it otherwise wouldn't possess.

Wishing a thing away doesn't make it not have happened, I thought, half-nonsensically, and started wading through the wreckage of the flowers toward the place where I'd been attacked. That was where I found Cooper, sprawled among the crushed vegetation with his eyes closed and his face turned toward the empty sky. The—the thing had bitten him several times, once on the shoulder, twice on the right arm. All three wounds were still leaking blood. I crouched down, reaching out to feel for a pulse.

It was there. Weak and thready, but there. He wasn't gone yet, although he would be soon if I didn't get him some medical care—and that didn't even touch on the fact that he'd been bitten. He could be a dead man walking.

That could be true for both of us.

"Time to move." The sound of my own voice startled me. I shied away from it, looking anxiously around to see whether I had attracted any unwanted attention. As before, nothing moved, and I finally realized what else was wrong with this scene:

The thing, the werewolf—I couldn't avoid the word forever, no matter how much I desperately wanted to—was gone. There was a crushed patch in the aconite where its body had landed, but there was no sign of the body itself. Massive footprints that were half human and half lupine led away from the crushed flowers. Which meant that either a) the werewolf hadn't been dead, which seemed unlikely, given how many bullets I had put into its head; or b) the thing that bit us had been a second werewolf, and it had been large enough to pick up its pack mate and carry it away.

Either way, there was a live werewolf in the area. I didn't want to be here anymore, and Cooper couldn't afford to be. That didn't mean I could run off without the things I needed to finish my work.

I moved away from Cooper, scanning the ground until I spotted the strap of my work bag. I picked it up and slung it over my shoulder before I resumed scanning. My pistol was harder to find, being small and darkly colored, but I eventually found the stock poking out from under a thick tangle of aconite flowers. I wiped the mud off the stock and jammed the barrel into my belt, and only then did I go back to hoist Cooper off the ground, bracing him into a fireman's carry despite the pain the action awoke in my injured arm.

"I'm really glad you're not Riley's size," I muttered, through gritted teeth. "I think I'd have to leave you here to bleed out." That wasn't true: I would at least try to improvise a travois before I'd leave a man behind. But the image was ludicrous enough to take my mind off the pain for an instant, and that was all I really wanted. This was going to be difficult. Anything that made it the slightest bit easier was to be grasped and clung to with both hands.

Cooper was a dead weight as I shuffled out of the meadow and into the woods. I must have looked like I was drunk, staggering from side to side, unbalanced and uncertain of myself. Every sound I heard signaled danger to my shock-addled mind, until I found myself flinching at birdsong. I didn't know the environment here. I didn't know what to *listen* for.

Thankfully, Cooper had led me in a relatively straight line from the medical station to the meadow, and the few twists we'd taken hadn't been enough to take us away from the general direction of the road. After what felt like an eternity, I stumbled out of the trees and onto the hard-packed dirt. The brilliantly manmade form of Riley's SUV gleamed in the afternoon sun about twenty yards away. Twenty short yards, after what I'd just been through. I walked toward it as fast as I could with Cooper still weighing me down, and let out a sigh of relief when I saw the medical station exactly as we'd left it, down to the closed and locked front door.

"Sorry about this, buddy," I said, and lowered Cooper until he was halfway on the hood, allowing me to rummage through his pockets. He kept trying to slide off my shoulders, forcing me to hoist him up again. I nearly dropped him twice. I was starting to be afraid that I wouldn't have the strength to catch him when the third time inevitably came, and then my fingers hit the rounded outline of his key ring, and I stopped worrying about silly little things like gravity. Playtime was over. It was time for me to really get to work.

After carrying Cooper through a forest and searching him for keys without dropping him on his head, balancing him on my shoulder while I unlocked the door was practically child's play. Jett immediately stuck her head outside, giving one of those shrill, piercing barks of hers as she took in the muddy, aconite-and-blood-covered outlines of her master and me. It must have been very confusing for her, because she barked one more time before retreating to her corner and sitting back down.

"Good call," I said, and carried Cooper inside.

The operating table was covered in the supplies I needed to save our lives. Pushing them onto the floor would be stupid to the point of becoming suicidal. Instead, I dumped Cooper in the station's one small chair before heading to the cabinet where I'd spotted the emergency first aid kits. I couldn't give him back the blood he'd lost. I could at least try to keep him from losing too much more.

Jett whined. I looked up, trying to sound sympathetic as I said, "I know, girl. It'll be okay, you'll see. I'll fix your human."

Assuming *anything* could fix her human. I might be able to keep him from dying before Riley and Shelby got back, but so what? Was it really fair of me to make that decision for him? We'd been bitten.

There it was, bald and bloody as the handprints I was leaving on the walls: we'd been bitten, both of us, by a werewolf. Possibly two werewolves, if the other one had

survived even after we'd poured so many bullets into it
that it should have qualified as a lead hazard. We'd been
unconscious and covered in werewolf saliva for an unknown period of time, and since we had open wounds, our
chances of contracting lycanthropy were even higher than
usual, and *that* meant—

No. That meant I had to do my job, and if Cooper
wanted to hate me for saving him, that was a problem for
later. I still took a few seconds to look around, searching
for a phone. I needed to warn Shelby about the werewolves, assuming she hadn't been attacked already.

I couldn't think about that. She could take care of herself, and I needed to focus on the situation at hand. Besides, there was no wall phone. I didn't have an Australian
SIM card for my cellphone yet, and a quick check of
Cooper's pockets showed that his phone had been lost
somewhere between the meadow and the medical station. I didn't have time to go out looking for it.

Grabbing the first aid kit from its place on the wall, I
moved to kneel in front of Cooper. "Again, I'm really
sorry about this," I said. "I didn't want us to be traumatic
injury buddies until much later."

There was a good pair of scissors in the kit. I carefully
worked the blades around the cuff of his shirt and began
cutting.

It takes a certain amount of skill to cut the clothing
off a living person without hurting them: you're basically
using conjoined knives right next to their skin. I focused
past the pain in my own arm, forcing myself to move nice
and slow as I stripped Cooper's upper body one piece of
fabric at a time. The more I cut away, the more of his
injuries were revealed. I knew from the way my own injuries pulled and ached that the werewolf had bitten
down hard on my arm, but that was where it had stopped;
for whatever reason, it hadn't decided to continue working until it ripped me open.

It hadn't been that kind to Cooper.

The entire front of his torso was covered in claw marks

and scrapes that could have been made by anything, but were likely to have been made by teeth. His right shoulder was a mauled mass that looked almost like hamburger. Images from *An American Werewolf in London* were all too happy to present themselves to me as I used a piece of peroxide-soaked cotton to wipe away the worst of the mud and aconite pulp before starting to wrap his injuries in gauze.

Even as field dressings went, this wasn't a good one. The chance of a secondary infection was ridiculously high, and no matter how much gauze I slapped on, I wasn't going to stop the bleeding completely. It was enough better than nothing that I kept going. Shelby and Riley would come back eventually; they had to, I had the SUV. When they got here, we could move Cooper to a better location, one with more advanced medical facilities. All I had to do was keep him alive until they showed up—and give us both a fighting chance at overcoming the infection.

I stood once the last piece of gauze was taped off and walked back to the operating table, my own blood loss making my head spin. My field bag was there, and the smell of crushed aconite flowers wafted out to greet me, sweet and acrid at the same time. I looked at them, swallowing hard. They were incredibly poisonous even in their untreated form. What I was going to do to them would only concentrate those toxins, making them even worse.

It was the only chance we had. I took a deep breath to steady myself and reached into the bag for the first handful of flowers.

The recipe for lycanthropy-w antiserum is surprisingly close to several of the old folk remedies that were supposed to either kill or cure a newly infected werewolf. As is so often the case, necessity had been the mother of invention, and while we might someday have something synthetic that does the job, for now, we stick with the tried and true.

I fed the aconite leaves in clumps into the small blender I'd packed for the purpose, stuffing it until the lid barely stayed in place. Two quick buzzes on the chop setting gave me a lot of diced vegetation, which I decanted into a larger bowl before stuffing the blender a second time, this time with flowers, which I proceeded to blend into a sort of horrifying aconite smoothie. The air turned sticky-sweet with the smell of crushed flowers. Normally, that would have been upsetting. At the moment, the fact that it was covering the smell of blood was a blessing.

I got down to work.

No matter what changes in my life, science is always there. Science has been the one constant of my existence. I wanted to know why the world worked the way it did before I had sisters, before I had a career in mind, even before I understood that for most kids the bogeyman was a scary story to tell in the dark, not a real thing that might be sleeping under their bed. (I had alienated myself from my elementary school peers *very* quickly by trying to tell them about my home life. My parents had told me not to, but I had believed, with the blind hopefulness of a child, that my friends would understand when I said things like "Grandpa used to be a bunch of corpses" and "Grandma killed a rock demon once, but we think it was actually a colony organism." My friends did not understand. My friends did not remain my friends for long.)

Science kept the terror at bay. My mind kept trying to present me with images of the werewolf in the field, the werewolf in the long-ago stable, and I kept shunting them to the side, focusing on science. Science would save me.

Bit by bit and step by step, I extracted the fluid from the aconite leaves, grinding them down and mixing them periodically with the other ingredients that were going into today's bad idea stew. Once they had been reduced to a dry, fibrous mass, I moved them to a beaker and added water before turning on the Bunsen burner.

It was getting harder and harder to force myself to keep moving, and to keep observing the necessary lab protocols. My own wounds weren't bleeding anymore, but they needed to be cleaned and treated, and I didn't have time for that right now. The pain of touching the bite would only slow me down; once I'd been sure I wasn't going to bleed in my ingredients and potentially contaminate them, I had left it alone. It didn't *feel* like the werewolf had severed anything essential. My arm was still working normally, if a little stiffly, and so I just kept going. It was better than the alternatives, none of which I really wanted to consider.

I must have blacked out at some point. I was watching the contents of the beaker bubble and reduce. Then I blinked, and the beaker had gone from two-thirds full to holding little more than two inches of liquid, poisonously dark and glittering slightly from the silver nitrate. It looked disturbingly like the mascara Antimony would put on before one of her roller derby bouts.

The thought was funnier than it should have been. That realization sobered me instantly. I was going into shock—if I wasn't there already—and I needed to move.

We didn't have a blast cooler, and we didn't have time to wait for the stuff to cool naturally. Cooper still wasn't awake. I poured the thick, viscous liquid into a waiting tray, creating as much surface area as possible, and added the final, most dangerous ingredient: mercury, which dripped silver and deadly into the mass, glimmering on the surface until I stirred it into the rest. I kept stirring for a minute and a half, timing myself on the wall clock, trying to ensure that everything was evenly mixed. Mercury's tendency to clump meant that using the blender wasn't a good idea, and was part of why we had to make such small batches, and use them so quickly. Not only would the aconite begin to lose its efficacy, and not only would the rabies treatments become gradually denatured by the things around them, but the mercury would pull away, forming clots of deadly toxins that weren't counterbalanced by the other deadly toxins the treatment was supposed to contain.

Jett watched me with narrow, wary eyes as I measured out a quarter teaspoon of sludge and shambled toward her unconscious owner. "You're pretty lucky, you know," I said to Cooper. "Most people pass out from the shock of this stuff, assuming it doesn't make their hearts stop—which it doesn't always, but this is Australia. You might have extra strong aconite here or something, and I haven't been able to test it. Your mouth is going to go numb. You may have long-lasting nerve damage on your tongue, although that's a relatively rare side effect. You will probably experience dizziness, unconsciousness, nausea, blurred vision, and either constipation, diarrhea, or both. Also you may turn into a werewolf anyway, and I am so sorry to do this to you without your consent, but with the amount of blood you've lost, it's going to be a while before you wake up, even with proper medical care, and this stuff really needs to be administered as soon after the bite as possible."

Cooper didn't wake up. I glanced to the door, wishing Shelby and Riley would appear and save me from needing to make this decision on my own. I felt like I was doing the right thing, but how could I be sure? How much of my motivation was based on the need to see someone else ingest the stuff before I risked myself?

Shelby and Riley didn't appear. I turned back to Cooper. "I guess this is it," I said, and raised the spoon. My hand was shaking. I raised my other hand to steady it, and missed my wrist twice before I realized what was happening.

I had waited too long.

Maybe I hadn't been bleeding the whole time, but I had still lost a lot of blood in that meadow, and had suffered a severe enough injury that I should have been seeking medical treatment immediately, not playing chemist in a one-room hideaway in the middle of no-where. The last of my reserves had been spent on making the treatment that I was even now failing to administer.

I almost felt grateful as my knees buckled and, for the second time in less than three hours, I plunged into un-consciousness.

This was getting to be a habit.

Jett's barking pulled me back into the world of the living. I had fallen on my injured arm, and as soon as I became aware of myself again, the pain took care of the rest, rocketing me straight from the pleasant fields of dream-land and into the cruel realities of Australia. I struggled to sit up, managing only to lift my head enough to see Jett standing in the open doorway—oh, God, I'd left the door open, I'd been so distracted by pain and the need to get the tincture mixed that I'd left the door open— barking her head off. There was a new urgency in those high-pitched yelps, lending them a weight that they had previously lacked. This wasn't barking for the sake of barking. Her *person* was in trouble, and to a dog, that meant everything.

Cooper was still propped in the chair. The spilled tinc-ture had left a dark splotch on his shirt. He didn't appear to have moved, and I couldn't tell if he was breathing. I didn't think he was breathing. I gave up the fight to sit and put my head back on the floor, closing my eyes and waiting for whatever was going to happen next. Giving up seemed strangely easy, like this was the way things were always intended to be for me. I would die here, and that would be the end of it. The mice would find their own way home. Poor mice. I would be one more death they'd have to remember for the rest of their lives, and for all the lives that came after. Knowing that I was go-ing to break the colony's heart hurt, but what choice did I have? I was done.

"Jett, what're you on about? Why's the door open?" Shelby sounded innocently curious, like she had no suspicions that things could have gone wrong. "Was it that Alex, hmm? Did he not do the latch? Cooper would do the latch for you, there's bunyip around these parts, you know."

More than just bunyip, I thought. I wanted to call out to her. I couldn't figure out how.

"Shelly, look at this." Riley. He sounded concerned, unlike his daughter. The reason why was quickly explained as he continued, "There's blood on the ground here, see? Someone's been hurt."

"Oh, God—Alex?" Shelby didn't hesitate. She shoved past the dog, her footsteps pounding on the thin wooden floor. I heard her gasp. I wanted to roll over and tell her that I was fine, I just needed someone to help me off the floor, but that seemed so hard. I decided to stay where I was instead. Much better. "Alex?!"

I couldn't ignore the edge of panic in her voice. She wasn't touching me. That was a good thing. Even upset, she was respecting proper safety procedures. The risk of infection would have been too great, given that I was sprawled in a pool of blood and unidentified black sludge.

Answering her was the only polite thing to do, much as it pained me to even think about moving. I shifted my head enough to free my jaw, and said, muzzily, "'M not dead."

Under the circumstances, it felt like a speech worthy of Shakespeare.

Shelby must have decided to hell with observing proper procedures, because I heard her step forward, only to stop abruptly. "Daddy, let me *go!* He's hurt!"

"Yes, and Cooper's dead." Riley's voice was grim. "Son, you want to go ahead and tell us what happened?"

It was difficult to think, much less follow an unspoken implication. Still, I did my best, and after only a few moments I reached the appropriate conclusion. "I didn't kill him." The more I talked, the easier it became. The words were coming back to me, clear and understandable, if a little bit dusty around the edges. "I tried to save him."

"So what's this sludge on his shirt? Some sort of toxin?"

Shelby's father had to be playing stupid to upset me. It was the only thing that made sense. "It's the toxin you sent us out here to make," I snapped, turning my head and glaring at him. Half a second later my body realized that I had just forced it to move, and rewarded me with a wave of staggering nausea. I fought through it, keeping my eyes on Riley. He filled the doorway, one massive hand clamped down on Shelby's upper arm as he forced her to stay with him. "I spilled the tincture when I was trying to administer it to him."

"Yeah? You're sure you didn't feed him a nice big dose to see what would happen?"

Shelby shook off her father's hand in a sudden, convulsive motion. He turned to blink at her, apparently as surprised by this as I was. "Stop it!" she said, grabbing a box of plastic gloves off the nearest counter and yanking them on. "Just you stop it! I know you don't like Alex, and I don't give a fuck! Look at his arm!" She pointed at me as she dropped the box. I obligingly twisted as much as I could to show him my left arm, and the shredded coat that covered it. "Something bit the ever-loving *crap* out of him, and now you're going to stand there accusing him of murder? Really? That's how you're going to deal with my bloody fiancé now?"

"Fiancé?" he said. He sounded like he'd been pole-axed. I knew how he felt.

Shelby didn't dignify his question with a response. She just glared at him and stalked over to where I was sitting, reaching down to offer me her hands. I glanced at them, alarmed. She smiled a little. "No open cuts, I'm wearing gloves, and lycanthropy is hard to catch, you said so yourself," she said, still holding out her hands. "I'd have to lick you all over to pick up any of the remaining werewolf saliva from your skin. You'll forgive me if I'm not interested, yeah?"

"Yeah, but you're still taking a shower after this," I said, and offered her my right elbow.

With her grasping my arm and me pushing off with my legs, we were able to get me to my feet with a minimum of trouble. The newly awakened pain in my left arm had dropped back down to a dull throb, allowing me to focus on other things. Like Cooper, whose eyes were still closed, but whose chest no longer rose and fell with the labored rhythm of his breath.

"Damn," I whispered. "You poor bastard."

"What happened?" Shelby's voice was gentle.

I turned back to her. "We went to the aconite field to gather flowers," I said. "There was this flat pond . . ."

"A billabong," said Shelby. "I know the one. There's bunyip down there."

"Cooper seemed to think he could handle them." And maybe he could have. Bunyip were business as usual for him: they existed in the environment they were made for.

"But that wasn't what attacked you, was it, Alex?"

Her tone was low and even: that, and the use of my name at the end, actually made me smile. "You're talking to me like a victim," I said. "That's good technique. Really soothing. You've been working on your people skills."

"I'll work on them even harder if you'll tell me what attacked you." She was smiling, but I could see the concern reflected in her eyes, and the hands that held me upright were trembling faintly. She was terrified.

She was right to be. I pulled away, shifting my balance to my own two feet, and much to my relief, she let me go. "We were ambushed by werewolves." I looked to Riley, who was standing stone-faced in the doorway, blocking all hope of escape. "I think there were two of them, both in wolf form. One attacked. We filled it with bullets. We didn't expect the second one. It came out of nowhere."

"How are you so sure there were two?" asked Riley.

I shook my head. "We shot the shit out of the first one, if you'll pardon my French. I never even saw the second one coming . . ." I closed my eyes. I couldn't help myself. The image of a wolf rising from the flowers was there, waiting for me, and I was suddenly glad I couldn't remember any dreams I'd had while I was unconscious. I shuddered, trying to shake off the thought, and opened my eyes as I repeated, "It came out of nowhere. There was no time for us to run. It bit me, and savaged Cooper. When I came to, I carried Cooper back here and bound his wounds. You can see what I did . . . I don't think I made things any worse. I did the best I could." My cheeks were wet. I was crying. That wasn't really a surprise, although I wished I could have held back the tears until Riley was no longer looking at me with those cold, judgmental eyes.

"What about your own wounds?" Shelby asked.

"I wasn't bleeding that badly, and I was afraid I'd make things worse," I said. "Cooper was out cold, he couldn't help me take care of myself. I figured it was better to stop his bleeding and get the tincture mixed up— we've both been exposed, Shelby. He's dead, but I could still be infected. You should get away from me." It would be weeks before I was capable of passing the infection on, but at that moment, rational thought was taking a backseat to the instinctive need to protect her.

"Not too likely, but thanks for trying to shove me out as soon as things went sour," she said amiably. She looked back to her father. "Can we call Mum, get some reinforcements and a cleanup crew out here?"

"A lot of people are going to find it suspicious that Cooper died as soon as we left him alone with your American," said Riley. "You should be prepared for that."

"And I would've found it suspicious if Alex had died when he was left alone with Cooper, except for the part where no, Daddy, that's not how this works," Shelby said, all traces of amiableness gone. She glared daggers at her father. "We're doing a dangerous job, in a dangerous place, and you want to stand there looking at a man with this sort of wound in his arm, implying foul play? If there was foul play, it's on us. We're the ones who *left* them here."

Riley stood there for a moment, expression not changing. Finally, he said, "I'll call your mother," and left the station.

The room lightened as the sun was allowed to flood back in. "You know, I'm starting to get the feeling your father doesn't like me," I said. Something brushed against my leg. I looked down. Jett was leaning against me, her ears pressed flat and her tail tucked between her legs. "Poor little thing. She doesn't know what's going on."

"She'll be taken care of," said Shelby. "We're good about taking care of our own. Now come and lean against the counter, I want to get a look at your arm."

"Not if there's even the slightest infection risk, I'm not—"

"The risk is minimal for me, but it's getting higher for you with every minute that passes without cleaning this thing out. Don't argue with me, Alex. *Please*." Her tone made me wince. It was agonized, full of longing and dismay and six different flavors of misery.

"Hey." I raised my right hand and peeled off my glove before touching her cheek gently with the back of my fingers. "This isn't your fault, you know. I knew the job was dangerous when I took it."

Shelby looked at me like I was speaking gibberish. "You wouldn't be in Australia if not for me insisting that we needed help. You'd be safe at home, playing with the things that want to turn you into stone. Take off your coat."

I shrugged out of my jacket, only wincing a little as the shreds of fabric that had been driven into my wounds by the werewolf's teeth pulled free. My shirt was going to hurt a lot more to remove. "And I wouldn't be playing with the things that want to turn me into stone if my parents hadn't raised me to be fascinated by the fringes of the scientific world. We can play the blame game as long as you want. It's not going to change anything."

"It never does," said Shelby bitterly. She leaned closer, studying the tears in my shirt. "This is ruined. Can I cut off the sleeve?"

"Scissors are on the table."

She nodded curtly and turned away. While I couldn't see her face, she said, "My dad doesn't like you. He's not going to, either. Apart from the whole 'I'm supposed to have been back in Australia by now' nonsense, I told him about your family when I was still trying to save you from them."

"Ah." Understanding suddenly dawned, no less painful for being so clear.

The human side of my family was known throughout the cryptozoological world for being defectors from the Covenant of St. George. That made us potentially untrustworthy, since we'd already proven that we'd betray our allies if we ceased agreeing with them. It also made us useful. But the cryptid side of my family consisted partially of cuckoos. Like werewolves, they weren't native to Australia. The Thirty-Six Society had never been forced to learn to cope with them. Which was why, a few years before Shelby and I met, a group of cuckoos had been able to infiltrate the Society and start killing people.

I still didn't have all the details—I might never have them, given Shelby's reluctance to discuss what had happened—but I knew that a lot of people had died, and that one of them had been Shelby's older brother, Jack.

"He knows I'm human, right?" It was an indelicate question, and even needing to ask it made me feel faintly speciesist. Why was human better than any of the other options? My grandparents and my cousins are wonderful people, and their various species of origin had never done anything to impact my opinions of them. But Shelby was a human girl, from a human family, and no matter how much some people try to say that species doesn't matter, it does. It always does.

"Makes you worse in his eyes." She started gingerly cutting away my shirtsleeve, moving with the sort of exaggerated care that she usually brought to working with her cats. "Now you're not driven by instinct or different neural programming. You're a *human*. You should be siding with your own species against the world, not coddling the sort of folks who think exploding other people's brains is fun."

"It sounds like he would have fit in well with the Covenant." I gritted my teeth as her tugging separated the shirt from my skin. She was only tugging on the edges of the wound, not working at the places where the fabric had been driven well and truly into the surface of the musculature, and the pain was already bad enough to make me feel nauseous.

"Let's talk about this later, yeah?" The question was forcedly light. "Alex, this is pretty bad under here. I'm going to need to dig a bunch of bits out of your skin before I can really see the wound. Are you . . . are you all right for that?"

"It's going to hurt like hell, and I may pass out, but I'm okay," I said, bracing myself against the counter. "If I throw up, I'll try not to throw up on you."

"You're so sweet," she said.

"I try," I said, and closed my eyes. I didn't want to see her looking at me like that—and if the moment came where concern turned to pity, I didn't want to see that either. "I anticipated the possibility of cuts and burns during the manufacture of our remedy. If you look in my supplies, you'll find some sealed vials of cuckoo blood. You can use those as a topical antibiotic."

"Oh, brilliant. That makes things much easier." Her lips brushed my cheek in a dry, almost perfunctory kiss, and she moved away. I listened to her footsteps, keeping my eyes closed. It would be better if I didn't have to see her face.

My parents raised me with the idea that species didn't

matter: people were people, no matter what other attributes they possessed. It was a fine ideal to put forward, and for the most part, it managed to stick. It can be hard to get used to the idea that some people photosynthesize, while others eat their prey alive, but given enough time, the mind can adapt to anything. And it was easy for me to say all that, because at the end of the day, I was human: I was a member of the current dominant species, king of the trash heap, and apex predator to the stars. We'd killed off everything that might threaten our supremacy, and now we had the freedom to sit around saying that everybody was equal.

You want to talk true equality? Talk about a spillover virus with the power to change everything you've ever known or cared about. In the eyes of that virus, everything mammalian really *was* equal.

"This is going to sting," cautioned Shelby. I hadn't heard her come back.

"Okay," I said, gripping the counter hard with both hands. "I'll do my best not to scream."

"I'll still love you if you do," she said, and got to work.

If the pain of the werewolf biting me had been unbelievable, the pain of my girlfriend trying to repair the damage was worse. She had produced a pair of tweezers from the first aid kit, and she used them to dig every scrap of cloth and piece of crushed aconite plant out of my wounds, setting me to bleeding again. I could feel it running down my arm, and I welcomed it. Part of what made lycanthropy-w so difficult to catch was the way victims of werewolf attacks tended to bleed all over everything. Our own bodies washed half of the danger away before it could get into our systems.

"Oh, my poor boy," she murmured. There was a clink as she put the tweezers down, and the next thing I felt was a damp washcloth being pressed against my skin. That was nice, for half a second. Then the peroxide she'd used to soak the fabric reached my nerve endings, and I bit my lip with the effort of keeping silent.

Shelby must have known how much this was hurting me, but she kept working, not slowing down or allowing her hands to shake. I kept my eyes closed until I felt her thumb against my chin, and then I opened them, raising my head just enough to meet her worried gaze.

"This bite needs stitches," she said. "Can I . . . ?"

"No stitches," I replied. "Cuckoo blood and gauze, butterfly clasps if you have to, but no stitches. We're going to want to cauterize the wounds with silver nitrate as soon as we're ready for me to take the tincture, and stitches would just get in the way."

Now she looked alarmed. "Cauterize—but Alex, that's going to scar something awful."

"Better scarred than a werewolf," I said. "I never much liked wearing tank tops anyway. They make my shoulders look all funny. Can you stop the bleeding?"

"I already mostly have," she said, alarm still evident. "I really don't like this, Alex."

"That's good," I said. "Neither do I."

"What in the blue suffering fuck have you people done to the place?" demanded a female voice from the doorway.

Shelby winced. "Hi, Mum," she called. "Sorry about all the blood." She didn't move away from me. I couldn't tell whether that was because she was still concerned, or because she was trying to stay between me and her mother. I wasn't sure which one I wanted it to be.

"This is worse than your father said it would be." Charlotte Tanner strode quickly across the medical station to where Shelby and I were standing. She stomped through the puddles of blood in her path, not seeming to care about the fact that she was leaving bloody footprints across the very few swaths of clean floor remaining. "Cooper's *dead*. How do you take a man on a basic forest recon and wind up bringing him home *dead?*" Her words were callous, but her tone wasn't: she sounded like a woman who was grasping desperately for sense, because the alternatives were too terrible to be borne.

"It turns out to be pretty easy," I said. "Hello, Ms. Tanner."

"Hello, Alex," she said, distracted momentarily by the instinct toward politeness. Her eyes went to my wounded shoulder. She grimaced. "That looks fairly awful. How does it feel?"

"Worse than it looks," I said. "As for the elephant in the room, yes, it was a werewolf that killed Cooper, and it was the same werewolf that bit me. If I didn't know better, I'd say it had been waiting there for us."

Charlotte nodded slowly. "Why do you know better?"

"What?"

"You said if you didn't know better. Why do you know better? Kangaroos can lay ambushes. So can most predators. Why can't werewolves?"

"Like I said before, the change makes most of them mentally unstable. They have impulse control issues, usually even when they return to their original forms. A fully transformed werewolf isn't thinking like any creature that arises in nature. They can't *plan*." And that, right there, was the source of my terror. Becoming a cuckoo like Sarah, or a gorgon like Dee, was biologically impossible, but it wouldn't have driven me into a quivering ball of fear. Lycanthropy was different. It not only stole your form, it stole your mind.

Science had been the one thing that got me through all the troubles and pains of my life. Science couldn't save me when I no longer had the mind to understand that it existed.

Charlotte nodded once, before asking, "How are you so sure?"

"What?"

"How are you so sure? Have you been a werewolf? Interviewed one? 'Excuse me, Mr. Big Bad Wolf, but when you ate all those people, were you in your right mind, or were you overcome with animal passions?' Maybe werewolves are smarter than we give them credit for being, and just don't want to tell you."

I stared at her. "I . . . I don't know. Werewolves are one of the only things we've never tried to make peace with. They're a disease. Diseases have to be wiped out, for the sake of everyone they might infect."

"I suppose so. Still, it's a very Covenant way of looking at the world—we show our roots in our own ways, don't we?" Her eyes dipped to the wound in my shoulder before moving to Shelby, who was standing red-cheeked and anxious between us. "How likely is it that you've been infected, Alex?"

Just like that, everything about her—her stance, her pointed questions, even her seeming lack ·of concern over Cooper's death—fell into place. "I have as much of a chance of being infected as anyone else who's been exposed," I said. "I have a fresh batch of antiserum. Now that you're here, we can move Cooper out of the chair and I can sit down long enough for the first stage of treatment. After that, we'll have twenty-eight days before we know one way or another. If I have been infected, and can't stop that infection before it fully takes hold, you'll have to put me down."

"No," said Shelby. "Shan't. Find another solution."

"Yes, *shall*," I said firmly. "Shelby, if I start to change, I won't be on your side anymore. I'll be a danger. To everyone, and to everything."

"Unless you manage somehow to prove that werewolves can think," said Charlotte. "Wouldn't that be a scientific achievement?"

"You know, a few seconds ago I was sure you were trying to convince me to kill myself," I said. "Can you please pick a line of argument and stick with it? Lots of good people have been bitten by werewolves over the years. Doctors and wildlife conservationists and yes, members of the Covenant who would've died before they'd allow themselves to become monsters. Not one of those people ever stood up and said 'hey, I'm a werewolf that thinks, let's not eat people.' They all became killers. *I* would be a killer. If I go werewolf, we have to stop me from hurting people."

"Good," said Charlotte, with a decisive nod. "You may continue to breathe for now, Mr. Price. Shelby, do whatever you have to in order to get him ready to travel. I brought the rescue truck, so we'll be able to lock him in the back where he can't hurt anyone. Your sisters are helping your father look for signs of the werewolf. I'm going to stay here and hold a gun on you both, to make sure your boyfriend doesn't try anything funny. Understood?"

"Yes, Mum," said Shelby.

"Yes," I said.

"Good. And Alex?"

"Yes?"

Charlotte smiled sadly, her eyes reflecting an infinity of regret. "I'm really sorry it had to be like this."

"Yeah, well." I shrugged, trying not to wince when it pulled on the wound in my shoulder. "I always knew that it was dangerous to come to Australia."

Eight

"Transformation doesn't always happen in an instant. Sometimes it comes slowly, infecting the body and the brain until you wake up and realize that you've been completely remade in something else's image. Only pray that whatever infects you will leave you better than you were."

— Thomas Price

Sitting in an animal rescue van, driving down the back roads of Queensland, Australia

THE VAN THE SOCIETY used for transporting injured wildlife around Queensland was big enough to have been a perfect base for a roving serial killer: much like the SUV, and like Riley himself, it seemed to have been designed to take up as much space as humanly possible while still being considered a "normal" example of the breed. A wire screen separated the front seat from the back. Charlotte and Gabby rode up front. Shelby and I rode in the back, seated on foldout benches on either side of the van.

"Thanks for leaving the cages home, Mum," Shelby said, her hands resting on her knees and her eyes remaining fixed on me. "It would have been awkward back here if we'd been crammed between enclosures."

"We could have just put your boyfriend into one," said Gabby. "Solve a bunch of problems in one go."

"I'd rather avoid cages as long as possible, if it's all right by you," I said. I could envision far too many of them in my future. We'd be putting me in one—or at least in a small locked room—as soon as we made it back to the house. After some brief discussion, we had mutually agreed to wait to deliver the antiserum until I was secure, since there was a chance it would cause convulsions. Better that we do something like that in a setting we could control.

"Alex," said Shelby softly.

I mustered a wan smile. "It's all right."

"No, it's not. None of this is all right. How have you even *lived* this long?" She looked suddenly angry, her sorrow transmuting into rage. "There's a cockatrice, you look at it. There's a werewolf, you get bitten by it. Did you ever meet a monster you didn't want to turn into? It's hard on the heart, Alex. It's just . . . it's so damn hard on the heart."

"Not just yours." I leaned my head back against the van wall, staring up at the ceiling. Riley and Raina were back at the medical station, disinfecting everything and wiping away all the signs of what had happened there. Including Cooper. "Did Cooper . . . did he have family?"

"No, thankfully," said Charlotte. "We'll have a private service, but we're not going to be explaining his body to anyone who would ask unfortunate questions. People disappear in Australia every day."

"People disappear all over the world every day," Shelby corrected. "It's not just here. It's sad, though. He was always sweet to me, in his own way."

"Every death is sad." I was so tired. My arm still ached, despite its swaddling layers of gauze and cuckoo blood. I closed my eyes.

"Alex, try to stay awake, all right? We'll be able to set you up a blood transfusion once we get back to the house." Shelby sounded concerned.

I frowned, not opening my eyes. "I haven't lost that much blood. And if you have the equipment to perform a blood transfusion at the house, why did we have to go to the middle of nowhere for me to break out the chemistry set? There was nothing at that medical station that I didn't have with me or couldn't have scavenged from a working kitchen."

"Dad doesn't trust you," said Gabby.

"Gabby!" said Charlotte.

"What? It's true, Mum, he doesn't. Shelly came home with a boy who was half Covenant and half the monsters that killed Jack, of *course* Dad doesn't trust him. He might as well have been completely covered in little mustaches he could twirl. So that's why, Alex." From the way her voice shifted, Gabby had twisted to look at me. I kept my eyes closed. "He didn't want you mixing up chemicals in the house when there was a chance you were up to no good. Then Cooper went and got killed, and you didn't, and now I don't think he knows what to think about you. Might be an improvement, really, as long as you don't turn into a werewolf."

"I'm going to hold you underwater in the next billabong we find," said Shelby, a low, dangerous note in her voice. "I'm going to hold you underwater until the kicking stops."

"You can give it a try," said Gabby. "I'll let you."

"It's all right, Shelby," I said, allowing myself a hint of a smile. "At least she's being honest." Honesty was the best policy. It was what I planned to use with the mice. They needed to know what had happened to me, so that they'd be able to explain it to my parents if they had to go home without me.

My parents. Honestly, I wasn't sure I knew what I was going to say to my parents. If I called and told them I'd been bitten, there was every chance they'd be on the next plane to Australia, and it wasn't like they could do anything to help me fight off the infection. Nothing could do that. If they came here, they'd be putting themselves into the line of fire, and they would make it harder for me to do what I might need to do. Could they stand by and watch while I put a gun against my head?

No. They couldn't, and they wouldn't. No matter how often they had said that our jobs—our lives—could be deadly, they wouldn't be able to accept that my infection meant that I was genuinely lost to them. "I can't tell them," I said.

Shelby sighed. The sound was soft and still in the enclosed van, filled with a deep and unquestioning sadness. "I know you can't," she said.

"What's that?" asked Charlotte.

"Alex can't call his parents," Shelby said. "They'd want to come here, and that wouldn't work out well for anybody."

"You got all that from 'I can't tell them'?" asked Gabby.

"I've been spending a lot of time with his family lately," said Shelby. "I'm starting to figure out how they think."

"That's what worries me," said Charlotte.

The van rattled down the back roads between the medical station and the safe house at what felt like unsafe speeds, especially given my current position in the back, surrounded by unsecured animal rescue supplies. I kept my eyes closed for the rest of the drive, trying to think about anything other than the aching throb in my shoulder, and the tiny psychosomatic fire ants scurrying in my blood. You can't feel lycanthropy taking hold, any more than you can feel rabies, but in that moment, I would have sworn I could trace the path of the infection as it radiated out from my shoulder and sought new homes in the tissue of my nervous system, spinal cord, and worst of all, brain.

I was sunk in my own depressed contemplation when the van finally jerked to a halt. One of the front doors slammed almost before we had stopped moving, and then the back of the van was flung open, sending light flooding into the previously dark space. Even through my closed eyelids, it was enough to make me shy away and raise an arm to shade my face—and then, because the mammalian state comes with some weird instinctual responses, I cracked my eyes open enough to see what was going on.

Gabby was standing in front of the open van doors with a gun in her hands, the muzzle trained on me. Her stance wasn't as good as it could have been; her feet were too close together, and the placement of her hands wasn't giving her any defense against the recoil. She'd be lucky if she didn't break a wrist if she had to fire. Of course, at her current range, I'd be lucky if she didn't put a bullet through my heart and solve the whole "I can't tell my parents I've been bitten by a werewolf" problem sooner rather than later.

"Please undo your belt and come with me," she said, before adding, "Sorry about this, Alex. It's basic quarantine procedure."

"I know about quarantine," I said, keeping my movements slow as I slid to my feet. The van was almost tall enough for me to straighten up inside. Only half-stooped, I walked toward the exit. Shelby remained behind me, not saying a word either to defend me or to support her sister. She'd been put into an awkward position, and I felt bad for her—or as bad for her as I could muster, given my own situation.

"It's a nice room," said Gabby. "You barely notice the bars on the windows."

"Lovely," I said. "Look, I'm going to need someone with me when I take the antiserum. It can cause heart failure and convulsions."

Gabby looked alarmed. "Well, none of *us* is going to do it. Not if we can't know for sure that you're not contagious."

I decided against trying to explain the difference between "contagious" and "infectious." Besides, I wasn't either. "I won't be able to pass the virus for twenty-eight days."

"We only have your word for that! We can't risk it."

Shelby would do it. Happily. And it would just cause more problems with her family, which was the last thing I wanted to do right now. I swallowed the urge to sigh. "Fine. Is there a local gorgon or wadjet community you can call? Maybe they can send a doctor."

"There aren't any gorgons in Australia," said Gabby, looking at me blankly. "I don't even know what a what-sit is."

I was going to die because the locals had shrugged off their Covenant influences enough to protect things that *didn't* look human, but not enough to work with things that *did*. "Hang on," I said. I twisted to look over my shoulder at Shelby. "Get my phone. Find the number for the Sarpas. Call Kumari, and tell her what's going on. Tell her I need a nonmammalian doctor within the next two hours, and tell her . . ." I took a deep breath. "Tell her I'll guarantee Chandi access to her fiancé every day for a month after I get home, if she does this for me."

"I'll do you one better," said Shelby. "I'll also tell her that if you don't make it home, Chandi gets her time anyway. I have the pull at the zoo to make it happen. Especially if I'm grieving."

"Thank you," I said, and turned back to Gabby, who was watching this exchange with a nonplussed expression on her face. "All right. Take me to the oubliette."

"It's not an oubliette," she said. "There's cable. Now march."

I marched.

It was becoming more and more apparent that I didn't know how large the Thirty-Six Society compound was, and just as apparent that they weren't going to make it easy for me to learn. Gabby marched me down a pleasant brick path until it tapered out, becoming a somewhat less pleasant dirt path that wound through another patch of thickly packed eucalyptus trees. Something whistled high overhead, and was answered by Flora's shrill, territorial shriek.

"Can I get a guide to the local birds?" I asked. "Since there's a window and all, it might be interesting to learn which call belongs to which thing I've never seen before."

"I'll tell Mum," said Gabby. "*Please* keep walking."

"If Shelby can't reach my contact, we're going to need to figure something out about my medical care, you know."

"We need to make sure it's safe before we do anything. We've been quarantining people, but we haven't been poking at them." Again, she sounded apologetic, and again, that didn't change anything. This was hard for her. I understood that. Anything that involved marching a visiting cryptozoologist to your secret isolation shed was going to be difficult. That didn't mean it wasn't difficult for me, too.

We stepped out of the trees and onto the calm green oasis of a lawn, dotted here and there with flowers I didn't recognize. There was a small two-story house there, complete with tiny porch and even tinier chimney rising from the roof. The door was ajar, and someone was waiting for us just inside. I glanced back at Gabby, who shook her head and gestured me forward with her gun. Her finger was resting on the trigger, I noticed: she was more than prepared to shoot me if she felt that it was necessary. She hadn't been keeping her finger on the trigger when Shelby was in eyesight.

"So I guess he's with us," I said, and kept walking.

The figure in the hall turned out to be another man I recognized from the previous night's dinner. He was of apparently Filipino descent, with long black hair tied into a ponytail and a scruff of a goatee covering his chin. He was also holding a gun large enough to make Gabby's look like a bad joke. I nodded to him. He frowned at me, his eyes focusing on my gauze-encrusted shoulder.

"Is this the one who was exposed?" he asked, looking back to Gabby for confirmation.

She nodded. "One bite. It's been thoroughly cleaned out, but . . ."

"You and I both know that doesn't mean anything," he said, and turned back to me. "My name is Angelo Magdael. I will have the extreme pleasure of being your jailer for the next twenty-eight days. If you have any weapons on you, please surrender them now."

I'd been waiting for this, which meant I'd had plenty of time to consider my reply. "No," I said, as politely as I could manage under the circumstances. "I appreciate your reasons for asking, but I'm afraid I'm going to have to refuse."

Angelo blinked. So did Gabby. Gabby—possibly because she had grown up with two sisters arguing with her over everything under the sun—recovered first, demanding, "Why not? I'm holding a gun, you know."

"Yes, and so is he, and neither of you has a proper grip," I said. "You shouldn't keep your finger on the trigger while you walk, either. I understand the necessity of keeping control of the situation, but I'm not going to run, and even if I've been infected, I won't be able to infect anyone else for twenty-eight days. We have a window. As for why I won't give you my weapons, I'm a Price. We *never* give away our weapons."

"Gun," repeated Gabby, like it made all the difference in the world.

"Two guns," I countered. "Also several knives, a garrote, one of my grandfather's poison rings, and the technique for making werewolf antiserum, which I have memorized and have yet to pass on to any members of your organization. For the moment, you *need* me. You're not going to shoot me until the need has passed. Now, I've come along with you willingly. I'm letting you put me in quarantine, although I'm going to have a serious talk with your father later about how long I'm willing to stay there. You're not getting my weapons. That's where I have to draw the line. Besides, if I'm infected, I reserve the right to fix the problem myself."

Angelo and Gabby exchanged a look that I recognized in concept, if not in its exact details. They'd clearly been working with each other for a long time; they'd just as clearly been expecting me to behave according to their script. To be fair, they had probably used that script on all the other people currently in quarantine, and it had no doubt worked every time. Unfortunately for them, those people were members of the Thirty-Six Society. They had a sense of duty to their fellow society members, and to the country of Australia, which would be better off without a bunch of heavily armed werewolves running around the place.

My sense of duty was to myself, and to Shelby, and to the idea that I was going to find a way to beat this: a way to go home human. And if that couldn't happen, I needed to be the one who decided when the battle was over. Allowing these people to disarm me, no matter how good their intentions were, was not the way to get what I needed.

"Mr. Price—" began Angelo.

"I don't think you should waste your time, or mine, with this argument," I said wearily. "Please. I just want to get to whatever room you're planning to keep me in, and take a nice hot bath while I wait for Shelby to show up with a physician who can take care of my wounds without having a panic attack. I don't want to stand here and fight with you. You won't win. We'll all lose."

"This is very irregular," said Angelo. He gave me a reproving look. "You're going to get us into trouble."

"Just tell Riley I was the one who wouldn't cooperate. I bet you he'll have no difficulty believing it." I paused as something occurred to me. Looking to Gabby, I said, "Do you think you could do me a favor?"

She blinked. "You're refusing to follow a simple request, and you want me to do you a favor? Did you hit your head when that werewolf knocked you over?"

"Asking me to give up my weapons is not a simple request, and you know it," I said sternly. "I need you to go to the room where my things are, and get the mice."

"Mice?" said Angelo.

"What?" said Gabby.

"I need the mice," I said, as patiently as I could. "I don't need my clothes or my books—although I'd welcome my books, it's always good to have something to read while you're in solitary confinement—but I need the mice. They need to hear what's happened to me."

Gabby nodded, understanding dawning in her eyes. "I'll ask if they'll come with me," she said. "How much do you want me to tell them?"

"Tell them the God of Scales and Silences needs them to be with him; say that it's a matter of holy writ," I said. "They'll come."

"All right," said Gabby. "He's all yours, Angelo." She turned and fled—taking her finger off the trigger of her gun, I noted, as soon as her back was to me. She was more frightened of the lycanthropy-w virus than she wanted to admit, maybe even to herself.

Angelo was staring at me when I turned back to him, an expression of utter disbelief on his smooth-planed face. "You called yourself a god," he said. "You're not really telling me those rumors about you having a colony of Aeslin mice were *true?*"

"Not a whole colony," I said. "Just six. Technically it's a splinter."

"Man, you won't give up your guns and you travel with a splinter colony of extinct theologians," he said, shaking his head. "Maybe you'll survive this after all. You're too damn weird to die of something as plebian as a werewolf bite."

"Here's hoping you're right," I said. "Which way to my room?"

Angelo started a little, seeming to remember his duty. "This way," he said, and indicated the stairs.

The décor in this house was as basic and IKEA neutral as it was in the main house, down to the same brightly colored vases lining the stairwell walls. It was like they wanted people to believe that their properties were lived in, but only to a point. There was something faintly off about the whole place, like a showroom that had somehow acquired a whole ancestral home's-worth of ghosts. A brightly colored rug blunted the edges of the stairs. It was the only thing that showed any signs of wear, with dull and patched spots breaking the lines of the pattern. That was almost soothing. Humans like to know that they live in the places where they exist.

The stairs led us to a narrow hallway lined with doors, all firmly shut. Angelo stopped. I did the same. "There are four bedrooms on the second floor," he said. "Two of them share the master bathroom. The other two have ensuite bathrooms of their own. We're putting you in one of the ensuite rooms, which means you won't have a tub, but you'll be able to take a shower if you like."

"Can I get some plastic sheeting to keep my injuries dry?" I asked.

Angelo nodded. "I'll bring it right up. You'll be locked in. The door is opened three times a day for the delivery of meals; I'll knock thirty seconds before I open the door. I never come alone, and I always come armed, so please don't get any funny ideas about rushing me. You don't have a phone, but there is a cell you can ask to borrow, providing you're willing to let one of us stay to monitor any calls you want to make. I'd normally say that we've removed everything sharp, but since you've got your share of sharp things, I don't think we really need this disclaimer. Do you have any questions for me?"

"Yes," I said, suddenly weary, looking at those four unmarked doors in this cheery, oddly distressing hallway and feeling like I was looking at my inevitable demise. "What happens when I tell Riley this isn't the way to go about things? Quarantine is important, but this is over-kill when you're talking about a disease that can't even be transmitted for the better part of a month."

"If Riley hasn't magically transformed into someone who takes advice from people who don't belong to the Society? Nothing happens, except you piss him off. You stay in your room, we figure out a way to pick your brain without letting you anywhere near anyone that you might hurt. Come the end of the month, either you're clean or you're a monster. If you're clean, we give you our apologies, maybe a fruit basket or something. If you're a monster, we give you three silver bullets to the head and three more to the heart, and then we feed your body to the drop bears."

"You realize that means you'll run the risk of infecting the drop bears," I said.

Angelo looked at me flatly.

I sighed. "Right. Okay, which room is mine?"

Angelo pointed to the first door on the left. I tapped my forehead with one finger in a quick semi-salute, walked over, and tried the knob. It was unlocked. There didn't seem to be anything left to say, and so I opened the door, stepped inside, and closed it behind me. The sound of a key turning in the lock followed only a few seconds later, sealing me inside.

I listened to his footsteps moving away in the hall outside my guest room-slash-prison before I finally allowed myself to sigh and relax. The tension I'd been carrying in my neck and shoulders didn't drain away—I doubt anyone who's just been bitten by a werewolf is capable of letting go that easily—but it did migrate down into my chest, where it formed an iron band around my lungs and heart. Breathe too deep and the whole thing might shatter. Rubbing my sternum with one hand in an effort to ease the constricted feeling, I took my first real look around the room.

If the guest room I'd been assigned before had been perfunctorily decorated, this one was positively Spartan. The walls were painted a soothing shade of beige that did nothing to make up for the bars on the windows or the cover bolted over the light bulb in the ceiling fixture.

There was a bed: it had two thin pillows and what looked like a hotel duvet, the kind designed to be bleached to within an inch of its life. There was a dresser with four drawers. I walked over and opened them, driven more by dull curiosity than anything else. The top two were empty. The bottom two contained a spare set of sheets and a Bible, respectively. Despite Gabby's joke about cable, there was no television, computer, or phone.

"This isn't going to do at *all*," I said, scowling. They could lock me in here at night, but during the day, I was going to need to be allowed out. I couldn't do my research without a working Internet connection and access to my books; I couldn't mix more of the only treatment that stood a chance of keeping me human without proper equipment. No matter how I looked at things, I couldn't stay here.

The attached bathroom was as small as possible while still holding toilet, sink, and shower, and the shower left no room for me to keep my dressings dry. Angelo didn't return with the promised plastic sheeting. I wasn't really surprised.

In the end, I had to settle for a sponge bath at the sink. There was no mirror. Someone who wanted out of their situation could use broken glass as a weapon just as easily as they could use it as an instrument of suicide; it was too risky. I could understand every decision that had gone into preparing this facility, and I could even understand why they had continued to seem like good ideas after people began being bitten. But this simply would not stand. People who were locked up in conditions this tight for a disease with this long of an incubation period would worry themselves to death long before they showed a single symptom.

When I was clean enough that I was willing to live with myself, I returned to the main room and stretched out on the bed, resting my injured arm on my chest and tucking my right hand behind my head. War is war, no matter what form it takes, and when you're at war, you get your sleep where you can find it. I closed my eyes and went under in a matter of minutes.

My dreams were full of teeth.

The sound of the door being unlocked jerked me out of my fitful doze. I sat up, my right hand going to the knife at my belt, and waited as the door swung open and Shelby stepped into the room. The mice riding on her shoulders gave a subdued cheer when they saw me.

"Brought you some visitors," she said.

"Shelby." I sat up straighter, letting go of my knife in order to run my fingers through my hair. It was still mud-caked, despite my attempts at a bath; I probably looked like some sort of horrifying genetic experiment involving a lab tech and a hedgehog. "I didn't think they'd let you come to see me."

"Oh, they weren't going to," she said, taking a step forward before crouching down to let the mice run off of her and onto the floor. "Dad came up with a good dozen reasons why I was never going to see you again, and Mum as good as said I'd let myself be swayed by emotion and let you out of here if I was the one to bring you the mice. It was a roaring argument; you should've been there with popcorn. Not that you would have enjoyed it much, since it was your fate we were mulling over, but at least you would've had popcorn."

"HAIL!" cheered the mice, with more enthusiasm this time. They scampered across the floor and swarmed up my legs, running the length of my body to get to my shoulders, where they spread out like a tiny prison lineup. They managed to avoid stepping on any of my actual wounds, although two of the six ran down my arm to sniff at the gauze.

One of them squeaked something too shrill for me to understand. The other four went to join the investigation. That was . . . probably something I would need to worry about in a minute. I turned my attention back to Shelby, who was still in her crouch, looking nonplussed by the activity on my arm.

"What made them change their minds?" I asked.

"I pointed out that if I didn't bring the mice, someone else would have to convince them to move," she said.

"Hail the Unpredictable Priestess!" piped one of the mice, drawing a cheer from the others before they went back to studying my wounds.

Shelby blinked. "That's a new one."

"That's . . . yeah." I shook my head. "About what you said back at the med station—"

"Hold that thought: the mice weren't the only reason I was allowed to come here."

I swallowed a groan. "I should have known there was something else going on. What is it? Are you under orders to shoot me?"

"No. But I thought you might like to meet your doctor." Shelby turned back to the door and called, "He's decent, wearing trousers and everything. You can come on in."

"Thank you for the confirmation of trousers," said a mild female voice. Its owner followed it into the room: a tall, slender woman of apparently Indian descent, dressed in tan slacks, sensible shoes, and a blue medical scrub top. Her long black hair was braided back from her face and tied off with a red hair tie, and if not for the way the mice stiffened as soon as she entered, I might have mistaken her for human. She smiled as she approached the bed where I sat, holding out her hand. "Dr. Helen Jalali, at your service. My cousin speaks well of you."

"Is your cousin Kumari Sarpa, by any chance?" I asked, taking her hand and shaking it.

Her smile broadened, showing the oddly curved sides of her incisors. It was a minor physiological difference, easily overlooked—unless she decided to extend her fangs. "She is. However did you guess?" She had a strong Australian accent, confirming my suspicions that the wadjet had been unable to resist establishing a community here. It was perfect for them: no Covenant, lots of space, no native cobras to complicate the issue, and plenty of venomous snakes they could eat without feeling bad about their dietary choices. Australia and Arizona were the modern wadjet's dream homes.

"I had a hunch." I released her hand. "Did Shelby tell you what was going on?"

"Yes, and I was fascinated to hear that we have a lycanthropy-w outbreak in our own backyards." Helen slanted a narrow-eyed glance at Shelby. "No one thought to notify the local cryptid populations. We don't rank for 'need to know' information, it seems."

Shelby held out her hands, palms facing Helen. "Don't shoot the messenger, all right? I've been in America the last eighteen months. I haven't been making any decisions about who tells what to who—and besides, I didn't even know you were here."

"No, but you were here before that, and you never came to tell us when there was a crisis," Helen replied. She didn't sound angry; just tired, like this was a conversation she had often had with herself, and now felt obligated to share with an actual person. "This place is less than four kilometers from my house. We weren't *hiding* ourselves from you; you just didn't care. I have kids, you know. They could've done with knowing that there was a group of rangers, however misguided, close enough to keep them safe."

"I'm sorry," said Shelby. "I'll talk to the rest of the Society. We'll try to be better."

Helen blinked, nonplussed. Apparently, that wasn't the reaction she'd been expecting. "Ah," she said. "Well, thank you. Now, as for you, Mr. Price . . ." She turned back to me, attention going to my arm.

That was when one of the mice decided to speak up. "Not sick," it pronounced.

Helen blinked. "Excuse me?"

"The God of Scales and Silences is not sick," said the

mouse. The others joined in with nods and sounds of rodent agreement. "He is damaged, yes, and will need Tender Care and perhaps Kisses for his Boo-Boos, but he is not sick."

"I wouldn't be sick yet, guys. Lycanthropy has a twenty-eight-day incubation period. It'll be weeks before we know one way or the other."

The mouse that had initially spoken turned and looked at me like I was being intentionally obtuse. "No," it said. "We know right now. Today or twenty-eight days, it will make no difference, because you are not sick."

"I don't think you can—"

"Hold on," said Helen. "The, ah, mouse may be on to something here. What are you, mouse?"

"Aeslin," squeaked the mouse proudly. "We Stand in Service to the Gods."

"Aeslin mice traditionally do," said Helen. "Can you detect sickness?"

"Not all sickness," said the mouse. "Some things smell wrong quickly, like flesh going sour, or breath going dank. If there were sickness here, we would know."

"You can't know," I insisted. "Okay, yes, you're pretty good at catching the early stages of a cold, and we've learned to listen to you when you say it's soup and juice time, but you've never been around lycanthropy. Let Dr. Jalali do her job."

The mouse looked at me, whiskers bristling. "The Spring was New, and the green leaves of the willow trees were coming into Bud," it snapped, in the rapid singsong that meant a point of scripture was being made. "And lo, the Patient Priestess did come to the God of Uncommon Sense and say Dear, Something Is in the Sheep Flock, and We Should Investigate. Then did the God of Uncommon Sense call upon the Sitter of Babies—"

"Wait." I held up a hand, cutting off the flood of rodent theology before it could build to an unstoppable pitch. "Are you saying that Great-Great-Grandpa Alexander and Great-Great-Grandma Enid took a member of the congregation with them to deal with *werewolves?*"

"He got all that from a mouse beginning a religious parable?" asked Helen, looking to Shelby incredulously. "How are these not the most protected species in the known universe? They ought to be everywhere."

"But they're not," said Shelby, looking regretful. "As to the parable bit, yeah. They go on, and he translates. Unless we're having sex at the time. Then I just chuck a pillow at them and tell him that noise was the wind."

I rolled my eyes but otherwise ignored her. I had more important things to worry about, like the mouse clinging to my arm and looking at me with surpassing rodent smugness. "Not one member," said the mouse. "A full *dozen*. We scattered through the grass and led them to the den, and oh! Such cheese! Such cake! We feasted well and thoroughly!"

"HAIL!" shouted the rest of the mice, exulting in the memory of a feast that happened generations before they were born.

"Hold on a moment." Helen leaned closer to the mouse, which held its ground surprisingly well, considering that she was a giant cobra that just happened to look like a human woman. "Before they became extinct, Aeslin mice were renowned for their ability to preserve institutional knowledge. We know they pass their rituals from generation to generation. Why wouldn't they also pass the descriptions of scents they wanted to catalog. Mouse?"

"Yes?" asked the mouse.

"What does lycanthropy smell like?"

For a moment, we all held our breath. The mouse didn't seem to notice. Calmly, it replied, "Like rabies, but sweeter, the way a spider's bite smells when it is fresh and hard to see. There is no smell of sweetness here, only torn flesh, and blood, and bruising. He is not sick."

"Do you mind if I proceed with preventative care

despite your no doubt excellent diagnosis? I'm sure you're right—you're talking mice, after all, and I honestly can't think of any studies saying *not* to use talking mice as diagnostic engines—but it's best if I do my job anyway." She leaned closer and whispered conspiratorially, in a voice still loud enough for Shelby to hear, "The local humans get shirty when they think we silly monsters know more than they do."

"Hey," protested Shelby, without any real heat. She knew the local attitude toward human-form cryptids as well as I did, if not better: she had shared it, on some level, until she'd met my family and friends. It was hard to keep thinking of people who didn't descend from monkeys as inferior when they were smarter than you were, or at least better read.

Helen looked at Shelby and shrugged. "Sorry, princess. I go with what I know, and what I know is that your people were going to let a werewolf run rampant through the state without telling anyone they didn't feel protective toward. It makes a girl a little cranky. And you, sir." She turned back to me as she stood, putting herself on higher ground. It was a snake instinct that the wadjet shared with their cobra cousins. Male wadjet sometimes used the females to become taller still, and if the sight of a woman in heels with a spectacled cobra balanced on her shoulder wouldn't strike fear into your heart, then your heart is made of sterner stuff than mine. "I'm told you have a treatment. Is this correct?"

"Yes, ma'am," I said, resisting the urge to stand and put myself on her level. It would just make her uncomfortable, and I needed her to stay in my corner, at least long enough to prepare her report to the Society. "It's in my bag. The nasty black sludge with the little sparkles in it."

"I'll get it," said Shelby, sounding glad to be of use.

"Be careful," I said, earning myself a sour look. I shook my head. "I mean it, Shelby. This stuff is incredibly toxic. If you get any of it on you, you could make yourself really sick."

"And you're going to swallow it anyway, aren't you, you silly man?" She crossed the room to my field bag and rummaged through it for a moment before pulling out the jar of antiserum that I'd managed to mix before collapsing. "What do you want done with this?"

"I'll take it," said Helen, holding out her hand. "You don't have to stay in here for the next part if you don't want to. I know that seeing your mate in pain can be troublesome."

"No," said Shelby, in a flat tone devoid of the humor she had been forcing herself to project only seconds before. "I stay."

"As you wish." Helen took the jar from her and turned back to me. "Please remove your shirt and assume a neutral sitting position. If you make any hostile moves, I will strike. If I feel threatened in any way, I will strike. If you attempt to reach for a weapon, I will strike. Do you have any allergies I need to be aware of?"

The change in tenor between the portions of her speech was abrupt enough to leave me blinking as I unbuttoned my already-ruined shirt and stripped it off, exposing my bruised and bloodied chest. Shelby made a little hissing noise between her teeth as she saw the damage without anything to obscure it or make it look less bad than it really was. "I don't intend to threaten you, but why did we just go from friendly to 'I'm going to pump you full of venom'?"

"I'm about to start doing things that could cause you a great deal of pain." Helen turned to Shelby. "I know you want to be here for his treatment, but I'm going to need that chair now."

Shelby scowled, but couldn't deny the lack of seating in the room. "I'll be right back," she said. "Don't start without me." Then she was out of the room, heading into the hall with irritated quickness.

Helen turned to me immediately, dropping her voice to something more conspiratorial than her earlier staged whisper. "Are they holding you prisoner?" she asked.

"My cousin vouched for you, and I am willing to get you out of here if that's necessary. We can discuss payment later."

I blinked at her. What tactics did the Thirty-Sixers use to keep the Covenant out of their continent? "No," I said. "I'm here voluntarily, because they asked for help, and it seemed like a good idea to keep werewolves from getting established in Australia. Didn't Kumari mention Shelby?"

"She said you traveled with a blonde girl from the Society, but I wasn't sure how much of that was keeping your friends close and your enemies closer." She set the jar of black sludge on the bedside table, abandoning her hushed tone. "I don't know how much you know about how things work here, but the Thirty-Six Society does not call in the local wadjet to play doctor."

"Then they should," I said. I moved into a sitting position as I spoke, sending the mice scattering for the relative safety of the bed, which at least wasn't moving. "I asked them to call you. You can't catch what I might have."

"You are not sick," squeaked the mouse who had diagnosed me, indignant. It took up a perch on my knee, wrapping its tail around its paws and fixing me with a stern eye. "You must learn to have Faith," it chided.

"I do have faith," I said. "I just have more faith in science than I do in, er, faith itself. It's a God thing. You wouldn't understand."

All the mice made a low "ooo" noise, clearly enthralled by the idea of being in the presence of divine mysteries. I was going to pay for this later.

Helen looked amused. "Your life is one long theological argument, isn't it?"

"You have no idea," I said. "But my point stands. You can't catch lycanthropy—which I do not have—" I added, before the mice could start objecting again, "but you understand human physiology and how to provide medical treatment. That makes you the best person for the job."

"It's nice of you to say so." Helen turned as Shelby walked back into the room, now lugging a folding wooden chair. "Thank you. I apologize for sending you away before, but I needed to speak to my patient in private."

"Gotcha," said Shelby. She plunked the chair down next to Helen before looking at me. "You didn't bite him. We're fine. What do you want me to do now? I'm not leaving, so don't even suggest that. Fighting isn't fun when one of us is venomous and the other is heavily armed."

"It's just like being at home," I said, garnering a cheer from the mice.

Helen didn't rise to the bait, thankfully. We could be here all evening if she really got Shelby going. "If you're not going to leave, you can help me with my equipment. I'd rather avoid any chance that you're going to come into contact with his bodily fluids, just to be safe."

The mouse on my knee made a small huffing noise, but otherwise didn't argue.

"Right," said Shelby. "I've already had two showers today, and I'd rather not take a third. I'm here for whatever you need." She sat on the end of the bed, close enough to be reassuring, but far enough away to be out of the logical splash range for anything that happened to come out of me.

Helen sat down in the chair Shelby had provided, setting her medical bag on the floor between her and Shelby. She leaned over to dig around in it, producing a pair of thick-lensed glasses and a suture kit. "Now," she said. "Let's begin."

I'll spare you the process of having my wounds cleaned—again—cauterized with silver nitrate, and stitched by Helen, who had a steady hand but didn't believe in painkillers. She was a general practitioner by trade, which meant she had an excellent grasp of human anatomy and where it differed from wadjet anatomy (like the part where I was a mammal, and not a big snake in an excellent human suit). She was a field doctor for cryptids by calling, and that meant that painkillers were something to be reserved for really *serious* accidents, the sort of thing where the person being worked on would be lucky to walk away, and thus didn't need to keep their wits about them. Since I didn't qualify as a severe trauma case, she just jumped right in and started searing my flesh.

There wasn't much conversation during that part of the process. It wasn't until she was putting in the stitches that she got chatty. "You're sure this was a werewolf?" she asked, as she sewed up a long gash on the back of my arm.

It was all I could do not to jump, from the combination of the pain and the question. "Yes, I'm sure," I said. "It looked like a werewolf, it moved like a werewolf, and it sure as hell wasn't a dingo."

"Dingos don't look much like wolves, actually," said Shelby, who was resolutely not watching as the needle darted in and out of my flesh. One corner of the room seemed to have become particularly fascinating to her, and she was staring at that instead of anything involving me, Helen, and the medical bag.

"That's ... odd," said Helen, and tied off her sutures. "Werewolves aren't supposed to be capable of thought once they've transformed, but whatever bit you did it like they knew exactly where to aim. None of the major arteries were involved, and while there's muscle damage from the bite, it's not severe enough to keep you out of commission."

"Meaning that if the infection were to take, I'd be primed to do a lot of damage when the twenty-eight-day incubation was up," I said slowly. "That's ... Shelby, do we have pictures of the other werewolf bites? I need to know whether this is coincidence or a pattern." Once would be a lucky accident that had kept my injuries from becoming too severe. More than once would mean we might be dealing with something impossible, and terrifying.

A werewolf that remembered how to think.

Werewolves were capable of spreading the infection that made them at a fast and deadly rate without tying human intelligence to their rage. Give them the ability to think, to plan, to work on any level above "beast," and we could be looking at the kind of outbreak the world had never seen before.

"I'll get them for you," said Shelby.

Helen picked up the jar of cuckoo blood—now more than half-empty—and began slathering it generously over my stitches. It would help keep the wound from becoming infected, since it would create a virtually anaerobic environment. Wherever cuckoos were from, it wasn't a place where our native bacteria thrived. "Wouldn't intelligent werewolves be a good thing?" she asked. "I mean, you could reason with them. Explain why their behavior is inappropriate, and convince them to stop."

"Rabies attacks the brain and central nervous system," I said. "People who become rabid have been known to kill their friends, their loved ones, even their own children. It's not universal—most rabies victims die without hurting anyone—but it happens enough to be a common fear throughout the mammalian world. Lycanthropy is worse. No one has ever encountered a calm or passive werewolf, and before you say that's Covenant teachings talking, I'd like to note that almost all werewolf killings can be classed as self-defense. The others have involved werewolves that have already attacked, more than once. We can't assume that an intelligent werewolf would be friendly."

"There are days when I am simply ecstatic to have come from a different branch of the evolutionary tree," said Helen, packing her suture kit away. "Now, your antiserum. You really want to go through with this? Even with your mice saying that you're clean?"

"My mice are, if they'll forgive me for saying this, mice," I said. "I have absolute faith in their teachings, and if they say I'm clean, I'm sure they're right. But I need to be able to go to Shelby's father and say I've done everything in my power to make sure I can't hurt anyone. That includes using the treatment I'm going to recommend for everyone else who's been exposed." Although I was also going to recommend the mice check everyone who was even suspected of harboring a lycanthropy-w infection. If they gave any result other than "clean," we'd have something resembling proof that they could do what they said they could.

"It's your funeral," said Helen. "Lay back on the bed, open your mouth, and think about something more pleasant than what I'm about to do to you. Because . . ."

"I know," I said, cutting her off. "This is going to hurt. Now do it."

And she did.

Nine

"That probably wasn't the smartest thing you've ever done. Points for style, I guess. Points off for being too stupid to live."

—Kevin Price

Waiting in one of the quarantine rooms in a secluded guesthouse in Queensland, Australia

THE FEELING STARTED COMING back to my tongue an hour after Dr. Helen Jalali administered the werewolf antiserum. There was still a sharp, almost burning sensation at the root of it, and I couldn't keep myself from drooling—not the best thing when you're a) trying to present yourself as a professional and b) dealing with people who are terrified of accidental fluid transfer—but at least my temporary lisp was gone. That was a good thing, given the pitch I was about to make.

The door was closed, and had been closed since Shelby had walked the doctor back to her car. Helen had grumbled about blindfolds the whole time, which made me suspect that the Society still wasn't playing nicely with the sapient locals. That was a bad sign. They needed all the help they could get to come through this reasonably intact—and that help included me.

I reached the wall, turned around, and paced back in

the other direction. I was getting tired of waiting for Shelby to come back for me, and knew that I couldn't move until she did. The inside of my mouth still tasted like aconite and ketamine, which accounted for the continued drooling. The body knows when it contains things that shouldn't be there, and will try to flush them out through whatever means are necessary.

The mice were arrayed in a loose circle on the bed, watching me pace. Every fourth circuit around the room they shouted "HAIL!" for no clear reason. It seemed to be keeping them happy, and while I was sure they had some religious explanation for their behavior, I was equally sure I wouldn't be able to get them to shut up about it if I made the mistake of asking. The last thing I wanted to do was have Riley walk in on the Aeslin mice in full-on religious ecstasy.

Although the look on his face might be worth the argument that would be sure to follow. I smiled a little at the thought, and was pleased to feel the muscles on either side of my mouth pull upward at the same time. Facial numbness and temporary paralysis were possible side effects of the antiserum. (They were among the milder, more desirable side effects, mind, since the others included fun things like "seizure," "heart failure," and "death." Modern medicine is occasionally deadly, but there's a lot to be said for having access to machines and lab technicians capable of refining deadly toxins to a slightly less deadly state.)

The mice cheered twice more in response to my circuits around the room, and I was beginning to give serious thought to asking them why they kept doing that—damn the consequences—when there was a knock at the door. I stopped dead, wiping the last of the drool from my chin as I called, "Yes?"

"Alex, it's Shelby. I've got my dad with me, and he says he'll only come in if you'll sit on the bed and promise to stay sitting the whole time we're in the room. Can you do that? Please?" There was a degree of anxiety in her voice that I very rarely heard from her.

I walked back to the bed, gesturing for the mice to get out of the way before I plopped down onto the mattress. Most of them ran behind the pillow. One—the one that had been the first to say I wasn't sick after they'd checked my wound for signs of the lycanthropy-w virus— scampered onto my knee and sat, tail curled primly around paws. It looked up at me, silently asking for permission.

I nodded. It wasn't like having the mouse there was going to hurt anything, and it might help, depending on how things went down. Besides, I appreciated the company. It made me feel a little less alone. "I'm sitting," I called. "It's safe to come in."

The door swung open, and Shelby stepped into the room. Her face matched her voice: anxious and drawn, tight with worry. She held the door for her father as he entered after her. Riley Tanner didn't look worried. He just looked angry.

"So quarantine is good enough for our people, but it's not good enough for you, is that it, Price?" he demanded, not bothering with pleasantries. "I don't see why you think you're going to change my mind about basic protocol."

"Hello, sir," I said. "I'm fine, thank you for asking."

He blinked, apparently taken aback. "I didn't ask."

"I noticed," I said, in my best "I am a scientist, don't fuck with me" tone. It was hard to fight the urge to stand and put myself on a level with him: like Dr. Jalali, he was using his height to assert dominance, towering over me because there was nothing I could do to stop him. And like Dr. Jalali, I needed to let him have that feeling of dominance. I had needed her to provide me with medical care without the risk of infection. I needed *him* to let me out of this room while I could still do some good. "As for why I'm asking you to change your mind . . . sir, I never said you had to quarantine your people, just monitor them closely. Keeping them—keeping *us*—isolated at night is a good idea for the sake of everyone's peace of mind, but there's no risk of transformation until twenty-eight days have passed. That's twenty-eight days of backup you're planning to waste, all because you don't understand this disease."

"You're drooling, son," said Riley. "Go ahead. Keep telling me you're not sick."

"This is a side effect of the mixture I ingested to make *sure* I wouldn't get sick," I said, fighting to keep my tone level. I wiped the side of my mouth with my hand. "It irritates the mouth, which can cause excessive saliva-tion."

"Well, you irritate me, so I guess you and your 'cure' have something in common."

"Dad," snapped Shelby. "You said you'd listen to him, not come in here trying to score points like this was some sort of . . . of sport. Why aren't you *listening* to him?"

"I don't know, honey, maybe because he was raised by Johrlac, nearly got you turned to stone, and got one of my best men killed within a day of showing up on this continent?" Riley wheeled on Shelby with unnerving speed. She felt it, too: she took a step back, letting go of the door. It swung shut. Riley didn't appear to notice. "He's been nothing but bad news since you got involved with him. I told you to cut ties as soon as you reported he had one of those heartless mind-suckers living with him, but you didn't listen. You had to save your boy-friend. Now he's here, wreaking havoc amongst the peo-ple who should be able to trust you to have their backs. So why don't you tell me, daughter dear? Why are you listening to him at all?"

"Because he knows what he's doing, and he's not let-ting personal feelings interfere with his work," she snapped, her normal temper surging back to the surface. "He'd do this job for anyone. That's a thing you should be glad of, because if you were treating me the way you're treating him, I'd sure as hell not be volunteering to help you with *anything*."

Riley glared at her. Shelby glared back. I looked at the mouse on my knee. The mouse looked up at me.

"Sometimes I wish I had the ability to conjure popcorn from thin air," I said.

The mouse flared its whiskers in amusement. "It is as in the teachings of the Noisy Priestess," it squeaked. "Always should popcorn be eaten when people fight over foolish things."

"Uh, Alex?" I looked up to see Shelby looking at me, a bewildered expression on her face. Her father wore a virtually identical expression. "Are you having a chat with your mice while we're arguing about whether or not to let you out of quarantine?"

"No," I said, standing. I did it slowly enough that the mouse was able to run up my arm to my shoulder, where it perched, whiskers quivering. "I'm having a chat with my mice while you argue about whether or not there's anything here to argue about. It seemed like less of a waste of time."

"Son, you want to sit yourself back down before we have a problem," said Riley. His tone was tight and cautioning.

"No, I don't believe I do," I said. "You're not stupid, are you, Mr. Tanner? I don't see how you could be. I've met your daughters, and intelligence is often partially genetic. More, I've met your people. The Thirty-Six Society doesn't listen to you because you're big, they listen to you because you're smart. You know your country, you know your territory, you know your local cryptids. You're the best man for the job you do."

"Flattery isn't going to make me stop telling you to sit down," he said. There was a note of confusion in his voice, like he couldn't quite figure out where I was going with this, and consequently didn't know how to make me hurry it up.

"Sir, if you're not stupid, why are you persisting in acting like you are?" It was hard to keep my tone level as I asked that question. Shelby's alarmed expression and "cut it out" hand gestures weren't helping.

Riley's eyes narrowed. "All right, forget sitting down. It'll be more fun to pound the stupid out of you while you're standing up."

"If I'm infected, you can't risk fluid transfer."

That stopped him. I smiled.

"So basically, if you 'pound the stupid' out of me, you're admitting the treatment worked, and I'm not an infection risk. Normally, I wouldn't endorse that, but with the mice also vouching for me, I think you'd be safe to take the risk. Or we can go ahead and try my plan, which involves less punching me in the face—disappointing, I know—but might have better long-term results."

Riley frowned. "What's your plan?"

"Ah, good." I smiled, hoping my slightly numb lips wouldn't make the expression too Heath Ledger-as-the-Joker for what I was trying to convey. "According to the mice, I'm not infected. Thanks to Dr. Jalali, who administered the antiserum I prepared after Cooper and I were bitten, we know that even if the mice are wrong, I'm in the best possible position for dodging the infection." I knew that most of my projected good cheer was mania: on some level, I was still scared out of my mind. There wasn't time to dwell on the fear. The fear was going to do me no good, and it could do me a great deal of harm if I surrendered to it. "Are we in agreement thus far?"

"I'll grant you that," said Riley grudgingly.

"This disease spreads through fluid transfer. You can't catch it by touching an infected person, or even drinking from the same glass." I sounded like a public health announcement. I forced myself to keep going. "I'm willing to return here at night. I'm willing to be locked in while I sleep. But, sir, I need to be able to help you with this situation—and not to be overly boastful of my abilities, you need me. You need *someone* who has dealt with lycanthropy before, and who can speak to the local cryptids. You don't have anyone else with my skill set."

His eyes narrowed again, this time accompanied by the tensing of the jaw that signified rage in almost all primates. Sometimes it's nice to be dealing with members of my own species. I understand them when they react to me. And that impulse explained everything. "You arrogant little—"

"Sir, there is arrogance in this room, but it's not *mine*," I snapped, stunning him temporarily into silence. I took advantage of the opening, stepping toward him—still not close enough to be an infection risk, but close enough that my presence would be impossible to belittle or overlook. I was also close enough that he could punch me in the face, but that was a risk I was willing to take. He probably wouldn't do it. My face was where I kept my teeth, after all, and he was worried about catching lycanthropy.

Riley stared at me, eyes narrowing further. I was starting to wonder if he needed glasses. Behind him, Shelby shook her head, her best "you better know what you're doing" expression on her face.

I really hope so, I thought, and said, "Dr. Jalali and her family live less than five miles from here. Where there's one wadjet family, there are more, because they need to be close enough to find husbands for their daughters. They're spread out by necessity, they're better gossip networks than the bogeymen if you can find your way inside, and they had no idea there was a werewolf in this part of Queensland, because the people who knew about it didn't tell them. They're your *neighbors*. They'd be your allies, if you gave them the slightest indication they were welcome. They *like* living in a place where they don't have to worry about the Covenant swooping in and shooting their children, but you're not giving them cause to like you, and it's cutting off one of your main sources of potential intelligence. It's speciesist and it's *stupid*. Sir."

Riley stood up a little straighter, silently reminding me that I was picking a fight with a mountain that walked like a man. "We don't need monsters to point out the holes in our security," he said. "We don't need anything inhuman to help us find husbands for our daughters. I'm still not seeing where you're offering me anything I can't find just as well without letting you out of this room."

At the word "husbands," Shelby winced. Oh, great.

"Mr. Tanner, how much of this is about my relationship with your daughter?"

Riley didn't answer.

"Mr. Tanner, the wadjet have doctors who can interact freely with the potentially infected Society members, with no fear of catching lycanthropy-w. They can't catch the disease, and because of that, they'll continue to treat your people like, well, *people*," I said. "If one of my mice travels with them to see the potentially infected, we may be able to provide reassurance for people who have every reason to be terrified right now."

"Great. Snake doctors and talking mice are the solution to all our problems." Riley wasn't yelling. It might have been better if he had been. "Sounds to me like I can have both those things without letting you out of this room."

"Would you ever have thought to look for them without me?" It had taken shamefully long for *me* to look for them. I'd known about the Society members in quarantine before I'd landed in Australia, but I hadn't thought to seek a nonmammalian doctor until my own life was in danger. I didn't like what that said about the scope of my focus. I had allowed myself to be overwhelmed by fear, and hence distracted from the greater mission. I needed to serve all intelligent life, not just the interests of the species I happened to share.

Again, Riley didn't answer. I watched his face, trying not to glare or show my desperation. This wasn't my field of expertise. Give me a thesis to defend, not a jailer twice my size to rail against.

Shelby stepped around her father, putting herself between us. He blinked and drew back slightly, startled by her movement. I managed to hold my ground, but only barely; I had seen her start to move.

"You're being a pompous ass, and I won't stand for it," she said. "I knew from talking to Raina and Gabby that you wanted to see Alex for yourself, and I figured the werewolf problem was a good excuse for you to do that, especially since we needed the help. What I didn't figure was that you'd be watching for a way to get my fellow out of the way."

That gave Riley something he could seize on. "Surely you're not implying I sent him out there to be *bitten*," he thundered.

Shelby scowled. "No, Daddy, although I might start implying it if you keep refusing to listen. Him getting bitten was a convenient accident. Otherwise, you'd have just kept shoving him into labs and hoping he'd stay out of the picture so you could grill me over and over on what I was doing with a Price from America, instead of coming home and settling down proper with someone from the Society. Did you ever consider that maybe I'm with a Price from America because I love him? It's a thought you might want to start having, along with the thought that maybe the fact that he's diddling your daughter doesn't mean he has no brains remaining in his head!"

"Uh, Shelby, maybe a little less emphasis on our, uh, after-dark activities?" I asked, as the red spread across Riley's cheeks and forehead. He looked like steam was about to start coming out of his ears, cartoon-style, and I really didn't want the accompanying anger to be directed at me.

"No, Alex, he needs to hear this," she snapped, her eyes staying on her father. "Yes, I'm sleeping with Alex, Daddy. Because I *love* him, all right? I'm going to marry him, and probably give you those grandkids Mum's always on about, and the fact that he's an American and from a family you don't approve of doesn't matter a toss, do you understand? This isn't *Romeo and Juliet*. Our households aren't alike in dignity, although they may be alike in pigheaded, head-up-the-bum-ness. You're going to stand aside and let Alex out of this room. You're going to let him do the job he came here to do. Or I'm going to stand in front of the whole Society and announce that you've locked away one of our best prospects, without valid medical reasons, because you can't stand the fact that he's fucking your oldest girl."

The word "fucking" seemed to break something in Riley. The color drained from his cheeks, replaced by a resigned pallor. He shot me a venomous glare before looking back to his daughter and asking, in a soft voice, "Is this really what you want?"

"I want to protect our people, Daddy, and you're not going about it the best way," she said. "Humans only isn't the best way. It's as short-sighted as anything else that says 'we should leave people out for their own good.' Alex is right, and if we want him to help us, we can't lock him up in here. It doesn't do anyone any good."

Riley looked at her for a few seconds more before turning his attention to me. "All right, Price: you get your way. You can move about freely during the day—but don't be mistaken, everyone *will* know that you've been bitten, and they'll be watching for signs that you're trying to spread your disease. Do you understand? And come bedtime, you'll be locked back in here, in case you decide to change in the night and start going for throats."

Werewolves could transform as easily during the day as they could at night, but somehow sharing that little piece of information didn't seem to be in my best interests. "I understand," I said. Then, pushing my luck a little, I asked, "Can we open discussions with the wadjet about coming here to treat the others who have been injured? They're unlikely to request much in the way of payment; mostly, they trade in information and in favors."

"I don't want to owe any favors to a snake," snapped Riley.

"Some people may feel differently," said Shelby. "Mary's

in quarantine, yeah? Her family would probably be happy to owe a snake a favor if it meant they knew she was as comfortable and well-tended as possible."

"Fine." Riley threw up his hands. "Fine. You do what you want—but you heed me, Shelby Tanner. If your precious boy there bites anyone, I'll put him down like the dog that he is. He won't get another chance from me. Do you understand?"

"Yes, Daddy," said Shelby.

"Yes, sir," I said, just in case my understanding mattered.

"I don't believe this." Shaking his head, Riley turned and stalked out of the room. He left the door open. That was good: at least he'd meant it when he said I was going to be allowed to continue moving about freely.

"Your father hates me," I said, sounding faintly dazed.

"My father hates everyone who dates one of his daughters." Shelby turned to me, smiling brightly. "I think that went rather well, don't you?"

For once, I had absolutely nothing to say.

A crowd had gathered in front of the quarantine house by the time we finished getting me dressed and shifting my weapons to better align with my injuries. I've always been right-hand dominant, which was good, but many of my knives were positioned to be backup weapons for my left hand, and that wasn't going to work when I didn't have full range of motion in that shoulder. Especially since most painkillers also fogged cognitive functions, which meant I couldn't use them if I was planning to go into the field.

Shelby and I stepped onto the porch and stopped, blinking at the people waiting for us in the yard. I didn't recognize most of them, and the few I had seen before at the previous night's banquet looked gravely worried, not welcoming in the least. Raina was sitting on the edge of the porch, her back against a pillar and Cooper's dog stretched out beside her. Jett had her head in Raina's lap, apparently unperturbed by the fact that the girl was playing with her Gameboy right above the dog's ear.

Raina looked up at the sound of footsteps. "Oh," she said. "It's you. Gabby owes me ten bucks. She said Dad would shoot you before he let you out."

"I think he was considering it," I said. I gave the crowd a sidelong look. "Why do we have this much company?"

"They wanted to see that you were still a people, and not a hairy, slavering killing machine." Raina cocked her head to the side in a gesture that reminded me of Shelby, especially Shelby in the early morning, when she wasn't quite prepared to be awake yet, and was thus overly critical of everything around her. "You don't *look* like a hairy, slavering killing machine. I guess you could've shaved. Are you going to rip our throats out with your teeth?"

"Not planning to, thanks," I said, and turned to face the crowd. They continued to watch us, staring and silent. I raised a hand and waved. "Hello."

"How come you're out here?" demanded a voice from the back of the crowd.

I frowned. "Do you mean 'how come I'm in Australia,' or 'how come I'm not in the quarantine shack with everyone else'?" I was reasonably sure they meant the second, but I wanted the conversation to *be* a conversation, not an interrogation. We were outnumbered, and I didn't know what Riley might have said to them on his way out of the house. We needed them to think that we were equals, rather than recasting us into predators and prey.

"How about both?" The owner of the voice pushed her way through the crowd to the front. She was a short, skinny woman with dark brown hair and a face like a fashion model, complete with lipstick, elaborate eye makeup, and enough foundation that I wasn't sure of her skin tone. She was probably Caucasian, based on the shape of her face, but I could have been wrong. "What makes you think you can solve our problems for us? You're not even here two days before you're a werewolf and Cooper's dead? Sounds to me like you should get right back on the plane!"

An ugly murmur spread through the crowd. This wasn't good. I took a breath, looking for my courage. It seemed to have stayed in the room, and so I went for the next best thing: my sense of duty. "I'm not a werewolf," I said. "I've been checked by a medical professional, and the consensus is that I am not infected." Mentioning the mice wouldn't do any of us any good, and it might confuse the matter. "Just in case the doctor was wrong, I've allowed myself to be treated with an anti-lycanthropy tincture. In addition, I'll be returning to quarantine each night, and will be locked in until morning. This will continue until the twenty-eight-day incubation period has passed." Unless I transformed after all, in which case a bullet to my skull would take care of the rest of my problems.

The crowd glared and muttered. I took a deep breath, glancing down at Jett, who seemed perfectly comfortable with her head on Raina's leg. I looked back to the crowd.

"Cooper's death was an accident. The werewolves attacked while we were gathering aconite flowers to make the treatment that we'll be offering to anyone who has been or happens to be bitten. I tried to save him. I failed."

Shelby stepped forward. "He's telling the truth," she said. "When my father and I found Alex and Cooper, they were both collapsed in the medical station, blood and flower petals everywhere. Cooper's wounds had been cleaned and irrigated to reduce infection, and the bleeding had been slowed. It was clear that Alex tried to intervene. He failed. Can you really blame him for failing when he was injured and standing up against impossible odds?"

The crowd muttered more. The mood seemed to be

lifting, turning away from anger and toward the easier to manage combination of mistrust and fear. Anything that kept them from breaking out the torches and pitchforks was okay by me.

"Cooper was a good man," I said, and I didn't have to force the wobble in my voice; it came naturally and almost against my will. Showing weakness could go either way when I was facing a potential angry mob. "Maybe he could have gotten away if he hadn't stayed to help me shoot the thing. Maybe not. We're never going to know. But I can promise you this: I will be staying here, and fighting beside you all, until we manage to remove this threat from your community. I will do everything in my power to make things right for you."

The crowd quieted further. This time, their muttering was barely distinguishable as words. Raina finally stood, dislodging Jett's head with a gentle nudge, and turned to face the people who'd come to confront us. She shoved her Gameboy into her pocket, almost as an afterthought, and crossed her arms as she demanded, "Well? Are you lot happy now, or do you need to see me hobble him?"

I gave her an alarmed look. If she decided to try, I was going to have my first full-on fight with a member of the Tanner family since the night when Shelby had drawn a gun on my cousin in the kitchen of my grandparents' house.

The crowd muttered and, for the most part, looked down or away—anywhere but at the girl who was now facing them all down. Shelby reached over and took my hand, lacing her fingers through mine. I squeezed her palm lightly, and just held on. Whatever was going to happen now, it was already done; all we were waiting for was the shape of it.

One by one, the people who'd come here to accuse me of somehow betraying them by being bitten turned and walked back toward the path separating this little isolation facility from the main house. The woman with the dark brown hair was the last to go, shooting glares over her shoulder at us all the while, until finally even she disappeared from view.

Raina blew out a breath, sagging. "You don't do *anything* by halves, do you?" she demanded, dropping her arms as she turned to me. "Can't just see a werewolf, no, you have to go and get yourself bitten by one. Can't just bring in an outside expert, nope, it has to be a snake woman with three university degrees that Dad can't pretend don't exist. Are you even a person, or are you a walking force for chaos?"

"My baby sister's the force for chaos," I said automatically. (Specifying which baby sister I meant would have been redundant: compared to me, they were both proof that entropy always wins.) "Dr. Jalali was just the closest medical professional who didn't need to worry about catching lycanthropy."

"Only that wasn't a factor, because you're clean," said Raina, a slight sneer in her voice.

"Yes," I said firmly.

"You don't have to be a snot, Raina," said Shelby. She still hadn't released my hand. "You know Alex didn't do anything wrong. There's no point in acting like he did, unless you're trying to get Dad on your side for something."

"Everyone else is going to act like he did something wrong," said Raina. She sounded much calmer now: she just sounded tired, too, like she couldn't believe she had to explain this to us. "He's your imported werewolf expert, he's the man who's going to save us all, and what's the first thing he does? Runs out and gets himself bit, like some amateur with trumped-up credentials trying to impress his girlfriend. Doesn't build faith in his skills, and doesn't build faith in your ability to assess the situation, either."

"But that's not all, is it?" Shelby frowned. "You've been prickly since I got home. What's wrong, Raina?"

"Are you home for good or not?"

The question seemed to come completely out of left

field. Shelby blinked at her sister. I did much the same. Raina looked at us both and groaned, shaking her head.

"You don't even get it a little, do you? She—" She stabbed a finger at Shelby, whose look of profound confusion deepened, "—was supposed to go to America, learn about manticores, and head straight back here. Instead, she sent a bunch of notes explaining how to deal with the problem, and she stayed gone. It took *werewolves* to bring her home, and she hasn't said word one about whether it's for keeps. You weren't supposed to leave us!" She whirled to her sister on the last sentence, making it clear that she wasn't talking to me anymore. "Jack left, and he was going to be Dad's replacement one day, so with him gone, all that fell to you. But you just had to go, too, didn't you? You weren't supposed to *go*."

"Oh, Raina." Shelby pulled her hand from mine. I let her go without hesitation, and even took a step back to place myself firmly out of the scene as the sisters embraced, holding each other so tightly that there was no space between them.

Something nudged my hip. I looked down to see Jett pressed against my leg, her ears forward, watching the two. I rested my hand on the top of her head, and we stood there silently, four lost souls, waiting for the future to arrive.

Ten

"A life that is lived carefully, calmly, with thorough preparation and sufficient resources, is likely to be healthy, long, and incredibly boring. Fortunately, I have never been in danger of living that particular life."

—Jonathan Healy

Tromping through the brush in Queensland, Australia, looking for signs of werewolves, which is a genuinely terrible idea

ONCE THE THIRTY-SIX SOCIETY decided on something, they didn't stand around talking about whether or not they'd made the right call. They barreled forward with little concern for the potential damage; it was like meeting a group with an institutional policy of "damn the torpedoes, full speed ahead." And that explains how, less than two hours after I'd been cleared to return to the field, on the same day I'd been bitten by a werewolf, and less than an hour after putting in a call in to Helen to ask her to come back and begin treating the Thirty-Sixers, I found myself walking into yet another unfamiliar forest.

Shelby was nearby, tromping gamely through the brush and offering helpful tips like, "Don't step on the anthill," and "There may have been a snake just now, I'm not sure, but if there is, try not to piss it off." Raina was a little farther ahead, with Jett tagging at her heels like a small black shadow. There had been no discussion of leaving the dog behind when we took off on this latest fool's errand: she was trained to help Cooper in the field, and that made her useful for our purposes, as long as we didn't mind the fact that she'd take off running if she saw a bat that needed snapping at.

I had asked why, if Jett was field-trained, Cooper had left her behind when we went to gather aconite. No one had been able to give me an answer for that.

Charlotte, Riley, and Gabby were farther along, having driven another two miles up the road before getting out and starting through the wood. We were all supposed to wind up in the same place: a sheep meadow that had already been the site of two suspected werewolf attacks. The hope was that we would arrive right around the time the moon finished rising, and—if the werewolves were really responsible for the carnage the shepherds had been reporting—catch the werewolves in the act. Their transformations weren't actually tied to the moonrise, but as most human werewolves *believed* that they were, they were more likely to subconsciously trigger the change when they saw the moon. The mind was a powerful thing. Sometimes dismayingly so.

(I had attempted to point out, several times, that this plan was predicated in part on our sharing a meadow with multiple werewolves, after just one had managed to wound me and kill Cooper. Of the Tanners, only Gabby seemed inclined to see this as a bad thing, and she had been voted down by the rest of her family. Of such democracies are horror movies born. Suggesting that we not split the party had been met with even more disdain. Two groups covered twice as much ground, and we were all armed. Discussion over. I would have stayed home and skipped the whole thing, but Shelby was going, and I'd be damned if I was going to let her walk into a massacre without me.)

Shelby fell into step beside me. "Raina's up ahead," she said. "We'll be there soon."

"That's good," I said. "It's always nice to get torn apart in the open, as opposed to getting torn apart in the shelter of the trees."

"That's the spirit." She bumped me gently with her shoulder. "It'll be all right. There's more of us this time. You're not getting bit again on my watch."

"The last werewolf kept coming until I'd almost run out of bullets," I said.

"You weren't packing silver then," said Shelby, entirely too reasonably. "You are now. It'll be fine, as long as you don't switch back to lead ammunition for a laugh."

"Right," I grumbled. Then I paused, giving her a sidelong look. "You know, I'd been hoping for the chance to talk to you without the rest of your family around."

"Yeah?" She sounded innocent, which meant that — knowing Shelby — she knew what I was about to ask.

"Why are you telling your father I'm your fiancé? I sort of thought one of us had to propose for that."

"Well, first, because he needed to see you as something I was properly attached to, not some summer fling. 'Fiancé' has more weight than 'boyfriend' when you're asking someone not be put down for the crime of getting bit by a werewolf," she said, again sounding entirely too reasonable. "Aside from that, you *did* propose. It just took me a while to sort out what my answer was going to be. Once I did, I figured I could go ahead and jump straight to fiancé. Was that wrong?"

"What?" I sputtered. "I didn't propose."

"Did so," she said. "In the woods, between the gorgon encampment and their farming community, after I killed that poor lindworm. You said 'marry me.' I'm saying yes."

I stopped walking. Shelby continued for a few more feet before she stopped and looked over her shoulder at me, raising her eyebrows.

"Well?" she said.

"You're saying yes," I said flatly. "It's been *months*.

That was on a different continent, during a completely different life-threatening situation. And you're saying yes now."

"What?" She walked back over to stop in front of me, spreading her hands as she asked, "Do you not want to marry me?"

"Don't be silly. Of course I want to marry you."

"Did you not propose?"

"Yes," I admitted, before adding sheepishly, "But I didn't think you'd noticed."

"Oh, I noticed." She leaned in to give me a chaste kiss on the cheek—an annoying but necessary observation of the "no fluid transfer" rule that was going to be in effect until I received my final clean bill of health, at the end of the twenty-eight-day latency period. "You can't blame a girl for thinking long and hard before she agreed to marry a *Price*, now can you?"

"Most of the girls I know on more than a superficial level are Price girls, so that question is a little unfair," I said. "I don't have a ring for you or anything. I was sort of not expecting this right now."

Shelby's smile was bright enough to light up all the forests of Australia. "That's all right. We can go to the jeweler's after all this is taken care of. Nothing says 'hooray, we didn't die' like watching the salespeople crawl all over themselves trying to convince you to buy expensive rocks you don't really want."

I blinked at her. Then, slowly, I began to smile, until my expression mirrored hers. "We're getting married."

"Well, sure we are, silly," said Shelby, before turning and sauntering off in the direction we'd been heading previously. "Won't you at least *try* to keep up?"

I tried.

We walked almost a mile before we came out of the woods atop a ridge overlooking a broad green meadow that looked almost artificial in its pastoral sweetness, like someone had transplanted it from a movie set in New Zealand. Fluffy clouds of sheep dotted the green, and we were far enough away that they looked a little dingy but not filthy—a beautiful trick of distance. (Sheep are some of the nastiest creatures in the world. They're smelly, stupid things that have been bred to have way too much hair, meaning that all their bodily fluids and drippings get felted right into the wool. If not for bleach, we'd all walk around covered in sheep shit all the time. Agriculture is not a pretty thing.)

Raina was already on the ridge, having beat us out of the woods by at least fifteen minutes. She had managed to find a stick somewhere, and was throwing it for Jett over and over again. The dog seemed willing to continue this game indefinitely, but Raina reclaimed the stick and didn't throw it again when she saw us come walking out of the tree line.

"I was starting to think you'd been eaten," she accused, although she didn't come anywhere near her previously acerbic tone. She still didn't strike me as one of the world's warmest people, but whatever had been broken between her and her sister was no longer festering. "There are drop bears around here, you know. Unless you've forgotten how bad an idea it is to mess with those?"

"Didn't see any," Shelby said brightly. "Needed to chat with Alex for a minute or two before we had to get back to business. Any sign of Gabby and the folks?"

"Not yet, but they had a bit more of a hike, so I'm not worried." Raina threw the stick again, sending Jett flying after it in an ecstasy of canine delight.

"I know this is a really awkward, ugly American sort of question, but do Australians not like roads that actually go where you're trying to *go*?" I asked. "We seem to do a lot of walking through woods and fields and swampy bits, and maybe it's me, but I'd expect the roads to take us to those places. It would be a lot easier to run away if we didn't have to navigate half a mile of hostile forest before we could get to the car."

"Car's two kilometers that way," said Raina, pointing across the meadow. "If we need to run away, we'll be getting our cardio for the week."

"Right," I said, putting a hand over my face. "I'm in a country full of Shelbys."

"I resent that," said Shelby. "I'm unique, thank you. It's not my fault if you've no appreciation for our culture."

I lowered my hand and gave her my best pleading look. It seemed to do at least a little good: she huffed, looking amused, and exchanged a quick glance with her sister, who snorted and flung the stick again.

"What she means by 'appreciation for our culture' is 'you have to understand how much conservation work we do.' A lot of the land around here is privately owned, and at least partially dedicated to preservation. This is sheep grazing land, yeah, but it's interspersed with billabongs and isolate tree patches, which provide habitat for a lot of endangered wildlife. Including drop bears." Jett brought back the stick. Raina threw it again. "So there are no roads because either the roads belong to people we don't feel like explaining ourselves to—like the rancher who owns this particular patch—or because running a road in would mess things up for the creatures who already live here."

"Ah," I said. "I should have thought of that. I just have trouble matching the care you take with the native animals with the disregard you have for the other native sapients."

Raina frowned at me before giving her sister a questioning look.

"Alex doesn't understand how we can be so good to the drop bears and bunyip and such when we don't have good relations with our nonhuman neighbors," translated Shelby. "Honestly, after spending the last year with his family, I have to ask the same question. We've been falling down when it comes to getting on with the other people who live in this country. We ought to be better."

"Tell it to the werewolves," said Riley. We turned to see him ascending the ridge, with Charlotte and Gabby close behind. Gabby looked anxious. She was darting glances up at the sky, watching as the sun sank slowly toward the horizon. Charlotte, in contrast, looked perfectly serene and fresh as a daisy, and not at all like a woman who had just hiked a mile through dense forest. "Animals are animals, no matter what they look like. They have instincts, and we can't blame them for that. People are different. People have to learn to control themselves. Any person who can't may as well be considered a monster."

I frowned. "So are you saying that any thinking cryptid that doesn't 'control themselves' into acting like a human being may as well be a monster?"

Riley shrugged, massive shoulders rolling under his shirtsleeves until I was afraid he was going to bust a seam. "You said it, not me," he said. "Raina, Shelly, you're with me. We need to set a line around the flock. Gabby, you stay here with your mum. Keep an eye on our 'guest.'" He turned and went tromping back down the hill. Shelby cast me an apologetic glance as she followed him. Raina didn't even do that.

"That could have gone better," I muttered, watching them go.

"That isn't likely," said Charlotte brightly. "Have you got a weapon?"

I turned to give her a blank look before reaching into my jacket and producing my backup handgun. It was small and compact enough that it didn't change the line of my clothing, which was important when there was a chance I'd be interacting with noncombatants, and it was loaded with silver bullets. "I'm sorry, I thought you knew," I said. "Shelby and I were discussing ammunition in the car."

"I wasn't sure whether that meant you were borrowing one of her guns, or whether you had one of your own," she said, not missing a beat. "Sometimes Gabby forgets to pack a pistol when she doesn't really want to be coming along on a hunt."

"Mum!" protested Gabby.

"It's true," said Charlotte. She turned to survey the flock, and the rest of her family. Riley was moving Raina and Shelby into position on the far side of the massed sheep. Either there wasn't a sheepdog working the field, or the Tanners were a familiar enough sight that the dog wasn't going on alert. Jett was a black speck bouncing along at Raina's heels. "Looks like we're good to move. Are you both clear on your orders?"

"Yes," said Gabby.

"No," I said.

"Good," said Charlotte. "Move out." She started loping down the side of the hill, moving with a speed and grace that spoke of absolute familiarity with the terrain. The sun, having dipped down to taste the horizon and found it good, was now descending almost as fast as Charlotte Tanner, dropping the visibility on the field more with every second. I exchanged a glance with Gabby. Then, without another word spoken, the two of us took off after Charlotte.

Gabby, like her mother, was graceful and gliding on the uneven ground, even though she never quite approached Charlotte's speed. Charlotte ran like a six year old, or an Olympian in training, and somehow managed to do both at the same time: every leap was perfectly planned and executed, every step found solid ground. I, on the other hand, fumbled along behind them like the tourist I was. The quality of the soil was unfamiliar to me, turning every footfall into something potentially treacherous. Only the mild but constant fear of the things that lurked among the Australian underbrush kept me from taking a header into the grass.

It says something when you're more afraid of falling down and maybe meeting a spider than you are of breaking an ankle, providing that broken ankle doesn't dump you on your ass.

The sheep were agitated when we reached the bottom of the ridge. They danced from one foot to another, heads up, ears flat, bleating into the twilight. Riley was a hulking shape on the other side of the flock, and I allowed myself a moment to wonder whether he might not be the problem. Sheep may be stupid, but they can sense hostility, and Riley had hostility to spare.

Then one of the rams reared up onto its hind legs, gave a low, bleating moan, like an animal in excruciating pain, and turned inside out.

"Oh, *fuck*," I said, and started shooting.

The most common comparison for the lycanthropy family of viruses is rabies. They cause a lot of similar symptoms in the people they infect, which is why we go back to rabies again and again when talking about anyone infected with lycanthropy. The uninformed might even start to think that a werewolf was just a person with a bad case of rabies, someone who turned almost animalistic in their rages. There's a reason we explain it like that. It's easier on everyone if we never couch things in more honest terms.

The ram—a big boy, maybe three hundred pounds of mutton on the hoof—shrieked as its skin warped and twisted, woolly coat being expelled from the skin with a speed that left it raw and bleeding, hence the appearance of having been turned inside out. The bones were distending and transforming so fast that I could hear them crackle and snap inside its body. Its flesh was changing too, shifting composition from marbled, fatty softness to rockhard, combat-ready muscle. The ram bellowed again as our bullets bit into its midsection. This time, it sounded less like a bleat, and more like a howl of protest against the world. How *dare* this reality exist? How *dare* we shoot at the ram, which was meant to be king of the newly born night?

I stopped firing wildly, forcing myself to take a breath

and steady my hands. Then, barely pausing to aim, I raised my gun again and fired at the werewolf, which showed virtually no signs of its ovine origins.

A hole appeared at the center of its face. It blinked yellow, lupine eyes dumbly, a bit of its original sheepish dullness creeping back in before those eyes went completely blank, and the werewolf collapsed. The untransformed members of the flock scattered, bleating. I let out a slow breath.

"All right," I began. "That takes care of—"

Something screamed. I turned, as did the Tanners. Five more of the sheep had stopped in their tracks—four ewes, and a second, juvenile ram—and were staring at us with yellowing eyes.

"Well, fuck," I said, shoulders slumping as my brief-lived hope died. "There's more than one."

Of the six werewolves among the flock, the old ram had been infected the longest: that was the only explanation for why he'd transformed so quickly, and so completely. The five that were now advancing toward us, stiff-legged and snarling, were still essentially sheep. Their eyes were yellow, and one of the ewes was starting to shed her fleece in huge, bloody clumps, but they still looked like barnyard animals, more suited to a petting zoo than to a horror movie. I took advantage of their slow approach, checking to see how many bullets I had left. Two more. It had taken four, plus however many the Tanners used, to take down a single werewolf that wasn't yet prepared to attack.

"Riley?" I began reloading as quickly as I could, jamming the bullets into place with my thumb. I had half a box of replacement ammunition with me. That didn't feel like it was going to be enough. "Was there a plan here, apart from 'let's all go to the meadow and get turned into confetti by the sheep'?"

"These weren't here yesterday—they've got the wrong

markings. This is a different flock of sheep," he said. I heard the click of his own chamber being slotted back into place. "Someone's setting us up."

"Oh, that's splendid." I aimed, fired, and sent the smallest of the ewes sprawling. In the aftermath of my shot, two more guns went off. I wasn't sure who they belonged to, but I was sure there was something wrong: while a bloody patch blossomed on the shoulder of the lead ewe, she didn't fall. She didn't even stagger.

As she approached, her skull began to warp and twist into a new shape, canine teeth pushing their way through her jaw and piercing her lower lip. She snarled, saliva dripping all around that newly terrible maw.

A sudden, horrifying comprehension seized me. I put the safety back on my pistol, flipped it around, and offered the butt to Shelby. "Trade me guns."

"What?" She stared at me like I was saying something completely unreasonable. She wasn't too far off with that.

"I need you to trade me guns." The werewolves were still stalking toward us, their short sheep's legs and ongoing transformations slowing them down. That wasn't going to last much longer. As soon as they were changed enough to break into a proper run, we were going to find ourselves rushed by a small pack of hungry, ruthless predators. The fact that they had started out as herbivores wasn't going to make any difference. Hell, it might just make them hungrier.

Shelby kept staring at me. I gestured at her with the butt of my pistol, not withdrawing it. If she didn't make up her mind soon, we were going to be in even more trouble, as I had just effectively removed two of us from the fight. If my left arm had been fully functional . . . but it wasn't, and introducing throwing knives into a gun fight was just asking for trouble, even if they *were* tipped in silver.

"Oh, you *asshole*," she finally snarled, and thrust her own pistol at me as she snatched mine out of my hands and unloaded two rounds into the nearest werewolf, sending it sprawling. There was a momentary pause as she stared at the weapon in her hands, stunned by what had just happened. Then she whooped and opened fire again.

Her family did the same, but I was unsurprised when only Shelby's shots seemed to have any effect. I opened the chamber on her pistol. The bullets inside gleamed in the moonlight with the uniquely heavy shine that one gets from weapons-grade silver. I shook them into my hand, allowing Shelby and the others to keep up the suppressing fire as I scratched at the surface of one bullet with my thumbnail. The dull silver sheen came away easily, revealing cleaner steel underneath.

"Motherfucker," I swore. "Shelby! Someone switched your bullets!"

"What?" Her gun clicked empty. She glanced at me, and I lobbed the box containing my remaining silver bullets at her underhand. She caught it, beginning to reload even as she asked, "What are you saying?"

"I'm saying I'm the only one here who actually brought silver bullets to the werewolf fight, and you don't have enough firepower without it! All you're doing with the lead is slowing them down and pissing them off!" I shoved Shelby's gun into my coat and pulled out a knife. It was a silly weapon, under the circumstances, but it was better than nothing. Much, much better than nothing.

There were only two werewolves still standing, and their ovine origins were almost completely obscured by the newly lupine lines of their bodies. One of them was still somewhat woolly, with a tail that hung between its legs like a fat white fruit. The other had a more sheep-like skull, but as it was filled with sharp predator's teeth and covered in thick gray fur, the shape of its skull didn't matter as much as the thought of what that skull might do.

"Alex?" said Shelby, seeing me measuring the space

between myself and the lead werewolf. "Don't do anything—"

The werewolf leaped. So did I.

Werewolves are, thankfully, creatures of instinct: with the exception of the ones that had attacked me and Cooper near the meadow earlier, I had never heard of a werewolf making a strategy or following a plan once it was transformed. *These* werewolves had begun life as sheep, bred for obedience and stupidity over the course of generations. It was jumping for a man my height, not for a person who was suddenly sliding on his knees under the arc of the werewolf's trajectory. I jammed my knife upward, turning my face away and screwing my mouth and eyes as tightly closed as I could. It wasn't squeamishness. I wanted to avoid fluid contact as much as possible.

My knife slammed into the werewolf's belly just below the rib cage. The creature gave a yelp of strangled pain and kept going, driven forward by its own momentum. A hot rush of stinking blood exploded over my arm, like a water balloon being popped, and the heavy, horrible feeling of the werewolf's viscera slammed down on me, landing on my head, chest, and shoulders like nothing I had ever experienced before. There was a yelp as the werewolf finally passed fully over me and impacted with the ground.

I didn't know whether having the majority of its internal organs removed would be enough to kill a leaping werewolf, but I was damn sure that it would slow the bastard down.

The gunfire continued as I lay there in the grass, covered in werewolf offal and stinking of blood. I heard someone scream. I didn't know who. I didn't think it was Riley or Shelby, but the other three were still basically indistinguishable to me in their distress: I hadn't yet had the time to learn what they sounded like when their lives were endangered. Then a foot hit me in the shoulder, hard enough to hurt. I made a small noise of protest, without opening my mouth.

"You *asshole!*" Shelby sounded furious. That was good: a furious Shelby was a breathing Shelby. Something soft and clean was dropped on my face. I sat up, scrubbing the worst of the blood away as she continued to rant. "You can't tell me I'm the only one with a working gun and then—argh, and then *unzip* a fucking werewolf everywhere like you're some sort of deranged action hero! You could have given me a heart attack!"

She kicked me again, this time in the hip. I finished scrubbing the blood off my mouth, coughed, and asked, "Can you stop kicking me long enough to get the blood out of my eyes? I'm afraid I'll just grind it in if I try, and I really don't want to increase the mucus membrane exposure."

"You're marrying a man who thinks 'mucus membrane exposure' is a thing to say right after you've got werewolf liver in your hair," said Raina sourly. "Oh, yeah, Shelly, you've got yourself a winner here. Can I be your maid of honor?"

"Is everyone all right?" I asked. "I missed the end of the fight." Ignoring Raina seemed like the best approach, under the circumstances.

Fortunately, I wasn't the only one who thought so. "No one was bitten or scratched," said Riley roughly. "Thanks for the bullets, Price."

"How did you know?" I heard Shelby kneel beside me. She lifted my glasses off my face. "All right, you don't have much blood actually on you—good thing you need corrective lenses, or this might be a much bigger problem. Keep your eyes closed, all right?" Something damp touched my eyelid.

Asking what it was seemed like a dangerous course of action, and so I focused on the question at hand. "Too many shots were being fired without any of the wolves going down. If we were all packing silver, that would have been a much shorter fight. Something had to be wrong."

"So why did *you* still have silver bullets?" demanded

Riley. The momentary gratitude I had heard in his voice was gone. That was a disappointment, but not really a surprise.

"Because I never let my weapons out of my possession," I said. It was hard to keep my face still while I spoke, but it was also necessary: Shelby was dabbing at the area around my eyes, making it clear that the blood had not yet been totally removed. I was going to *bathe* in hand sanitizer when we got back to the house. "In order for someone to have switched my silver bullets for lead, they would have needed to knock me out, distract the mice, and manage the exchange without leaving anything out of place. I'm assuming you have a more centralized means of storing your weapons?"

Riley's silence was all the answer I needed.

"You should be able to open your eyes now," said Shelby, slipping my glasses back onto my face before she pulled away. "Just try not to wipe at them until you've had access to better sterilization tools, all right?"

"All right; thank you," I said, and opened my eyes, blinking at the suddenly bright world around me. Even moonlight can seem blinding if you've been in total darkness for long enough. "We came out here alone, a family group and a visiting cryptozoologist who had already been exposed once. That seemed a little strange to me, but I'm not native, I don't know how you do things. *Was* it strange?"

"Yes and no," said Charlotte. Riley shot her a sharp look. She rolled her eyes and spread her hands, indicating the abattoir that the meadow around us had become. "For God's sake, Riley, there's no harm in telling the man how operations are usually managed, given the circumstances. Can you really look at him and say he's not at least trying to keep us all among the living? No, Alex, this is not unusual: the Society is very wide-spread under normal circumstances, so most families or local groups survey and hunt alone. Waiting for backup to arrive from another city or state could mean someone gets killed."

"But when we're all together, we usually work together," chimed in Raina, not to be left out. "So it's weird that only five of us came out, instead of everyone."

"It was your mother's idea," said Riley, sounding suddenly defensive.

Charlotte went still. It was a trick I'd seen her daughter pull more than once: all animation drained out of her, taking the sparkle from her eye and the tension from her lips as she slowly turned to stare at her husband. "What did you say?" she asked dangerously.

"I got your text," said Riley. "You're the one who proposed we spend some time with the family and the boyfriend," here he indicated me with a sweep of his hand that somehow managed to imply his disgust, even though his facial expression didn't change, "before things got really out of hand."

"Yes, and *I* got *your* text, saying you wanted to observe Alex in the field so that we could convince Shelby to end her association with someone who was so clearly unsuitable for her—no offense, Alex," Charlotte added hastily.

"None taken," I said. "It's almost a relief to know that neither one of Shelby's parents likes me. It puts me on level ground."

"I didn't send that text," said Riley.

"Well, I didn't send the text you're describing either," said Charlotte.

"I didn't text anyone; you can check my phone," said Raina. Gabby didn't say anything. She stood close by her sister, looking distressed—and more, looking like she understood what was going on, which put her ahead of the rest of the family. She had been away at school before the werewolves came. She had something the rest of them couldn't get for love nor money. She had perspective.

"No one here sent any texts," I said. "Someone's playing you. The same someone who swapped your silver bullets for regular bullets that had been spray-painted the color you expected to see when you checked your ammunition. I really hate to be the one who says this, because God knows I can't afford to lose any more credibility with you people, but you have a traitor in your midst.

"Someone sent you out here tonight to get the entire Tanner family killed."

Riley and Charlotte exchanged a glance. In the distance, a wolf howled. And none of us said a word.

Eleven

"Ah, traitors. Like taxes, politics, and discussions of the weather, they remain an unavoidable, unwanted part of the human condition."

—Thomas Price

Back in the SUV, which is a major improvement on the meadow full of dead werewolves, no question about it

WE WEREN'T MOVING.

That wouldn't have been so frustrating if we hadn't been sitting in the family SUV, parked off behind a stand of trees where passing motorists would be less likely to see us and wonder what we were doing out in the middle of nowhere. Even worse, we'd been parked there for the better part of an hour, which meant I'd been in an enclosed space with Shelby's entire family for the better part of an hour. I was beginning to wonder how she'd feel about being an orphan. From the way her lip had started to twitch, I suspected she'd feel pretty good about it.

Sadly, the logic behind our temporary hold was sound. By the time we'd hiked out of the bloody meadow and back to the car, the noise would have attracted one of the local shepherds; even if they didn't bring their flocks in at night, they had to have been monitoring them somehow, just due to the density of local predators. Once a shepherd showed up, we could count on the local authorities being called—the real authorities, not all of whom were aware of the Thirty-Six Society's existence. We'd barely had time to move the SUV to a more well-hidden location before the emergency response vehicles came blasting down the road, their sirens running and their lights flashing, just like emergency response vehicles anywhere in the world.

"Well, that tears it," Charlotte had said, with no real surprise in her voice. "We've got too much blood on us to risk the road until we see them go by again. Relax, you lot, we're here for the haul."

It might not have been so bad if the elder Tanners had been willing to discuss the traitor in their organization while we waited. At least then we would have been *doing* something. But they had shut down all attempts to raise the topic, until I became frustrated and sank back in my seat, not saying anything. Shelby had put a hand on my arm, shooting me a look of resigned understanding. No wonder she'd been so amazed when she met my family and learned that we believed in talking things out—a necessity, when your immediate family includes two telepaths and two empaths, not to mention Antimony, who wasn't psychic, but was easily irritated enough that she was practically the next best thing.

When I'd first arrived in Australia, I had looked at the Tanners and seen only their similarities to the people I knew and counted on back home—and there were plenty of similarities, don't get me wrong. Now that I'd been here long enough to see how they responded to crisis situations, the differences were looming larger all the time.

"Are you really marrying Shelby?" Raina's question would have been abrupt under the best of circumstances. In the dark, silent SUV, it sounded like the start of an interrogation.

I looked up at her. She was just an outline in the gloom.

That actually made things a little easier, since I didn't have to see her face when I said, "I was hoping to, yes. I did propose, and it seems polite to go through with it."

"Aren't you supposed to ask her father for his consent?"

"No, he's not," said Shelby. There was steel in her tone. "That would imply that I was property, and that someone could give me away to someone else. That's not true. That's never been true. Only person Alex needed to ask was me, and you know what my answer was."

"Could've told us." Gabby's comment was much softer; I might not have heard it, if we hadn't all been shut in the car. "You've emailed me at least once a week since you left, and you never said you were getting married."

"I wanted it to be a surprise," said Shelby. "So . . . surprise, I guess. I'm getting married."

"Will the ceremony be here or in the United States?" asked Charlotte. Then, as calm as an assassin sliding a knife between someone's ribs, she added the question I'd barely started formulating: "Where are you intending to live? Alex could apply for Australian citizenship. It's a difficult process, but being married will make it easier, and it would keep you near your family."

Riley hadn't said a word, but I saw his hands tighten on the wheel, and imagined I could hear his teeth grinding.

"I'm going to get murdered and dumped in a bog before I even have this conversation with my parents," I said, tilting my head up so that I was staring at the ceiling, and not the vaguely menacing shapes of Shelby's family.

"They probably already know, you know," said Shelby. "Sarah's no doubt told them—and Mum, I don't know yet where we're going to live. We haven't started having those conversations yet."

"Oh, God," I said, almost philosophically. "I'm going to die."

"Maybe those are conversations you should have before you go announcing that you're going to marry some boy your family's only just met," snapped Charlotte.

"Maybe we should wait to have *any* of these conversations until we're not dealing with lycanthropy-infected sheep and people setting us up to be slaughtered," I suggested.

They ignored me.

"She's going to move to America, obviously, or she wouldn't be hedging," said Raina.

"No, she's not," said Gabby. "She wouldn't do that. She knows how much we miss her already, and that's when we have good reason to expect her to come home. Tell her, Shelly. Tell her you're not moving to America."

"Still the werewolves prowl, hungry for human flesh," I said. Again, they ignored me.

"I don't know *where* we're going to live, all right? Alex gets a vote, too." Shelby was starting to sound annoyed.

She wasn't the only one. "There are plenty of nice boys in Australia, Shelby Tanner," said Charlotte. "Why couldn't you find one of them? No offense, Alex, you're lovely, for a Price, and I'm sure you'd be an excellent husband for some girl who wasn't my oldest daughter."

"Offense taken, and did I mention there were *werewolves?*" I kept my eyes on the ceiling. At least if I was watching the ceiling, I would miss any rude gestures thrown in my direction. "I really, really think werewolves are more important than our eventual mailing address."

As expected, they ignored me for a third time. "Australia's great! You'll love living here," said Gabby. "We have beaches, and you can come see me in the opera after I graduate, and there are lots of really *interesting* monsters for you to study."

"Like werewolves?" I asked.

"I hate to agree with the Price boy, but maybe this conversation can wait until another time," said Riley, who sounded about as happy about the situation as I felt.

I didn't make the mistake of thinking this made him an ally. I heard the rubber squeak as he tightened his hands on the steering wheel again. "Believe me, it's a conversation we *will* be having, as a family—but I'd like to live that long."

"Can't live anywhere if we're all dead," said Shelby. She sounded incredibly happy, like this was the best thing that had ever been said, by anyone. Then again, it was distracting her family from grilling us about our long-term plans. Maybe that *did* make it the best thing anyone had ever said. "Who had access to the bullets, Dad?"

Riley twisted in his seat enough to jerk his head toward me. "I already told you I didn't want to discuss private matters in front of our visitor."

"He's my fiancé, Dad, and that makes him family. Plus, whoever set this up was trying to kill him, too, which I figure makes this his business." Shelby looped her arm through mine to illustrate her point. I would normally have enjoyed having her snuggle up against me like that. I wasn't normally worried that her father was going to throw me to the wolves—literally. "Who had access to the bullets?"

"Everyone," said Charlotte. "They came out of the central stock. There's no way anyone could have known for sure which boxes we'd grab."

"Which means either your luck was very, very bad when it came to picking up ammunition for this little jaunt, or you don't have any silver bullets left," I said. "How hard would it be for me to walk into your central stock and swap things around?"

"You? Dead hard. No one would let you in there unescorted. But me, or Shelly, or anyone who's known to be a member in good standing of the Society? Dead easy." Charlotte hesitated before she added, "The door's always locked, and everybody has a key. We'd notice if someone like you tried to stick your head in, but that's just because you're not supposed to be wandering around alone."

"So I—assuming I was a Thirty-Sixer—could have walked in with my pockets full of silver-painted bullets, and swapped them for the actual silver bullets without anyone noticing me or realizing what I'd done. Is that what I'm hearing?" I looked around the car. I couldn't see expressions in the gloom, but I could see postures, and no one looked very happy.

"Could a werewolf have done that?" asked Gabby.

"If they wore gloves," I said. "Silver is a contact poison to them, and they might have developed a rash like poison oak if they'd touched it directly, but it wouldn't kill them or even cause enough immediate pain to be obvious to someone who saw them walking out of the supply area. The better question is whether a werewolf would be able to plan that far ahead. Is there some sort of log that people are supposed to sign when they take things?"

"We've never needed one," said Riley. "Do *you* have a log?"

"No, sir, but there aren't nearly as many of us, and we generally have a good idea of our resources." And we always knew what our visitors were doing, didn't we? When Uncle Mike and Aunt Lea came by, or when Aunt Mary was haunting the house, we knew, and we kept a close count on our bullets. It was a little mistrustful of our allies, maybe, but it meant that we didn't encounter any nasty surprises.

"Did you have silver bullets before, Dad?" asked Shelby. "I know you killed the werewolf that bit Tim."

"We did," said Riley. "I bought them from a supplier on the Gold Coast, and I checked them myself before I allowed anyone to take them into the field. They worked like the records said they would, and I didn't look any further."

"Then whoever swapped the bullets did it after they saw what they could do a werewolf," I said. "Someone who was there. How many people went with you on that trip?"

"Eighteen or so," said Riley. "More knew where we were heading. I thought werewolves were just dumb beasts. All the records we had said that they were monsters, not opponents. You even said it yourself."

I hadn't put it quite like that, but arguing with him seemed like a bad idea under the circumstances. "A werewolf that has transformed is a monster. A werewolf in the default shape of its species is a member of that species, just . . . a little more temperamental, a little faster to react and judge, a little more oriented toward survival of the self. They don't make choices for the greater good, because the disease they carry won't let them. New werewolves transform often and uncontrollably, like those sheep we saw tonight. Werewolves who manage to survive through their first cycles of transformation tend to be less functional, but more in control of their transformations. They can hide themselves a hell of a lot better."

"So they could have been with us this whole time," said Shelby. "It could be someone back at the house."

"Not 'could be'; almost certainly is," I said. "They had to have had access to the ammunition, to your cellphones, and most importantly, to information. If you're trying to set a trap like this one, you need to know who you're dealing with, and how they're likely to react. I *really* don't want to reopen this topic, but when the two of you received the texts you thought were from each other, was there any mention of Shelby and me being engaged?"

"No," said Charlotte.

"Absolutely not," said Riley.

"Then we're in luck: we can move Raina and Gabby lower on the list of potential suspects—er, sorry." I glanced at Shelby's sisters. "Add in the fact that I don't think you're foolhardy enough to set up a trap and then walk into it, given the historical lack of loyalty on the part of most werewolves, and we can take you off the list completely. Those sheep would have eaten their puppet master as cheerfully as they would have eaten us."

"No offense taken, but just you wait until the toasts at your wedding," said Gabby, in a mild tone. "It's going to be *all* about how the first thing you did in Australia was damn near get yourself killed. See how you feel about baseless accusations then."

"We can write Mum off for similar reasons," said Raina. "She'd never have walked into a trap, but if she'd been trying to get a rise out of Dad, she would *definitely* have mentioned the engagement."

"And Dad's not stupid enough to walk into a field full of lycanthropic sheep just because he wants to see you get introduced to your lungs," chimed in Shelby. Then she paused, a sour look crossing her face. "The only person not being cleared by this run of logic is me, you realize. Please come up with some clever reason that I can't be the werewolf, all right? Just so I feel better."

"The mice still like you." Shelby looked relieved. The rest of the Tanners looked bemused, their expressions barely visible through the gloom. My eyes were adjusting. I shrugged. "The mice were able to tell from my wounds that I hadn't been infected. They adore Shelby—they consider her a priestess, which makes her holy, and makes anything that endangers her a very big deal. Even if she'd been in Australia during the initial attacks, which she wasn't, the mice would have freaked out if they'd smelled infection on her. She's clean. She can't be our traitor."

"I could've told you that, but it's nice to hear you stand up for my girl," said Riley. He still didn't sound terribly impressed with me. That wasn't a surprise. Honestly, the only things I could think of that might get him on my side were martyrdom and grandchildren, and I wasn't ready for either one.

The road in front of the car suddenly lit up. We all froze, barely allowing ourselves to breathe as the police cars that had earlier rushed by on their way to the meadow went roaring in the other direction. Apparently, there was only so much they were willing to do about a bunch of dead sheep after dark, even if the field looked more like a slaughterhouse than it had any right to.

"Right," said Riley, and started the engine. "Let's go see who's unhappy to see us."

Everyone was unhappy to see us.

We pulled up in front of the temporary headquarters of the Thirty-Six Society to find the whole place lit up like a Christmas tree, to the point where our little walk through the woods—something these people seemed ungodly fond of—was a joke: no one was going to drive past this compound and not realize that something was going on just past that thin layer of foliage and forestry. There were too many angry voices raised from the direction of the house, and the floodlights weren't even in the neighborhood of what I'd call "subtle."

"Oh, what are these bastards doing now?" Riley scowled and barreled forward, shoving his way through the underbrush. It sprang back with almost cartoonish speed, closing the path behind him.

"Sorry, kids, I need to go make sure Riley doesn't murder anyone for no good reason," said Charlotte. She started to dart after him.

Shelby grabbed her mother's elbow. "What if there's a good reason?" she asked.

"Then I'm going to help him hide the bodies." Charlotte shook off her daughter's hand and dove into the brush. Again, it snapped back into place behind her with frustrating quickness, leaving no path for us to follow.

"They do this," said Raina, continuing forward at an only slightly hurried pace. "It's best if you just let them get it out of their systems."

"Daddy's frustrated because he can't punch were-wolves without getting infected, and Mum just wants him to stop being tempted to try," added Gabby, pulling back a branch. "It's business as usual. I'm surprised

Shelly didn't tell you about it before she brought you here."

"I'm not," I said, flashing Shelby a quick, tight smile. "She wanted me to actually come."

Shelby shrugged, an unrepentant smile on her face. "You were going to have to meet them eventually."

"It might have been nice to do it under less crisis-ridden circumstances," I said, and pushed forward through the brush, following her parents. When I reached the other side I stopped, blinking rapidly against the glare, and just stared. I heard the Tanner sisters come crashing out of the woods behind me; then all three of them stopped as well, and we were briefly, unexpectedly united in our sheer bemusement at the scene in front of us.

What looked like the entire Thirty-Six Society was gathered on the lawn. The question of how they moved their equipment through the woods was answered by a row of little red wagons—literal little red wagons—laden with guns, ammunition, and some more exotic weaponry. I had to admire the *Evil Dead*-level dedication that went into thinking "I'll take a chainsaw into battle against a werewolf," even as I wanted to find out who thought it was a good idea and shake them until they realized the error of their ways.

Almost everyone was shouting. Some were shouting at each other; some were shouting for the sake of shouting; and a ring had formed around Riley and Charlotte, all of them gesturing wildly while they shouted at the Tanners. It was the very picture of chaos, and for one ignoble moment I was tempted to grab Shelby's hand, skirt the crowd, and return to the quarantine house, where we could lock ourselves in and let the Thirty-Sixers shout themselves out.

The moment passed. I started forward, ignoring the twinging from my injured left arm, and pushed my way through the ring that had formed around Charlotte and Riley. Roughly half the people who had previously been yelling at them stopped dead, looking confused by my sudden appearance. I kept pushing, finally coming to a stop next to Riley. "What's going on?" I had to half-shout to make myself heard, thus continuing the vicious chain reaction of the crowd.

"Someone told *all these people* that we were dead!" Riley roared. There were no half-measures for him: he was making sure that everyone in range heard him as loudly and clearly as possible. I had to admire that, even as I started really wishing for a pair of earplugs. "Said we'd been ravaged by werewolves in the south meadow, and now no one wants to believe what's in front of their eyes!"

"Wait, *who* said that?" I asked. "I mean, that seems sort of important—"

"You're standing there *with* a werewolf!" someone shouted, not waiting for me to finish. "You expect us to believe you when you're standing there *with* a werewolf?"

"Fuck off, North," shouted Charlotte, somehow manage to make the suggestion sound almost genteel. That was a talent she definitely shared with her daughter, who could sound perfectly pleasant while suggesting anatomical impossibilities. I'd just never heard it done quite so loudly before. "Alex has a clean bill of health from a doctor *and* the Aeslin mice."

North—whoever that was—didn't reply. Apparently, "the mice said he's okay" was starting to carry weight with these people, probably because they were desperate and the old books all said that Aeslin mice were trustworthy. I made a mental note to give the mice extra cake at their next banquet.

Sadly, the rest of the shouting just redoubled in the wake of Charlotte's words, becoming a loud, muddled mess from which only the occasional syllable could be picked free. Shelby pushed her way through the crowd next to me, a worried look on her face.

"I think these folks are likely to get violent soon," she said. "Not that I mind a little rumble, but does anybody know how to calm them down?"

"They're your people," I said. "When my whole family fights, we do it in one room, not an entire yard." Maybe there was something to be said for not having that many members. Fewer people to help, sure, but that also meant fewer people to fight with you. "Who told them we were all dead?"

Shelby scowled at me for a moment before her eyes lit up and her scowl became a grin. "You're right! They're my people! Daddy, cover your eyes."

"What—" began Riley. Charlotte, who was slightly faster on the uptake, reached up and clapped her hand over her husband's eyes, interrupting him before he could say anything else.

Shelby whirled to face the crowd, and shouted, in her best "I am in charge of this tiger show, and all you visitors better shut up and sit down" zoo employee voice, "We have not been bitten by any werewolves! Look!" And then she pulled her shirt off over her head and spread her arms, putting every inch of her torso not covered by her polka dot lace bra on display.

The shouting stopped instantly. You could have heard a pin drop. Then Raina pushed her way past me, snorting laughter all the while, and stopped next to her sister. Jett followed, tail wagging, and stopped next to her new mistress. A nice wall was building between me and the hostile parts of the crowd, really.

My left arm gave another twinge. I resisted the urge to apply pressure to the wound. Reminding these people that I couldn't pull the "take off your shirt to prove you haven't been bitten" trick didn't seem like a good idea at the moment.

Shelby continued, "We were set up, and someone wants you to think we all got torn to bits, but since we're all here, and mostly not too covered in blood—"

"—except for Alex," interjected Raina.

"—yes, all right, except for Alex, but that's because he gutted a werewolf and got the insides all over his clothes, *thanks Raina*," said Shelby, giving her sister a poisonous look. "He wasn't bitten a second time. None of us were bitten, even though we were out in a meadow full of werewolves without any silver bullets, thanks to some-one on this property. So can you all calm the fuck down and let us tell you what happened?"

The crowd still wasn't shouting, although they weren't quite as quiet anymore. A low murmur ran through the assemblage. It could have meant anything. It was un-likely to mean total acceptance of Shelby's words, which was potentially a problem for us. I'd never been lynched before. I wasn't looking forward to starting now.

"For the love of God, Shelly, put your shirt back on," said Riley, pushing in between his daughter and the crowd. A few people were gauche enough to make disap-pointed noises, and in that moment, I think Riley and I finally found common ground in the desire to beat those people into pulp. He scowled at the assemblage, hands balled into fists, and shouted, "We were set up! Someone sent us out there to get eaten by werewolf sheep. One of *our own people* sent us out there. I knew that some of you didn't like how I've been running things, but I always thought better of us. I never thought any of us would be *cowards*."

"Werewolf sheep?" asked one of the Thirty-Sixers, looking confused. "That doesn't even make any sense."

"They were sheep that had been infected, so they turned into wolves," said Raina. "How does that not make sense?"

"What kind of wolf bites sheep and doesn't eat them?" demanded the Thirty-Sixer. "Wolves kill sheep. Everyone knows that. They don't just have a nibble and trot away."

I blinked.

"We don't know what werewolves do," snapped Raina. "Maybe the werewolf wasn't hungry. Maybe it hated farmers. Maybe it just didn't like the taste of mut-ton. You can't look at wolf behavior and apply it whole-sale to something that isn't actually a *wolf*." Jett made a small buffing sound, as if to support her new mistress' point.

"One sheep maybe, but how many are you saying attacked you?" The Thirty-Sixer folded her arms, and I suddenly realized why I recognized her: she was the model from before, her face now scrubbed clean of makeup to reveal a spotty olive complexion, complete with bags under her eyes and freckles across the bridge of her nose. It was like Verity always said—the best disguise a woman had was makeup, well-applied, and removed when necessary. "I don't think it makes sense."

"It does, actually." I pushed my way between Shelby and Raina. Shelby still hadn't put her shirt back on. For once, I didn't allow that to distract me as I focused on the woman with the folded arms. "What's your name?"

She blinked at me, looking taken aback. "I beg your pardon?"

"I asked your name. You were at the quarantine house earlier, telling me off for having been bitten, and now you're here, stirring everyone up again. I like a little dissent, but you seem very focused on causing it. Now, what's your name?"

The woman scowled. "Chloe," she said. "Chloe Bryant. If you think I like dissent, you must love it. You're causing it everywhere you go."

"It's a gift," I said. "Look: we have established that whoever sent the Tanners—and me—to that meadow was trying to set a trap. They *wanted* us to be hurt, even killed. Werewolves are only bestial when transformed. Even if a wolf-form lycanthrope would be more inclined to shred sheep than infect them, that doesn't mean our werewolf couldn't have gone there while he or she was human, and injected the sheep with saliva, or bled into their open mouths, or something." The more I thought about it, the more sense injections made. Lycanthropy is hard to catch. A syringe and a supply of infected blood or saliva would increase the odds of a successful infection—and even then, our plotting werewolf could easily have injected the entire flock, only to get the six that had attacked us.

Or maybe only to get one: the old ram that had been the first to change forms. He could easily have turned the other five members of his flock without even intending to, nipping at them during ordinary sheep things, or spraying them with saliva during his first partial transformations. Maybe our werewolf had only needed to infect a single animal in order to turn the herd . . . and maybe that had been the plan.

"The Covenant boy is right, but that's not the whole of it," said Riley. "The sheep had been turned before he or Shelby even got to Australia. Somebody's been planning this for a while. Somebody wants to change the way things work around here. Is it you, Chloe?"

Chloe glared at him. "I want to change the way we do things," she snapped. "I've never made any bones about that. But that doesn't mean I'm going to use werewolves to do my dirty work, you bastard." She spun on her heel and stalked away, elbowing and shoving her way through the crowd.

Her exit seemed to take the last of the steam out of our burgeoning mob. The muttering increased, but the tension and potential violence was gone, replaced by a group of confused and even frightened people who didn't know quite what they were supposed to do.

Riley continued to eye them angrily. "So? Who said that we were dead? Speak up, I'm waiting."

"Everybody," said a man, stumbling forward. "I don't remember who said it first. It was just everywhere all of a sudden."

Great: a whisper game. The man didn't seem to be lying. He met Riley's eyes anxiously, searching for approval, before he melted back into the crowd.

These people were still too worked up to tell us anything useful. They needed to feel like normalcy was returning. That, at least, was something I had a reasonable amount of experience with, thanks to working with school groups back at the zoo. I turned to Charlotte, lowering my voice, and asked, "Is there any way we can move people inside?"

"I think I can manage," she said, before turning back to the crowd, cupping her hands around her mouth, and shouting, "Tea, coffee, and Tim Tams in the main hall in ten minutes! Anyone who wants to come in and help me brew things gets first crack at the goodies!" Then she strode forward, heading toward the house without a second glance. The muttering increased again, but dropped in volume as what looked like half the crowd peeled off to follow her.

"Clever boy." Shelby kissed me on the cheek before pulling her shirt back on over her head, tugging it into place.

"I try." I looked to Riley. "Who is in charge of the central stock? I'd like to talk to them."

"I can do you one better," he said. "I'll take you there."

"I'm coming with you," said Shelby.

"Gabby and I will help Mum with the coffee and see if we can't find out who started the rumors," said Raina quickly. "Not trying to ditch you, Shelly, but if Dad's going to kill your boyfriend, I'd rather not be there to witness it."

"Thanks," said Shelby dryly.

"No worries," said Raina, and trotted off after Charlotte, Jett tagging at her heels and Gabby following at a somewhat more subdued pace, shaking her head and looking wearily up at the sky.

"This way," said Riley.

We followed him.

Riley led us around the house to a door I hadn't seen before, set flush with the foundation and accessible only by descending three shallow stone steps. "We used to have flooding issues here, before we got the drainage systems up to date," he said, producing a key from his pocket and unlocking the door. "Probably would have again if there were a really major storm."

"You could hire a siren to waterproof the place," I suggested. "They can't work miracles, but they're good at convincing basements not to flood and houses not to float away." They were also good at luring men—mostly men; some sirens lured women, and that was okay, too, except for the part where it wasn't okay at all—to watery graves. I figured that part probably didn't need to enter our discussion of do-it-yourself home improvement.

"You really do like turning to monsters to solve your problems, don't you?" asked Riley. He opened the door, revealing the barren hallway on the other side. He stormed inside, leaving me standing with Shelby on the steps.

"I'm really starting to understand why you nearly shot my cousin in the chest," I said.

"Things here aren't like they are in America," said Shelby, almost apologetically. She followed her father inside. "If it's any consolation, you've convinced me to appreciate monsters for what they are."

"I honestly don't know whether that helps," I said. "Should I shut the door?"

"Nah. It stays open when there's someone in here. Tells people to shout before they come stomping around the corner, reduces the odds of anybody getting stabbed without a good reason."

"What a lovely way of doing things," I said, trying to keep my voice low enough that Riley wouldn't hear me. "Do you get a lot of accidental stabbings around here?"

"Not as many as we did before we started leaving the door open," said Shelby, and followed her father down the hall. After a pause to absorb this information, I went after her.

The hallway leading to the central stock was as clean and generic as the rest of the house, if not more. No effort had been made to pretend that this was a place where people lived: the walls were barren, the carpet was industrial gray hardpack of the sort usually found in auto shops and hospital waiting rooms, and the air smelled faintly of gun oil. It was a sweet, indelible scent that seemed to have been worked all the way down into the walls, becoming a permanent part of the house. From cleaning out ammo dumps and helping my grandmother—Alice, the dimension-hopping one with the grenades—reorganize her stockpiles, I knew that it would take more than just soap and elbow grease to wipe that scent away. They could sell the house, and three families later, people would still be asking about that funny metallic scent in the basement.

I caught up with Riley and Shelby in short order. They were waiting for me in front of a large door with reinforced hinges. "The frame was built by one of our folks who used to rob banks for fun, before he decided to go straight and start working with the conservation movement," said Riley, without preamble. "The hinges are designed to be impossible to remove without damaging them, and there are patterns on the metal that couldn't be replicated without contacting the man who did the initial install. Anyone who opened this door did it with a key."

"Or was the man who did the initial install," I said, more out of reflex than because I thought it was an important concern. We already knew that whoever was trying to feed us to werewolves was working with, and hence a part of, the Thirty-Six Society. Since I was the only nonmember on the premises, and the only person not allowed to have a key, their security was a nice afterthought, but not anything that would actually keep our adversary—whoever it was—away from the bullets.

Riley snorted. "Have to throw aspersions wherever you can, don't you, Covenant boy?"

"Since you've started calling me 'Covenant boy' when I have never belonged to the Covenant of St. George, and am definitely of legal age, I don't think I'm the only one casting aspersions," I said. "We already know that whoever swapped out the silver bullets for painted lead ones is a part of the Society. Which means the only reason I can think of for you to be bragging about your security is because you don't want me to think I can just waltz in here and start shopping for a new set of throwing knives. I'll stop being a suspicious bastard if you will."

"Which means you're not going to stop, because Daddy's been a suspicious bastard since he was born," said Shelby. She turned to her father. "Alex isn't going to steal from us, all right? He has plenty of weapons of his own. Lots of nice sharp things he can stab people with if they annoy him. Lots of nice sharp things I can borrow, since we're getting married and that means I have a common-law claim to his knives. Now can we *please* get on with opening the door?"

Riley scowled—more at me than at Shelby—and produced a keychain from his pocket. It bristled with keys, flashlights, tape measures, and all the other pieces of detritus that tended to build up on a keychain that was used regularly. My father's keychain was quite similar. I swallowed the urge to smile. Riley probably wouldn't understand it, and I didn't want to cause any more trouble.

And then he unlocked and opened the door to the central store, and I stopped thinking of anything beyond gazing in impressed delight at the room—or rooms, really—on the other side.

"All right," I said. "This is excellent." The way the Tanners had been describing their storeroom had led me to picture a really big closet, impractical as that would have been for supplying the entire Thirty-Six Society with ammunition, weapons, and the other assorted pieces of gear they needed to do their jobs. I'd been off by a factor of at least ten. The room on the other side of the door looked like it took up most of the footprint of the house, an impression that was reinforced by the large support beams that appeared every eight feet or so, lending strength to the foundation. The space between those beams was packed solid with shelves. Fluorescent lights hung overhead, switching on as we moved into the room.

"Motion detectors," said Riley proudly. "They make sure we're not drawing too heavily on the local grid, and also prevent someone from forgetting to turn off the light when they just swung through to grab a fresh spool of fishing wire."

"We make little shopping trips constantly," added Shelby, walking past me to examine a shelf loaded down with nets of various sizes. All of them were carefully organized, and matched up with helpful labels identifying their weight, manufacturing material, and any special features. "If you're passing through Melbourne, you buy a few bales of chicken wire, or some fishhooks, or a bunch of dried meat and bottled water. Then it all gets funneled to the various stores around the continent. That way nobody ever has to buy so much that it sets up a red flag in some government computer somewhere."

"It's uneven, of course," said Riley. "When our girls were younger, Lottie and I could barely afford to contribute enough to pay back what we'd taken, much less help build against the future. As they got older, and we got more free income, we've increased our contributions. To each according to his or her need."

"I've been sending money home," said Shelby. She sounded distracted. It wasn't hard to see why: this place was like a cryptozoologist super store. I found myself taking internal notes to share with my family when I got home. There was a lot here that we could learn from, when it came to organizing and preparing ourselves for any disaster the world happened to throw our way.

"The specialized ammunition is this way." Riley started down one of the aisles, clearly expecting me and Shelby to follow. We did, past rows of knives, hanging racks of khakis and bulletproof vests, and into a square-shaped construction of shelves loaded down with ammo boxes. Again, the omnipresent labels made it clear what each of them contained. The shelf labeled "silver" was conspicuously denuded, with only about twenty boxes of ammo remaining, spread out across a variety of calibers.

"May I?" I asked, indicating the shelf.

Riley nodded, not saying a word. I took that for consent, and reached for the first box that came to hand. The label identified its contents as .9-millimeter, and the weight of it supported that; it was heavy enough to have contained silver bullets, and it rattled appropriately when I hefted it in my hand.

I opened the lid. I looked at the bullets. I scraped one of them gingerly with the edge of my thumbnail. And then I shook my head in disgust, replacing the box on the shelf. "Painted," I said. "We'd need to do chemical composition tests to be sure, but I'm willing to say that I don't think there's a speck of real silver in that box. Your bullets are gone."

"How can you be so sure?" Riley demanded. "They weigh the same. They shoot the same."

"Yes, but you don't usually wrap real silver bullets in embossing foil," I said. "They're fakes."

Silver bullets are expensive as all hell, in part because their manufacture is so difficult. They can't be pure silver: the metal's too soft, and it would warp inside the barrel of the gun, either causing a dangerous misfire or resulting in a slug too twisted to have any real force behind it. Bullet makers who want to work with silver need to find the exact right balance of alloys, silver, and lead to come up with something that will be effective against the sort of things you hunt with silver—lycanthropes, for instance—but will still work in a standard gun. Even a "pure" silver bullet will generally be at least half lead by weight. That means you can't tell them apart just by lifting the ammo box.

Just by lifting the ammo box . . . I turned a thoughtful eye on the other shelves. "Someone who stole this much silver ammo would have trouble carrying it out without being seen, even under this sort of security setup," I said thoughtfully. "How much stock do your people put in the labels?"

"When I was seven, I got into the stores and swapped a bunch of twine weights around. I thought they looked better that way," said Shelby. "I was grounded for a week without desserts."

"We take our organizational system very seriously," said Riley. "Why?"

"Because if I were planning to try sabotaging you, I'd need a heat source—maybe some sort of portable lamp, you can buy them at most camping goods stores—and a bunch of silver foil." I turned my eye toward the other shelves, looking for anything that seemed out of place. All the little cardboard boxes were neatly labeled with the caliber of the bullets they contained, stacked in even towers and pushed back until they formed level planes. It was a good system. It would make it easier to put things away; no wasted space, no mess, no inefficiency. And nothing to betray someone who really understood how it was supposed to work. Anyone who had been involved in the restocking process would know how to move things, how to conceal them . . . how to hide whatever they'd purloined in plain sight.

"What's the most common caliber among the Thirty-Six Society?" I asked.

"We use .300 for most of our hunting rifles," said Riley. "It works on kangaroos and emu, and they're the things we're most likely to feel all right about shooting if we have to. Plus they're delicious. I won't pretend that's not a factor."

"Good to know," I said, still scanning the shelves. "How common is .45?" That was the caliber I habitually carried for city work. I'd be able to tell if anything major had been done to the bullets without more than a cursory inspection.

"Not terribly. Too big to be good for a small carry weapon, too small to take out a charging buck that wants to see your intestines on the ground."

"Okay." I crouched down and began moving boxes of bullets aside on the shelf labeled LEAD—.45. Riley made a noise of protest. Shelby shushed him.

The first two layers of boxes looked like they belonged there. I pushed them aside, continuing to dig. The third layer . . . the boxes there looked ever so slightly newer than the ones in front of them, like they had spent less time on the shelves. That should have meant they'd be at the front, unless someone came down here and rotated the contents of the shelves on a regular basis—and if they did that, then there shouldn't have been older boxes visible to the back when I pushed another column aside, releasing the dry, dusty smell of aging cardboard.

"Gotcha," I said. I pulled a box of bullets out of the middle stack and straightened, opening it. The top layer was normal, lead bullets in simple brass casings. I picked them up, revealing a second layer where the casings gleamed dull silver, like dimes that had transferred hands too many times. Scraping my thumbnail against these bullets didn't bring up any scraps of foil; they were the real deal. I tilted the box toward Shelby and Riley, showing them what I'd found.

"No one saw anyone carrying out a bunch of stolen silver bullets because they didn't carry them out," I said. "They just moved things around to make sure no one would realize what had happened."

"They mixed the bullets, too," said Shelby, looking horrified. "Oh, God, we're going to have to do a complete inventory."

"Do you keep medications down here? Herbal supplies? Antivenin?" The looks of increasing despair on both Shelby and Riley's faces were enough to tell me that I was on the right track. I resisted the urge to groan as I made the box of silver bullets disappear into my pocket. We were going to have plenty of evidence of what had happened here, and I was raised never to pass up an opportunity to reload—especially given the number of my silver bullets Shelby had used out in the meadow. "I don't recommend using *anything* down here until it's been thoroughly looked over. We don't know what our antagonist's goals are, and that makes this whole room potentially dangerous."

"They tried to kill us," said Riley.

"I noticed," I shot back. "The question is, were they trying to kill *you*, and your family, or are they planning to take out the entire Society like that? If I were the werewolf—"

"Oh, good, this is exactly the sort of thing you should be saying to my father who doesn't like you," muttered Shelby.

I ignored her. This wasn't the time to be worrying about Riley's desire to introduce me to a shallow unmarked grave. He would have plenty of time to plot my death, but only if we survived the next few days. I started again: "If I were the werewolf, I'd be looking to take out the people I was sure would fight my authority, and then I'd start trying to infect the rest. Imagine what a thinking werewolf could do with the resources of the Thirty-Six Society at his or her disposal. Since the local cryptids don't really know you, they wouldn't notice the change. Not until your people came for them in their beds."

"Why would my people do that?" asked Riley. "Even if they'd been turned into werewolves, they'd still know that the policy regarding monsters is hands-off and eyes away."

"Because infected humans are monsters, plain and simple," I said. "They kill without remorse when they're transformed, and without consideration for how it may look on the global stage. And most sapient cryptids hate lycanthropes for that reason, so you can bet they'll talk if the werewolf outbreak here becomes bad enough—which means the Covenant *will* hear about it, and they *will* step in. They'll have to. They're murderous bastards who overstep their mission statement on a regular basis, but they're good at what they do. Saving Australia from lycanthropy would fit the bill."

"How would the Covenant even find out? We're isolated here. Besides, why would the Covenant listen to anything a bunch of monsters had to say? And that's assuming they have a line on rumors coming off this continent to begin with." Riley shook his head. "I think you're borrowing trouble."

I took a deep breath, trying to find something—anything—else that I could say.

It wasn't there. "My sister is marrying a man who used to belong to the Covenant of St. George. I bet he still knows how to get hold of his former coworkers. If I die here, that will be a tragedy, but it's not going to cause my family to take any permanent steps. If the entire Thirty-Six Society goes radio silent, at the same time that the local cryptids begin reporting an out-of-control mob of werewolves rampaging across the continent . . ." I let my voice trail off, trusting Riley and Shelby both to be smart enough to understand what I wasn't saying.

Shelby's look of slow dismay told me that she understood. I focused on Riley. Instead of opening up in comprehension, his face shut down, becoming so smooth and expressionless that I could no longer guess at what he might be thinking.

"It would be a bloodbath," he said, voice gone hollow. "They'd have no one to stop them. They could cleanse this continent the way they wanted to a hundred and fifty years ago. You have to contact your family. You have to tell them not to contact the Covenant. I was a fool to think we could trust you, even for a few minutes. You should never have been allowed out of the airport."

"I'm sorry, sir, but I won't do that." Quickly, before Riley's mood could turn murderous, I explained, "If the werewolves overrun the Society, they'll overrun the continent. They'll kill everyone. Maybe that would be considered an acceptable loss by some people—we have a lot of humans, and we only have one Australia—but werewolves are human when untransformed. They'd get on planes. They'd get on cruise ships. They'd *spread*. Australia would become an unending plague pit spreading destruction and despair across the world. The ecosystem would be devastated by the introduction of that many apex predators, and more, the Covenant would still get involved. It would just happen later, after the veil of secrecy that keeps their business from the eyes of the world was shattered." It was hard to force the words out. I felt like a traitor. And everything I was saying was the truth.

Shelby put a hand on her father's arm. "They used to work in the open, Daddy. They used to go wherever they wanted, killing whoever they wanted, because all they had to do was point a finger and say 'monster' if they wanted to be believed. If we let the werewolves have Australia, the Covenant will get all that power back again. Do you want to be responsible for that?"

Riley turned and looked at her, face still expressionless. Then, calmly, he reached up and removed her hand from his arm, pushing her away before he let go. "I knew when I let you go to America that it would change you," he said. "I assumed you'd come back a little less angry, a little wiser, a little more ready to accept your responsibilities. I thought, God forgive me, that you'd come home and help heal the wounds Jack left when he was taken from us. But all you've done is make things worse for yourself, and for us. You've been corrupted. If I can take any consolation from this situation, it's that your brother didn't live to see it."

He turned away from her, leaving her white-faced and gasping, and fixed his attention on me. "We'll do a full inventory; we'll find the missing silver bullets, and we'll determine how much other damage has been done. I will support whatever you propose for finding the wolves in our flock, and for resolving the threat that they pose. And then I will drive you to the airport myself. You will never come back here. Do I make myself perfectly clear?"

"Yes, sir," I said.

"Good." He turned and strode away into the maze of shelves, heading for the distant door.

I slumped, leaning against the nearest shelf. "That didn't go as well as I'd hoped." The lights came on as he walked, marking out his progress in a brightly lit chain of electrical reactions.

"You did threaten to call the Covenant on his country," Shelby said, moving to lean next to me. "You can't blame a man for being a little shirty when you hold up his worst nightmare like it's something reasonable to threaten him with. Even if it *is* something reasonable; even when it's not a threat." She sighed deeply. "Alex, what are we going to do?"

"Honestly, I don't know." I watched the lights. "If the werewolves have decided to start some kind of organized attack, we're in for a world of trouble. You get that, right?"

"In this particular situation, the world can go hang," said Shelby. "I'm worried about my country. Don't get me wrong—if Daddy is serious about manually deporting you, I'll be coming along, and we'll settle the 'where are you kids going to live' conversation the cheap and easy way. But Australia will always be my country. I can spend the rest of my life in America. I'm ready to do it, if it means staying with you. That isn't going to change where I come from."

I didn't say anything. I was watching the lights, which were continuing to blink on as Riley walked across the warehouse-like room.

Shelby nudged my knee with her own. "That would be a good wedding slash engagement gift, you know. You could play St. Patrick, only do it with werewolves in Australia, instead of snakes in Ireland."

"Hang on a second," I said, and frowned. Something about the lights was bothering me. They were on motion sensors, but the way they were turning on and off . . .

"What?" Shelby followed my gaze to the lights. Out of the corner of my eye I saw her frown mirror my own. "Well, that's silly. Something must be wrong in the circuitry again, we haven't been anywhere near that corner of . . . the room . . ." Her voice trailed off as understanding struck her. It struck me in the same instant, and then the two of us were running after Riley, moving in perfectly matched silence as we raced against those changing lights.

Riley hadn't gone anywhere near the far corner of the room, not unless he'd gotten turned around on his way to the door, but that didn't make any sense, since there was a clear path of lights leading back the way we'd all originally come, marking his progress. No, these lights had another source. Someone else was in the room.

We ran.

Twelve

"Little pitchers have big ears, and sometimes that means they also have big guns.
Be careful what you say, when you say it,
and know who might be listening."

—Alexander Healy

*The underground survivalist stockroom of an isolated
house in Queensland, Australia, running like hell*

WHEN I WAS A child, my parents used to put my sisters and me through every kind of drill imaginable.
Other kids played games. We prepared for a war everyone prayed we'd never have to fight, but that everyone
involved knew wouldn't show us any mercy if we were
unprepared. We learned how to navigate by the stars, by
the patterns of moss on trees, and by the calls of certain
types of bird. We learned how to lay snares and dig pit
traps.

And of course, we learned how to reload a gun while
running full-tilt across a basement full of blind alleys and
obstructed views.

I pulled the box of pilfered silver bullets from my
pocket and snapped my pistol's chamber open, slotting
bullets into place as I ran. It was tricky work, but I'd done
it before—those drills had been good for something after

all—and I only dropped one, despite the pain in my arm. We didn't stop running to pick it up. Our lives, and Riley's life, were worth more than a single silver bullet.

We didn't dare yell: if Riley was being stalked, but not actually attacked, any noise could make things worse. Not that it made a difference. We had just come around another corner and could finally see the wall when the screaming started. *"Daddy!"* shrieked Shelby, putting on a burst of speed that would have made any track star proud.

It was a burst of speed I couldn't match. I did my best to catch up, putting my head down and running like hell, but the gunshots still beat me. I swung around a set of shelves, making a split-second assessment of the situation. There was Shelby, gun in her hands, standing over her father, who was crumpled on the floor in a spreading pool of blood. He was clutching his left arm; the werewolf in the basement had bitten him in the same place that the one in the woods had bitten me.

The werewolf itself was about five feet from Shelby, black-furred and red-eyed and gathering itself to spring. Its lips were drawn back, revealing a jaw filled with sharp canine teeth. The drool pooling at the corners of its mouth made my heart skip a beat. Lycanthropy spreads via fluid transfer. A dry bite—like the one I'd been lucky enough to receive—won't necessarily spread the infection. A good juicy bite, on the other hand . . .

"Shelby! *Down!*" I shouted. She didn't turn. She just hit the ground on her elbows, going down hard in the pool of her father's blood. The werewolf's head whipped around to face me, lips drawing back even farther, a growl vibrating up from the depths of its chest. I took a deep breath, stabilized my stance, and opened fire.

My first bullet caught the werewolf in the center of its chest: I had aimed for the point of greatest mass, judging it as the best way to stop the thing before it slammed into Shelby. It howled. I fired twice more, hitting it in the shoulder and the forehead.

The third shot did it. The werewolf collapsed in a heap, emptying its bladder onto the floor. The smell of hot urine filled the air, overwhelming the smell of blood. That was a good thing, disgusting as it was: it meant the beast was almost certainly dead.

"Almost" doesn't count for a damn thing. I strode past Shelby, much as I ached to stop and help her up, and emptied my gun into the werewolf's head. The body jerked with every bullet, but that was all. It didn't twitch or try to get up. It was well and truly dead.

"Daddy!"

The werewolf was dead, but Riley wasn't . . . and given the amount of drool the beast had been generating, that might mean we had another werewolf on our hands. I turned, arms hanging loosely at my sides, to see Shelby now huddled against her father's chest, her arms wrapped tight around him, sobbing. Riley wasn't holding her. He was just sitting there, a befuddled expression on his face, bleeding on the floor and staring at the crumpled werewolf.

"Shelby." She didn't move. I tried again: "*Shelby*. I need you."

"Is it dead?" Shelby peeled her face away from her father's shoulder and twisted to follow his gaze to the fallen werewolf. "It's dead." The relief in her voice was indescribable, and it made me want to hug her, almost as much as it made me want to get her out of the room. "You killed it. Thank you, Alex. Thank you so much."

"Don't thank me yet," I said grimly. I tilted my head back and checked the ceiling. The lights seemed to be behaving normally now: they were only on in the small slice of room that we occupied. That didn't necessarily mean anything. This space was massive, and the trouble with motion detectors is that most of them aren't sensitive enough to pick up on someone who decides to hold perfectly still. Breathing is not going to keep the lights on. I started reloading my gun as I swung my attention back around to Shelby. "I need you to go find your mother and bring her back here. Bring at least two people with guns, and have someone call Dr. Jalali. We're going to need her."

Shelby blinked, relief melting into incomprehension. "Why do we need Dr. Jalali? The werewolf is dead. You killed it."

"This isn't a movie, Shelly," rumbled Riley. He sat up a little straighter, seeming to snap out of whatever fugue he had fallen into. "Killing the master werewolf doesn't make everyone it's bitten go normal again. If it did, we would have wiped them out centuries ago. It's a virus, and I've been bitten."

"Dr. Jalali isn't a mammal, and that means she'll be able to treat your father without worrying about blood-borne contamination. He's not infectious yet, but not all the blood is his." As I spoke the words, I finally *saw* how much blood was on Shelby's skin and clothing. She was practically marinating in the stuff, and it was all I could do to hold my position rather than running over and yanking her to her feet, away from her father, away from possible contamination. I resisted. "Shelby, you need to go, and you need to take a thorough shower before you come back here. Please."

She would also need to be checked for open wounds, for cuts on her hands and face—what if she'd skinned her palms when she fell? Oh, God, what if she'd hit the floor so hard that she'd broken the skin on her elbows? She'd been *kneeling* in the pool of blood, and there was no way of telling Riley's blood from the dead werewolf's. They could both be infected. I could lose her.

I'd only been in Australia since yesterday, and was not very impressed with it thus far.

"Please, Shelly," added Riley. "I've got Alex to watch over me. He'll make sure I don't get eaten by anything else that might be lurking."

Shelby looked from him to me, uncertainty plain, before climbing to her feet. She slipped twice in the blood, smearing it across the industrial carpet, and I had to once again fight to keep myself from running to her side. "I will be *right* back," she said. "Daddy, don't you do anything stupid while I'm away. Alex, don't you let him do anything stupid. I'll never forgive you if you do." Then she whirled and ran out of the room, leaving bloody footprints in her wake. They were going to need a full decontamination crew in here, and even then, it might be a good idea to rip up and burn the carpet. There was no telling how long lycanthropy could live in cloth.

"We need a virologist," I muttered. "Why didn't I ask Helen if she could find us a virologist?"

Riley was scowling at the fallen werewolf. "In the movies they always turn back when they die," he said. "How are we supposed to know who this fucker was if it doesn't turn back into a human?"

"We don't know that it started off as a human," I said— although if it hadn't, that meant someone would have had to let it in, which left us with at least one werewolf unaccounted for. I really, really hoped this one had been human when it started. "I think it's likely, but it could also have been a large dog, or a kangaroo, or even a sheep. When Helen gets here, after she takes care of you, I'll see if I can get her to perform a superficial examination. We can at least determine whether the werewolf was male or female, which cuts our potential suspect pool in half. What did Shelby mean by 'don't do anything stupid'?"

"She was telling me not to shoot myself." Riley sounded calm, like admitting that his own daughter was concerned he would commit suicide was perfectly normal. "We don't have much experience with infectious monsters here, but we have plenty of venomous ones. A few of them, there's no treatment, there's no cure; there's just rotting from the inside out while you wait for your family to give you permission to die. Most people who get bitten choose to take the easy route to the grave, and no one blames them. It's one hell of a way to go." His gaze flicked back to the dead werewolf. "Of course, so is this. It might be kinder if I shot myself."

"Please don't," I said. "I don't want Shelby to be that mad at me."

To my surprise, Riley actually laughed. "Believe me, son, neither do I, and under the circumstances, I'd probably wind up stuck haunting the place. I won't swallow my gun. Besides, the way I'm bleeding, it may be a moot point."

Bleeding. Shit. "Are there medical supplies in here? There must be, you told me that there were. Where are they?"

"We don't know—"

"I know how to check the seal on a package of gauze. We can stop the bleeding, even if we can't trust any of the medications. As long as you keep an eye on the lights and shout if anything changes, I should be safe to go and come back."

"And if there's another werewolf out there, just waiting for you to split the party?" The look Riley gave me was calculating and calm. "How do I explain your corpse to Shelby?"

"I could ask you the same question, you know." I shrugged. "Someone's explaining something either way, and I'd rather be able to at least say I tried to make sure you could attend our wedding. Now, which way do I go to find the first aid?"

Riley raised a hand—which was shaking slightly; the blood loss was getting to him, even if he was struggling not to show it—and pointed down the row of shelves to my left. "Go six shelves that way, make a right, and you won't be able to miss what you're looking for."

"Good." I stepped close enough to put my box of silver bullets down at the edge of the spreading bloodstain. "Reload, and be ready." Then I turned and took off running, heading in the direction Riley had indicated.

The Thirty-Six Society took their stockpiling *very* seriously. I swung around the corner six shelves in, and found myself confronted by three racks of nothing but gauze, bandages, antiseptics of various kinds, suture kits, and other basic first aid supplies. Even if our werewolf or werewolves had been sabotaging the place, they couldn't possibly have damaged as much as was in front of me. I began quickly grabbing things off the shelves, checking to be sure that their seals and packaging were intact, and then moving on to the next item I thought I might need. In the end, I had several rolls of gauze, a bottle of hydrogen peroxide, a suture kit—for Helen, not for me, as there was only so much I was willing to do in the name of saving Shelby's father—and a box of latex gloves. I spared one last glance at the overhead lights, confirming that they hadn't changed, and then went running back.

Riley was still sitting up in the same position when I raced into view. He lifted his head, eyes gone dull and tired, and said, "Took you long enough. What, did you have to run back to America for just the right brand of cotton ball?"

"I still beat Shelby and the others back," I said, walking to the edge of the bloody puddle and kneeling. I rolled the hydrogen peroxide toward him. Let it get covered in blood. It wasn't like he presented a biohazard to himself. "Uncap this and pour it over your wound. We want to try flushing it out as much as we can."

"What, I didn't die passively, so now you're actively trying to kill me?" asked Riley, brows rising.

I shook my head. "The hydrogen peroxide won't hurt you, it will flush the wound. It's not antiviral, but it will still remove at least some of the virus that hasn't entered your body yet. Please, work with me here." I opened the box of gloves, pulling out a pair.

"I haven't given you much reason to *want* to work with me," said Riley, uncapping the bottle. He sniffed its contents once, suspiciously, before upending it over his injured arm. "Damn, that stings," he said, clenching his teeth. The hydrogen peroxide bubbled and foamed as it came into contact with the blood.

"Good," I said. "Now take off your shirt."

Riley gave me a flat look.

"I need to see the wound if I'm going to stop the bleeding." I held up a roll of gauze. "Shirt. Off. I'm not going to do anything Dr. Jalali will object to when she gets here, I promise. You get to keep your arm, and you'll have some fun scars to show off a year from now."

"Assuming I'm not big, hairy, and dead by then," said Riley, his gaze drifting back to the dead werewolf. He hauled his bloody shirt off over his head, revealing a torso that was ridged with the lines of scars both old and long-healed and relatively new. The wound on his arm stood out red and angry against the rest. "Are you seriously planning to marry my daughter?"

"As long as she'll have me, yes," I said. I walked over to crouch beside him, careful not to lose my balance. "Lift your arm. I need to get this tied off."

Riley obliged. Blood loss must have been making him suggestible. "She's always been my favorite, you know. A man tries not to play favorites with his kids, but it just can't be helped, and Shelly . . . ah, she was special from the start. Jack was my friend, but she was my angel. I didn't like her leaving. I certainly didn't like her coming back with a man from a Covenant family."

"Sorry," I said. Wrapping a werewolf bite was a lot like wrapping a snakebite, only larger. I wanted to cut off the bleeding without trapping any venom—or werewolf saliva, as the case might be—inside the wound. I focused on that, rather than looking at Riley's face. "And I'm not from a Covenant family. We quit generations ago."

"Ah, not your fault." Riley shifted positions slightly, making it easier for me to get at his arm. "I'm never going to like you. We're not the sort of men who get along. You probably won't like me either, once you're safely married to my daughter and allowed to admit it to yourself."

"Believe me, sir, I have no trouble admitting that I don't like you right this second. I don't need to be married to Shelby to tell you that I don't care for the way you've behaved toward me, or your attitude toward sapient cryptids. But that doesn't mean I don't understand." I tied off the gauze and sat back on my haunches. "I also understand about playing favorites, and not wanting to let the people you love out of your sight."

"That's not going to stop you taking her away from me."

I raised my head and looked at him solemnly before I went back to applying more gauze to his arm. "That's because I'm *not* taking her away from you. Shelby's a grown woman. She makes her own choices. I'm lucky in that she's choosing to spend at least part of her life with me, and I'm going to do my best to make it the rest of her life—and before you say something about my getting her killed, I'd like to note that I'll be working with her to make that life as long as possible. I never thought I'd meet a woman like her, and I'm not stupid. I'm not going to gamble with her heart, because there's no guarantee I'll ever get this lucky again."

"So you're saying she's taking herself away from me."

"No, I'm saying that you're shoving her." I tied a last loop of gauze in place and stood, moving away from him. "I'm going to marry your daughter, Mr. Tanner. I'm going to work very hard to be a good husband, and to give her the life she deserves. If you want to be a part of that life, maybe you should stop pushing, and start listening."

Riley opened his mouth to answer, and was cut off as Charlotte, Raina, and six other Thirty-Sixers hurled themselves through the doorway and into the room. They stopped shy of running into the bloody puddle, proving that they understood contagion. "Riley!" cried Charlotte, and the sound of her voice nearly broke my heart.

"Hello, sweetheart," he said, mustering a wan smile.

I moved around the puddle to the other side, where I caught the eye of one of the men—North, I realized—and said quietly, "You need to move him to the quarantine building, and then you need to search this whole room. The werewolf was waiting in here for us. I don't think there are any more unpleasant surprises, but there's only one way to know for sure."

"On it," said North, with a quick, decisive nod.

"Thank you," I said, and walked past him, out into the hall, and away.

I found Shelby in the downstairs bathroom of the small house being used for quarantine. She was sitting, still fully-clothed, next to the tub, her head in her hands. She raised it when she heard my footsteps, just enough to see that it was me, and then dropped it back down. "Is he alive?" she asked.

"He is," I confirmed. I had removed my bloody shoes when I got out of the already-contaminated basement hall. I tossed them into the bathtub, and followed them with my shirt, which needed to be either sterilized or burnt, depending on what our resources looked like. I moved to the sink to start washing my hands. The latex gloves had protected me from the majority of the biohazard risk, but it was better to be safe than sorry. "I managed to stop the bleeding, and your mother's with him now. Did you reach Dr. Jalali?"

"I did," she said. "She's going to meet us here."

"Good. How are your elbows?" I tried to make the question as light as possible, but it fell into the space between us like a lead balloon, heavy with meaning and with weight I didn't want it to have. Some things are unavoidable.

"I didn't break the skin, if that's what you're asking." Shelby finally raised her head. She leaned against the side of the tub, looking at me dully. There was a bloodstain over her left breast. "Is he going to be all right?"

"I don't know." I shook the water off my hands and moved to crouch next to her. "You need to take that shirt off. Please."

Shelby looked down, saw the blood, and sighed before pulling her shirt off over her head. It joined mine in the bathtub. "Can she check me, too?"

"Once we're finished examining and treating your father, I think that would be a good idea." It wasn't a good idea for me to touch her, under the circumstances; we still didn't know whether she'd been exposed, or whether a few specks of infected blood might have somehow made their way under my bandages. I still reached out and rested the back of my hand against her cheek for a moment. "Are you all right?"

"No," Shelby admitted in a small voice. "I'm really not. He's my *daddy*, Alex. He's not supposed to get ripped up by werewolves right in front of me. That's not . . . this isn't how any of this was supposed to happen. Why is everything happening like this?"

"I don't know," I said quietly. "I think sometimes the world doesn't really care about how we feel. It just keeps on turning, and we're expected to do whatever we have to in order to keep up."

"Fuck the world," Shelby said, and buried her face in her hands again.

For once, I didn't have anything to say, and so I didn't say anything. I just stayed in the bathroom while she stripped down and showered, washing the chance of infection away. I kept the door open just a crack, waiting for the sound of Riley and the others arriving. Then we changed places, letting me get cleaned up while Shelby went and got me a change of clothes.

We had so much work to do, and we still didn't fully understand what the enemy wanted. We just had to hope that we could figure it out in time.

Thirteen

"There is evil in the world. Things might be easier if there wasn't, if good and evil were just concepts men invented to justify themselves; we could ignore them, then. Sadly, good and evil are both very real, and very inconvenient."

—Martin Baker

Sitting on the front porch of a secluded guesthouse in Queensland, Australia

IT WAS A BEAUTIFUL night. I could see the lights on in the main house from where I sat on the guesthouse porch. Jett was stretched out next to me with her head down on her paws, while my hands rested limply on my knees. The front door was open, and noises drifted down the stairs as Riley and his various companions dealt with their own issues. Technically, since it was full dark and the moon was up, I should have been locked in my own room, waiting for morning to prove that I wasn't a werewolf yet: that was the deal I'd agreed to in order to buy my own transitory freedom. Deals seemed to have fallen by the wayside, under the circumstances.

Someone stepped on the porch beside me. I held up my hand, and was rewarded with a cool glass bottle being pressed into my palm. I lowered my arm and took a swig. Ginger beer. Sharp, sweet and bitter at the same time, and nonalcoholic. A good choice.

"All right, now you need to explain yourself." Dr. Helen Jalali sat next to me, giving me a quizzical side-long look. She had a ginger beer of her own, and her lab coat was pristinely white, serving as a symbol of her office and a "do not shoot the person wearing me" at the same time. "How did you know it was me, and how did you know I was bringing you a drink?"

"Wadjet have a very specific stride," I said. "It took me a while to figure out how you distribute your weight, but after spending a year dealing with Chandi and her constant demands to see her fiancé, I caught on. There's only one wadjet here, so it had to be you."

"And the drink?"

"Lucky guess." I took another swig. "What did the mice say?"

Helen sighed. "They said the infection was in him. I've patched his wounds and given him the anti-lycanthropy treatment, and I've agreed to come back the next three days to treat him again. He's still very much in the woods. We could lose him. I'm not going to lie to you about that."

That explained why Shelby hadn't come out. All three Tanner sisters were inside, as was their mother, and they had more than enough on their plates at the moment. I would have been a distraction. "How's he taking it?"

"Surprisingly well," she said, shaking her head. "He thanked me for my service. Thanked me! A Thirty-Sixer! Honestly, that alone was worth getting involved in this whole sordid mess. I never thought I'd live to see the day."

"This isn't the time to go into the whole history of colonization in Australia," not with God only knew how many werewolves still roaming Queensland, "but what is the deal with you and the Society? I thought they had rejected Covenant teachings."

"They did and they didn't." Helen took a swig of ginger beer. "This happened before I was born, all right? I wasn't here for any of it. My family didn't even move here until two generations ago."

"Secondhand knowledge at least gives me someplace to start," I said.

"Just so we're clear," said Helen. "The Thirty-Six Society rejected the Covenant not because they were perfect paragons of equality and enlightenment. They just didn't like the idea of killing everything that already lived here. They sort of went 'Adam and the Garden' conservationist. Taking care of all the poor, misguided, unprotected animals that needed the benefit of their wisdom and experience and firearms."

"I'm guessing 'animals' that were capable of talking back didn't fit that mission statement," I said.

Helen nodded. "They've never been particularly nasty. I mean, we don't have to deal with being hunted through the streets or 'cleansed' out of our neighborhoods, not the way it would have been under the Covenant. But when the Covenant was first sent packing and the Society was getting itself organized, we had some rough elements show up thinking Australia was the new wild frontier, and that they could do anything they damn well wanted. The Society closed ranks damn fast after that happened. Said if something wasn't human, it deserved conservation, but it didn't get a voice in how that conservation happened. Between that and their approach to 'invasive species' . . ." Her tone turned bitter. "As if European settlers weren't the most invasive species this continent has ever seen. There are fewer than three hundred wadjet in the country, but some of the Society would be happy to send us all packing, because we don't 'belong here,' and somehow they do."

"That's not going to happen," I said. "I don't care if I have to move to Australia and spend all my time yelling at people; no one's getting deported or sent away. You're Australian citizens by virtue of birth, same as anyone else who was born or hatched or budded here. No one gets to tell you differently."

Helen smiled a little. "I knew there was a reason Kumari liked you. And it's not just that fabulous mammalian butt of yours."

I blinked at her, not sure what to say to that. Helen's laughter split the night like an ax, and we sat for a little longer in silence, waiting to see what the night was going to bring next.

It was nice to have a little bit of a break. I needed the time to think. Most of my life is lived in laboratories and offices, places where things go slowly enough that I can really consider my next move and what it's going to mean for the situation at hand. Since getting to Australia, it felt like I'd been rolling from argument to crisis to argument again. And that wasn't good. That wasn't how I did my best work.

"You're a doctor," I said abruptly. "What kind of doctor are you?"

"See, that's the sort of question I would have expected someone to ask before I was providing emergency medical care to the lot of you," said Helen. "I trained as an oncologist before I came out here as a general practitioner. It's an odd specialization, I'll admit, but it meant I didn't have to deal with as many humans before it was time for me to settle down and start a family of my own. The ones I saw, I saw a lot, and that let me learn how to deal with mammals better. I've been a GP long enough now to be quite good at it, if that's a concern. I can't catch most of the diseases you mammals carry. I get to do some good for the human populace, and keep admitting privileges and access to certain pharmaceuticals that my people have real use for."

"Sounds like everyone wins, then," I said. "How much do you know about the lycanthropy family?"

"Nasty business, related to rabies, and this is the first major outbreak I've heard of on this continent," she said. "We've had some issues with a few nasty strains in India, but I've never been there, so I don't have frontline experience."

"Right. Everything we have says that once someone is infected and capable of transforming, they're not really rational anymore—that they're essentially beasts in their transformed state. But the werewolves we're dealing with here are showing complex planning behaviors *while* transformed. They're capable of lying in wait while they let their targets get into position. It doesn't feel right somehow. It doesn't mesh with what we know about this disease."

Helen took a swig of her ginger beer, expression going thoughtful. "Didn't this start off as spillover from the therianthropes?" she asked. "It was their disease first."

"Yes," I agreed. "We think it originated with either the wulver or the faoladh. We've never really spent the time or resources to try to nail down the origins of the infection. Most of the likely origin points are firmly within Covenant territory, and knowing where rabies lurks naturally hasn't enabled us to cure it."

"Right. See, here's the thing. I've never met whatever that second one you said was, but I've met wulver. They're perfectly nice people, and they're not ravening beasts when they're transformed. A little impulsive, sure, and really offended if you try to play fetch with them—mostly because they *will* play fetch, and then they feel bad about letting their instincts take over—but still people. They're just people who look different."

"That doesn't match the data we have on werewolves," I said, a sick feeling starting to form in the pit of my stomach. "I think we've made a terrible mistake."

"What's that?" Shelby sounded weary. I turned to see her standing behind us. She had replaced her bloodstained shirt with one pilfered from the clothing we'd moved into my temporary room. It hung around her like a shroud, save where it caught on the slope of her breasts and became slightly, distractingly too small. She smelled like strawberry shampoo and industrial soap.

"How's your father?" I asked.

"Stable. He's kicked everyone out of the room except for Mum, and they're having a serious talk. There's going to be a flood of people through here as soon as everyone finishes regrouping. Raina's locked herself in the hall toilet. I think Gabby wants to do the same, except there's only one hall toilet. We still don't know who sent us to the meadow, and now everyone's so upset that I don't see how I'll be able to get them asking again, which puts it all on me." Shelby shook her head. "It's a mess, Alex, it's a stupid, horrible mess, and I don't know how we're going to clean it up. What was the terrible mistake?"

I blinked. "What?"

"Just as I came out here you said that we'd made a terrible mistake, and I know you're not as dumb as you sometimes want people to think you are, so whatever it was, it's something you don't want to say in front of me." Shelby wrapped her arms around herself like she was trying to ward off a chill, even though it was a pleasant, even balmy night. "What mistake? What did we get wrong?"

"Ah." I put my ginger beer aside and stood, trying to collect my thoughts. I would have had to tell her what I'd realized eventually: that was the nature of both our work and our relationship. Secrets get people killed. But I'd been hoping, on some level, to have a few minutes to work things through on my own. "Remember when I said that most werewolves were killed within the first month after their infection, when we followed the trail of carnage back to their lairs and put them down for their own sake?"

Shelby's expression hardened. "Yes," she said coldly, and I immediately regretted my words. Until we knew whether Riley was going to successfully fight off the infection, talking about werewolves in such absolutist terms was going to be a minefield.

"Helen just pointed something out to me. Lycanthropy

began as a therianthrope disease, and therianthropes aren't beasts when transformed. They may have different instincts—the mind is to some degree a plaything of the body—but they're still people." What I was about to say went against everything I had been raised to believe, and I had to wonder on some level whether my grandfather had known. Grandma Alice always said Grandpa Thomas was the smartest man she'd ever met, and he was the one who'd written most of our response plans for werewolf attacks. He'd also known, by then, that we were morally opposed as a family to anything that smacked of killing people for the crime of being dangerous.

Had he understood that werewolves were *too* dangerous to coexist with humans, thanks to the disease that made them, and written his instructions accordingly? He'd married into the family. He'd helped to shape it, both with his genes and with his teachings. But he'd never quite embraced the Healy line's odd form of pacifism.

"What are you saying?" asked Shelby slowly.

"I'm saying that therianthropes are people when they're transformed because they were people to begin with. We've always believed that werewolves became animals when they transformed, but maybe that's not the case. Maybe the problem is that we've always been dealing with *new* werewolves, who were still disoriented and panicked by their own transformations, and hence reacted like animals." And then there were the *actual* animals to be considered. Turning into a wolf didn't make a sheep or a cow any smarter—and once they had reached the stage of fully transforming, we wouldn't be able to tell them from a werewolf that started out as a human being. All werewolves looked essentially the same in their lupine forms, and they didn't change back after they were killed. So every infected animal reinforced the idea that werewolves were irrational killing machines, and meanwhile, we continued to ignore the threat of werewolves that had originally belonged to sapient species. Their heads might be muddled when they first got sick, but after . . .

After, they would be able to plan, if they lived long enough. They would be able to consider their actions, and adjust their tactics according to the way the people around them reacted. They would *learn*. And through it all, they would be motivated by two desires: to survive, and to spread. We knew from our interactions with lycanthropes of all kinds that they shared that much at least, regardless of their starting species or how long they had been infected. All lycanthropes wanted to spread the disease that had created them.

"Wait," said Shelby. "I thought you said werewolves couldn't think. That they were just dumb, violent animals. That's what you *said*."

"That's what I thought," I said. "We know the disease makes them short-tempered and angry, and we know they want to spread their infection—that's one of the major goals of *any* disease, and the various strains of lycanthropy are no different. But I think we can safely say, looking at what the werewolves here in Australia have been doing, that they're not just dumb animals. They're still capable of at least some degree of planning and tactical thinking while they're in their lupine forms."

"I'd guess the initial confusion probably lasts for two transformation cycles, maybe three," said Helen.

"That would account for eighty percent of the people infected with lycanthropy. Most werewolves don't make it past their first full cycle, much less two more," I said grimly. "We kill them when they're at their most bestial, and we never realize they could remember how to think. We've been winnowing out the most primitive werewolves from outbreak after outbreak, for centuries. How long had the outbreak been going on before we got here?"

"At least a month," said Shelby slowly. "We don't know when it started. It's not like the werewolves sent a card to let anyone know that they'd arrived in Australia."

A slow, sick certainty was beginning to gather in the pit of my stomach, too concentrated—too *right*—to be ignored. "The infection had time to become established, even if it didn't have time to spread very far," I said. "Members of the Society are trained to deal with various types of bite. You told me so yourself. What happens if someone gets bitten by something they don't believe is venomous?"

"Flush the wound, monitor it for signs of infection," said Shelby. "Most wouldn't even seek medical care. That's a silly thing to involve anyone else over."

"Which means a member of the Society could easily have been bitten and infected before anyone even knew that was a risk. Werewolves are infectious even when not transformed. Whoever it was treated their own wound and didn't tell anyone, because who wants to report being nipped by a sheep or a collie when they have bigger things to worry about?" The more I talked, the more reasonable this all felt, like this was exactly what had happened. It made sense; it matched up with all the facts we had. "Then, when their twenty-eight-day incubation was up . . ."

"If they were on patrol, they might not have been near anyone when they turned," said Shelby. "There's a lot of unpopulated land in Australia. If something got into the sheep, everyone would assume it was a dingo or a wild dog. Nobody jumps straight to 'werewolf.' That would just be silly."

"So our werewolf turned for the first time where there was no one around to hurt, woke up the next morning and . . . what? Just decided to keep it a secret?" I frowned. "That doesn't make sense."

"Of course it doesn't make sense to you, Alex. You were raised to think of monsters as if they were people," said Shelby, sounding frustrated. She glanced to Helen. "Sorry. No offense meant."

"Offense taken," said Helen, in unknowing echo of myself right after the incident in the sheep meadow. It would have been amusing under other circumstances. In the moment, it was just one more layer of tension on what was already an unbearable mound of discomfort and dismay. "I am not a monster. I am not a mammal, and maybe that's a problem for some people, but it doesn't make me a *monster*."

"I know," said Shelby. "I'm sorry, I'm a little stressed right now. Things aren't coming out like I mean them. I know you're not a monster. I've met your cousin, and her daughter, and they're very nice people. I've even met her husband, and while it's a little harder for me to think of him as a person—what with him being a giant snake and all—he was perfectly pleasant and didn't pump me full of hemolytic venom even a little bit. But I was raised with the word 'monster' on heavy rotation, and it's difficult to just cut it from my vocabulary overnight."

"Try," suggested Helen pleasantly.

"I will," said Shelby. She looked back to me. "If you got bit and turned into a werewolf, you'd go to your family, right? Tell them 'we have a problem,' and set up some sort of containment plan, something to keep you safe. They'd still look at you as if you were a person, because you'd still *be* a person to them. Your essential personhood isn't tied up in what species you are."

"But it doesn't work that way here," I said. More pieces were falling into place. "Someone gets bitten, not knowing they've been exposed to lycanthropy-w, transforms for the first time under conditions that don't lead to any homicides, turns back, and says 'well, I'm still the same person. I can't let those assholes back at home put a silver bullet in my head just because I went and caught a therianthropic cold.'"

"Lycanthropy acts on the brain the same way rabies does," said Helen. "They'd become paranoid, suspicious, violent, all without losing their original intelligence."

"All while surrounded by people who throw around the word 'monster' like it isn't a racial slur," I said. "That's basically a recipe for convincing a werewolf not to turn him or herself in."

"I'll take it one step worse for you," said Charlotte, emerging from the quarantine house. It wasn't clear how long she'd been standing inside and listening to our conversation. Long enough, judging by the pinched expression on her face. "If *I* were bitten by a werewolf, and *I* wanted to be able to keep myself safe from the people who'd been my allies, I'd start recruiting. After all, I'd know the selling points of the infection—all assuming I'd need them. Once someone's been bitten, they're probably a lot more willing to listen to a sales pitch that doesn't end in a shallow grave."

Graves. I stiffened, looking from Charlotte to Shelby and back again before I asked the question that was going to make me the least popular person on the porch—and that included Helen, who was still viewed as less than a person by most of the Society. "What did we do with Cooper's body?"

Charlotte stared at me, an expression of dawning horror on her face. "This way," she said, and started for the steps. The rest of us followed her, again, including Helen. Under the circumstances, she may have thought that staying with the group was the best way to stay alive. Honestly, I couldn't have advised her one way or another.

Given everything else the Thirty-Six Society had on the property, I had halfway been expecting them to have a proper morgue, complete with stainless steel storage drawers for the bodies of their fallen comrades and a convenient drain in the middle of the floor. It was almost a relief when Charlotte led our makeshift posse to a tin storage shed that looked like it had been purchased from a mail order catalog.

Helen was less reassured. "You keep dead bodies in *here?*" she demanded, gesturing to the shed doors with a sweep of one hand. "Actual dead humans? The sort you're not intending to eat later?"

"See, things like that are why some people have a less than positive view of nonhumans," said Shelby. Helen glared at her. Shelby shrugged. "I'm just saying."

"We can't afford the sort of refrigeration units that would keep bodies better preserved, and it's not like we ever keep them for long anyway," said Charlotte, undoing the padlock on the door. "As soon as we're sure the coast is clear, we'll take him out into the nearest billabong and feed him to the crocs." She was clearly hoping the body was still there. I shared the sentiment.

"What about his family?" Helen sounded scandalized.

"Cooper didn't have any family left, and if he had, they would have been allowed to come with us for the feeding." Charlotte swung the doors open. I tensed, waiting for the smell of rotting flesh to come wafting out. It didn't. Human bodies decay fast when they're actually dead. The absence of the stench was . . . well, it wasn't a good thing.

Charlotte took a step forward, squinting into the gloom. Then she stopped, and sighed, and said, "The rest of you ought to come and take a look at this. I think we have a problem."

"That's good," I muttered. "We needed a problem tonight. Everything was going far too smoothly, so it's obvious that we were people in need of a problem." I stepped up behind her.

Somehow, it wasn't a surprise when I saw the hole that had been ripped in the shed's rear wall. Whatever had made the opening had peeled the tin back like they were opening a can of sardines. I frowned at the jagged tears in the metal and stepped inside, ignoring the vague protests and exclamations of distress from my companions. The danger was past. Our werewolf had long since fled for more welcoming climes.

"Didn't any of you think to check for a *pulse?*" asked Helen. "I'd have thought that was basic logic."

"I checked," I said. "But I was bleeding out at the time. Did anyone else check?"

"Riley did," said Charlotte. She hesitated before adding, "Through gloves and a plastic sheet. We were taking precautions against infection, and you'd already said that he was dead."

"Again, bleeding out at the time," I said, turning back to face them. "There's no tearing from the outside. Cooper must have woken up once he'd recovered from his blood loss—and that's a good trick, really, I would have thought the amount of blood he'd lost would keep him out of commission for at least a little bit longer, even if it didn't kill him—and then torn his way out, rather than risking being caught here. Is there any way to unlock the door from the inside?"

"Why in the world would there be? No one ever gets stuck in there," said Charlotte. She sounded affronted, like I had just accused her of locking her children in the shed. That hadn't been my intention, but this didn't seem like the time or the place to get embroiled into another "what I actually meant was . . ." conversation. Speaking a common language didn't do much good when there were cultural and societal gulfs between you. "The door is always locked from the outside."

"Right. Then he would have had to tear his way out, even if he was trying not to be noticed." I snapped my fingers. "The ruckus when we got back from the meadow run. Everyone was there, ready and eager to accuse us of things, and it made so much noise that a little tin being torn on an isolated part of the property wouldn't even have been noticed. We know he has at least one accomplice. They could have whipped everyone into a frenzy."

Shelby leveled a flat look on me, eyebrows raised. I blinked.

"What?" I asked.

"If he had an accomplice capable of getting everyone

all worked up and mad, why not ask that same accomplice to open the padlock from the outside?" she asked. "Much easier. No need to rend metal for no good reason, less chance that someone's going to take a wrong turn and see the great gaping hole you've ripped in things."

"Yeah, but this was a fair scare, wasn't it?" asked Helen. We all turned to look at her. She shrugged. "I'm just saying. You open a door you thought was safely keeping things inside, and what you find is that a dead man has come back to life and ripped his way out through a wall. So now he's terrifying."

"And terrifying men are usually men you don't want to mess around with," I said, nodding. "Cooper knew that if we figured him out, we'd be coming here to confirm it—if he was just gone, what good would that do him? He'd be passing up a chance to scare the pants off us."

"We might have thought something stole his body to eat, and given him a little more time to get away," Shelby said.

Charlotte snorted. "Cooper? Nah. If he was going to do something like this, he'd do it as flashy as possible. He liked to come off quiet and then surprise everyone. That's the sort of fellow he was." Her face fell. "Is. And now he's a werewolf. Has he been a werewolf this whole time?"

"He was probably infected before you had any idea there was a risk. Now, he has control over his transformations," I said. "He's been a werewolf for at least three months, maybe longer. I'd say that he's been recruiting people from within the Society to help him out, based on what we've seen so far."

"Oh, my God." Charlotte put a hand over her mouth. "I think I'm going to be sick."

"I think I'm going to go back to the house and get the mice," I said. I shook my head. "We have to check everyone for infection. Anyone here could be a werewolf."

"Anyone except me," said Helen. "It's been lovely seeing you all, but I think I'm going to get the fuck out of here before something rips my head off. Please be sure to call if anything else that might kill us all fetches up, all right? A little advance warning would be *wonderful*."

"I'll make sure someone calls you," I said.

Helen nodded before turning and walking, with admirable briskness, back toward the road. I would have been uncomfortable about letting her go off alone, if not for two things: out of all of us, she had the least to fear from a rogue werewolf, and any werewolf had quite a bit to fear from *her*. Wadjet venom could rival taipan for strength, and at her age and general level of physical fitness, she was generating more than enough to kill anything that decided to cross her. It wasn't a solution to everything, as the wadjet of the world learned when the Covenant first entered India with guns in hand, but it would be enough to get her safely to the car.

"Mum, come on." Shelby took hold of her mother's arm, tugging gently. "We need to go with Alex. We need to call everyone together and explain what's going on."

"And while we're having meetings, how many of our new enemies will we be telling exactly what we know?" Charlotte shook her head, giving me a plaintive look. "Are you sure Cooper is our werewolf?"

"I don't think he's the original, no," I said. "Something bit him. Something brought the infection here. Maybe it was a game animal smuggled into the country by someone with more money than sense—that's how you got the manticore problem, isn't it? Or maybe it was a person, somebody who got bitten and then came here thinking that there was enough open space for them to disappear and never endanger anyone. Lycanthropy is rare enough that even most victims don't realize they can infect other mammals. They think that as long as they avoid humans, they're taking the proper precautions."

The sheep, and how calm they'd been about the Tanners, made me sure that Cooper was behind the ambushes. Looking into either the folklore around lycanthropy or the scant research that had been published (thinly veiled as explorations of a variant strain of rabies) would have made the spillover connection quickly evident to anyone who knew how to ask the right questions. He'd figured out that animals could be infected, and he'd used that knowledge.

"Still a cryptozoologist, even after changing species," I murmured.

"What's that?" asked Shelby.

"Nothing." I shook my head. "We need to move. I don't like us being out here on our own." Between the three of us, we had the silver bullets in my gun and whatever other weapons we happened to be carrying. I knew Shelby had a pistol and several knives, as did I; while I wasn't sure what Charlotte carried as a matter of course, Shelby had to have received her training *somewhere*, and I was willing to bet Riley hadn't been the one to teach his eldest daughter how to hide a pair of brass knuckles in a bra. And none of that would do any good, if it wasn't silver. Cooper had already shrugged off severe enough blood loss that he'd been pronounced dead, and one of the werewolves that had attacked us both—me sincerely, Cooper as part of whatever double-blind scheme they were trying to pull—had gotten up and walked away after being shot with almost a dozen lead slugs. Silver was the answer. Without it, we were sitting ducks.

"Agreed," said Charlotte. She turned and walked back toward the house. Shelby and I followed, not letting the space between us stretch to more than a couple of feet. Sending one scout ahead of the group was just asking to be cut off or separated, and we didn't need that tonight.

Shelby stuck close to me as we made our way back to the guesthouse, which I appreciated very much. I resisted the urge to take her hand, less because I was afraid of showing affection in front of her mother, and more because I needed to keep both my hands free in case of trouble. I should probably have been taking point, but I didn't think leaving our rear flank unguarded was a good plan. With no ideal options open to us, I was going to stay where I felt like I could do the most good, and that was next to Shelby.

Gabby and Raina were on the porch when we arrived in the yard, talking intently to Chloe. We were too far away to hear what they were saying, but judging by their posture and the sharp, unceasing motion of their hands, it wasn't anything they were going to repeat with their mother in range. Jett, who had been pressed against Raina's leg, pushed away from her new mistress and barked once in our direction, announcing our arrival. Gabby and Raina stopped talking as they turned to look at us. Chloe took advantage of the break in their concentration, first stepping back from the two, and then bolting down the porch steps.

It was really too bad for her that Shelby did the bulk of her work with large carnivores, and was accustomed to thinking like a predator. By the time Chloe's foot hit the pavement Shelby was there, a gun in her hand and a smile on her face. She shoved the muzzle of the former into Chloe's chest, digging it in with enough force that I knew the thinner woman was going to have a bruise.

"Going somewhere?" asked Shelby.

Raina hopped down the porch steps, coming to a stop behind Chloe. "She wanted us to shoot Dad," she reported, in a low, dangerous tone. "She came in here to say that if we didn't do the right thing on our own, she'd go to the Society and get them to *order* us to do the right thing."

Shelby looked horrified. "What about the quarantine period?" she demanded. "We've had people locked up in there for days!"

"*He* proves that you don't think the rules apply to you and your family," said Chloe, stabbing a finger at me to punctuate her statement. "Your little American boytoy should be shut away like the rest, but he's running free, because the rules don't apply to the high and mighty Tanner family. You really think anyone's going to believe that you'll keep Riley caged? He'll be free by morning, and then we're all doomed!"

"Shelby, can you keep her here?" My words seemed entirely out of place, given the situation. I needed to say them anyway.

Thankfully for me, Shelby understood the way my mind worked at least well enough not to question me. "Yeah," she said. "Go take care of whatever you need to do."

"I'll be right back," I said, and ran for the porch.

Even if the guesthouse hadn't been small and mostly comprised of closed doors, I would have had no trouble finding my room: all I had to do was follow the sound of high-pitched rodent voices chanting liturgies. I swung myself through the open door and found the entire congregation standing in a circle on the floor, some of them holding brightly colored feathers from unidentified local birds, others holding small candles of the sort commonly found on birthday cakes. Shelby's garrinna, Flora, was curled up on the bed with her forepaws crossed in the classic feline manner and her head cocked hard to the side in a perfect expression of avian fascination. All the mice stopped chanting as they turned to look at me. Flora raised her head and mantled her wings, giving a screech of welcome.

I was, for once, speechless. It seemed the mice were, too. Then, as one, they began waving their feathers and candles and shouting, "HAIL! HAIL THE GOD OF SCALES AND SILENCES, CONQUEROR OF WERE-WOLVES!"

"That is *not* going to become a part of my official title," I said sternly. I crouched, putting myself more on a level with them. "I need three mice to come with me. The mission will be a dangerous one. I cannot guarantee the safety of any who choose to volunteer. I can promise you that I will do my very best to keep you from harm, and that should I fail, I will carry the weight of my failure for the rest of my living days."

Aeslin mice never forget anything. They don't hold the rest of the world to the same lofty standard, which is a good thing, or we would be forever breaking their tiny, fragile hearts. For them, an offer of memory by one of their gods was the greatest of all possible honors. I just hoped I wouldn't have reason to make good on my promise. "What do you need us to do?" squeaked the priest, lowering its feather. "We are at your Service."

"The werewolf we came here to find is cleverer than we suspected, and has done more damage than we feared," I said. "We need to check people for signs of infection. We suspect that it's been biting them and then coaching them through their first change, bringing them back only when they can control their tempers." It occurred to me that there might be some sort of master schedule I could consult, something that would tell me who had taken sick or vacation days, and when. Back home, it would have been virtually impossible for one of us to be bitten by a werewolf and disappear for a week without someone taking notice. Maybe I'd get lucky, and it would work the same way here.

I hadn't been getting lucky very often.

"No bitten thing can control their temper," said the priest, sounding dubious. "It may Seem So, but that will be Mere Illusion. Given time enough, they will slip. The bonds they construct around themselves will break, and the Beast will be Freed."

"That's what I'm afraid of," I said. "Will you help me?"

"A moment," squeaked the mouse gravely, before turning back to the congregation. The circle constricted, becoming something more closely akin to a huddle, and they began murmuring, squeaking, and otherwise talking amongst themselves. I resisted the urge to lean closer and try to listen in. They deserved to make this decision without feeling like I was judging them.

Finally, all six mice turned to look at me expectantly.

"We will Come," squeaked the priest. "But you must Choose."

I blinked. "What?"

"I cannot claim this Honor as my own, for I am responsible for the Lives under my Care," said the priest. "But you are responsible for the Heavens and the Earth, and the lives of mice and men must be as tools to you. So you will Choose the three who will accompany you, whose lives will be risked for this Sacred Task. Thus will we know that the correct souls have been selected for such a Holy Undertaking."

My mouth went dry. I had known when I asked the mice if they would be willing to do this for me that I would be risking their lives—and while Aeslin mice are superheroes compared to their more mundane cousins, they're still mice. They can be killed by cats, or poorly placed human feet . . . or werewolves. I had been hoping, on some level, that they would choose their own best and brightest, and save me from the responsibility.

They were all still watching me with bright beady eyes, clearly excited by the idea of going on a holy mission, even as the thought of initiating that same mission made me feel slightly sick. "You, you, and you," I said, stabbing my finger almost at random into the congregation. "You're the ones I choose."

The three mice who had been selected for this great honor—and this incredible risk—squeaked with startled delight, throwing their feathers (and in one case, lit candle) aside. The candle was quickly retrieved by another mouse, I noted, before it could set the carpet aflame. That was a small mercy, as the three chosen mice swarmed onto my palm and then raced upward to my shoulder, their squeaks and chitters of joy completely unintelligible to my human ears.

I remained in my crouch, briefly meeting the eyes of the young priest. It looked more tired than it had when we left America, and I realized with a pang that I didn't know its name, or whether it was male or female, or whether it was mated. It was a cypher to me, and I was a god to it, and that suddenly didn't seem fair.

"Do you want to come along?" I asked the priest. I couldn't figure out how to broach the bigger questions. I had never been as good at talking to the mice as my sisters were, and maybe that went both ways: Verity and Antimony were priestesses, not gods, and that made them objects of less reverence to the colony. There was room for conversation there, and maybe that same room didn't exist for me.

The priest flattened its whiskers, looking pleased by the offer. At least I'd gotten that much right. "No, but thank You," it said. "I will stay here, with the congregation, and Pray for the Success of Your endeavors."

"All right," I said, and straightened. The mice on my shoulder gave another brief cheer. "You are hereby free to go wherever you need to go in order to keep yourselves safe. If danger comes into this house, go to the walls, and keep yourselves safe."

"We Shall," squeaked the mouse priest, and the two remaining members of the congregation cheered as loudly as their tiny lungs allowed, sealing the compact.

Still feeling as if I were somehow betraying their trust in me, but with no other evident solutions, I turned and left the room as the mice atop my shoulder cheered.

The hall was empty. The other doors were closed—including one that had been open until very recently, where Riley Tanner was being quarantined. I hesitated as I passed it, unable to fight the idea that I should stop and knock and tell him what was going on; that Cooper was a traitor, or at least was no longer on the side of his former allies. That we were going to check the Society for other turncoats, and find a way to track Cooper down before he could spread his sickness through the whole continent. I would have wanted to know, in Riley's place.

I would also have wanted to help. And the only way Riley had left to help was to stay locked in that room with the virus in his veins, waiting for my makeshift treatment to either cure him or fail him. He couldn't come out. He couldn't protect his family. Telling him what was really going on wouldn't just be futile, it would be cruel, and much as I didn't like the man, I didn't want to torture him.

Sometimes there are no easy answers in our line of work. Sometimes there's no way to prevent people from getting hurt. I sighed, looking away from the door, and kept on walking.

It was the only thing I had left to do.

Fourteen

"Family matters more than anything else in this world. Family doesn't have to love you. Family doesn't even have to like you. But when you need them, family has to have your back."

—Kevin Price

Once again on the front porch of a secluded guesthouse in Queensland, Australia, really wishing there were some excuse to make all parties involved take a nap

CHARLOTTE HAD LIT WHATEVER version of the Bat Signal the Thirty-Six Society used because when I stepped back onto the porch, I was greeted by yet another sea of Australian cryptozoologists. It was becoming a common enough occurrence that their sheer numbers didn't throw me—I was more amazed by the fact that she'd managed to rouse this many people at two o'clock in the morning.

It helped that most of the Thirty-Sixers were standing very still, casting nervous glances at their neighbors and looking like they didn't know whether they should be declaring their own uninfected status or avoiding contact with everyone they couldn't be sure of. I scanned the front lines, looking for familiar faces. I hadn't been in

Australia long enough to learn everyone's names, but I had been there long enough that at least a few people had started standing out to me.

I found about half of them. The rest were either farther back in the crowd, protected from casual observation by the surrounding bodies . . . or they weren't here. And if they weren't here, there was every chance they were with Cooper.

This was going to be harder than I'd thought.

Charlotte turned when she heard me step onto the porch, a spark of animation coming into her otherwise empty eyes. "There you are," she said. "Good. You can explain the plan from here." And then she stepped to the side. Charlotte Tanner—who already looked like she'd been widowed, even though her husband was alive upstairs, waiting to see what the end of his incubation period would bring—stepped to the side, indicating that I should move forward. Raina put a hand on her mother's shoulder, bolstering her up.

In case that wasn't clear enough, Shelby made a small beckoning gesture. Her gun had been holstered, and Chloe was gone. I swallowed the urge to turn and bolt for the safety of the upstairs as I squared my shoulders and walked to stand between them. The eerily silent crowd turned its many eyes on me. The urge to run rose again. I swallowed it back down.

"Where's Chloe?" I murmured, as I stepped into position.

"Mum wanted us to form a line, so I asked Gabby to take Chloe inside and lock her in one of the quarantine rooms," said Shelby. "We can question her when this is done, yeah?"

"Yeah." I kissed her on the temple before turning my attention to the crowd. "This is what we know," I began.

It took about fifteen minutes to explain the situation, from what we had found (or hadn't found) in the tin shed that was *not* a suitable substitute for a morgue to all the reasons that the werewolf in the basement's behavior was abnormal. Gabby returned somewhere in the middle of my explanation. I stressed, several times, how important Helen Jalali was going to be to the Society's recovery, since she was the only doctor we knew of who didn't have to worry about potential infection, and who could thus treat anyone who had been exposed. And then I stopped talking, and I waited for the inevitable questions.

The first one was something I hadn't been expecting, although I probably should have been. A man shouldered his way to the front of the crowd and demanded, "Well, how do we know if we've been exposed? Cooper helped with dinner the other night! Maybe he put something in the soup!"

The people around him erupted in anxious mutters. I put my hands up, waiting for silence. Inch by slow inch, it fell. I lowered my hands.

"Lycanthropy is spread via fluid transfer," I said. "You can't catch it from a toilet seat or by sharing a glass. It can't be cooked into food without denaturing the virus and making it ineffective." Technically, Cooper could have drooled or bled into something cool, like salad dressing, but even then, there would only have been a risk if the people who consumed his "specialty dishes" had had open sores or wounds in their mouths, throats, or stomachs. The odds of an infection via that route were perishingly small, and I decided quickly that it was better not to mention them at all. I was already struggling not to start a panic.

Shelby stepped up next to me. The crowd, which had been starting to mutter again, calmed, looking to her with a degree of trust that they would never show to me. I was an unknown quantity. She was the daughter of their current leaders, the heir apparent, and even if she'd been away for a long time, she was still someone they knew had their best interests at heart.

"We have a test for lycanthropy," she said. "It doesn't require bleeding, which is good, since we've seen enough blood shed in the last few days, yeah? It just needs you to come over here and let the talking mice get a whiff. If they say you're clean, you're clean. If they say you're not, well. We have plenty of space in the quarantine house," she nodded over her shoulder to the building behind us, "and we'll be offering the best possible care. We want to help you get better."

There was no "getting better" for someone who'd been infected long enough to have experienced their first transformation. The body the new-minted werewolf returned to was no longer fully human, having grown the necessary circulatory backups and additional nerves to survive repeated changes. There was no point in going into any of that under the circumstances. We wanted anyone who had been infected—or suspected they might have been—to come to us willingly, not turn and bolt for the hills.

"Why do we trust a bunch of talking mice?" shouted someone.

To my surprise, it was Gabby who stepped forward and said hotly, "Because they're Aeslin mice, and Aeslin mice can't lie! Unlike you, Patrick Hester. Don't think we've forgotten about you trying to catch that drop bear last year." The target of her rage was a large, towheaded man. The people around him stepped away, creating a bubble of open space that was extremely visible in the middle of the otherwise packed crowd. "You were going to sell that poor thing to a private collector, and for what? A little money? You should be ashamed of yourself. We trust the talking mice because they're talking mice, just like we mistrust you because you're an arsehole."

"That's my sister," said Shelby, looking amused.

Raina didn't look so amused. "That's not right," she said. She reached forward, putting a hand on Gabby's shoulder. "Hey. I'm the angry one, remember? Dial it back a little, we need to keep these people on our side."

Gabby's head whipped around so fast I heard the

bones in her neck crack. She bared her teeth at Raina in a human parody of a dog's snarl. Raina's eyes widened and she took a step back, almost colliding with me. Jett matched her motion, ears going flat.

"Gabrielle?" said Charlotte. "Honey, what's the matter?"

Bit by bit, Gabby's snarl faded into a look of wide-eyed dismay. Then, before any of us could gather our wits enough to react, she turned and flung herself from the porch, shoving through the crowd as she fled toward the woods.

"Gabby!" Charlotte jumped after her middle daughter, giving chase. I had to give her this: she was in her late forties at the very least, she was a mother three times over, and based on the speed with which she pursued her fleeing child, I would have been happy to have her represent me in a triathlon. The crowd, which had parted somewhat to let Gabby through, closed again around Charlotte, not to protect the fleeing girl, but because they were all starting to demand answers at once.

Shelby was standing frozen, a horrified expression on her face. I turned toward her, and said the words I most wanted to avoid:

"She's been exposed." They were cold, cruel words, and they fell hard into the space between us, seeming to create a chasm that could never be bridged. "The temper, the physiological response—it's the only thing that fits."

"She's my *sister*," snapped Shelby.

"That doesn't make her immune." It hadn't made her father immune. It hadn't made me immune. All any of us could do was roll the dice and take our chances.

"I know where she's going."

Shelby and I both turned to Raina. She was still standing where she'd been when Gabby ran, Jett pressed against her legs like the small black dog thought that her new mistress was the only remaining source of safety in a world that had suddenly turned confusing and cruel.

"What's that?" asked Shelby.

"I don't think she's working with Cooper—not voluntarily—and I know where she's going. The same place she's always gone when she was scared." Raina's expression went hard as she focused on me. "I can take you there, but you have to promise you won't hurt her."

"I don't know if I can promise that," I said, tracking Charlotte's progress—or lack thereof—through the crowd. Gabby was gone, leaving nothing but confusion and shouting in her wake. "If she attacks one of us, I'll have to react accordingly. But I can at least try to make sure she isn't hurt."

"If you can't promise, I can't take you," said Raina stubbornly.

Shelby sighed. "And when Mum gets back here? Do you put the same requirement on for her? If Gabby's been infected, we're going to need to deal with it, one way or another. If we go now, maybe we can talk her down before Mum makes things worse. She means well, you know she does, but . . ."

"But she'll pick and pick and agitate the situation." Raina shook her head. "This is such a mess," she practically moaned. "I should have seen it. She's my sister. I should have *seen* it."

"We promise," I said, before the conversation could continue. I lifted the mice down from my shoulder, setting them on the porch railing. They looked up at me with wide, trusting eyes. "When Charlotte comes back, help her," I instructed. "Let her take you around to sniff out the infection. All right? She is the mother of your newest Priestess. Until I return, obey her as you would *my* mother. Understand?"

"It Shall Be So!" squeaked one of the mice, while the others shivered in religious ecstasy.

We could deal with the issue of whether I had just deputized Charlotte Tanner as an official Mouse Priestess later. I turned to Raina. "Please," I said. "Take us to your sister."

Raina nodded, eyes bright with the tears she wasn't

allowing herself to shed. Then she turned and bolted back into the house, leaving Shelby and me to follow her or be left behind. Jett ran at her heels, ears folded flat against her head and long canine legs eating up the distance with ease.

We ran through the front room and down the hall, until we came to a small, boxy kitchen that hadn't been included on my earlier tour of the house. There was a door on the far wall, half-blocked with boxes and kitchen detritus. Raina tore into the barricade like a wild thing, raining down cardboard and boxed pasta on Shelby and me, until she wrenched the door open and flung herself through it in turn, vanishing down the back porch steps. Shelby and I exchanged a look before we pursued. We had already come far enough that turning back seemed impossible.

Trees loomed up on the other side of a narrow strip of uncultivated lawn that was half wildflowers and half snarled scrub that snatched at our feet and ankles as we ran. I didn't recognize any of it, and I didn't remember enough about the local flora to know if we were charging straight into the Australian equivalent of poison sumac.

If that was the case, the Tanners would no doubt have the Australian equivalent of calamine lotion in their medicine cupboard. I kept running.

Eucalyptus forests are not like evergreen forests in any but the most general of senses. We ran until we could no longer see anything but trees in any direction. The space between trunks remained broad enough to feel like something out of a Hollywood film. It was like we were running through a soundstage, and not an actual wood, and that only made me more uneasy.

"This is ridiculous," muttered Shelby. She put on a burst of speed, grabbing Raina by her elbow before the younger Tanner girl could vanish into yet another thick copse of trees. "Stop! Raina, just stop, all right?"

Raina stumbled to a halt, turning to glare mulishly at her sister. "You said you wanted to help me. You *said*."

"Yes, and we even ran off half-cocked to do it, but where are we even going? We're in the middle of nowhere, and there are *werewolves* on the loose!" Shelby let go of Raina's elbow. "This isn't a good place to be without a plan."

Jett leaned against Raina's leg and whined. I looked at the dog, a sudden, horrible thought occurring to me. She had been with Cooper when I first met her. Who was to say that the sweet little black canine wasn't a werewolf in waiting?

Bringing it up now wouldn't do any good. I made a mental note to have Jett checked for lycanthropy as soon as we got back to the mice.

"I have a plan," insisted Raina. "We're going to find Gabby and make her come home. That's the plan. We're going to fix her."

Shelby cast me a sidelong look. I shook my head. I was staying out of this one for as long as possible. Having two younger sisters of my own has left me well-equipped to know when to shut my mouth.

Sighing, Shelby turned back to Raina. "And when we all come crashing through the brush and scare the life out of her, how's that going to help her? We need to have a real plan. I need to know where you're taking us."

Raina frowned. "You *have* been away too long," she said. "Dad said you'd gone native on us, but I thought if I dragged you out here, you'd catch on and snap back to being normal. Gabby *needs* you, Shelly. She needs you to be on top of your game and looking at things like a Tanner, not like some pretty Covenant trophy wife."

Shelby slapped her.

The noise echoed through the eucalyptus trees. Somewhere above and to the right, a bird screeched, and then everything was silent. Raina stared at her sister, slowly raising a hand to touch her reddening cheek.

"You hit me," she said.

"You don't call me a trophy wife," said Shelby. "You know better than that. Our mother raised you better than that. Now where are we going?"

"You hit me in front of *him*." Raina dropped her hand. "I don't know you anymore."

Shelby audibly groaned. "Don't. Just don't. This isn't a soap opera, no matter how much it may look like one, and we don't have time to piss around out here. Gabby's in trouble. She needs us. And I need to know where you're taking me. Alex is already hurt."

"Alex is also the only one here with silver bullets," I said. This earned me a glare from both sisters. I paused, reviewed the statement, and amended, "I'm not intending to harm Gabby in any way unless she presents a clear and immediate threat to one of our lives. In that case, yes, I will shoot; being your sister doesn't mean she gets a free pass to murder either one of you. But we don't know if she's alone. Cooper may have told her there was a cure, and said he would provide it if she'd just go along with whatever it was he told her to do. If he's here, then yes, I'm going to do my best to at least incapacitate him. We need to know how many werewolves we're dealing with."

"If you shoot my sister, I'll scalp you," said Raina, with the utmost civility. She looked back to Shelby and said, "She's gone to the old playhouse."

Shelby's eyes widened. "Oh, lord. Right, Alex, come on: we're running again." Then she took off, and Raina took off with her, leaving me to try to catch up with them—and leaving any questions I might have about the nature of the "old playhouse" blithely unanswered. The Tanner sisters knew the score. I was just the man who got to trust that they weren't going to get us all killed.

The trees grew larger and closer together as we ran, and other things began to appear alongside the eucalyptus. Twisting-trunked trees with glossy brown bark and broad green leaves; smaller, scrubby trees that looked almost like a form of evergreen. Still we ran, until the trees opened up around us and we were standing on the verge of a large, green-surfaced pond that stretched away into the distance, canopied by more trees I didn't recognize. There was a small dock near where we were standing, but there was no boat there; no, the boat was anchored some twenty yards from shore, at the base of a particularly large and impressive barrel-shaped tree. In the tree was a fort-like construction which looked like it was made mostly of plywood. I stared.

"Oh," I said finally.

"She's taken the boat," said Shelby. "How are we supposed to get to her if she's taken the boat? I'm not swimming in that water; it has things in it."

"Things?" I asked. I wasn't sure I wanted the answer.

"Eels," said Shelby. "Turtles. Sometimes really big snakes, although not as many as you'd think, on account of the bunyip around here eating them."

"You built a playhouse in bunyip territory?" I couldn't stop myself from squeaking slightly. Both Raina and Shelby turned to blink at me.

Finally, Raina said, "Where else would you suggest we build a playhouse? New Zealand? Everywhere is bunyip territory, except for maybe the middle of Sydney, and that's because even the bunyip don't want to deal with the fucking funnelweb spiders. Those nasty bastards will kill you as soon as look at you."

". . . right," I said. "I'm sorry, for five seconds, I forgot we were in an unholy murder paradise. What do you suggest we do if we don't have a boat and the water is full of 'things'?"

"We ask the things." Shelby cupped her hands around her mouth and shouted, "Hey! Basil! Hey! I know you're out there! Gabby's gone and snitched the boat again! Come on, you lazy bastard, haul your ass out of the substrate and come help us out!"

Her call echoed over the swamp. I frowned at her, then at the playhouse. Nothing moved. If Gabby was there, she had to hear her sister shouting, but it wasn't drawing a visible reaction from her. I didn't know whether or not I should be regarding that as a good thing. Under the circumstances, I was no longer sure how I should be regarding much of anything.

"He's not going to come out," said Raina. "He hasn't been answering us lately."

"Did you keep bringing him Tim Tams and *Doctor Who Magazine*?" asked Shelby.

"No," said Raina. She pushed her lower lip out in a pout. "Dad cut my allowance when I refused to go on survey for those blasted manticores that you were supposed to be helping us get rid of. Like I should go and get myself stung to death because you couldn't be bothered to come back and do your job? I had to make cuts in the budget."

"So you cut Basil's Tim Tams? Oh, real smart, Raina, real smart." Shelby turned back to the swamp, taking a deep breath. She cupped her hands around her mouth, and shouted, "I brought Raina and I will let you hit her with an eel if you'll come out and help us get the boat!"

"I want my Tim Tams," said a sullen voice from what looked like an undifferentiated patch of swamp. Then, with no further fanfare, the swamp . . . stood up. What I had taken for floating water weeds became hair; an upturned branch became an impressively pointed nose, and the rest became a tall, stocky, aggressively male humanoid wearing nothing but whatever had happened to adhere to his olive green skin while he was submerged. He scowled at the three of us and Jett, scratching one muddy buttock with his left hand. "Who's the fellow? And the dog?"

"Basil, meet Alex Price, my fiancé. Please do not drown him, bury him in mud, or attempt to feed him live frogs because you think it's funny when humans scrunch their faces up. Alex, meet Basil, our local yowie. The dog is Jett, she belongs to Raina." Shelby gestured between us violently. "There, now you've met. Basil, will you please go get the boat? Raina and I need to talk to Gabby."

"Hi, Basil," said Raina.

"Fuck off, Raina," said Basil. He stabbed a finger in my direction. "How come I get told all the things I can't do to him, but he doesn't get told what he can't do to me? You're favoring the humans again."

"Well, yes, I am," said Shelby. "I generally do. As to why Alex doesn't get a list of thou shalt nots, it's because he's a gentleman, and he knows that it's rude to attack your new friends. You've never shown that sort of civility. If you start, maybe I'll stop giving you commands."

"It's nice to meet you," I said, before the argument could proceed. "I've never met a yowie before. I'd love to discuss your ecological niche, after the current crisis has passed. I can bring Tim Tams to pay you for your time."

Basil blinked. A small frog fell out of his hair and leaped for the swamp, choosing freedom over remaining on Basil's head. Basil snatched it out of the air and jammed it into his mouth, crunching twice before he said, "I like this one, Shelby, he understands basic commerce. All right, Price, you can come back here and talk to me. I'll let you open your own tab, rather than drawing on this pair's." He jerked a thumb toward Shelby and Raina. "Their credit's shot. Which is why I'm interested to hear what makes them think I'm going to bring the boat over here for them. Strikes me that watching them go wading might be a great way to spend an afternoon."

"I wasn't even in the country when Raina decided to stop paying you," protested Shelby. "You can't punish me because she's an unthinking brat!"

"Can, will, am," said Basil. "You're the older sibling. You should have drilled it into her head that she needed to keep paying me while you were away. You didn't, and now you're paying the price. Sucks to be the eldest, doesn't it?"

"Yes, it does," I said. All three of them turned to look at me. "I'm the eldest in my family, and I'm betting you are too, Basil. You know it's your job to make sure your younger brothers and sisters are taken care of. That they understand right and wrong. Don't you?"

Basil frowned slowly before he nodded and said,

"That was my job before we all left home, yeah. Someone's got to do it."

"Well, we're here, and asking you to please, ah, get the boat," I gestured toward the boat, just in case he was the sort to interpret my words to mean "any boat he could find" and dredge one up from the bottom of the swamp, "so that we can go and help Shelby and Raina's *other* sister. The one who isn't standing here in front of you, being very sorry that she didn't get your cookies when she was supposed to."

On cue, Shelby dug her elbow into Raina's side. Raina reddened, looking down at her feet, and said, in a staccato rush, "I'm sorry I didn't bring you the Tim Tams I promised. There was a new Pokémon game and I really wanted it, but I should still have kept my word to you before I did something for myself and I'm sorry."

Basil blinked. "See, that's all I wanted," he said. "Apologies are the glue that makes the world go 'round. Wait here, you lot, and I'll expect everything that's coming to me to be delivered here before the full moon, or it's no more Mister Nice Yowie." He stood up still further, rising out of the muck until it became very clear that the hypothesized evolutionary link between yowie and Sasquatch was more truth than fiction. Scratching his mossy bottom one more time, he turned and lumbered toward the boat.

"Do you think he'd give me some hair and maybe a blood sample for later analysis?" I asked, transfixed by the sight of the giant green man wading through the swamp.

"That's my little scientist," said Shelby, sounding amused. "Tell you what, how about you come back here and negotiate that with him after we've finished handling the current crisis? I'll bring popcorn."

I blinked, the strangeness of the scene finally crystalizing into something logical, if bizarre. I turned to Shelby. "Your father didn't even want us to call Dr. Jalali, because the Society doesn't treat nonhumans as people.

How is it that you and your sisters are friends with a yowie?"

"We found him," said Raina. Her head was up again, and her coloring was back to normal. Embarrassment was apparently not a long-term thing with her. "He'd been bit by a snake. Was all sick and moaning and making a muck of things here on the bank. Right over there, in fact." She pointed to a spot a little farther along.

"Luckily, Jack and I were with them that day, and since he was already training to be Dad's assistant, and I wanted to do anything he was doing, we both had our snakebite kits and medical supplies on us," said Shelby, smoothly taking up the story. "Basil never did tell us what had bitten him, and we thought he'd die even after we suctioned the venom out and gave him some basic medical care, since we couldn't provide antivenin if we didn't know what he needed. But it turns out yowie are tougher than anything living has the right to be. As soon as we got the bulk of the poison out of him, and some fresh water into him, he bounced right back. Was up and moving about normally by the end of the afternoon."

"Jack insisted we come back here to check on him; said that once you've saved something, you're responsible for it, even if it's as smart as you are. Basil started asking for Tim Tams after the third time we came by. He helped us build the playhouse, and the skiff." Raina paused, looking down again. "They were real good friends. He hasn't been the same since Jack died, you know? He's still friendly enough, but it's like he's not really glad to see us, not like he says. He's just going through the motions so we don't get upset enough to tell our parents he's down here. So we haven't visited much."

Which explained why Raina had been willing to seize on the excuse afforded by the reduction in her allowance. They couldn't come to visit Basil. They couldn't afford the cookies, and that meant they had no business bothering him. Keeping my voice as gentle as I could, I asked, "Did you let him come to Jack's funeral?"

"No, of course not," said Raina, sounding baffled by the idea. "He's not a people. He's just Basil."

I looked to Shelby. She looked horrified. Good. At least one of the Tanner sisters understood why the yowie was angry—and while I could forgive Raina for not seeing him as a person when she first met him, I couldn't forgive her for continuing to see him as something less than she was after spending all the time she had described in his company. Basil wasn't human. He should still have been allowed the opportunity to join in the mourning for his friend.

Shelby's thoughts seemed to have run along similar channels. When the yowie waded back to the bank, now dragging the small boat in his wake, Shelby ran and splashed a few feet out into the water, throwing her arms around as much of his thick, weed-covered torso as she could manage. "I'm so sorry!" she exclaimed. The water swirled around her ankles as Basil blinked bemusedly down at her. She continued, "I should have realized you missed Jack almost as much as we did. I should have told my father you were coming to the funeral, so that you could say good-bye, and damn anyone who thought you didn't belong there. I didn't realize I was being horrible, Basil, and I'm *so* sorry. Can you forgive me?"

"Ah," he said, and raised one muddy hand to pat her shoulder, awkwardly—less, it seemed to me, because he didn't want to offer comfort, and more because he was so much bigger than she was that he was afraid of hurting her. He could easily have crushed her, but all he did was pat twice and then pull his hand away. "It's all right, Shelby, don't cry on me, all right? You know how I hate getting wet."

Shelby lifted her head and laughed thickly. She *was* crying, and the funereal look she always had when she wasn't smiling had deepened, becoming an almost overwhelming sadness. "You're always wet, you swampy bastard. You haven't been dry a day in your life."

"And I hope never to be," Basil said. "I brought your boat."

"Thank you." Shelby swiped a hand across her eyes and turned to me. "You should probably stay out here. The boat's only built for three. We used to have to play ferry to get all four of us over."

"No problem," I said. "I'll keep watch for more werewolves." I didn't want to let Shelby and Raina go to the playhouse without me, but I knew that neither of them would stand for being left behind, and if anything would convince Gabby to come out and let us help her, it was the presence of her sisters.

Raina seemed to sense my reluctance. She paused as she walked toward the water, long enough to touch my arm and murmur, "Thank you." Then she was joining Shelby in the boat, and the two of them were producing oars from the bottom of the vessel and rowing away, leaving me and Basil standing on the shore. Jett sat down on the bank nearby, whining as she watched her mistress row away.

Basil looked at me. I looked at him. Neither of us said anything. Shelby and Raina reached the tree that housed their rickety hideaway. They tied the boat in place and got out, swarming up the boards that had been nailed to the tree trunk like gravity and the Tanner sisters were not well-acquainted.

Basil snorted. "When we first put those boards up for the girls, they used to fall off every time they tried to climb," he said. "I was forever catching them before they could hit the water."

"Oh?" I asked, neutrally.

"Yeah. This water's no good for humans to be splashing around in. You people take sick so easy, there's no point in making it any harder on you, is there?" He crossed his arms, forcing a few drops of water out of the moss that covered him. It dripped back into the swamp at his feet. "I always caught them. Put them back in the tree. They just needed to learn how to climb on their own."

"It sounds like you did a lot for them. Thank you. I'd be sad if Shelby had drowned before I got to meet her."

"I'd say you would be. Fiancé, huh? I don't suppose I'll be getting an invitation to the wedding." It was impossible to ignore the bitter note in the yowie's voice. He'd been so important to the Tanners when they were children, and Shelby had never thought to mention him to me, because she'd never really considered him a person.

Wait. "I thought Shelby and her family weren't from around here," I said. "How did you know them when they were kids?"

"They came here for training, Society business, all that," said Basil. "I only saw them once or twice a year most of the time, but that was more than enough for me. They were always smiles and laughter when they were little. Makes me want to go find a nice girl and have some kids of my own, you know? And don't think I didn't notice you dodging the question."

Shelby and Raina had vanished inside the playhouse. I watched the side of the building, searching for any hint of what was going on in there. "I wasn't dodging it, I just don't know yet," I said. "We only got engaged a day ago, and I need to talk to my family, find out where the wedding is even going to happen . . . if we get married in Australia, you're more than welcome to attend. Given how little her parents seem to like me, I'm expecting we'll get married in the United States, or maybe on a ship in international waters where no one can say we're starting things off by favoring one side of the family over the other."

Basil laughed. "Oh, you humans. You sure do know how to muck things up, don't you?"

"We're pretty good at it," I admitted. Something banged inside the playhouse, causing bits of sawdust to detach from the bottom and drift down to the swamp. I tensed. "Did you see that?"

"They're just slamming around. They do that." For all his calm words, Basil kept a tight eye on the tree. "What's going on, anyway?"

If the Tanners hadn't told the local wadjet community about the werewolves, I doubted they'd told the yowie either—and Basil weighed four hundred pounds if he weighed an ounce. The idea of something that large catching lycanthropy was enough to make my blood run cold. "Have you ever heard of werewolves?"

"Oh, that lot? Nasty bunch. They tried to bite me a few days ago. I drowned three in the swamp before they realized it was a bad idea." Basil sounded utterly calm.

I blinked at him, mentally adding "drowning" to the list of things that would kill a werewolf, rather than just inconveniencing them for a little while. "You do realize they're contagious, yes? If they'd bitten you, you could have turned into one of them." Yowie are mammals. Big, intimidating mammals.

"Oh, yeah?" Basil shrugged. "No one told me that. Besides, it's not like they managed to break the skin."

Something rustled in the trees behind us. The sound was followed, an instant later, by the long, low rumble of a lupine growl. Jett was behind me like a shot, pressed against my legs and whimpering. I went stiff, feeling my blood chill in my veins. "Well, it looks like they're back for another try," I said. "Don't let them bite you." *And please, Shelby, stay in the playhouse,* I thought, wishing more than I had ever wished before that I had Sarah along to play telepathic relay and keep everyone informed as to what was going on. *Take your time with your sisters, and don't come out.*

I'm not a telepath, and Sarah was on another continent; Shelby wasn't going to hear me pleading with her. That thought all too firmly in mind, I turned to face whatever was coming out of the wood.

Fifteen

"Most people would very much like to believe that humans invented the ambush. It makes them feel like we're special. Smart. Try telling that to the trapdoor spider, to the octopus, or to the wolf. They'll be delighted to hear how special you are, as they're draining the marrow from your bones."

—Jonathan Healy

Standing on the bank of a swamp in Queensland, Australia, probably about to be attacked by werewolves

EVERYTHING WAS ABSOLUTELY STILL. Nothing rustled; nothing moved; no birds sang. The growling from the trees had stopped, however temporarily, and it was almost possible to convince myself that I'd imagined it. I might have made that fatal error, if it hadn't been for Jett hiding behind my legs and Basil standing at the edge of the water. He'd heard the growling, too, and he looked as uneasy as I felt.

"You sure that was your wolves?" he asked. "Maybe we scared them away."

As he spoke his final word, the woods exploded.

Three wolves bounded into the open, all of them displaying the foaming drool that would increase their odds of successfully infecting us with a single bite. I didn't know how much of that was intentional—but if all our theorizing about intelligent werewolves was accurate, and not just paranoid delusion, they might be working themselves into a froth on purpose. If you can't beat them, recruit them. Once we were infected, we'd probably be a lot less enthusiastic about the idea of killing all werewolves.

I pulled the gun from my belt and clicked off the safety, but kept it low, pointed at the ground rather than at any of the approaching wolves. They were eating up ground, their legs churning as they flung themselves toward us. I still had a few seconds. "If you stop where you are, I will not shoot you!" I shouted.

They didn't stop. "They're not stopping," observed Basil.

"I noticed!" I raised my gun and fired once into the ground a foot or so ahead of the lead wolf. That got its attention, even though words hadn't been able to do the trick. It yelped and scrambled away from the impact site, almost falling over in its hurry to retreat. The other two wolves dug their paws into the ground, bleeding off speed at an impressive clip, and pulled back into an uneasy circling motion. The lead wolf drew back its lips and snarled at us. Saliva dripped from its jowls, pooling on the ground in foamy puddles.

"They stopped," said Basil.

I risked a sidelong glance in his direction. "Are you always this fond of stating the obvious, or am I just the lucky recipient of your sarcasm?"

"Bit of both," said Basil.

"Right." I refocused my attention on the wolves. "I'm going to lower the gun now. I'm not going to put it away, but I'm going to lower it, and if you don't make any threatening moves, I won't either."

The wolves didn't do anything but continue to pace and circle. I took that as at least something of a good sign. Taking a long, slow breath, I lowered the gun.

"I know you can hear me, and I'm hoping you can understand me," I said. I was unable to prevent myself from speaking slowly and clearly, like I was trying to make myself heard and understood by a quarry golem. (They don't have ears, and mostly function through lip reading, sign language, and throwing things. It works out reasonably well for them. Being ten feet tall probably doesn't hurt matters.) "I don't want to hurt you. I'm hoping you don't actually want to hurt me. Please. Can you shift back to human? I need to talk to you. This will be an easier conversation if you can talk back."

"So talk."

The disappearance of Cooper's body had been enough to convince me—mostly—that he was one of the werewolves, if not the source and patient zero for this particular outbreak. But there had still been a small amount of doubt, a small chance that I was wrong. The sound of his voice put any lingering questions to rest.

He walked calmly out of the woods into the open, still dressed in the bloody remains of the clothes he'd been wearing when we were attacked. He'd had plenty of opportunities to change since then, if he'd been able to reconvene with his werewolf buddies. He was making a point, and I didn't like it.

"Hello, Cooper," I said, keeping my gun pointed resolutely at the ground. I didn't want to bait him any more than I had to. "You're looking a lot less dead than I'd expected, given the way I last saw you. Didn't know the Society had a 'resurrection' policy."

"Didn't die," he said, with a broad shrug. "Lost a lot of blood, which dropped my pulse low enough that you lot didn't find it. I was hoping that would be the result. I guess I got lucky."

"I guess I did, too," I said. "I'm still clean."

Cooper blinked slowly, looking bewildered. Then he whistled once, short and sharp and shrill. The three werewolves—the *other* three werewolves—stopped circling and prowled over to sit down in front of him, forming a loose, protective semicircle of lupine bodies and narrowed, feral eyes. "What do you mean, clean?"

"I mean the treatment I brought with me kept me from getting sick, Cooper." There was no point in telling him that the infection hadn't managed to take hold of me in the first place: letting him think we had a guaranteed cure for lycanthropy could only work in our favor. "I'm not going to transform. I'm not contagious. I'm not *infected*."

"Then we'll try again." Cooper made the statement sound perfectly reasonable, like he was proposing a dinner date. "We'll try again, and if that doesn't work, we'll keep trying until we manage to bring you over to our side. I want you, smart boy. You're quick, you're loyal, and you've got science in your back pocket. That's going to come in handy."

"You really think you're going to live long enough to benefit? Even if I don't shoot you, the human body wasn't designed for shapeshifting. Therianthropes survive their transformations because they're adapted to them on a cellular level. The disease you have is breaking the laws of nature every time it rewrites you. You know what most werewolves die of?"

"Silver bullets," said Basil. "Even I know that one."

Cooper laughed. "I like your friend. He's gonna be a wolf the size of a pony. That's going to be something to see, don't you think?"

"Werewolves die of heart attacks," I said, refusing to allow myself to be baited. "They die because when they go from biped to quadruped and back again, sometimes their spinal cords restructure the wrong way, and they snap their own necks. They die because their livers explode. Do you understand me yet? Werewolves die because they have a *disease*. You have a *disease*, Cooper, and the fact that you're spreading it to your own people on purpose—well, that's sick. No pun intended."

"They stopped being my people the moment I got bit," said Cooper calmly. "Ask your friend there how the

Thirty-Six Society deals with monsters. Ask your girl-friend. Shelby Tanner was always the worst of a bad lot, even when she was a little girl. Bigots, all of them."

"I don't think she's so bad," said Basil.

"They're conservationists," I said.

"Sure. They conserve. In pens and paddocks and aviaries, they conserve. In zoos and museums and private collections, they conserve. They love their koalas and their kangaroos and all those other nice creatures for the tourists to coo over, but anything that isn't native—anything that seems like a danger—those things, they're more than happy to lock away forever." Cooper shook his head. "They weren't going to lock me up. I've been one of them for too long. I know what their hospitality looks like."

"So why didn't you quit?" I asked.

"Didn't mind it so much when I was on their side of the cage. Things have changed."

"You still didn't have to . . ." I trailed off. "Infecting the people you used to work with is wrong. Even if you know they'd treat you like a monster, you shouldn't have done that. That was what made you a monster. Not the virus. Not the things you did when you were transformed and didn't understand yourself. The choices you made."

"Then I'm a monster," said Cooper calmly. "That gun you're holding, it has what, six shots in it? There's four of us. I think I like those odds."

"Cooper—"

"I like you well enough, Covenant boy, and I know you came a long way to help us. I figure if anyone can find a way for this virus not to kill us all, it's going to be you—and my people deserve that chance, don't you think? They deserve a chance at long, healthy, productive lives. We can do better work for this country as monsters than we ever did as men." Cooper turned, walking back toward the woods. "Get him, boys. Infect, not kill. We need him."

"Wait!" I cried.

Cooper stopped. The wolves, which had been tensing

to spring, froze. If there had been any question remaining as to whether transformed werewolves were fully aware, that moment would have answered it: only thinking creatures would have reacted that way. "What, you willing to come quietly?" asked Cooper, twisting to look over his shoulder at me. "That would be the sensible choice. Much less chance that we'd accidentally damage you. I'd like to take you as intact as possible, since men who've just had their arms ripped off always need help in the lab, and that seems like a waste of resources."

I didn't shoot him. No one was going to reward me for that, and I would probably regret it later, but in the moment, the fact that I didn't go ahead and shoot him felt like the most self-control I had ever shown. "Gabrielle Tanner," I said. "How long ago did you have her bitten?"

"Ah. You found out about that one." Cooper smiled slow and languid, showing more teeth than he really needed to. "Not that long ago. Did it myself, actually. I picked her up from school. She seemed suspicious. Watching me, yeah? She caught me sneaking off the property when I was supposed to be dead, so I gave her a little nip and pointed out what her family would do to her if they found out. She wasn't willing to see the sense of my words right away, but she was willing to conceal her condition and my survival, so that's something, right? Imagine the look on Riley's face when his precious little girl went for his throat."

"All I needed to know." She had been infected within the last forty-eight hours. She hadn't transformed yet. She could still be saved.

I raised my gun, and had the satisfaction of seeing Cooper's eyes go wide in his suddenly bloodless face before he threw himself at the trees, and the wolves threw themselves at me.

Then a hand was grabbing the back of my shirt, and Basil's voice was saying, "Sorry about this, but you seem like a fellow who enjoys air," and I was flying backward through the air, hauled by that same hand. Jett was in

Basil's other hand, balled up and whimpering. The wolves skidded to a stop at the edge of the water, apparently unwilling to follow Basil into the swamp. They had been Australian naturalists before they became werewolves; they knew better than most what could be lurking in those waters.

The yowie strode through the water, churning it into a froth around his tree trunk-thick legs. Snakes, frogs, and what looked like a small crocodile fled from the disturbance he made—and many of them fled toward the bank, creating a second barrier between us and the werewolves. I hesitated, gun still in my hand. On the one hand, I now knew that werewolves were intelligent creatures, capable of moral decisions and ethical thought. On the other hand, they were disease vectors, and these werewolves were specifically targeting their former friends and companions out of the accurate belief that failure to turn them all would result in a widespread monster hunt.

Too much of my training had been focused on sympathy for every living thing. I was still debating whether or not to pull the trigger when Basil ran into a thick stand of swamp-growing trees and dumped me unceremoniously on a wide branch about eight feet above the surface of the water. He dumped Jett in my lap. She promptly tried to hide her entire head in my crotch. I wasn't Raina, but I'd do for now.

"Sorry to pull you out of there, but I didn't really want to dance with the werewolves," he said. "You all right? I didn't suffocate you or anything, did I?"

"Not quite." I rubbed the front of my neck, where the collar of my shirt had dug into the skin, and shook my head. "I need you to go back and get the girls. Please. We can't leave them there with Cooper in the area, there's no telling what he'll do when they go rowing back to shore."

"In a minute." Basil crossed his arms, looking at me flatly. "Why weren't you shooting, huh? I know you humans and your guns. It's cute, how you've made up for a total lack of natural defenses by coming up with a few hundred unnatural ones. You should have been filling that arsehole with bullets the second you figured out he was coming for you and the girls. What gives?"

"I . . . my family believes that everything has a right to live," I said. "We just try to keep things as fair as possible. To smooth out the edges where we collide with one another."

"Wow." Basil shook his head. "I mean, wow. I knew humans were inherently fucked up, and I thought the Thirty-Six Society were top of the heap there. I mean, they can look at folks like me—just folks, yeah? Just trying to get along, maybe have a little fun, maybe find a nice billabong that doesn't already belong to a bunyip or a croc too big for eating, settle down, have a family—and think that we're monsters. That's pretty screwy. But you lot! You look at everything and think 'that has a right to live, even if it's going to eat me.' Screw that. You have a right to defend your species. You have a right to keep breathing. There's a middle ground between 'everything's a monster' and 'everything has a right to live except for me.'"

I blinked at him slowly before asking, "So next time, you think I should shoot?"

"The man flat out said he'd been infecting humans to get them on his side," said Basil. "That means he's taking things that *are* human and making them into things that *aren't* human. You can be as nice a fellow as you want to be, but I don't think you should sit idly by while your species gets replaced. That's not being nice. That's being stupid."

"So noted," I said. "Now will you please go get the girls?"

"I'll be right back," he said. "Try not to get eaten by a bunyip because you think it needs a square meal, a'right?" He turned and lumbered back into the swamp.

I leaned back against the trunk of the tree I was seated in, resisting the urge to close my eyes and think.

Basil was right: I'd been so interested in confirming whether or not the werewolves were still intelligent in their changed forms that I hadn't considered that I'd been essentially baiting four large apex predators while holding nothing but a handgun. I had killed werewolves before. Knowing that they weren't just dumb beasts shouldn't have changed things—or if it did, it should have made me even more enthusiastic about killing them. Werewolves that could plan and execute complex maneuvers were terrifying, and they couldn't be allowed to exist. So why had I hesitated?

It wasn't like my family didn't understand the need to kill things for the sake of the human race, however much we disliked doing it. Grandma and Sarah were the only "good" cuckoos we knew of. All others came with a permanent order to shoot on sight, unless they did something to indicate that they, too, might be capable of showing things like mercy and affection. We knew there were monsters in the world, real monsters, not things like gorgons or bunyip or yowie that inherited that title from urban legends and folklore about them killing people for fun. We knew that sometimes, monsters had to be stopped. So why had I hesitated?

Riley's voice echoed in my head, calling me "Covenant boy," talking about how much they didn't need me or my family's teachings. Just like that, I had my answer.

I had hesitated because I didn't want to be what he thought I was. On some level, I had been willing to let myself be seriously hurt to prove that point. I wasn't Covenant. My parents raised me better than that. I understood mercy. And mercy was the thing that was likely to get me killed.

"Oh, I can already tell I'm going to *love* having in-laws," I muttered.

The sound of sloshing alerted me to something approaching through the swamp. I tensed, turning my head toward the sound, and was relieved to see the great green form of Basil come slogging through the trees, hauling the small boat belonging to the Tanner sisters behind him. All three of them were there. Jett pulled her head out of my crotch and barked, tail beginning to wag as she saw Raina. At least someone was having a good day, even if we still needed to check her for infection.

Raina was in the middle of the boat with her arms around Gabby, who was crumpled against her sister and sobbing, face buried in Raina's shoulder. I fought the urge to wince at the sight of such casual contact between someone who was almost definitely infected and someone who wasn't. Gabby hadn't been infected long enough to have changed, and lycanthropy didn't spread through tears. Most werewolves didn't take a lot of time to cry.

Shelby was at the front of the boat, standing with one foot on the stubby prow to counterbalance the rest of her body. She had a gun in her hand, and was watching the swamp warily. I smiled at the sight of her. I couldn't help myself. I might not be thrilled by the idea of in-laws, but they were a package deal with Shelby . . . and I was more than thrilled by the idea of *her*. No, that wasn't right. The idea of her was pleasant enough. The reality of her, on the other hand, was worth moving mountains for.

"I see you managed to survive sitting alone for five minutes," said Basil, once he was close enough that he didn't have to shout. "Anything interesting happen?"

"Nothing tried to eat me. I'll call that a win." I leaned forward, waving my free hand. "Hello, the boat. Is everything all right down there?"

"Not in the slightest," said Shelby. Her face was fixed in funereal mode. It made me want to put my arms around her and tell her everything was going to be all right now, that we had solved all our problems and were going to go live happily ever after. It was a pity that both of us would know I was lying. "Gabby's been bit."

Behind her, Gabby gave a convulsive sob and burrowed even deeper into her sister's arms. Raina raised her head to look at me, but didn't say anything. She just narrowed her eyes, clearly waiting for me to respond.

"I know," I said. "But she wasn't bitten long enough ago to have turned; the treatment I brought with me should still work for her."

"What if it doesn't work?" asked Raina. "Are you going to shoot our sister?"

"No." I hadn't been certain—not really—of what my answer would be until I heard it spoken aloud by my own voice. It was a relief. "We know from dealing with Cooper that werewolves are capable of controlling themselves when transformed. If Gabby is going to turn, we can find ways to manage it. It will mean a certain amount of compromise, and locking her up on full moon nights, to avoid her accidentally infecting anyone else, but it can work."

Gabby pulled her face away from Raina's shoulder, looking up at me with large, liquid eyes. "But . . . opera school," she said weakly. "I was going to sing *Carmen*."

I winced, doing my best to hide it. "We'll find a way," I said.

"I may have one," said Basil. All four of us turned to look at him. He focused on Gabby. "Do you trust me?" he asked.

"Don't quote *Doctor Who* at me," said Gabby, and wiped her eyes with the back of her hand. "Of course I trust you, Basil. You're our Basil."

"All right." Basil looked first to Shelby and Raina, and then to me. "There's a wagyl near here. Its bite can cure just about anything. I'd wager lycanthropy is on that list. But you have to let me take her, and you have to promise you won't try to follow."

Given the situation we'd fled when we ran after Gabby, we were needed back at the Thirty-Six Society. We didn't know how many werewolves Cooper had created, or how they were going to react to the fact that the Aeslin could quite literally sniff them out. Charlotte needed backup. And yet . . . "Is this wagyl something that could come back here? Gabby isn't the only one who's been exposed."

"Asking a wagyl for a favor is a big deal," said Basil. "Getting it to bite one person is going to be hard enough, but I'm willing to negotiate because it's Gabby, and she's as good as family to me. I'm not even going to ask about anyone else until she's bitten and it can't be taken back."

"Is there any risk to her?" asked Shelby. "Wagyl may be awesome healers or whatever, but they're still ripping big snakes. I don't want my sister getting hurt."

"Your sister's already been hurt," said Basil.

"I'll do it," said Gabby. She stood up, the boat rocking beneath her, and took a step toward Basil, raising her arms like a much smaller person, like she expected him to sweep her up and carry her, piggyback, into the trees. Maybe that was exactly what she *did* expect. She'd been smaller when they first met, after all. "I don't care about risks, and I don't care if it could hurt me. I want to finish opera school. I want to see the world. I want to have children someday. I can't do any of those things if I'm stuck here, being a werewolf."

"Gabby . . ." said Shelby.

"It's my choice." Gabby turned to her sister, sticking her chin out in what was apparently a hallmark of the Tanner sisters when they were deciding to be remarkably stubborn about something. "I don't have any better options. Alex's 'cure' isn't guaranteed to work for me, and I refuse to be a pet monster for the Society. I'm not the new Tasmanian wolf."

"Can I go with you?" asked Raina, before looking up to Basil. "Can I?"

He shook his head. "No, dear, you can't. It's not because I'm punishing you, either: I'd take you if I didn't think it would make it even less likely the wagyl would help her. They don't like humans much, as a rule. Too many dead, and their memories are long."

Raina nodded, crestfallen. "That's what I was afraid you'd say."

Shelby opened her mouth, like she was going to object again. Then she stopped, mouth snapping closed, and nodded. "All right," she said. "Go with Basil. He'll keep you safe. He'll make sure no harm comes to you, unless it's unavoidable. And if harm *does* come to you, Raina and I will both make sure it's understood that this was your choice: no one forced you, no one coerced you, and no one told you that you had to go."

"Thank you," said Gabby, smiling through her tears. She flung her arms quickly and wildly around her sisters, managing to catch all of Raina and half of Shelby's torso. Then she let them go and stepped up onto the side of the boat, holding her arms out for Basil once more. He picked her up like she was a toy and set her on his shoulder, where she fit, not well, but compactly, putting one arm around his head to keep her balance.

"Down you go," he said, reaching for me once his hands were free. I barely had time to stuff my gun back into my waistband before he was grasping me around the waist and lifting me down to the boat, which settled and rocked under my weight. Then Shelby was there to steady me, and Jett, tail still wagging, was cramming her nose into my crotch, examining all the new smells I had accumulated since she last checked me over.

"When will we know?" asked Shelby, her eyes remaining on Basil and Gabby.

He mustered a small smile. It looked like it hurt him, and I realized then that whatever a wagyl was, it wasn't a magic bulplet: there were no guarantees, and Raina and Shelby were allowing their sister to be carried away, without backup, to what might be her certain death. "It should take a few hours to get to the right spot, and a few hours more to negotiate a bite. It'll take about eight hours for the venom to clear her system. One way or the other."

"You don't have to do this," said Raina. Her eyes were fixed on her sister, and the look of bleak despair on her face made me revise every thought I'd ever had about Shelby's occasional expression of funereal gloom: this was what it really looked like when a Tanner girl's heart was breaking. "We can find another way. A less danger-ous one."

"I won't live in a cage," said Gabby. She sat up straighter on Basil's shoulder, and the moonlight slant-ing through the trees made a halo of her pale hair, mak-ing her look like some sort of fairy-tale heroine getting ready to embark on her big quest. *Gabby and the Were-wolves* wasn't likely to be coming from Disney any time soon, but maybe it should have been. "I love you, and I wish I didn't have to risk this, but I won't live in a cage. Not for you, not for anybody. I'll be home as soon as I can."

"Take care of our girl, Basil," said Shelby.

"I will," pledged the great green man, as solemnly as if he was promising her the moon and the stars. Then he turned, Gabby still riding easy on his shoulder, and slogged away into the swamp. The three of us stood si-lently in the boat, watching them go until we couldn't see them anymore. Raina sobbed, a short, cruel sound that cut off abruptly at the end as she swallowed the rest of her sorrow, forcing it to stay penned inside. We were alone.

Shelby was the first to move. Raina was in a state of something resembling shock, and I knew it wasn't my place to try to force the matter: she wasn't my sister. Shelby had no such compunctions. She picked up both oars, thrusting one of them at me, and said, "We need to get back to the house before Mum loses control com-pletely. Alex, you're going to help me row. Raina, you're going to sit down, and hug your dog, and stop looking like someone's just died. Gabby will be *fine*."

"You don't know that," snapped Raina.

"You're right; I don't," said Shelby, which stopped Raina in her tracks. The younger Tanner looked from her sister to me, clearly confused as to how she was meant to proceed. Shelby didn't give her time to figure things out. "She could die from the wagyl's bite. We know next to nothing about them. We don't know whether their venom is hemolytic or neurotoxic, we don't know whether they can control how much they deliver—it's a gamble. But Basil wouldn't have taken her if he didn't truly believe that he could help, and our mother needs us. Dad's in quarantine. We're all she's got."

"This would never have happened if you hadn't brought him here," muttered Raina, directing a sharp glance at me as she fell back on what I was starting to think of as the Tanner family's favorite song.

"Oh, because Alex is a mad virologist who traveled backward through time to invent lycanthropy and spread it through the therianthrope population, thus leading to a situation where Gabby would get bit? Don't be daft, Raina. It's not becoming. Alex isn't at fault here. Cooper is, for having her bitten. We're going to shoot that man until he's more holes than skin, and then we're going to shoot him again a few times, just to be sure." Shelby sat down on the boat's center board, dipping her oar into the water, and motioned for me to do the same. "Now let's get the hell out of here before something else decides to have a go at eating us."

I sat down next to Shelby, falling somewhat awkwardly into the rhythm of rowing toward the distant, unseen shore. She was better at this than I was, thanks to what must have been years of practice; I had only ever rowed the little rental kayaks around Puget Sound, and once in Lake Washington, when we had taken a trip up the coast to chat with the local sirens. My left arm shouted and moaned in protest at the repetitive pulling motion. It hurt like hell, but it wasn't enough to burst my stitches, and so I kept rowing. My discomfort was less important than giving Raina the time she needed to pull herself back together for the dangers that we had yet to face.

Dangers . . . "I saw Cooper," I said.

Shelby's head snapped around to face me, eyes so

wide that I could see the whites of them even through the gathering dark. "What?"

"He and three of his werewolves came after me—and Basil—while we were waiting on the bank. Didn't you wonder why I was sitting in a tree in the middle of the swamp?" I found myself mildly but irrationally annoyed at the yowie, who should have told them what was going on when he went to fetch them from the playhouse.

Maybe he'd assumed we would have more time together. Or maybe he just didn't care about making things easier for me. Either way, he was gone, and I was here, with two Tanner sisters staring at me in the dark.

"Three werewolves?" demanded Raina. "Who were they?"

"I don't know," I said. "They stayed in wolf form the whole time. If I've met them in their human forms, I don't know about it." That would have been too easy. Cooper knew that. Things were chaotic enough back at the house that he could easily have pulled three, or five, or a dozen of his people from the fringes of the crowd without being noticed; all they'd have to do was return clothed and clean and join the others in shouting, and no one would remember that they'd ever been gone.

"Bastard," muttered Shelby.

"It's worse than you think," I said, and took a deep breath, watching Raina carefully as I continued, "He's the one who bit Gabby. In a way, though, that's a good thing."

"I'm going to slit your throat and bathe in your blood," said Raina serenely.

"Alex, you'd better explain yourself fast, or I'm not sure I'm going to be able to stop her from making good on her threats," said Shelby, a warning note in her tone. In that moment, she didn't sound like she *wanted* to stop Raina from making good on her threats—and I couldn't blame her. If it had been my sister, I would have felt much the same.

"Cooper's cover only got blown when he was 'killed'

during the encounter that saw me bitten," I said. "He must have been planning the attack before we went out there. Let himself get wounded so we wouldn't suspect him, and then get put into quarantine with me. It would have given him free access to convince me to break out with him. All he'd have needed to do was play up the Thirty-Six Society reaction to things that weren't—or were no longer—human, and I might have listened. I'm sorry. It's true." Discovering that I had a toxic but effective treatment for lycanthropy would have accelerated his timeline. The tincture made me sick, but it could kill someone whose infection was already far enough along to allow them to transform. "When that didn't work out, and he'd been forced to 'die' to avoid being treated for his disease, he took the first opportunity he had to get away. That's when he went for Gabby. We know when she was infected. We know how far along she is."

"So this *is* your fault." This time, Raina sounded resigned, like she'd always known that if she followed the narrative for long enough, she would be able to blame everything on me.

"I think it's more ours," said Shelby. "We knew Basil. We knew that people could be nonhuman and still be, well, *people*. And we didn't say anything. Not even when we grew into positions of vague influence, we didn't say anything. We helped create an environment that made men like Cooper almost inevitable."

"Jack said—"

"Jack was going to change things after he was in charge, Ray-Ray. He was going to remake the Thirty-Six Society for the modern world, and no one was going to be able to stop him. But that didn't happen, did it? A Johrlac came here and killed him, and we all got so wrapped up in being sad and paranoid that we stopped thinking about being better. We should have kept thinking about being better." Shelby's voice broke a little on the last word. I glanced over, and saw tears gleaming on her cheeks, catching glints from the moonlight.

I didn't say anything. Those tears weren't mine to betray.

Raina sighed, deep and slow and pained, like the sound was coming up from the very center of her body. "I miss him so much," she admitted.

"So do I," said Shelby, and kept rowing.

My strokes got less ragged and more effective as we rowed through the swamp. I wasn't ready to try out for the Olympic team, by any stretch of the imagination, but at least I wasn't actively hindering our forward motion. Creatures chirped and hissed and hooted in the dark, making me wish for a floodlight. Something that sounded almost as large as Basil splashed off to our left, and I was suddenly just as glad we *didn't* have the floodlight. Seeing our neighbors wouldn't have made them go away, but it would have forced me to admit that they really existed.

I don't know how long it took for us to reach the bank, and the little dock where Gabby had originally launched the boat. Shelby took over both oars in order to guide us to where we actually needed to go, and Raina climbed up onto the dock to tie us down. That was a relief. We would have been there all night if they'd tried to leave things up to me.

"Come on, you," said Shelby, pulling herself up onto the dock and then turning to offer me a hand, which I accepted gratefully. My family worked hard to give us all the skills that we would need to survive in our chosen professions, but my lessons had never involved much to do with boats. Maybe that was something to consider for the next generation.

Nothing growled or lunged out of the bushes at us as we walked into the woods and started toward the house. I drew my gun, carrying it low against my thigh as I scanned the trees and waited for something to attack. All my vigilance was for naught: either we were alone, or we were being watched by Cooper and his wolves, who we would never see coming.

The trees up ahead began to get lighter, brightened by

the bleed from the house beyond them. We sped up a little, and voices began to trickle back to us. The argument was ongoing, then, and probably had been the whole time that we'd been gone. I realized I had no idea how long that had actually been. It didn't feel like it had been more than an hour—probably more like thirty minutes—but it was hard to say. Fear and adrenaline do funny things to the body's sense of time.

The back door was still standing slightly ajar. Raina was the first one through, followed closely by Jett, with me and Shelby on her heels. The voices got louder once we were inside, apparently coming through the open door, and we half-walked, half-trotted the rest of the way back to the porch, where all three of us stopped dead in the doorway. Jett danced a few feet farther, bouncing on the pads of her feet as she gave one ecstatic bark.

Charlotte, who had been in the process of lowering one of the Aeslin mice toward the face of a waiting Thirty-Sixer, turned to blink at us. "Oh, hello," she said. "You decided to come back. That's brilliant. Just let me finish this, and then we can have a nice chat about what made you think this was a good time to run off."

I blinked at her. So did Shelby and Raina.

"Mum, are you okay?" asked Shelby slowly. "You didn't ask about—"

"Is Gabby alive?" A note of fierce need overwhelmed the serenity in Charlotte's tone for a moment.

Shelby nodded.

"Then I trust you to have done what needed doing. So am I." She waved a hand, indicating the lawn, where the rest of the Society had formed itself into a long line that snaked across the grass like a bizarre conga. A few stood off to the side, not joining the conga; they seemed oddly relaxed, as if their troubles had all faded away. The reason why became apparent as Charlotte turned back to the Thirty-Sixer in front of her and finished lowering the Aeslin mouse to the level of his face.

The mouse sniffed. The mouse pushed its whiskers

forward as far as they would go, forming a bristled fan that brushed the tip of the man's nose and caused him to exhale with the effort of not sneezing. That had apparently been the goal: the mouse sniffed again, more rapidly, before squeaking proudly, "Not infected!"

"Uh . . ." I said.

"Well, it *is* what we told her to do," said Shelby, as the cleared Thirty-Sixer trotted off to join the others on the side of the yard. Apparently, those were the ones who had already been cleared by the mouse jury, declared free of infection and released back into the safe haven of their human lives.

There were a lot of problems with what we were witnessing, but I decided to go straight for the big one: "Is there any way of knowing that *everyone* is here?" I asked.

Raina shook her head. "No," she said grimly; she had looked at the yard, packed with people and not organized in any coherent fashion, and come to the same conclusion I had. "We can ask, but people have been on and off the property all day. 'Did you see so-and-so' is going to get a positive response no matter who we ask about, because *someone* will have seen virtually everyone we can think of."

"And someone else will be right there and ready to say that so-and-so was going somewhere predictable, but was definitely going to be back before the infection checks began, so they must be clean," said Shelby, keeping her voice low. "Someone needs to be taking names."

"That's not happening," I said. I stepped forward before the next person could step onto the porch, clearing my throat. "Charlotte? Can we have a moment?"

"Sure thing," she said, setting the mouse back on the porch rail. She clapped her hands together, eyes still on the yard, and called, "Everyone, hold tight and don't give up your spot in line. I'll be right back with you, all right?"

Some grumbling greeted this announcement, but not

enough to be dangerous. After the rest of what we'd been through, I was willing to take that.

Charlotte dusted her hands against her thighs as she turned to face us, eyes still bright and glossy with too many shocks, packed too tightly together. I spared an instant to wonder whether she even knew what she was doing, or whether she was just going through the motions because it was easier than stopping and really thinking about what was happening to her family, to her world. I dismissed the thought just as quickly as it came. Regardless of whether Charlotte understood her actions, she was going to have to live with them. That meant we all would.

"Well?" she said brightly, looking from face to face. "Where's Gabby? You did find her, didn't you? She shouldn't have run off like that. She scared the life right out of me."

"We found her," said Shelby. "Mum, she's been bitten. Cooper bit her. He passed the infection on to her."

"No, he didn't," said Charlotte, almost serenely. "She would have told us if she'd been bitten. She knows better than to hide something like that."

"Apparently not," said Raina. "She ran because she'd let the cat—or wolf, I suppose—out of the bag, and she was afraid of being locked up. I bet that's why Cooper's found support among the Society, you know. Anyone who'd been exposed saw the world getting narrower around them, and they took the only option they saw left."

Charlotte frowned at her daughter, but didn't say anything. Instead, she turned to me, raising her eyebrows, and asked, "Well? Where is she?"

"She's with a friend who may be able to offer her some unique treatment options," I said. "It was her choice, and we decided to allow her to make it. Charlotte, how are you organizing this line? Have you been keeping track of who's in it, or who's been cleared by the Aeslin mice?"

Charlotte blinked, frowning again, before she said, "The Aeslin mice haven't found anyone who's been infected yet. I don't think the situation is as dire as you've made it out to be."

"Mum, that doesn't answer the question," said Shelby. "Have you been keeping a list? Making notes? Anything that lets us know who's already been cleared?"

The mice on the rail began squeaking and squawking, saying something I couldn't make out over the sound of the humans on the lawn. I tried to peer unobtrusively around Charlotte, who was blocking my view of the rail.

She shifted positions as soon as she saw me lean, blocking my view more effectively. "Look at me while we're talking," she snapped. "Didn't your mother teach you any manners?"

"Please leave my mother out of this," I said, as politely as I could. "I have done nothing to question your parenting skills, and I'll thank you to do the same for her."

"No, but you're questioning everything else, aren't you? 'Did you keep a list' and 'we've taken your daughter for a new sort of treatment' and 'the werewolves are infiltrating your organization, good thing I'm here to save the day.'" She took a step toward me, jabbing her finger at my chest. There was a cold, glossy look in her eyes that made it clear she'd been looking for a good target, and thought she had found one in me. "Got anything else you'd like to question, Mr. Price, or shall I get back to the business of saving my people?"

An unearthly screech rose from behind her, high and shrill and agonized. It had barely registered with me before I was moving, shoving Charlotte out of the way and diving for the rail.

I was already too late. The sound cut off a short second later, while I was still lunging forward. A large Thirty-Sixer stood frozen on the top step of the porch, red leaking from between his closed fingers. One of the mice was nowhere to be seen. The two others had raced halfway up the porch support with the uncanny gravity-defying powers shared by terrified rodents the world over. They were clinging to the wood with all four paws, shrieking.

As my lunge ended, carrying me into range of their tiny voices, I finally made out the words: "MURDER! MURDER! HELP! MURDER!"

I didn't stop. I didn't think. I didn't consider the fact that the man in front of me was easily a foot taller and a hundred pounds heavier than I was. I just let my momentum carry me into him, burying my fist in his nose with a satisfying crunching sound that did nothing to lessen the sickening dread in my belly. The man stumbled back, losing his balance as his heels went over the step, and toppled backward into the crowd—less because of my awesome pugilism skills, and more because gravity does not like being treated as a toy.

His hand came open as he fell. It would almost have been a mercy if it hadn't. The body of the crushed Aeslin mouse was too small to make an audible sound when it hit the porch.

It may as well have echoed through the entire world.

The mice on the support beam raced back down and along the rail. I put out my hand, and the two of them jumped a full six inches to huddle in my palm, shaking, sides heaving as they struggled to breathe through what must have been a full-blown panic attack. I brought my hand to my chest, sheltering the mice, protecting them from any further attacks. I didn't say anything. I just looked at the fallen man with the bloody fingers, who was now being helped up by his compatriots, and waited.

"I wanted to show that I was clean," he protested, raising his clean hand to rub the side of his face. He carefully avoided touching his nose, which was leaking blood and looked like it might have been knocked askew. Good. I wanted to punch him again, and keep punching him until he looked like the broken thing I was refusing to let myself see. "The damn mouse wouldn't check me.

Said it wasn't right to check me until you said it could continue. I just wanted to show that I was clean."

He looked from side to side as he spoke, looking for support among his compatriots. They drew away, not meeting his eyes. I watched this edifying sight for a few seconds before I took a breath, steeling myself against what needed to be done, and knelt.

The mouse he had closed his hand around looked no different than any of the dead mice I had encountered in my life, the ones purchased from pet stores to feed to my snakes, the ones carried into the house by Crow, croaking proudly about his skills as a hunter. (He knew better than to hunt the Aeslin. The Aeslin had a nasty tendency to hunt back, and they could carry a grudge for a long, long time.) So no, there was nothing special about this mouse, save for the small necklace of buttons it wore around its thick rodent neck, and the fact that only minutes before it had been a talking, thinking, intelligent creature with a life and a future of its own.

I couldn't bring myself to pick it up. I looked at it, lying there broken and motionless, and I couldn't do it. Instead, I cupped my other hand over the Aeslin mice that were still alive and straightened, turning to face the Tanners. All three of them were staring at me, Shelby with her hands clapped over her mouth like that would somehow keep the tears inside, Charlotte and Raina with matching looks of wide-eyed horror.

"Someone needs to bring the body to my room," I said quietly. "The mice will have funeral arrangements to make, and rituals to observe. Now, if you will all excuse me, I need to go and explain to my colony's head priest how I've failed them."

Shelby dropped her hands. "Alex—" she began.

I shook my head. She stopped. "I failed them," I repeated, and walked through the open front door, the remaining Aeslin mice a small, shivering weight in my palm.

The door to my room was open when I reached the

second floor. The mice were nowhere to be seen. I stepped fully inside, took a deep breath, and said, "I need to see you, please. Come out. It's important."

"All right, mate," said Cooper, in an exaggerated Australian drawl. I had time to turn toward his voice, a look of horror spreading across my face. Then something was clapped over my nose and mouth, and the smell of chloroform obscured everything else. The last thing I saw was Cooper's smile, broad as a Cheshire cat's, and twice as dangerous. Then my vision went black, and Cooper, along with everything else, was gone.

Sixteen

"Ah, ambushes. Those take me back. The best ones are the ones that start with chloroform and handcuffs, and end with death threats and knives. And by 'best' I mean 'most irritating,' you understand."

—Thomas Price

Waking up in an unknown location that is hopefully still in Queensland, Australia, but might as well be on the moon

WAKING UP WITH A chloroform headache wasn't a new experience for me, and hadn't been since I was eight years old and my father spent the better part of a summer ambushing me at various points around the property. (When I got good enough at avoiding him to go a week without being knocked unconscious through some mechanism or another, he called his mother to come spend the rest of the summer with us. Waking up to the sight of Grandma Alice grinning maniacally while she cleaned her guns was sobering, and more than a little disturbing, in a "maybe my parents should not have been allowed to have children" sort of way.)

After taking a few shallow breaths to be sure my head wasn't going to explode at the slightest provocation, I dared to sit up a little straighter. The motion betrayed the fact that I was strapped to whatever it was I was sitting on; my wrists and ankles were no doubt restrained as well, if the numbness in my extremities meant anything. People who weren't in the habit of taking hostages always made things too tight, at least at first. It was like they didn't care about loss of circulation and gangrene.

Oh, wait. They probably *didn't* care.

"Are you awake, or are you just having a dream about your pretty girlfriend? It's been three hours. That's long enough for a sleep." The voice was Cooper's; judging by his calm, conversational tone, he was no more than five feet away. Something nudged my calf, causing my numb ankle to rub painfully against something that felt like a length of twine. They definitely weren't worrying about my losing circulation. Either they weren't planning to keep me for long, or they didn't care whether I ever walked again.

It's a sad fact of my line of work — cryptozoology, not herpetology — that waking up tied to an unidentified piece of furniture, being held captive by a werewolf, was nowhere near as upsetting as the idea that I could have been unconscious long enough to need medical attention before I'd be able to stand unassisted. That was just disrespectful.

"Hey." My calf was nudged again. I adjusted my thoughts on where Cooper was in the room. Since he was apparently kicking me, he was probably a lot closer than five feet. "Now I know chloroform doesn't last this long, and I know you've probably built up some sort of resistance to the stuff, so why don't you go ahead and stop playing dead? Unless you'd like me to start taking off fingers as an incentive to opening your eyes."

"Did you jump to violence this fast before you became a werewolf, or is it a side effect of the infection?" My voice came out slightly slurred. I swallowed hard to try to get the dry, cottony feeling out of my mouth, licked my lips, and continued more clearly, "I am genuinely interested. For science, if nothing else."

"I think it's a side effect. But it's one I'm capable of controlling, as long as I'm given a good reason to. You're not giving me very many good reasons, Covenant boy. I'd start, if I were you."

I opened my eyes. As expected, Cooper was standing in front of me, a frown on his face. He did not, it seemed, care for my continued disrespect. Poor him. My parents raised me to be polite and considerate of others. They did not, however, raise me to be particularly respectful of people who thought that drugging me and tying me to a—I took a quick glance to the side—to a chair was a good way to start a conversation.

Cooper was expected. The four people standing behind him were somewhat less so. Chloe Bryant—the woman with the face of a swimsuit model, and the attitude of a pissed-off bus driver—was one of them. That wasn't a surprise. I vaguely recognized two of the remaining three; they'd been around the Thirty-Six Society compound, although neither of them had done anything to really stand out. They had been backgrounders, extras in the great adventure that had been my time in Australia. The fourth . . .

My eyes focused on him for almost a second before they processed what they were seeing and transmitted that information to my brain, which really didn't want to accept it. Sadly, denial is not a strong suit of mine. I lunged against the ropes that held me, sending the chair rocking forward before it thudded back to the floor. The twine dug into my ankles, and the thicker rope that was tied around my waist and throat threatened to knock the wind out of me.

The tall, broad-shouldered man with the obviously broken nose took a step backward, eyes going wide, before he realized I wasn't magically breaking free of my bonds and coming after him. Then he grinned, the slow, sly smile of a man who suddenly felt like nothing could threaten him. "Yeah, I thought not," he said. "Not so tough now, are you?"

"Mick, you idiot." Chloe smacked him in the back of the head. He flinched away, sulking at her. I made a note of his mulish expression. He was the low man on their totem pole, then, the one who was most likely to yield to pressure. That was good to know, even as I still felt the burning desire to slit his throat for what he'd done to my mouse.

"Don't torment the doctor," continued Chloe, raising her hand as if to go for another smack. Mick cringed away. The blow didn't come, but her voice sharpened further as she continued: "He needs to be willing to help us, and he's not going to help us if you've got him all pissed off."

"I'm already pissed off," I said coldly. "If your goal was keeping me calm and relaxed, you shouldn't have started with chloroform. I've never had a date involving chloroform that didn't end badly." I swung my attention to Cooper, moving my head as much as I could against the rope. "Did you tell him to do it?"

Cooper frowned. "Do what?"

"Your man, Mick. He killed one of my mice. Reached up, wrapped his fingers around it, and crushed the life out of it. Was that your idea?"

Cooper blinked, and for just a moment I saw the man I'd thought I met before the attack in the meadow, the man who loved his dog and took everything at his own pace. "Why would I tell him to do something like that?"

"I don't know," I said. "I don't know why you do anything. I don't know why you bit Gabby, or whether you infected your own dog, or why you think that the answer to not wanting to feel like a monster is spreading a disease among the people who are supposed to be your colleagues. So for all I know, you could have given him the order."

"Well, I didn't," said Cooper stiffly. "I didn't infect Jett, either. I love my dog."

"It was just a mouse," I said. "It was just trying to do what I'd asked of it. They think my family . . . they think we're gods. It couldn't tell me 'no,' not even if it was scared, not even if it didn't want to do what I asked. How many of us can look our gods in the face and tell them we're not going to do their bidding?" The Aeslin mice did refuse us, from time to time, but never without good reason, and never about something that mattered.

Maybe that was going to change after my fragment of the colony made it home from Australia. Maybe I was going to be the one who finally, after decades of living with us, taught the Aeslin that we were fallible.

"Lottie had that damn thing sniffing out werewolves," protested Mick, seeming to sense the mood in the room shifting against him. "She was holding it up to people's faces and letting it check them for infection. You said, Cooper, you said do whatever it took to keep our people from getting caught out. Well, that mouse was going to catch *everybody* out. Sniffing like that."

"You also said we needed to get Mr. Price here away from the Tanners," said Chloe. "Killing the mouse accomplished that. It was a necessary loss."

"I see. It's funny how you're taking that approach now, when just a moment ago you were so invested in keeping our new friend from becoming too angry to work with us. It's almost like you're changing your allegiances to suit whatever you think will go over best at any given moment." Cooper turned to look thoughtfully at Chloe. "Is that what you're doing?"

Chloe's eyes widened. "No. No, sir. I would never do anything that disingenuous."

"See, I would have bet that none of you knew any words that big," I said. I flexed my hands, trying to keep the motion from echoing in my arms and shoulders. It was difficult; I had to restrict myself to even smaller movements of my wrists than would normally have been my preference. Still, my hands moved freely, with no more impediment than the rope. That was what I had been hoping for. "You didn't go for the organizational brain trust, did you, Cooper?"

"Brains are a liability when you're trying to build an army," said Cooper, sounding unconcerned. He began circling Chloe and Mick, cutting them off from their unidentified compatriots. The two remaining werewolves fell back, relieved expressions on their faces. Whatever punishment Mick and Chloe were about to face, they'd be spared. "It leads to having too many generals, and not enough soldiers. That's just bad planning. We'll have plenty of time for recruiting smart people to our side—starting with you. You're smart enough to know that you'll not be leaving this room still believing yourself to be a human being."

"You'll like being a werewolf, once you get used to it," said one of the unnamed werewolves. She was tall, brunette, and spoke with an accent that marked her as coming from somewhere outside Australia, although I couldn't have named her country of origin. "It's nice to know that you're bigger and badder than anything that might come after you."

"The running around naked part's nice, too," said Mick. He sounded uneasy, and his eyes were tracking Cooper. I couldn't decide whether the joke was a defense mechanism or a bad attempt at ingratiating himself with his chosen pack. It didn't matter either way.

I kept working my hands in slow circles, ignoring the way the twine bit into my wrists. These people weren't professionals: I'd known that as soon as I woke up with numb feet, still fully clothed. No one who catches a Price and wants to *keep* us captive leaves us with our clothes on. It's just practicality. The weight of the mice against my chest was gone. Either they had run out of my pocket when I was chloroformed, or Cooper had had them removed. I wanted to ask him if he had them. I couldn't give him that card. If he didn't have them, and I asked, he would know that he could lie. "I'm not an exhibitionist, thanks," I said.

"So which one, hmm?" Cooper turned to look at me. I slowed the motion of my hands by half, reducing it to a painful crawl. "The man who did the deed or the woman who laughed about it? Which one do you blame?"

I didn't hesitate. "The man who did it. If you didn't give the order, then he crushed the life out of a living thing because he thought it would be expedient. This is his fault. He's the one who committed the crime."

"Good enough for me." Cooper started to turn away from Mick. Then, grabbing the knife from his belt, he whirled back around. He moved with preternatural swiftness, faster than anything human could have hoped to achieve; I didn't see the cut so much as I saw Mick's throat open in a wet red smile, blood spraying from his severed carotid artery. My glasses protected my eyes, and I kept my mouth closed, turning my head away to try to minimize my exposure to his blood. I still saw him hit the floor on his knees, hands clutching his throat in a desperate attempt to stem the bleeding.

He slumped forward. Cooper produced a gun from the other side of his belt and fired twice, putting both shots into the back of Mick's head. The big man went limp, the smell of his emptied bowels mixing with the equally unpleasant odors of blood and cordite. Cooper kicked him in the leg. Mick didn't move.

"Big bastard seemed like a grand idea, but he wasn't," he said. "Never buy in bulk if you're hoping to get quality goods, that's what I'm taking away from this one."

I was probably meant to be stunned by the fact that he would kill one of his own people so easily. He'd clearly never dealt with harpies in the middle of a territory dispute. I raised an eyebrow, squinting to see through my blood-spattered lenses, and said, "That sounds like an excellent moral."

"And here I was afraid you'd be no fun." Cooper walked across the room to me. I stopped working on the rope that held my hands, holding perfectly still as he removed my glasses, spat on the lenses, and wiped them clean on his shirt. Then he replaced them on my nose, pushing them gingerly into place. "Sorry about the mess.

We're hard as hell to kill once we get going, and I wanted to make sure he didn't have a chance to make things any messier than they had to be." His three remaining werewolves had drawn close together, forming a small, terrified huddle.

Cooper was setting himself up as the unquestioned alpha of his little pack — a power dynamic that had a lot more to do with human psychology than it did with animal behavior. I didn't know about werewolves, for obvious reasons, but real wolves don't follow that sort of hierarchy. People just think they do, and if there's one thing people are good at, it's projecting their own distorted desires onto the animal kingdom.

"I'm drenched in blood and you're intending to turn me into a werewolf against my own stated preferences," I said. "I'm not seeing how this could get any messier."

"I promise, you'll enjoy being one of us." Cooper smiled, showing off all his teeth. "It's the best of all possible worlds."

"That's nice," I said. "If you bite me or infect me through any other means, I won't help you."

Cooper blinked. "What?"

"You heard me. I didn't come to Australia to become a werewolf. My family would probably be tolerant, since they're good that way, but it would interfere with my plans for the future. I would thus very much rather not."

Cooper blinked again. He didn't seem to be fully processing what I was saying. "You can't just refuse to become a werewolf."

"I didn't refuse to become a werewolf, I refused to help you if you turned me into one," I said. "I appreciate the fact that you've moved on to threatening me indoors like a civilized person, but my answer remains the same. I do not wish to become a werewolf. Thank you, but no thank you."

"Is he serious?" demanded Chloe. "That isn't how this works."

I leaned a little to the side in order to get a clear look

at her. "Actually, yes, it is," I said. "I'm assuming you wanted me because you're looking for information about your condition. There are some negative side effects, after all, and if I were you, I would very much want a trained biologist on my side. And if I am intentionally infected, I will fight you until you either have to kill me or let me go, at which point I will return to America to be cared for by my own family, and any chance you might have had of exploiting what I know will be gone. Bite me, and you lose."

Chloe stared at me. "I—I don't even know what to say."

"Oh, you'll help us," said Cooper, dragging my attention back to him. Chloe's interjection had apparently given him time to recover his train of thought. Pity. I preferred my assholes confused and easily manipulated. "See, what you're forgetting is that you're not the only one I can sink my teeth into. So you say you won't help us if we bite you? I say you're going to be *begging* for it after we bite your fiancée."

"Shouldn't I be begging you to bite me instead of biting Shelby?" I asked, struggling to keep my tone neutral. I couldn't let him see how much the question had upset me. If I did, he'd know he was on the right track. "And don't think I missed how you stopped referring to her as my girlfriend and started calling her my fiancée as soon as you thought you could use her against me."

"Nah." Cooper grinned. "I'm going to bite her no matter what you do. But once she's one of us, you'll help, just for the chance to keep her alive. Maybe that'll be my wedding gift to the pair of you—a little nip so you can make healthy pups." He turned and started to walk away.

"Where are you going?" This wasn't in the plan. Much as I wanted to be alone—it would make it easier to get out of these damn ropes—I didn't want him going after Shelby.

"You know where I'm going," said Cooper. He opened the door leading out of the room. I caught a glimpse of empty, unfurnished hallway. We were in another safe house, then; what little I had seen had the unmistakable hallmarks of the Thirty-Six Society's absolute lack of design sense. "Shelby will be thrilled to know that you've been found. Chloe, Trigby, you're with me. Blithe, you stay here and keep an eye on our guest."

Chloe and the previously unnamed male werewolf fell in behind Cooper, following him out of the room. Chloe cast a grin back over her shoulder at me, blowing a quick kiss before she stepped into the hall and slammed the door.

The remaining werewolf—Blithe—smiled apologetically. "Sorry about all this," she said. "Cooper said there'd be some resistance, and maybe his methods aren't the nicest, but he really does have our best interests at heart. You'll see. Once you've had a chance to take a couple of deep breaths and think about it, you'll understand."

"Cooper just killed a man in front of you," I said, slowly. "He slit his throat and then shot him in the head. Isn't that a problem for you?"

"Nah," said Blithe, shrugging. "Werewolves always have issues, no matter where we're at. I mean, back in New Zealand, I got accused of harrying sheep. As if I would. No point in bothering the flocks when they belong to the people I know. Tourists are much tastier."

This time, her smile seemed to contain substantially more teeth, and those teeth seemed substantially sharper.

I stared at her. "It was you," I said. "You're the one who brought the infection to Australia."

"Brought it to New Zealand first," said Blithe. "I was on vacation in California when I got nipped. Flew home before I shifted the first time. Didn't I get a shock! Ate the cat. Ate one of the neighbors, too." She didn't sound remotely sorry about either. "New Zealand's a bit small when you're a big, healthy predator, you know? I needed a place where I could run, where there were other dangerous beasts to keep people from fingering me for everything that went wrong. I'd worked with the Thirty-

Sixers before, and I managed to stick it out six months before anyone caught me. It was an accident that I came across Cooper while I was changed. I didn't mean to bite him, but he frightened me, and I did what came naturally."

"You should never have come here," I said.

"Yeah? Where should I have gone?" Blithe spread her hands in a beseeching gesture. "Look at it from my perspective: I didn't ask to get bitten. I didn't volunteer to be changed. Why should I have to give up my life because of a stupid accident? And look, I did my best to minimize the damage. I kept an eye on Cooper until I was sure he was going to change, and then I made sure he went through the first few transformations when he was somewhere nice and isolated, with no one around for him to hurt. He never had the opportunity to become a danger, you can be sure of that."

"You were the second werewolf in the meadow, weren't you?" I shook my head, using the motion to distract from the fact that I was working my hands harder now, picking and pulling at the rope that held them. I was starting to get some give in the knots. If I was going to be tied up and held captive, these were the sort of people I wanted doing it: people who had no idea how to take prisoners. "You're the one who bit me."

Blithe shrugged. "Cooper explained what you were here to do. I couldn't let you get a good look at me—it was hard to say whether you'd be able to spot me in my human form, I keep my eyebrows plucked and most people haven't noticed my hands—but I could help with recruitment. We figured you'd trust him after that. We didn't count on you being able to mix up your witch's brew after you'd been wounded, and we definitely didn't figure on you killing poor Donny. Lead works, if you use enough of it."

I looked at her blankly. "Your hands?"

She held them up, backs toward me, fingers pressed together. Her index and pointer fingers were the same length. "Some of the old stories are truer than I ever thought. I figured you might catch it if you looked."

"We usually kill werewolves before they have a chance to undergo any permanent physiological transformations," I said. Assuming I made it home alive and with my fingers intact, I was going to have a lot of updates to make to the field guide. We'd never realized that werewolves changed like that.

"Oh, then you'll love this." She stuck a finger in her eye. I cringed, waiting for gore—and only relaxed a bit as she withdrew her finger, now with a contact lens resting on the tip, and blinked one suddenly lupine, amber eye at me. Her grin was delighted. "You're a lot more squeamish than I thought you'd be."

"How is your color vision?" I couldn't resist. Maybe I should have . . . but it's not every day that a genuine scientific curiosity decides to try selling me on the idea of becoming part of its pack. Everything Blithe told me was going straight into the guide. Hopefully.

"Not so good," she admitted. "It's been getting worse since my irises started changing. I figure there's something structural happening in there. I used to need glasses, though, and now my vision is better than twenty-twenty. I can see for miles, and you'll be able to do the same. No more specs for you, brainy boy. Won't that be a nice change?"

"You know, I like my glasses," I said. The first knot let go. "I've been wearing them for most of my life, and I'm used to them at this point. Besides, they can be useful. They've kept me from getting blood, cobra venom, all sorts of things into my eyes. They even helped keep me from being turned to stone once."

"Too bad." Blithe smiled toothily. "I know you think this is a bad thing. I know you feel like we're forcing you. But it's for the best, you'll see. We're a family, a pack. We're better than what you'll be losing."

"Did Mick feel like that?" I kept working at the second knot. It felt like I was going to dislocate my thumb.

I was willing to do that, if I had to, but things would be easier if I didn't. It's hard to shoot people when your thumb doesn't feel like working anymore.

Not that I was actually sure I still had a gun, and it wasn't like I could ask Blithe if they'd taken it off of me: asking would be a good way to get frisked, assuming I hadn't been already.

Blithe's lip curled upward in a sneer. "Mick was a fool," she said. "He didn't appreciate the pack. He didn't appreciate what he'd become. He only went along with it because he thought it would make him stronger, and he thought it would help get him into Chloe's pants. I suppose that's been a bit of a shock for him on both counts, hmm? Not only did he not get laid, he got weaker. He wasn't meant to be an alpha."

"Am I?"

Blithe's sneer became more pronounced before she abandoned it in favor of laughing out loud. "Heavens, no. You don't have the right combination of viciousness and wanting to be an alpha. Cooper did. I did. We're going to lead this pack forever, and you're going to work for us willingly once you've been bitten and the instinct kicks in."

I frowned, thinking. Cooper hadn't mentioned Blithe; hadn't introduced her to me, hadn't brought her forward as his co-leader. Hadn't done anything but allow her to stay behind and try to sell me on the exciting werewolf lifestyle. There had been three wolves with him when he came to see us in the swamp. Mick couldn't have been among them—none of them had been particularly larger than the rest, and more, he'd been in the line, within Charlotte's line of sight, the whole time. Someone like Chloe or Blithe could move through the crowd without making a fuss, but Mick? He had been a mountain. When mountains move, people notice.

"If you're his co-leader, why didn't he tell you to bite me?" The second knot gave way. One more to go. I began working faster, trying to keep the motion from traveling into my arms and betraying what I was doing.

Blithe's eyes narrowed. "What?"

"I'm just saying, Cooper never told *me* he was sharing leadership with anyone. He seemed pretty sure that this whole pack belonged to him. He came up with the current plan all by himself. Leave me human, infect my girlfriend, make me beg to be one of you—that was all him. How come he didn't tell you to convince me?"

"He didn't have to," she said. She was starting to sound uncertain. Good. "He knew that when he left me here to keep an eye on you, I'd start working on bringing you around. I'm not some pup who needs constant guidance."

"Or maybe he didn't think you'd disobey him, because he doesn't think you're an alpha." The third knot was beginning to slip. Not much—not enough—but there was give in the rope now. I kept working, praying she wouldn't smell the blood from my increasingly raw fingertips.

While I would never be glad that one of my mice was dead, I did find myself thankful Mick had crossed a line and justified Cooper killing him—even if the justification was only in Cooper's mind. Mick had bled enough as he died that my little scrapes shouldn't attract any attention. I hoped.

"Shut up," said Blithe.

"I thought you wanted me to talk to you," I said. "So we could discuss what it's like to be a werewolf. Wasn't that the plan? I'm interested in your insights, since you're the one who decided to bite a man who was smarter than you were. Did you secretly know that you weren't an alpha? That would be a good way to go about replacing yourself. You wouldn't even have to admit what you were doing. You'd just need to stand back and follow orders while the pack slipped away from you and toward him. I applaud you, really. I couldn't have done it better myself."

"Shut *up*." This time Blithe chased the word with a snarl. There was a wild look in her single amber eye; the blue contact covering her other iris kept it from portraying quite so much of her turmoil. It was almost a snapshot of the werewolf condition. She was human and animal at the same time. Again, I wondered whether I had any right to do what I was about to do. If she had been willing to keep her teeth away from people, to go into quarantine and live out her life without hurting anyone, could I really have called her a monster?

But those weren't the choices she'd made. She'd bitten Cooper, knowing what might happen, and she'd helped him with his whole delusional plan to create a pack from the bodies of the Thirty-Six Society. She was a person, yes. She was also an enemy.

"Make me," I suggested.

She lunged, snarling—

—and stopped, looking in confusion at the throwing knife that was sticking out of her abdomen, just below the rib cage. It was a good shot, if I did say so myself. That's not an easy mark to hit, especially when your target is in motion.

"You little bastard," she said wonderingly. "I knew we should have searched you. I *knew* it. But Cooper said you'd be more cooperative if you felt we'd been respectful." She raised her head and growled, ropes of froth beginning to form at the corners of her mouth. "I'm done being respectful."

"Good," I said. "So am I."

Her one amber eye made a perfect target, distinct as it was from the rest of her face. Knife-throwing was never my focus—not the way it was for Verity, who practically specialized in the things, or Antimony, who regularly carried knives belonging to our great-grandmother, and considered them more accurate than bullets in many situations. But it was a family tradition, and I knew how to handle a blade with sufficient skill as to not be an embarrassment. I aimed. I threw.

Blithe stopped, the menace leaking out of her face like it was a punctured balloon. "Ah," she said, reaching up to touch the knife's hilt with one shaking hand. Vitreous humor was beginning to leak down her cheek like thick, terrible tears.

"Silver-tipped throwing knives," I said, pulling my other hand from behind my back and beginning to cut the ropes holding me to the chair. "Always carry them when going into werewolf territory. Unless you're trying to commit a very painful form of suicide."

"Ah," said Blithe again. She started trying to close her fingers around the knife, and found that she couldn't: the silver on the blade was already interfering with her motor functions.

"Cooper was right: people are generally happier when they feel like they've been treated with respect. But the way to do that would have been to not do this in the first place. Nothing about this situation is respectful." Pins and needles flooded my feet when I cut the ropes away. My circulation was going to take a while to return to normal. Bastards. I forced myself to stand anyway, testing my balance. "I truly am sorry this happened to you. I'm sure you were a lovely person before you got bitten."

"Ah," she said, dropping her hand. She looked at me beseechingly, or as beseechingly as it was possible for someone to look when they had a knife protruding from one eye.

"I understand," I said.

The third knife caught her in the hollow of the throat, severing her airway and coating the wound with silver at the same time. Whatever regenerative properties she possessed—it was unclear exactly how much healing werewolves were capable of, but all the legends agreed it was there, and it was always best to trust the folklore when fighting something you couldn't risk studying in depth—they wouldn't be able to work around the silver.

The sound she made when she hit the floor was small and somehow sad, like she had been intended for a grander ending. I walked across the room to where she lay sprawled, and knelt, rolling her onto her back. Her single remaining eye stared sightlessly at the ceiling. I checked her pulse, and found it absent. I still used one of my remaining knives to slit her throat, and waited for a count of one hundred before I reclaimed the others. It was always better to be safe than sorry, especially under circumstances like this one.

I wiped my knives clean on a patch of carpet that no one had yet had the chance to bleed on. Then I straightened, checking the rest of my weapons. They were all present, save for the pistol that had been at my belt. I guess Cooper's ideas about "respect" didn't extend to leaving me with silver bullets. That was all right. I'm a Price. I was raised knowing how to improvise.

With three throwing knives ready in my left hand, I walked to the door, and pulled it open.

Seventeen

"Empathy is a beautiful thing. It's also a luxury. When your back is against the wall, remember that survival comes before sympathy, and if you can only save one person, you have to save yourself."

— Alexander Healy

Stepping into the hall in an unknown location that is probably still in Queensland, Australia, but might as well be on the moon

COOPER WAS EITHER ARROGANT or stupid, or put too much faith in Blithe—or possibly and most likely, some combination of the three. The hall was empty, stretching out in either direction like an invitation to freedom. I stopped in the doorway, tucking my chin against my chest and closing my eyes as I listened to the house, trying to decide which way was going to lead me to the outside world. Voices drifted from the left, distant and distorted, but audible enough to make me think they belonged to living people, rather than to an unattended television set. I raised my head, opened my eyes, and started walking.

The nice thing about being in a house with an unknown number of people is that while it's still best to be reasonably stealthy, there's no need to muffle every step like some sort of ninja in a video game. Most small sounds will be dismissed as either a sign of the foundation settling, or the result of someone else moving around. There's a downside, of course—I could come around a corner and find myself nose to snout with one of my werewolf captors—but the positives outweighed the negatives, at least in my situation.

The impression that this was a Thirty-Six Society safe house intensified as I walked along the hall. The walls were bare, save for a few small, geometric paintings in cheap black frames, and the carpet, while a cheerful shade of lemony yellow, was clearly designed to be easily cleaned, more practical than plush. I would have laid odds on it having been Scotchgarded against bloodstains. Whoever did their interior decorating wasn't creative, but they were practical enough to make up for any lapses.

Following the voices led me to the top of a flight of stairs. I stopped and pressed my back against the wall, listening.

They were arguing about something. I couldn't make out what it was, but the female voice sounded angry, and the male voice sounded more placating. Cooper wasn't there, or if he was, he was sitting by silently, observing his people while they fought.

Cooper had taken Chloe and Trigby with him when he went to get Shelby. My stomach sank. Either there were more werewolves than I had suspected, or Cooper was already back with my girlfriend. Neither option was good. To be honest, I had hoped that Cooper's people wouldn't come back at all. Shelby wasn't some defenseless little flower, and with her mother and sister right there, she stood a good chance of taking out any attacker. But Cooper knew her. He might know how to get around whatever security the Tanners had in place.

Bastard. I didn't enjoy thinking of myself as a killer, but I couldn't deny that I would enjoy seeing him dead.

Slowly, I peeled away from the wall and began creeping down the stairs, so tense that my shoulders felt like they had been replaced by iron bars. The knives in my hand were no real comfort. I still couldn't use my left hand for knife-throwing, and this wasn't the sort of situation I wanted to walk into one-handed and without a gun. I listened even harder as I descended, hoping for something to indicate how many werewolves were beneath me, and whether they were the two I had seen before.

The step beneath my foot creaked loudly.

I froze, pulling back a step, but it was too late: the alarm had been sounded. "Blithe?" a man's voice, much closer than it had been only a few seconds before: he was approaching. Dandy. That was just what I needed. "Did you need something? You know you're supposed to stay with the Price fellow until Cooper gets back."

Maybe this *was* just what I needed. Now I knew that Cooper hadn't returned with Shelby, even if this confirmed the existence of at least two more werewolves. Like Blithe, this man sounded faintly familiar; I had probably walked past him at some point, maybe even been introduced to him, and failed to register anything out of the ordinary. Assuming I got through this alive, I was going to recommend the family seriously improve our werewolf detection training.

A narrow male face appeared around the wall separating the stairwell from the front room. He had time to widen his eyes and open his mouth in preparation for shouting for help, and then a knife was in his throat, making it impossible for him to do more than choke. He staggered backward, out of my line of sight, before I could throw another knife.

"What the *fuck*—?!" shrieked the female voice.

So much for stealth. I ran the rest of the way down the stairs, whipping around the corner into the living room to find a skinny teenage girl holding up the man with the knife in his throat, a terrified expression on her face.

"We didn't do it," she said rapidly. "We didn't kidnap you we didn't touch you we didn't do anything please. Please don't do this. Please we haven't hurt anyone please." The man was still choking and clawing at the knife in his throat, and for a moment, I was afraid I had acted too quickly: that I had killed, or at least direly injured, an innocent bystander.

Then I noticed her hands. They were shortening, the fingers becoming stubby as the nails became more pronounced, stretching into claws that dug into the man's skin without quite breaking it. These people were werewolves. Whether they had chosen this or not, they were, for the moment, the enemy.

She proved it a second later, when she shoved the man aside, revealing the reshaped angles of her legs, which had stretched and bent while his body had blocked them from view, giving her a wolf's jumping power while leaving her with a human's height and versatility. She snarled, showing a mouth full of teeth, and leaped for me, clawed hands extended.

I flung a knife at her, aiming for the dark triangle of her open mouth. She batted the blade aside while it was in the air. Shit.

With only two knives remaining and no chance of getting more, I did the only sensible thing: I turned and ran, trusting panic to grant me greater speed. There was a door only a few feet away. I wrenched it open, revealing a dark porch, the night spread out beyond it like a prayer—and Cooper, Shelby slung over his shoulder, standing there. The look on his face must have mirrored mine, all stunned confusion and disbelief. Then it hardened, and his eyes flashed amber.

Well, shit.

Cooper recovered first. "Don't kill him!" he barked, directing his words to the girl behind me. I raised my knives, preparing to throw, and stopped as clawed hands seized my arms and yanked them painfully behind my back. "Disarm," Cooper snarled.

The hands tightened, compressing until I could no longer keep my right hand closed against the pain. The knives clattered to the ground.

"He put one of those in Albert's throat," said the unnamed female werewolf, her words garbled by her mouthful of lupine teeth but still intelligible. "Albert's not getting better."

"Silver throwing knives?" asked Cooper, looking back to my face. I didn't answer him. He smiled. "Clever. I'm assuming Blithe is dead?"

"You're next," I said. "Shelby—"

"Not bitten yet. Thought I'd show you I mean business and give you one more chance to come along willingly. That way you can bite her yourself, once you understand what we're offering you." Cooper's smile was full of teeth, but they still looked mostly human. He was keeping himself under control, for now. "And before you start thinking that we're easily fooled, remember, I left Blithe with you for a reason."

I stared at him. It had seemed awfully convenient, me left alone with a single werewolf, especially one who was so cocky that she'd let herself get into range. "You set her up."

"She thought she was in charge. I thought you might have something up your sleeve." Cooper shrugged. "Guess I was right and she was wrong. Thanks for cleaning up that little mess for me. Now we have a better understanding of how far you'll go, and I don't have to kill her myself."

"Albert," whined the werewolf who was holding me.

"He should've known better than to go investigate a strange noise—I'm assuming that's what happened, yeah?" Cooper didn't wait for an answer. He pushed past us, carrying Shelby inside. The door remained open, but there was no way I was making a break for it: not now, not with Shelby in his control. He might be willing to refrain from biting me until I consented. I knew he wasn't going to offer her the same courtesy.

Besides, Chloe and Trigby appeared on the porch almost as soon as he'd vacated it, prowling out of the darkness as naked as the day they'd been born. Chloe smirked at me when she saw me. "Like what you see?" she purred. "Tanner girls don't know how to have fun. Maybe once you're properly one of us, you and I can play a little chase-the-rabbit around the meadow, hmm?"

"Business first, pleasure later," snapped Cooper. "Deb, keep hold of him. Chloe, come help me tie her down."

"You're no fun at all," complained Chloe. She stepped past me. "Ew, what happened to Albert? Is he dead?"

"He will be soon," said Cooper, sounding unconcerned. "Deb, come on. Kitchen, now."

Deb growled, apparently too upset to continue using words. Her claws were breaking the skin on my arms. I winced, but did my best not to struggle. She was on the verge of losing control, and I didn't want to give her any reason to disobey Cooper.

"Better move, Deb," said Trigby, not unkindly. "You know the boss doesn't like being kept waiting."

"Hate him," spat Deb, her voice now so distorted that it was virtually incomprehensible. She turned, yanking me along with her. I caught a glimpse of Albert, lying in a pool of blood in the middle of the floor—and apparently quite dead—and then I was being shoved across the room and down a short hallway that I hadn't had the opportunity to see before. It ended in a small, homey kitchen with a tile floor and floral wallpaper. A dining set took up a large portion of the available floor space. Shelby, still unconscious, had been dumped into one of the chairs, and Cooper was in the process of tying her hands behind her.

"Put him down," he said, jerking his chin toward an open chair.

Deb shoved me into the seat, harder than she had to, ripping my arms even more in the process. This time, I didn't bother to conceal my wince. Cooper was watching. The more hurt he thought I was, the better my situation was going to be.

"You've killed two of my people," he said. "I hope you understand that you're going to replace them. I am a fair man. I know you may have had other plans for your life. At the same time, I can't allow you to weaken us like this."

I stared at him. "You put me in a situation where it was her or me."

"Yes, and you could have chosen to let her kill you and thus spare yourself a lifetime on all fours. You elected to live. That's good for me—I wanted you to make that choice—but it's not necessarily best for you." Cooper smiled. "At least you'll still be together."

"It didn't have to be like this," I said. "It still doesn't."

"I think you'll find that we're well past the point of no return," said Cooper. He moved to stand behind Shelby, licking his lips once, and then bent forward, like he was going to kiss her neck.

I couldn't help it. I jerked against Deb's hands, cutting myself worse in the process, to no avail. Her grip was too tight. I wasn't breaking free.

Someone rang the doorbell.

The entire room went still. Cooper snarled, straightening again, and looked first to Chloe and Trigby—who were naked—and then to Deb, who was half-transformed and had shredded much of her clothing. Seeing no useful flunkies, he lowered his voice and said, "Be quiet. I don't know who followed us here, but they don't know for sure that anyone's inside."

The doorbell rang again. Shelby groaned, beginning to stir. Cooper checked the knots on her hands, looking flustered for the first time. Too much was happening at once; his plans might be elaborate, but they didn't cover anything like this.

"We can kill whoever it is," said Chloe, in a mild, almost disinterested tone.

"And then we have one more body on our hands," snapped Cooper. "How many of those do you think we can feed to the bunyips before somebody notices that the locals have started disappearing? We need to be careful, until we're the dominant species."

"As I told your former boss back at the Society, the Covenant is not going to tolerate an entire continent of werewolves," I said. "They're going to find out, and they're going to stop you." And even more people were going to die. No matter how we sliced things, a lot of lives were going to end if this fight continued.

"Let them come," said Cooper. "They're only men, by their own design, and we'll be something so much more that they won't stand a chance."

Someone knocked on the back door.

Every head in the kitchen swung toward the sound, except for Shelby's; she was still unconscious, slumped forward in her chair to the limits of the ropes that bound her hands behind her. Everyone was silent, even me. Crying for help would endanger Shelby, and might get whoever was standing outside killed.

The knock came again. And then, to my surprise, the doorknob turned.

"You didn't lock the door," said Chloe, in a surprised tone that would have sounded more natural coming from the ingénue in a horror movie than it did from a naked werewolf. "We're hiding in the middle of nowhere, and you didn't lock the door."

There wasn't time for Deb to answer. The door swung open to reveal Helen Jalali, dressed in tan slacks and a cream-colored sweater, holding what looked like a Bible against her chest. She smiled pleasantly as she looked around the room at the stunned werewolves, unperturbed by the blood and nudity. "Hello," she said. "Have you heard the good word of Wadjet, Protector of Egypt and great snake of the Milky Way?"

The stunned silence stretched on. Pagan missionaries were not, it seemed, on Cooper's docket for the evening.

"I have some pamphlets, if this is a bad time," Helen continued. "I think you'll find that when you're looking for a patron goddess to consume your eternal soul and save you from the fires of your current religion's afterlife, Wadjet is absolutely the best choice available."

"Get out," growled Cooper.

Helen's expression cooled as she looked at him. "That isn't a very charitable reaction to a neighbor expressing her religious freedom," she said.

"Get *out!*" Cooper shouted, and stepped toward her, menace evident in his posture.

"Oh, if you're going to be like *that*—Alex, cover your eyes!" Helen whirled, throwing her book as hard as she could at Deb's face. The cover came open on impact, and a glass jar full of my lycanthropy treatment fell out, shattering as it hit the edge of the table. Aconite and silver nitrate sprayed everywhere. Deb howled and fell back, clutching at her arms where the liquid had hit. Chloe danced away from the spill.

Cooper growled. So did Trigby, who stalked forward, the bones of his spine beginning to distort. Helen hissed, her fangs descending from the roof of her mouth and gleaming with amber beads of poison. Trigby and Cooper were both Australian; they knew better than to mess with a snake that was determined to stand its ground. They stopped where they were, apparently too perplexed to continue.

That was the pause I needed. I jumped to my feet before Deb could grab me, pulling another knife from my belt and whirling to jam it into her chest. Throwing knives aren't designed for stabbing people, but that doesn't mean you *can't* use them that way, if you have to. Deb's eyes went wide, and she clawed at me before she collapsed, fingers scrabbling for the knife.

I have an excellent grasp of human and demi-human anatomy. She wasn't transformed enough to have moved her lungs. Whether she died of silver poisoning or oxygen deprivation didn't matter to me; what mattered was that she stopped moving in a matter of seconds, leaving me with only three werewolves to contend with.

Three werewolves, and an immobilized girlfriend. Chloe jumped up on the table before I could move, grabbing Shelby by the hair and snarling, "I'll break her neck, don't you push it. I will kill the little bitch!"

Her declaration appeared to be what Cooper and Trigby needed to hear. They started moving again, stalking toward Helen with the calm, practiced precision of wolves going for their prey. For Helen's part, she smiled, the expression only slightly twisted by her fangs, and shouted at the top of her lungs, "THAT'S A GO!"

The shout preceded the front door being kicked open by less than a second. "Get the fuck away from my sister, you asshole!" Raina was the first Thirty-Sixer into the kitchen. When she saw me standing, she yanked a pistol out of her belt and lobbed it at me, yelling, "Think fast!"

I caught the gun without thinking about it. The safety was on, thank God. Raina might be a little more cavalier about safety than I liked, but she wasn't *trying* to get us all killed.

Charlotte was the next into the room, followed by three men I didn't recognize. One of them shot Trigby in the face as he was turning, and he went down. Cooper tried to lunge for Helen, but she was already dancing backward, out of the doorway, and slamming the door behind herself. He was too slowed by shock and confusion to stop her. I was glad of that. She was an ally, and a good person, and she didn't deserve to get caught in this crossfire.

Chloe howled in dismay when she saw Trigby fall. She lunged for the man who had shot him, and three of us shot her. She went down with a perfect trio of holes in her breast above her heart, hitting the ground like a sack of dead meat. In a matter of seconds, we had gone from three werewolves to one.

Cooper turned, snarling, and froze when he realized that every gun in the room was aimed at him. "How ... ?"

"Turns out it's pretty hard to hide a god," said Raina. She dipped her hand into the pocket of her coat, pulling out the priest of my Aeslin colony, who sat on her palm and glared with tiny black eyes at Cooper. "Shouldn't have started taking hostages."

"It's over, Cooper." Charlotte sounded exhausted. "Give up, and maybe we'll let you live."

"In quarantine? In *captivity?* Never." He bared his teeth. "You'll have to kill me—and if you're going to kill me, I think I'll make sure you've got something to remember me by."

I knew what he was going to do even before he moved. That was why, when he threw himself at Shelby, my gun was already aimed at the space above her head. My shot caught him cleanly in the neck, and he had time for one startled glance in my direction before four more bullets hit him, and he went down.

Silence, and the smell of blood and gunpowder, fell over the room. It stretched on for almost a minute, none of us quite sure what to say, no one wanting to be the first one to move. Then Shelby lifted her head and blinked at the rest of us, eyes bleary and unfocused in that "I just woke up after being hit with chloroform" way.

"Did somebody get the number of that bus?" she asked.

Raina snorted. Then she began to laugh. The back door opened, and Helen stuck her head inside.

"Is it over?" she asked.

"Yes," I said, moving to take the mouse priest from Raina's hand and letting it run up into the safety of my collar before I crossed to Shelby and began untying her hands. "I think it is."

Epilogue

"The best thing you can ever do for the people who love you is to make it home alive."
— Kevin Price

Getting ready to head for the Brisbane Airport in Queensland, Australia

Twenty-nine days later

"YOU'RE SURE YOU CAN'T stay longer?" Charlotte fussed with the collar of Shelby's shirt, pulling it up another quarter inch to cover the healing scratches on Shelby's collarbone. "We'd be happy to have you, you know that."

"I do know that, but I promised Alex's family I'd bring him back, and we have to tell them we're engaged." Shelby gently pushed her mother's hands away. "They're going to worry if we don't show up soon. Do you want them coming over here to make sure he's all right?"

"It would make wedding arrangements easier," commented Raina, without looking up from her Gameboy. Now that the werewolf threat was past and her sister wasn't going to transform, she was back to focusing almost exclusively on the needs of her Pokémon, which were many and never-ending. "Get everyone on the same continent, kidnap a priest, problem solved."

"No one's kidnapping a priest," scolded Charlotte. "It's rude to abduct the clergy."

"Let's not start another crisis right this minute, all right?" asked Riley, walking in from the hall. He was still slow and shaky, and his injuries had been more severe than mine: it would take months for him to fully recover, if he ever did. But he hadn't changed, and he wasn't going to. Our anti-lycanthropy treatment had worked, thank God. After everything they'd been through, I didn't think the Tanners could have survived shooting their patriarch.

Cooper hadn't turned as many people as he'd wanted us to think—that, or most of them had chosen suicide over life as a free monster. Of the Thirty-Sixers who had been put into quarantine, only two had shifted, and both of them would be working with the Tanners and Dr. Jalali on a quarantine and containment protocol. They wouldn't live long or healthy lives; the strain on their hearts would kill them years before they would otherwise have died. But they would live until then, and they would do it with the full support of the Society. If Cooper had believed he'd have that, maybe he wouldn't have done what he did.

Or maybe he would. He'd been happy as a monster. Maybe some people are just looking for the excuse.

"But, Daddy, without a crisis, how are you to know we love you?" Shelby walked over and put her arms around his neck, careful of his healing injuries. "I'll miss you."

"Come home sooner this time," he said, hugging her with equal care. "Gabby's going to sing *Carmen* next semester. You should come hear her."

"I will," Shelby promised, and squeezed briefly before letting him go.

"And you." Riley turned his focus on me. "Take good care of my little girl."

"Daddy," Shelby objected. "That's patriarchal and rude."

"I will, sir," I said.

Gabby came thumping down the stairs with Flora on her shoulder, dragging Shelby's suitcase. She moved surprisingly well for someone who had come home in the arms of a yowie, with two puncture wounds the size of quarters in her side. The wagyl's venom had come with some sort of accelerated healing: the punctures had been covered by scar tissue inside of a week, and to look at her now, you would never know that she had been saved from becoming a werewolf via the intervention of a giant snake.

"Here's the last of it," she said. "You're *sure* you can't stay longer?"

"Positive," said Shelby.

"You owe me five dollars," I said.

She gave me a long-suffering look, and I laughed.

The rest of her family was looking at me in confusion—even Raina, who apparently thought that frowning at me was more important than whatever Pikachu was doing. "I bet her five bucks that you'd all ask," I explained. "Gabby was the last one I was waiting for."

"Should've gone for twenty," said Riley.

I smiled. He smiled back. We might never be friends—our differences were great, and foundational—but he'd admitted that I wasn't bad for his daughter, and that was all I'd ever really wanted. Well, that, and not turning into a werewolf. So far, I was batting a thousand.

Flora screeched and launched herself at Shelby, who caught the little garrinna and cradled her against her chest, making cooing noises. I watched her. This was her home, and her family: this was the world that had created her. I liked it more than I had expected to. One way or another, we'd be back, and probably sooner rather than later. The Thirty-Six Society was going to need to monitor the local livestock and wildlife for the next few years, to be sure lycanthropy wasn't slumbering in the population, and an expedition to New Zealand was already in the offing. Basil needed his magazines and Tim Tams. Raina had promised to introduce him to the rest of her family, but that was going to take time. And while I trusted Charlotte and Riley to make an effort, they would probably need help learning how to relate to their local sapient cryptids. It's hard to shrug off generations of training just like that.

But all those things were for later. Right here, right now, it was time for me and Shelby to go back to the States. We had records to update. I had a mouse memorial to attend—the funeral was long since past, but the rest of the colony would need the chance to mourn their fallen companion. And maybe most importantly of all, we had a wedding to plan.

Not too bad, for an Australian vacation.

Price Family Field Guide to the Cryptids of North America and Australia
Updated and Expanded Edition

Aeslin mice (Apodemus sapiens). Sapient, rodentlike cryptids which present as near-identical to noncryptid field mice. Aeslin mice crave religion, and will attach themselves to "divine figures" selected virtually at random when a new colony is created. They possess perfect recall; each colony maintains a detailed oral history going back to its inception. Origins unknown.

Basilisk (Procompsognathus basilisk). Venomous, feathered saurians approximately the size of a large chicken. This would be bad enough, but thanks to a quirk of evolution, the gaze of a basilisk causes petrifaction, turning living flesh to stone. Basilisks are not native to North America, but were imported as game animals. By idiots.

Bogeyman (Vestiarium sapiens). The thing in your closet is probably a very pleasant individual who simply has issues with direct sunlight. Probably. Bogeymen are close relatives of the human race; they just happen to be almost purely nocturnal, with excellent night vision, and a fondness for enclosed spaces. They rarely grab the ankles of small children, unless it's funny.

Coatl (Coatl arbore). The coatl is a classic example of the plumed or feathered serpent. They are morphologically similar to boa constrictors (with feathers), but are likely evolutionarily derived from large monitor lizards. There are more than twenty-seven separate subspecies of coatl known, and many more have probably gone extinct, victims of urban expansion and people having an atavistic aversion to the idea of flying snakes.

Church Griffin (Gryps vegrandis corax). A subspecies of lesser griffin, these small, predatory creatures resemble a cross between a raven and a Maine Coon cat. They are highly intelligent, which makes them good, if troublesome, companions. They enjoy the company of humans, if only because humans are so much fun to mess with.

Cockatrice (Procompsognathus cockatrice). Venomous, largely featherless saurians approximately the size of a large chicken. This would be bad enough, but thanks to a quirk of evolution, the gaze of a cockatrice causes petrifaction, turning living flesh to stone. Cockatrice are not native to North America, but were imported as game animals. Again, by idiots.

Dragon (Draconem sapiens). Dragons are essentially winged, fire-breathing dinosaurs the size of Greyhound buses. At least, the males are. The females—colloquially known as "dragon princesses"—are attractive humanoids who can blend seamlessly in a crowd of supermodels. Capable of parthenogenic reproduction, the females outnumber the males twenty to one, and can sustain their population for centuries without outside help. All dragons, male and female, require gold to live, and collect it constantly.

Garrinna (Ochigrypas gilaa). Sometimes referred to as "the marsupial griffin," these small, brightly-feathered creatures fill the same ecological niche as the miniature griffin. They just do it in Australia. The garrinna is best described as a cross between a Tasmanian wolf and a pink and gray parrot. They are roughly the size of Corgis, and capable of dismantling cars with their clever beaks. Their habitat is small, and shrinking by the year.

Gorgon, greater (Gorgos medusa). One of three known subspecies of gorgon, the greater gorgon is believed to be the source of many classic gorgon myths. They are capable of controlled gaze-based petrifaction, and mature individuals can actually look a human in the eyes without turning them to stone. They are capable of transforming their lower bodies from humanoid to serpentine. This is very unnerving. Avoid when possible.

Gorgon, lesser (Gorgos euryale). The lesser gorgon's gaze causes short-term paralysis followed by death in anything under five pounds. The bite of the snakes atop their heads will cause paralysis followed by death in anything smaller than an elephant if not treated with the appropriate antivenin. Lesser gorgons tend to be very polite, especially to people who like snakes.

Gorgon, Pliny's (Gorgos stheno). The Pliny's gorgon is capable of gaze-based petrifaction only when both their human and serpent eyes are directed toward the same target. They are the most sexually dimorphic of the known gorgons, with the males being as much as four feet taller than the females. They are venomous, as are the snakes atop their heads, and their bites contain a strong petrifying agent. Do not vex.

Johrlac (Johrlac psychidolos). Colloquially known as "cuckoos," the Johrlac are telepathic hunters. They appear human, but are internally very different, being cold-blooded and possessing a decentralized circulatory system. This quirk of biology means they can be shot repeatedly in the chest without being killed. Extremely dangerous. All Johrlac are interested in mathematics, sometimes to the point of obsession. Origins unknown; possibly insect in nature.

Lindworm (Lindorm lindorm). These massive relatives of the skink have been found in Europe, Africa, and North America, which makes them extremely well-distributed armored killing machines. They tend to pair off at maturity, and while adult lindworms will have very little territorial overlap, they are constantly aware of the location of their mate and any juvenile offspring still being tolerated in the area. Lindworms are very difficult to kill, more's the pity.

Oread (Nymphae silica). Humanoid cryptids with the approximate skin density of granite. Their actual biological composition is unknown, as no one has ever been able to successfully dissect one. Oreads are extremely strong, and can be dangerous when angered. They seem to have evolved independently across the globe; their common name is from the Greek.

Screaming yam (Ipomoea animus). The screaming yam is exactly what it sounds like, and no, we don't know why. The screaming yam is also delicious. That may explain why they scream so much.

Wadjet (Naja wadjet). Once worshipped as gods, the male wadjet resembles an enormous cobra, capable of reaching seventeen feet in length when fully mature, while the female wadjet resembles an attractive human female. Wadjet pair-bond young, and must spend extended amounts of time together before puberty in order to become immune to one another's venom and be able to successfully mate as adults.

Wagyl (scientific name unknown). One of the great snakes of Australia. Virtually nothing is known about them, save that their bite can heal all ills, and that they are intelligent enough to bargain with.

Werewolf (species varies). Werewolves are not a species: they are the victims of a disease, lycanthropy-w, a form of therianthropic rabies which causes uncontrollable transformation, neurological dysfunction, and eventually death. Pity them, and avoid them at all costs, or their fate may be yours.

Yowie (Gigantopithecus yowie). These close relatives of the Sasquatch are found only in Australia. A fully grown yowie will stand somewhere between seven and nine feet in height, with dark brown skin which sometimes trends to olive green due to a biological process we do not fully understand. They tend to be swamp dwellers, although it is unclear whether this is voluntary, or a matter of "that's where we can remain mostly hidden." Yowie tend to be very pleasant. They also tend to be nudists. Approach at your own discretion.

PLAYLIST:

Everything's better with music! Here are some songs to
rock you through Alex's Australian adventure.

"Lucky Ones"	The Band Perry
"Man On the Moon"	Phillip Phillips
"I Will Hold On"	Moxy Fruvous
"Learn to Fly"	Carbon Leaf
"Hard Candy"	Counting Crows
"You're A Wolf"	Sea Wolves
"Wolves and Werewolves"	The Pack A.D.
"Do You Recall"	Royal Wood
"Winding Road"	Bonnie Somerville
"We Shall Come Home"	Oysterband
"Crystal Creek"	Dar Williams
"Bride of the Wolfman"	Ookla the Mok
"Better Sorry Than Safe"	Halestorm
"Bad Moon Rising"	Rasputina
"Sweet Hell"	Gin Wigmore
"Tear You Apart"	She Wants Revenge
"This Is Why We Fight"	The Decemberists
"Put the Gun Down"	ZZ Ward
"Nobody Flying"	We're About 9
"You Tell Me"	Thea Gilmore

ACKNOWLEDGMENTS:

Wow. Four books in and we're still going. This was Alex's last big adventure for a while: thank you all so much for coming along to see how it would go and how much trouble he would get himself into. He's a Price boy through and through, and that means a certain amount of chaos is inevitable. For book five we'll be looking in on Verity and Dominic as *Dance or Die* gets ready for its first all-star season. I, for one, can't wait.

Big thanks to my Australian betas, Gretchen McGhie and Amy Mebberson, without whom Shelby would sound a lot more Californian and a lot less like herself. They also double-checked my Australian sequences: while there are some intentional mistakes in Alex's narration, since he didn't have helpful Australians to correct his thoughts, the accidental mistakes are much rarer than they might have been otherwise. Thanks to Phil Ames, who will always be the man to blame, Dr. Bustos, who does his best to look like he understands a thing I say, and Nikki Purvis, latest target of my Mina-vations.

The machete squad continues to be amazing, and I really couldn't do this without them. Kory Bing illustrates the fantastic Field Guide to the Cryptids of North America, which you can visit at my website — beware the drop bears — while Tara O'Shea's dingbat and website design remains top-notch. I am the luckiest author in the world. Big thanks to my agent, Diana Fox, the entire team at

DAW, and to Aly Fell, who brings these people to life in the most incredible way.

Thanks to my Disneyland darlings—Vixy, Doc, Amy, Jovanie, Amber, Sarah, and Margaret—and to the fine people of Pixie Hollow, who are remarkably tolerant about Faces With Pixies. Thanks to Borderlands Books, for putting up with me. Thank you, for reading.

Any errors in this book are my own. The errors that aren't here are the ones that all these people helped me fix. I appreciate it so much.

Seanan McGuire
The October Daye Novels

"...will surely appeal to readers who enjoy my books, or those of Patricia Briggs." —*Charlaine Harris*

"I am so invested in the world building and the characters now.... Of all the 'Faerie' urban fantasy series out there, I enjoy this one the most."—*Felicia Day*

ROSEMARY AND RUE
978-0-7564-0571-7
A LOCAL HABITATION
978-0-7564-0596-0
AN ARTIFICIAL NIGHT
978-0-7564-0626-4
LATE ECLIPSES
978-0-7564-0666-0
ONE SALT SEA
978-0-7564-0683-7
ASHES OF HONOR
978-0-7564-0749-0
CHIMES AT MIDNIGHT
978-0-7564-0814-5
THE WINTER LONG
978-0-7564-0808-4

To Order Call: 1-800-788-6262
www.dawbooks.com

DAW 142

Diana Rowland

"Rowland's delightful novel jumps genre lines with a little something for everyone—mystery, horror, humor, and even a smattering of romance. Not to be missed—all that's required is a high tolerance for gray matter. For true zombiephiles, of course, that's a no brainer."

—*Library Journal*

"An intriguing mystery and a hilarious mix of the horrific and mundane...Humor and gore are balanced by surprisingly touching moments as Angel tries to turn her (un)life around."　　　　　　　　　　—*Publishers Weekly*

My Life as a White Trash Zombie
978-0-7564-0675-2

Even White Trash Zombies Get the Blues
978-0-7564-0750-6

White Trash Zombie Apocalypse
978-0-7564-0803-9

How the White Trash Zombie Got Her Groove Back
978-0-7564-0822-0

To Order Call: 1-800-788-6262
www.dawbooks.com

Michelle Sagara
The Queen of the Dead

"Brilliant storyteller Sagara heads in a new direction with her *Queen of the Dead* series. She does an excellent job of breathing life into not only her reluctant heroine, but also the supporting players in this dramatic and spellbinding series starter. There is a haunting beauty to this story of love, loss and a teenager's determination to do the right thing. Do not miss out!"

—*RT Book Reviews*

"It's rare to find a book as smart and sweet as this one."

—Sarah Rees Brennan

SILENCE
978-0-7564-0799-5

TOUCH
978-0-7564-0844-2

And watch for the third book in the series, *Grave*, coming soon from DAW!

To Order Call: 1-800-788-6262
www.dawbooks.com

DAW 192

Gini Koch
The Alien *Novels*

"Gini Koch's Kitty Katt series is a great example of the lighter side of science fiction. Told with clever wit and non-stop pacing, this series follows the exploits of the country's top alien exterminators in the American Centaurion Diplomatic Corps. It blends diplomacy, action, and sense of humor into a memorable reading experience." —*Kirkus*

"Amusing and interesting...a hilarious romp in the vein of 'Men in Black' or 'Ghostbusters'." —*VOYA*

TOUCHED BY AN ALIEN   978-0-7564-0600-4
ALIEN TANGO   978-0-7564-0632-5
ALIEN IN THE FAMILY   978-0-7564-0668-4
ALIEN PROLIFERATION   978-0-7564-0697-4
ALIEN DIPLOMACY   978-0-7564-0716-2
ALIEN vs. ALIEN   978-0-7564-0770-4
ALIEN IN THE HOUSE   978-0-7564-0757-5
ALIEN RESEARCH   978-0-7564-0943-2
ALIEN COLLECTIVE   978-0-7564-0758-2
UNIVERSAL ALIEN   978-0-7564-0930-2

To Order Call: 1-800-788-6262
www.dawbooks.com

DAW 160

Tad Williams

The **Bobby Dollar** Novels

"A dark and thrilling story.... Bad-ass smart-mouth Bobby Dollar, an Earth-bound angel advocate for newly departed souls caught between Heaven and Hell, is appalled when a soul goes missing on his watch. Bobby quickly realizes this is 'an actual, honest-to-front-office crisis,' and he sets out to fix it, sparking a chain of hellish events.... Exhilarating action, fascinating characters, and high stakes will leave the reader both satisfied and eager for the next installment."   —*Publishers Weekly (starred review)*

"Williams does a brilliant job.... Made me laugh. Made me curious. Impressed me with its cleverness. Made me hungry for the next book. Kept me up late at night when I should have been sleeping."

—Patrick Rothfuss

The Dirty Streets of Heaven: 978-0-7564-0790-2
Happy Hour in Hell: 978-0-7564-0948-7
Sleeping Late on Judgement Day: 978-0-7564-0889-3

To Order Call: 1-800-788-6262
www.dawbooks.com

DAW 207